Dreams of Mar

Dreams of Maryam Tair
Blue Boots and Orange Blossoms

Mhani Alaoui

Interlink Books

An imprint of Interlink Publishing Group, Inc.
Northampton, Massachusetts

First published in 2015 by

Interlink Books
An imprint of
Interlink Publishing Group, Inc.
46 Crosby Street
Northampton, Massachusetts 01060
www.interlinkbooks.com

Library of Congress Cataloging-in-Publication Data

Alaoui, Mhani.
Dreams of Maryam Tair : blue boots and orange blossoms / by Mhani Alaoui.
-- First edition.
    pages cm
ISBN 978-1-56656-091-7 (alk. paper)
I. Title.
PR9170.M53A53 2015
823'.92--dc23
                                2015014303

Cover illustration by Pam Fontes-May

Printed and bound in the United States of America

CONTENTS

I

II

III

To my parents

Sheherazade and the Little Girl

*T*he Old Woman is smoking a long wooden pipe. She is sitting with folded legs on a rock in the Atlas Mountains. Footsteps draw near, dragging her away from her dream-state. She raises her head. There, standing in front of her, with bright blue eyes and delicate frame, is a little girl. The Old Woman smiles.

"Here you are, my daughter."

"Here I am, Old Mother."

"I've been waiting for you a long time."

"I've been looking for you all this time."

"And now you are here, and we can begin. The story cannot wait any longer."

"So we must begin. I'm listening, Old Mother."

The Old Woman puffs and puffs on her pipe until the fumes penetrate her lungs and mind. She sets down the pipe, which continues to smoke and cough on its own. Though she is now a weathered woman who lives in a small house hidden in the rough North African mountains, she was once a great queen known to all as Sheherazade.

It is said that before the Old Woman became a great queen, she had been the mad king Shahriar's bride. Shahriar was known to decapitate his brides the day after their wedding ceremony. But Sheherazade led Shahriar to forget about cutting off her pretty head. Every night, Sheherazade told Shahriar a story but stopped before the break of dawn. Little did the Sultan know that his new bride had an imagination forged in a cage of ice and gold, and that, in her mouth, words became bastions against his death-desire. "Kan ya makan…Once upon a time, there was…oh there was not," she would begin every night. Night after night, for one thousand and one nights, Shahriar listened to Sheherazade's stories and fell in love with them. Night after night, Sheherazade ended a story and began a new one, and night after night, he postponed her beheading. After one thousand and one nights, Shahriar married Sheherazade. And after one thousand and two nights, Shahriar died and Sheherazade became queen. She reigned for hundreds of years and brought prosperity to her people. But every night, she would sit by the window and look at the stars, moons, and planets, and dream of other worlds. Finally, one night, she mounted her steed, Silver Moon, and left the palace, never to be seen again. That is, until today, when a little girl finally finds her.

The Old Woman empties her pipe, throws the ashes into the air, and watches as they rise. Then she cradles the little girl in her arms and begins.

"Here is the story of Adam and Leila, and of their daughter, Maryam, a child most extraordinary, hidden in the folds of time and now about to be born. Listen to how she came to be and to the story without which you wouldn't be here."

She lowers her voice.

"Kan ya makan…Once upon a time, in Casablanca…"

Leila

Summers were always hot in Casablanca. And that summer of 1981, the summer of the Bread Riots, was one of the hottest the city had ever known. Wave upon wave of heat hit the city, the price of bread soared, and the balance tipped.

While the old Centre Ville tried to slumber through its remaining days, students and factory workers, dreamers and the unemployed raised their banners and voices in front of its white walls and gardens. They rose against a world that had forgotten about them. They left behind them their blackened homes in the slums and working-class districts, in the Old Medina, the Sultan's Hub, the Prophet's Cave, and in the Central Quarries, where nothing was ever mined, and they marched into the city. And so the city burned.

There was no joy and barely any hope in their uprising. In Casablanca's streets, raw life was at stake. This was not a celebration of a world to come but a grim march against a failed way of life. And the riots—because this was Casablanca—were doomed to fail.

For this was a city where history surprised itself, a city that never saw a triumphant victory or a clear defeat. Grey were the days, years, and eras. Ups and downs, climaxes and nadirs were all suppressed under a monotonous rhythm that could kill time itself. Things simply disappeared or ceased to be relevant. Casablanca was a city of shades and shadows aspiring toward forgetfulness and dreamless sleep. Already, since that morning, the cracks on the elegant prewar buildings had deepened, and an ashen residue had settled on the facades. In a matter of hours, a dark green moss had grown on the newly formed crevasses. Soft and inviting from afar, the decaying Centre Ville had aged a hundred years in one day.

~

On that hot June day of 1981, at the height of the Bread Riots, Leila Nassiri had a vision. It seized her, moments after she stood in front of the window and stared at the gathering storm below. She saw the riots failing. She saw them quelled in blood and tears. Then she saw an old woman telling a story. The old woman beckoned to Leila and asked her to see behind the words. And behind the wall of words, Leila saw a little girl, a child whose destiny was unlike any other. Radically different and as old as the universe itself, she was a child with extraordinary powers and the ability to alter the course of worlds and stories. And Leila knew that this little girl had once been hers.

Leila emerged from the vision, drenched in sweat. She had trouble breathing and seeing. Her senses in disarray, she longed for fresh air and blue sky. This longing deepened into a nostalgia for happier, simpler days. She put her fingers in her mouth and, closing her eyes, tasted the acrid bitterness of the orange rind and the sticky sweetness of the ripe orange. She braced herself for the brutality to come and mourned for a world she knew was already lost.

She picked up her black cigarette holder and lit a cigarette. Feeling stronger, she walked slowly, barefoot, around the apartment. The wooden floor creaked lazily as she paced back and forth.

Leila

Leila had never felt at peace in this apartment that had been her home for the past thirteen years. She had let it slip away from her, untended and uncared for. The place, with its lacquered wood floors, black mosaic-tiled hallways and bathroom, its arabesques and granite fireplace, had once been beautiful. Now, the furniture was worn, the mirrors were blackened, and the brass doorknobs had an uneven red color from overuse. It felt like a borrowed home. And in many ways, that was what it was. An apartment given to her by an aristocratic father who, upon her return from Paris with a poor man at her arm, could not bear to see his daughter struggle too hard or too long in life.

Her father, Ibrahim Nassiri, had sat quietly at his desk while she asked for his legal permission to marry Adam Tair. There were many ways to treat daughters in Ibrahim's world, most of them profoundly cruel. But he knew that Leila would never survive his cruelty and that he would therefore lose her forever. That would surely kill him. So he gave her this old apartment, a remnant of his past wealth, situated on a high floor of an art deco building, with a wide veranda overlooking the Wilaya and the old post office to the right, the Park of the Arab League ahead, and the decaying cathedral at the end of the boulevard.

When Leila was much younger, she believed that she controlled her life. She believed in greatness beyond the curb. There was nothing spectacular about the way her life had settled into a groove. There was no fire-to-ashes chronicle, no secret unveiled to crush her spirit, no visible oppression pushing her down into her daily routine. Like a singer lowering a key, Leila had let her life quiet down. Here she now was, an empty life and an empty womb, and the riots were hitting the hot asphalt Casablanca streets.

Thirteen years already, Leila thought to herself. Thirteen years of her own prohibition, her not so roaring twenties of gradual detachment, of growing old without ever maturing.

What now roared was not her spirit but her unspoken regret. She blamed herself for being back in Casablanca, all because of a dream she had one night, thirteen years ago, of the orange tree and the pure, incomparable scent of its flowers. When she woke up from that dream, she knew that they, Adam and she, had to come back home. It was a dream, and a desire, that should have been hushed, no matter what the burning need for home pressed her to do. And Adam had agreed to come with her, leaving everything behind. She was to blame for the way their lives had turned out.

She walked to her bedroom, stood in front of the mirror and observed the lost years on her face and body. She held in her disappointment and sadness. Looking into the mirror, she unleashed her longing to return to the past, to the small Parisian apartment, and to purity. Leila was elsewhere, restless, unfulfilled. Her life was a constant denial of the present.

She stared at her flat stomach and understood why her belly wouldn't fill with child. It was rumored that she was bewitched, whispered that the evil eye was playing tricks on her. But the truth was that Leila was not sure she even wanted a child. She too began to believe that she was cursed. Yes, sometimes, in the dead of night, when her husband succumbed to one of his seizures and her belly curled in upon itself, she believed in the curse. And yet she could still smell, as she did now, the orange blossoms of her childhood over and beyond any sense of a dream deferred.

She opened the large glass windows that led to the balcony and stepped out. Hidden behind the plants and birdcages, Leila watched as the central plaza became an arena of violence. A fog descended on the plaza. The sky swirled into a dark grey cloud, and the air thickened. Leila froze. Unmarked white vans had begun to circle the plaza, while giant-looking blackbirds hovered above. The doors of the vans broke open, and the blackbirds swooped down from the sky. Large creatures, with red eyes and fur-covered bodies, formed a tight battalion. The sheep-skinned demons had come, and they were hungry.

They burned, crushed, and ate whatever they found. They danced around fires they had built for their pleasure, they dug great holes, threw bodies in with rubbish, made their witnesses insane. With their massive fists, they hit children, killed with glee, and disappeared men and women into their white vans. The demons grabbed protestors and, flapping their wings of dank wool, rose with them into the sky.

No one ever found the bodies of the disappeared. Thousands dead, thousands arrested, few would ever return, and they would never be the same. The demons had injected a leaden poison into their blood to dull their spirits and lull them into weary resignation.

The demons exist. They are real. They are here. Leila shuddered, chilled to the bone. She wondered where Adam was and if his body would ever warm hers again. She saw people surrendering to the demons and knew that the uprising had failed. The uprising failed for it resembled the city that was its home—beautiful, sprawling, cocky, and already defeated.

As Leila was about to close the balcony doors, a demon looked up at her. Instead of lowering her gaze and hiding, she looked into its cold, unfeeling eyes. She would never know why she looked into its eyes. A sparkling moment of recklessness, a jolt of courage in a woman who had forgotten what courage meant, a flicker of remembrance for a paradise lost before it was ever created. Come for me, her eyes flashed. Come, lest you regret me.

And now, the demon was looking deeply into her. Slowly, it smiled its terrible smile.

Adam

Adam taught math at the University of Science of Casablanca. He had been teaching there for thirteen years, ever since he and Leila had returned from Paris. Day in and day out, he stood in front of his students and taught them math. It's possible that at first he did get through to them. But as the days and years passed, the gulf between Adam and his students widened. It became more and more difficult for him to look his students in the eye. Most of his students were poor. Their families had placed their dreams in their education. But they soon realized that the bridges between the university and the real world had long since crumbled. The classroom was, for Adam and his students, a prison they willingly checked into every morning.

Fog and a grey vapor seeped, unchecked, into the classroom. The walls were humid, and the windows filtered a dirty light from outside. The large blackboard was hard. The chairs and tables were unstable and the paint rotten. At regular intervals, a high, shrill sound interrupted the professor's lecture or the students' musings. It was the drill of a factory that had been built near the university. It called the workers to work, to break, to lunch. Feeling the blues deep in his bones, a student once cried out to Adam, "How can we be expected to study when all we can hear is our brothers and sisters trudging off to the factory?" Adam saw talent fizzing out of them, just as it was fizzing out of him.

He roamed the deserted university halls and encountered peculiar characters. Men with dark glasses leaning against walls, taking notes; young boys and girls who pretended to be students but who rarely attended classes; university rectors in heated conversations with military officers. Boots hit the ground, and words were spoken beyond meaning or restraint. Students and professors were escorted out by the police, never to be seen or heard from again. Some students buried their hair under black veils, others grew austere beards and muttered strange incantations, still others debated politics and class warfare, abandoning probabilities and complex numbers. His balance tipping, Adam could only think to himself, What a masculine classroom...A cold sweat rolled down his spine. The university—far from the universal, far from tolerance and knowledge, a jail for the unwanted, a pit for the extremes, a political game for brutes.

There were rare times when he saw a light in one or two of his students. He would recognize it in a paper, an argument, or a comment. The fury in his head would subside, and he would be filled with deep, quiet respect for the fleeting balance of things. When discovering this light, he would frantically write to an old professor or to a colleague in Paris, encouraging them to offer the student a position in a lab or an institution. Indeed, he had started to believe that brilliant minds must be saved by sending them abroad and that it was his mission to do so.

He wrote these letters like a prisoner planning an escape, feverishly, in secret, with pounding heart. In his small office with the high, barred windows, Adam wrote like other men prayed. A scientist trapped in a world of fogs and wolves, he had found a glitch in the system, a way out. He wrote, stamped, and mailed letters that were odes to talent and hope. He felt the walls closing in on him and the floor tremble beneath his feet, and still he wrote, trying to make sense of things, imagining what the world out there must taste like.

~

That hot June day in 1981, at the height of the Bread Riots, and at the very moment of Leila's vision, Adam left his office, closed the door behind, and headed home to Leila and to the apartment they shared in the plaza of the Casablanca Centre Ville. Adam was going home, like he did every night, because he had nowhere else to go to. At first, he had been attracted to the woman he went home to. His heart beat and his footsteps rang on the sidewalk. He was in love with her. As time passed, however, something inside him began to quiver, and he became filled with want. Adam's desire for Leila was too normal, their love affair too banal. He never possessed her, he communed with her. He never dominated her, he communicated with her. Hidden from view was a deep craving for sexual possession. He thirsted for a carnal knowledge that Leila could not, or would not, give him. He desired desire, the objectifying fantasy of man on top. He never tried another woman, though perhaps he should have in light of future events, and his want grew, unchecked and unbalanced. But today, as he was walking home, Adam heard a voice call out his name.

"Ustad, Professor. Ustad Tair."

He stopped and turned to see a young man standing in front of a mint and vegetable stall. The peddler's smiling face and lanky build looked familiar to Adam, but he could not quite place him.

"Ustad. I am Mohamed Bouzid. I was your student two years ago."

"Yes, yes. I'm sorry, Mohamed. How are you?"

"I am well."

"Is this your cart?"

"Yes. My life is different now, as you can see."

"You left university?"

"My family needed the money, and so here I am."

"But you would have become an engineer! You could have helped them then."

"How many years would they have had to wait? I wasn't a bright student."

"We could have found a solution for you."

"Do you know how many of me there are out here, dragging carts or working assembly lines? At first, I believed that you would call me to your office and offer to write that letter for me. But after three years, I knew it would never be sent."

"The letter was for the very best, the exceptions. That doesn't mean all the rest should drop out. You would have become an engineer."

"Yes, but that's not how things work."

"Not everyone drops out."

"No, people stay as long as they can. Some have their families to help them. Some find work. Others find politics, or religion. Some stay because they have nowhere else to go. But I've found nothing except mouths to feed."

Adam was quiet. He hid his hands in his pockets and lowered his pounding head. He wanted to hold his breath for all of eternity.

"It's not your fault, Ustad. What can you do against God's will."

~

Adam put his hand to his forehead to ease the terrible headache that was submerging him. Sneering voices and wailing furies vied for control of him. He thought he saw the peddler pushing his cart uphill. When the cart reached the top, it rolled back down. Then the peddler pushed it back, over and over again. Adam saw other peddlers relentlessly pushing carts uphill. At first, the peddlers were young and gentle, their skins smooth and brown. Their patience knew no bounds. But as time passed, they became mightier, and their anger grew. If they were ever to burn, would the city burn with them? The space in front of Adam filled with pieces of papers—letters he never wrote, diplomas he never awarded, contracts he never honored. The piles swirled and rose in the air until he found himself in the eye of the storm, while the silence raged all around, and a mint-tea vendor who used to be a university student showed him the world to come.

Adam began to lose himself, slipping into an abyss of pain. Then the cold-eyed demons swooped down toward Adam and Mohamed the peddler. Under Adam's trembling eyes, they grabbed the peddler and swept him off into the air. But then they turned and stared back down at Adam, delivering a brutal promise before disappearing.

Leila and Adam

Leila and Adam were never meant to be. Leila was urban, wealthy, and upper-class. Adam was poor and orphaned. They were from different castes, and had they remained in Morocco, their paths would never have crossed. But they met in Paris where differences could be temporarily abolished by a shared drink, a kiss, and a walk along the Seine.

There they were far from the shame of the love affair in their home country. Leila and Adam found themselves irresistibly drawn to each other and ignored all advice to end their story before they ruined their lives. They were their own impossible beginning. When they returned to Casablanca, they braced for resistance and active opposition. Instead, they were met with silence, desperation, and then pragmatic acceptance of their union. Gradually, they were pushed into banality.

Leila heard a key turn in the lock and saw Adam come in. He was shaking and shivering. He carefully placed his keys and papers on the table by the door and paused, hesitant, in the middle of the room. The living room was in penumbra, and he could not see Leila. She rose from her seat by the window and took him in her arms. She could sense his weakness. She covered him with a blanket and rubbed his hands with jasmine oil.

"It's done," he said. "We lost."

"Yes. How could we win?"

"*They* were there. They spared no one. The chill that comes."

"I saw them too. I saw everything. They are real. The sky turned grey, and they closed in on the rioters. They spared no one?"

"I saw them. They made me a promise."

Leila saw the emptiness in his eyes. What he had just witnessed had erased a lifelong attempt to defeat his childhood terrors. Today, the demons of a loveless childhood had escaped from the dark, solitary corners of his mind and irrevocably proved that his repressed agony was real. They would keep their promise, that he knew.

"Did they see you?" Adam asked.

Leila thought for a minute.

"Yes, one of them saw me. He looked up and smiled. Will they come for us?"

"Yes."

"When?"

"Soon."

They fell quiet. Their silence echoed the silence outside. Sirens, metallic wings, and tires crushing gravel, all sound had ceased. The end may come soon but not tonight, not right away. As they stood silently together, they noticed a piece of paper on the tiled floor at their feet and bent down to look at it. It was a note written in small, tight, black letters and addressed to them. Adam picked it up and read.

> Dear Mr. and Ms. Tair,
>
> Please join me tonight after curfew. You will find me beyond the dead end inside the Portuguese Medina if you take the entrance facing the sea. Follow your footsteps, you cannot miss me.
>
> Most Gracious Regards, S.

Adam and Leila paused to think, but they could not find a reason to ignore the summons. Besides, tonight, they still had some time left. Tonight, they could still heed the city's pull and walk its streets. Tonight, for one last time, they could let its inner song, part-blues and part-Fairuz, fill their minds. They left their apartment and closed the door behind them.

~

Adam and Leila went down into the street. Curfew had been imposed on Casablanca, but they didn't care. The streets were almost silent but for the distant swoosh of a wing and the crackle of the wind. They left their apartment and walked into the blue-grey June dawn. Despite the disappointments and heartaches it had caused them, the fissured, half-abandoned city still held sway on Adam and Leila. Divided against itself, sprawling, crumbling with rare gardens and destructive nights, it was beautiful and harsh all at once.

Its roads were jammed, and the waves breaking on its shores clean and high. It was violent and cruel, rarely kind and compassionate. It was a city forged in second-hand steel, barely able to resist decay. Trees and green spaces were few and interspersed. The moist, full earth had been chased by the architects of a utopian city of industrial workers and colonial administrators. The very rich rubbed shoulders with the very poor, while the middle classes were a glitch in the imagination of a mad economist. Casablanca was dark, humid, and closed in upon itself despite its buzzing harbor and eclectic population. But its pull on its inhabitants, both visible and invisible, was undeniable. Adam and Leila walked in silence.

The cracks in the walls ran deep and wide. Howls broke the distance. They shuddered but knew that the howls were not for them, yet. They crossed the central plaza with its fountain, garden, Grand Tribunal, and Wilaya. They left the plaza to their right and walked toward the Medina. Leila briefly yearned to turn the other way toward the Place of Dying Palaces, where her family's house stood. She felt the need to press against her mother's chest and close her eyes for a while. But the note had said into the Medina, the Arab and Portuguese Old City. She lifted her head and continued walking. All they could hear were her heels on the pavement.

Adam and Leila walked into the sodden, humid air of the Old City. They smelled corrosion, saltwater, and rust. Here, too, the windows were shut and the streets deserted. They walked in silence with their arms wrapped tightly around each other, closer to each other than they had been in a long time. With silence all around and within, new sounds emerged. They heard a dull pulse that became more and more distinct the farther they walked into the Medina. They went deeper and deeper into its twisted streets and dark alleyways. Their shadows stretched wisplike on the broken walls before being lost to the night. The beat of the pulse was now so overwhelming that their bodies shook under its vibrations. Suddenly, deep into the heart of the Old City, they stopped.

They had reached the dead end. They stopped and waited, but nothing happened. Then Leila bent toward the dead end and saw, carved in the very walls of the Portuguese fortress, a small brown door with a bronze hand of Fatima, the prophet's daughter, her palm facing upward. She placed her hand on the sculpted hand of Fatima and pushed.

~

They soon found themselves in an oval-shaped room that looked like a cave. But the cave did not smell dank and peaty. It smelled crisp and earthy, as though the cave were located in the loveliest and greenest of forests instead of the dead end of a crumbling Medina.

There were tables by a fire and low couches embroidered in crimson and gold. A man was standing by the fire, his face hidden behind a veil as blue as night. He was a giant, with one hand green and one grey. At his side was a mighty sword with the name Zulkitab inscribed across its length. He held a small carving tool in his grey hand and what looked like a writhing serpent in his green hand. He was scraping delicately at the serpent-like thing to make an object that, upon closer look, happened to be a smoking pipe.

Then they saw two figures sitting with their legs folded on one of the crimson and gold couches: an old woman and a little girl. The Old Woman was telling a story to the child who was listening intently, her head lowered. When the Old Woman saw Adam and Leila, she stopped and smiled.

"Greetings, my children."

"Greetings, Old Mother."

"You have received my note. I was expecting you."

"Why are we here?"

"Because it is the end."

"The end?"

"Yes, but it is not written that it is over."

"Will we be lost?"

"You will be lost for a while in the wordlessness of the abyss, but perhaps you will return."

"It would be a miracle."

"Yes."

Leila turned to the little girl who was looking at her with curiosity in her large almond-shaped eyes. They smiled at each other, and Leila's senses were overwhelmed by the most wonderful of scents: the scent of windy steppes, cedars, orange blossoms and rose water, of half-moons, white stars, and emerald planets, of warm skin, beginnings, and pure joy. Leila touched the little girl's hair.

"What a beautiful child," she said softly.

Adam felt the taste of saltwater, lemon, and honey in his mouth. He felt a sense of shame and bitterness. The little girl got up and gave Adam and Leila the two brass bracelets she wore around her slender wrists.

"These will protect you from the darkness and will bring you back. Look, there's writing inside. It's magical and will engrave itself in your skin, and no one will be able to pry the bracelet away from you, unless that is your wish."

Sheherazade looked closely at Leila, Adam, and the child, her eyes sparkling.

"Oh yes, you will meet again," she said. "You will be everything to each other. Yours will be the tie that binds. That is my decision. Well, I decided, but you chose. Ha! And it is a good choice."

The man with the blue veil put down a bottle of clear, bubbling liquid. The Old Woman filled three small glasses.

"Drink of lamahia," she said, "the elixir of life. It is the drink of poets, condemned men, and humble peasants. The fig tree from which it came was itself drunk. Its roots, sap, bark, and branches were drunk before the fig was plucked. It was gorged in alcohol and forgetfulness. Drink to the bottom, that it may grant you peace. It's the end, my children. You will walk through other doors leading to other stories, but you will remember the door that you opened tonight and the hand of Fatima that warmed yours. And know also that the more violent *they* are, the more fragile *they* become. Their violence and cruelty will be your new beginning. Thus will you plant the seed of a new world."

Adam and Leila drank to the dregs. They felt the sweetness and bitterness of life course through their veins and shoot through their hearts. The bracelets attached themselves firmly to their wrists, and the inscriptions hooked themselves to their skin—hot-white tattoos of talismanic protection. When they looked up, the veiled man had disappeared, while the little girl was once again intently listening to Sheherazade's words. Their silhouettes faded like pale apparitions in the moonlight.

"Wait, Old Mother," Adam cried. "Why are they coming for us? Under what pretense, and with what proof? What will be the accusation and what could be the defense?"

"This is not a system of proof and defense," she answered. "This is the realm of fear and accusations. It is not a logic of laws and crimes—well not the laws you know and not the crimes you can fathom. It is about hearsay and instincts. About an unacceptable story that must be quelled. You were seen tonight. Don't be mistaken—you were seen as you are, as you dream yourself to be. The love of Adam and Leila should never have been. Their story should never have been told. From their love, their words, arises the possibility of a child, one whose birth must be avoided, for her powers could overwhelm the world. But if this child is ever born, and how could that ever be, she will smell of orange blossoms and walk the earth with soft boots of blue. Go. It is time."

~

A ringing sound echoed through the air, and the storyteller and her disciple were gone. Adam and Leila were back in front of the dead end in the Medina. The small door and the bronze hand of Fatima were gone. All that remained were the bracelets around their wrists and the embers in their veins.

Later that night, back in their home, Adam turned to Leila.

"A child? he said softly. "There was never a child for us. If only that mad old woman knew."

"She knows. She has her certainties. And she has left us with our doubts and our fears."

"And now to say goodbye to you, to our life that barely started, which I see now for what it could have been."

"They are coming. They are here."

~

The demons took Leila and Adam Tair. They burst into their home and destroyed everything: books, music, pictures, memories, and hope. Their world was violated and obscured. Leila and Adam disappeared, and everyone thought they would never return. But the demons' ways were mysterious, and death was not always the worst fate that they could imagine for their prey.

The Myth of Adam, Lilith, and Maryam

*A*n ageless woman sits on a high rock in a burning desert. Her hair is long, and an owl's wings are wrapped around her body. She has a face as wrinkled as time. A smoking pipe is draped lazily around her forearm. Next to her sits a little girl with blue boots and a blue dress. The older woman's voice rings clear and golden.

"Listen to the forgotten tale that is your heritage. Listen to the story of Adam, Lilith, and Maryam."

Kan ya makan, when the universe was young and the stars were spinning the night sky, God created a man and a woman from clay and water. He made them alike, each other's equals, and infused in them the same paradoxes and divisions. For a time, God was content with his creation. Adam and Lilith were His mirror to the world, and their existence was a proof of His greatness. He attached a golden bell to the mirror so that each time Adam and Lilith sang His praises, or looked within it up at the heavens, the bell chimed its golden song. But soon God became restless. The golden bell sang less frequently, and the mirror itself lost its pure transparency. The angels told him that the couple's love for each other was so great that they were forgetting His existence. God's ire was deep and his jealousy even deeper.

As the seasons passed, Lilith and Adam decided to have a child. They each bore her essence in their souls and breathed that essence on molded clay and fresh water they gathered from the spring. They were about to utter her name when God came down from His throne, His chariot wheels on fire and thunder in His stead. His wrath was terrible. "You have usurped my power. You have given life and name to your creation and done so without my permission." To punish Adam and Lilith for their terrible sin, God turned them against one another. He said, "Choose between eternity together as Adam and Lilith in the wastelands of hell, or knowledge and ease in the Garden of Paradise with a creature I will make even more perfect and more seductive than either of you."

The stars, moons, and planets suspended their work across the universe, as Adam and Lilith paused to consider God's offer. Lilith was still hesitating when Adam bowed his head in submission to his Lord. At that very moment, the love of Adam and Lilith broke. And ever since, lovers must break and conflict must arise.

God then said, "This child who should never have been born, the first child born of man and woman before they were man and woman, I will call her Maryam, the Disobedient One. She is your rebellion and your disobedience. She is your doubt, your resistance, and the chaos you have brought upon us all. I will exile her to the farthest corners of the universe, inside the emptiness. She forever will be forgotten, will be oblivion, namelessness, the world before the word. She will be the amphora that must never be opened and the black line drawn under the eyes of the bride forced to marry against her will. Her defiant heart will be quelled by millions of years of stardust in the cemetery of the universe.

"You, Lilith, will be punished for resisting your God. You will never have another child. Maryam will be your punishment, the poisoned fruit you loved and lost. You will be remembered through the ages as the succubus who fought with her lover and disobeyed her Lord. Dark wings will grow on your back, and you will never know rest. You will be feared by wives, mothers, and infants. You will be the lack that is *the power of night, the one without a man. The jackal, the owl, and the raven will be your only companions as you wail through the tapestry of the world.*

"But you, Adam, will be rewarded for your submission. You will be the one through whom the story is created. You will start a new family whose triangle will be suspended from the heavens with golden strings. You will have sons, and your new wife will be as beautiful and gentle as the sleeping dove. Her name will be Eve, she will make you forget about Lilith and Maryam, and she will teach you that the world is about domination."

Adam remained silent. But Lilith—cheated, betrayed, her heart broken—lashed out. "I'm here. I will always be here. I'm the dream of the unfulfilled. You want me gone, but I will always be here. So will Maryam, and she will come back when you least expect it. When you think the world is fully asleep under your dominion, she will dream the world anew." Only then did she go into the night.

Sheherazade hesitates, then stops.

"I must confess something to you. I have been sitting here for centuries, wondering why did Lilith not bow her head in submission to the Lord."

"Perhaps she was going to. Perhaps Adam moved faster," replied the little girl.

"Imagine that an infinitesimal unit of time may have forged our history and defined our future. What would the world have been if Lilith had bowed down first? Or again could it be that he who bows becomes Adam and she who thinks becomes Lilith? Or maybe she called God's bluff and understood that if neither bent to the Lord's will, they would remain free for all eternity."

"Perhaps God was not Himself that day," said the girl.

Sheherazade bristles with excitement.

"Yes why not? A faded shadow enacting a story of loss and betrayal that is older than time itself, a broken mirror reflecting a past

history through its crystal shard. In the holographic memory of the world, there lies an old God who no longer is, one whose light still bounces off the stars he once created and that are now dead. This God conflicts with every other God that once was, is, or will be, and it is He who appeared to Adam and Lilith that day."

"Or perhaps it was not God at all?"

Sheherazade gazes admiringly at the child.

"Well, that is the question. It's actually a fascinating theory. So…I heard that God wasn't alone that day, and that he wasn't quite himself either."

"He wasn't?"

"No, not at all. Apparently, someone was with him. A snake. They say that there was a hissing in God's voice when he spoke to Adam and Lilith. Something He of course would never do if He were himself."

"So we're here because of a snake?"

"Let's blame the snake, that works for me.

The Old Woman stops. She sees how affected the child is.

"It's just a story. Don't read too much into it, darling."

"But why did Adam betray Lilith and Maryam?"

"God only knows."

"What happened to Lilith?"

"She was punished for her disobedience by being written out of the book."

"How strong she must have been. Where is this story from?"

"It's from my wild delusional mind."

"If you say so. But perhaps one day you'll tell me the truth."

"The truth?"

Finally, the little girl asks the question she has wanted to ask all along, but only now finds the courage to.

"And…Maryam?"

"Ah, that's where you come in. There's something that you must do. It's a dangerous thing."

Sheherazade leans forward and whispers in the child's ear.

The Lair

*T*he light rises once more on the house in the middle of the world. Sheherazade has let down her dark, beautiful, jasmine-studded hair. She is wearing a long black kaftan and bright red stiletto heels, which she is quite proud of. She is strumming a Fender guitar, which she claims she found in the depot for lost and found objects on the other side of the hill. The little girl, too, has changed. She seems older and less frail. She is wearing boots and a military jacket that is too large for her.

"Your feet are muddy and you are soaked, little one. Come by the fire. Tell me what you've seen."

"I went to the lair where Adam and Leila are held. I became a falcon but couldn't enter because I was too large to squeeze through the demon gates. I became a small bird, and only then could I fly in. The lair was a labyrinth of stone and steel. I began my journey and flew into eternity. Finally, I found Adam's prison cell. His hair was long and white, and he looked a thousand and one years old."

"Did you give him the message?"

"Yes. I told him that he would be out soon and that his trials would be behind him. I told him that his suffering wasn't in vain. But he just smiled and turned away, as though the sight of me was too painful. Then I flew another eternity across the sea of darkness and into a lunar mountain range. There I found Leila. Her suffering was much greater than Adam's, for she wasn't allowed to find peace and *forgetfulness. Her belly was round. I curled myself around her neck and whispered in her ear that she would be out soon and that we would be together again. She too smiled but with infinite tenderness. She touched my feathers and gave me orange seeds to peck on. They were most delicious, but bitter. I don't know where she found them, but the scent of oranges in her cell was overwhelming."*

"You did well, my darling."

Zohra

After three months, which translated to a thousand and one years in the demons' lair, Adam returned. He went to his in-laws, in the old house in the Polo, because he had nowhere else to go. Their large gate opened for him. No one had seen or heard word of Leila. He himself had not seen her since that night when the cold-eyed demons came for them. Adam and the Nassiris had no other choice but to wait. Meanwhile, in the lair, two demons looked up into thin air and blinked their cold eyes once. They stopped working Leila and, to their own confusion and for no reason they could fathom, grabbed her, loaded her into one of their white vans, and threw her out onto a dirt road leading to the Central Quarries. They had obeyed an order, or so they thought. Then they filed their papers: "death under interrogation."

~

The Central Quarries was Casablanca's oldest, most infamous slum. It was the place where things were sent to die, where nothing was ever mined, but where beginnings abounded. It lay at the heart of the Prophet's Cave, a vast, sprawling workers' district. Men and women from all over the country left their families and tribal homelands to become the new workers of

Casablanca. They believed that one day they would return to their tribes and pastures, but they were wrong.

Where once their lives had been lived to the beat of the herd, the mosque, or the crop, they were now regulated by the siren and the alarm clock. The French bosses had arranged lodgings for a certain number of local workers and for their foremen—rough men who had left their native Greece, Italy, or Spain to try their luck in the African colonies. Foreign, industrial, and brand new, these lodgings—called the Cités— were imaginary replicas of traditional homes. Whitewashed and with small inner patios, they echoed the delusional utopia of the colonials.

But the vast numbers of rural migrants who came to work, or wait for work, in Casablanca needed more. The Quarries was the local, spontaneous, and irrepressible answer to the Cités. It rose from the ground in a matter of days, built from necessity and industrial waste, to become the labyrinthine entrails of a modern city. It was the other Casablanca, neither white nor enclosed, a city of tin cans and vibrating plastic.

Sheets of grey iron were welded together to become walls and ceilings, wooden crates torn up for windows and doorways. In the cold half-winters of Casablanca, rain sang softly on the flat roofs and seeped into the endless twilights of the bidonville, Casablanca's version of the shanty town. Electricity, when available, was poached from the city's electric poles, gas bottles were shared, and water was pulled from nearby pumps and sometimes boiled. Carts, mules, chicken, and sheep meandered on the dirt roads. Children played in dark ponds, and animals survived on thin air. Vendors sold their wares and brought news from beyond the margins. Rooms were added to backyards, squats popped up like mushrooms during a wet night. A happy few even became rich—landlords of hectares of previously unclaimed, unwanted land.

Zohra

Here was the new working class—created in a day, scrambling to be defined and regulated, with hearts still dreaming of tough mountains and starlit nights, and nostrils still breathing in the scent of wild flowers and of hair coiled around henna and musk, forgetting that it was from their poverty that they had fled. Here was the Central Quarries, where nothing but tin and plastic were ever mined, where things brought to die breathed life anew. The Quarries that became central without anyone knowing for whom they were central. And it was here, at her doorstep, that Zohra of the Ait Daoud stood waiting for the demons to bring Leila Nassiri Tair to her.

~

Zohra took Leila in and nursed her body with herbs and ointments. As the herbal fumes twisted up the walls of her hut, she felt a ferocious bond to the devastated body that the demons had brought her. But truth be told, Zohra had always known Leila. She had been dreaming of her since Leila was a little girl. She did not know where the dreams came from, but she had always known that they were not like other dreams. They were a thread tying Leila's destiny to hers. This was all she could be certain of. A fortnight ago, she dreamt of a small bird entering the demons' lair and curling itself around Leila. She pushed behind it and penetrated the impenetrable. She saw Leila at the hands of two cold-eyed demons, and she understood that Leila was drawing her last breaths. Zohra—dream-Zohra—was now a soberly dressed bureaucrat who ordered the immediate release of one Leila Nassiri Tair.

Now here she was, in wounded flesh and fragile bone. Zohra saw the explosion of violence, the bandaged nights and cold floors that had swallowed Leila up. She looked to the signs for answers—the cards, the coffee mark, and the animal entrails all told of grief and sterility. But Zohra saw something else

33

there. Deep within the quivering entrails and the mark, she saw what she had secretly hoped to find. It was something she remembered from old wives' tales and ancient songs that the men and women used to sing long ago when the young slum still smelled and breathed of exile and loss, green and potent songs that held the promise of miracles, freedom, and a world healed.

While Leila was deciding whether to live or die, Zohra shared her knowledge of the place they were in. She told her the story of her family and the Central Quarries. And this story would help Leila heal by infusing into her veins the pulsing, working-class resilience of a place that was the city's heart.

~

My world, where you have come to fall, is the Central Quarries. My family was among those who founded the Quarries. I was a hundred fifty years old when my tribe decided to leave our ancestral homeland. The youngest and ablest of our young men and women were chosen to lead the way, and I was one of the elders who guided them. My tribe's homeland is the land of the Seven Saints, seven brothers who came from the Mashreq, the Muslim East, to found the holy city of Abou Jaad and its seven guardian shrines. There, in that magical, mystical land, everyone is a Sharif, rebellion is a way of life, and the outlaw is protected. Or so they claimed.

My own clan, the Ait Daoud, was believed to have an even more ancient descent. They too came from the Mashreq, but word had it they were Hebrews. It was said that they came to the Maghreb after the destruction of the Second Temple, twenty-five hundred years ago. No one knows for certain. But this I know. In my grandfather's house hung a key. This key, he said, could open the gates of the ancient Jewish shrine tucked away in the Atlas Mountains.

Why did the grandfather have this key? The elders said that when the Jews left the valley for Israel, they entrusted their keys to their Muslim friends and made them promise to look after their shrines and holy places. Others said that the Ait Daoud had always held this key, that they brought it with them from the Mashreq, along with a rose-colored Jerusalem stone that would be used to build the shrine. My mother Hafsa, heeded and feared for her strange powers and acute mind, and one of the few women to sometimes sit in the men's circle, believed that the Ait Daoud were descendants of the oldest tribe in the world.

But that was then. Now they too had to leave their tribal homeland for the city. They gave up their bodies for paid work and machine time at the thermal power station of the Roches-Noirs, then at the cement and sugar factories of Lafarge and Cosumar. Some proved exceptionally smart at handling the machines, while others immediately understood how to harness the new power. When the colonial bosses decided to lower the wages and put greater chains on worker and colony, we, the makeshift inhabitants of the Quarries, were the first to rebel. Angels black as soot hovered above our heads as we stood up against factory, town, and administration. It is here, in this urban swamp, that our independence from the colonials was won.

Resistance began with us—old, young, man, woman. Sometimes colonial workers themselves joined the strikes and coined words to echo those of workers and slaves around the world. Once our independence was won, we were told to return to our mines and factories. We, who expected to rise from the ashes of the burning colonial town, were forced aside and pushed down. We were dispersed throughout the city, and our neighborhoods were destroyed. Only the Quarries was slow to transform, slow to bend. We remained the beating heart of the margins, the living reminder that the city had never completely absorbed us, the rurals who came to stay.

Zohra continued her story long into the night, watching as Leila warmed to her touch and as her heart became stronger.

~

Zohra Ait Daoud had her own shack in the central land of the Quarries. Her walls were of corrugated iron and rotten wood. But don't be mistaken. She understood, quite early on, the potency of books. One day, when she was very young, she heard of the vast Green Book that engulfed many minds and created forests, mountains, and citadels. She became so fascinated by this book that she decided to steal it. She was caught and publicly beaten by the bearded old man who guarded it. He warned her to stay away from it. Did she not know that it was the most sacred of all sacred emanations? She was an insolent, ignorant girl. He said to her that one day she may be given the permission to learn by rote some of its verses, but she would never be able to read it for herself. Though she was made to kneel in penance to the man and the book in the dusty square of the slum, it was too late, for her mind had already taken in the book's symbols and signs.

Her mother taught her how to create talismans from discarded words and objects. And Zohra knew, instinctively, that the small pieces of paper or raw leather that were given to barren women and impotent men were covered with the very signs and symbols that she had glimpsed in the Green Book and that were forever inscribed in her memory. She poached in the green pastures of endless phrases and wisdoms with her own chants and incantations. She transformed old men's fortresses into wild pastures where jealousy, love, and revenge acted out their own tragedies. She conjured magic by dismantling the text, cutting words and sentences out, creating fury out of order. Symbols became portals to the wild green pastures of long ago, to the golden sands below, and to the high mountains to the east and north. When she ripped words out or scribbled letters on animal hides, she felt life rush through her veins and voices thump against her temples. The corrosive smell of iron and sewage that permeated her slum was forgotten, and the scent of roses filled her nostrils to oblivion.

But Zohra also knew that roses had thorns and that a talisman once made could unleash both good and evil. Perhaps she relished that spiraling out of control, where life came to claim its banal chaos. She warned her clients of a talisman's unforeseen consequences. But the soft husband wants an erect penis and the shunned lover her revenge. The conned associate wants to see his old partner burdened by debt, and the unjustly accused wants her predator lost at sea. The mother looks for ways to heal her child, and the servant dreams of becoming the master. People came to Zohra looking for revenge, fortune, or love. They trusted talismans and enchantments to make right a world that had gone wrong. Men and women were haunted by the quest of their own uncompromising justice— that ultimate, most sensuous of pleasures. But one day, perhaps not immediately, the client would have to pay the price. Zohra always warned her clients of the unforeseen consequences or great bitterness that would hold their days and nights if they resorted to magic, but none ever cared.

~

At the time when Leila was brought to her, Zohra had become a solitary being. But there had been a time when she had plunged into the heart of the world head first. She took lovers as she pleased, sometimes those very men who came weeping at her doorstep. She slept with them in the half-glow of her home, wrapping her legs tightly around their backs. It was whispered that she was Aisha Kandisha herself, that she-devil who played with men and took them with her to hell. It was even rumored that she was indifferent to men and had once been in love with a foreign woman who left her behind.

She refused to marry. Her freedom, however, came at a price—there would always be a man with a long beard and a closed mind pointing a stick at her, telling her to stay away. But this type of man never came too close. He had learnt to stay away. He warned against her but feared her all the same. He took her money as protection taxes but never took it all. He insulted her, his rage heightened by his terror of the otherworld, but he never dared destroy her completely.

For this man's religious faith had been nurtured amid stories of phantom trees and invisible beings, and he knew that Zohra's world was never too far from his own. Upon hearing the wolves howl, had not his grandfathers once crouched in the snows of the Atlas Mountains, shaken with premonition of the forces at bay? And did not the Green Book itself speak of spirits and djinns, and their constant interference in human affairs? His mind was a confused swirl of fear—fear of women, of spirits and djinns, and of God. Fear made him angry, and his anger was in turn deafened by a glass cage of burning hatred.

~

The day that Leila was healed, Zohra took her by the arm and closed the door to her house behind them. She knew that she would never return to the Central Quarries, just as she knew that she would never leave Leila's side.

A neighbor, known for her roughness, yelled out to her, "Stay, Zohra Ait Daoud. You will never survive out there. Your home will always be here. You will die and be forgotten like the ugly witch you are. Let the little bird go. Her world is not your world."

Zohra did not look back, but the words burned her heart. True, what did she know of the world out there? She had left the Quarries only once, a long time ago. One day, when her mother Hafsa felt that she was close to death, she took Zohra back to their village near Abou Jaad and had her tattooed in the manner of their ancestors. The women tattooed her chin and forehead with the symbols of her tribe—two triangles crossed by a thin line on her chin and a small circle on her forehead, between her eyes.

Now Zohra left the Quarries once again never to return, holding the hand of a young woman who reminded her of what may have been and may still be. A young man who secretly believed that Zohra was a queen drove them in his yellow R4 to the Place of Dying Palaces and dropped them in front of Leila Nassiri Tair's family home. Then he bowed low and left quietly.

The wrought iron portico of the Nassiri residence loomed high above their heads. Zohra rang the doorbell, and they waited. As Zohra and Leila waited, two men walked toward them. They were elderly men in long white djellabas and red felt hats, in heated discussion with one another. When they reached the wrought-iron portico of the Nassiri residence, they stopped, peered at the address on the wall and, satisfied, turned to the two women standing there. Zohra took a close look at them and thought they looked familiar. They bowed to her and introduced themselves as Scholar and Gossiper, respectively and alternately. "If you will listen," they spoke as a duet, in identical treble, "we will tell the story, big and small, known and unknown, of the House of Nassiri." After consecutive bows, they brandished the scrolls hidden in the folds of their clothing. The Scholar unrolled his scroll and, trembling, asked to begin first.

Zohra stood still, as the family's history and secrets rushed at her. Leila closed her eyes in pain.

Aisha and Ibrahim

S o, the Scholar began.

To begin somewhere, to begin where stories emerge from rivers of words, to tell you of a history that runs its course without you, Zohra of the Central slum, we begin in Granada.

It all began in Spain in 1492 when Granada fell to the Christian King and Queen, and the Moors fled their paradise. They followed their king, Boabdil, into exile to the lands south of the great blue sea. The Nassiris, high dignitaries in the Granada court or illegitimate children to Boabdil, or perhaps both, I cannot say, sewed emeralds, rubies, and diamonds to their clothes, close to their skin, and they too followed their king into exile. It is said that at the very moment the Moors were watching their world die before their eyes, a Genoese adventurer was setting sail for a new world beyond the horizon. It is also said that Boabdil, once king and now poet, cried for the kingdom he had lost in one long, mournful sigh.

To their new lands in the Maghreb and the Ottoman Empire, the exiles brought their wondrous talents and spiritual daring. While some, like the unfortunate Boabdil, wandered deeper and deeper into their melancholia, others forged new lives out of their sadness.

The Nassiris, companions to Boabdil, settled in Fes, joining the thriving community of Andalusi exiles. They built homes around patios and fountains to remember their lost Spanish gardens. They dreamt universities, hospitals, and a new adoration of the divine. But gradually, with fear of the outside world closing in on them, religiosity took precedent over science, and they became erudites and mandarins rather than creators and discoverers. They delved into the detail of the phrase and lost themselves in the drop of alchemy. They became the eighteenth and nineteenth-century Machiavellis and Medicis of the southern Mediterranean, but they left the geniuses outside the city gates.

By the time the colonials conquered them, they had turned conservatism into an art form and self-preservation into a political science. Some still had the blood of Boabdil in their veins, and they swayed under nostalgia and the inability to adapt. Others played a subtle game of bravery, pragmatism, and impeccable penmanship. Women hid bombs under their haiks, while men wrote pro-independence tracts. Young nationalists were sent to jail, tortured, and killed. Independence from the colonials was won here, according to them. It was here that they won their freedom. Then it was here that the decision to remain a kingdom was sealed.

The Nassiris, who survived the centuries by remaining close to their caste, saw their power and finances decline with the country's modernization. Like many Andalusi families, one of their branches left Fes in the 1950s to try their luck and skill in Casablanca. This branch, headed by Ibrahim Nassiri, Leila's father, invested in a plastic factory bought from a colonial who had understood that the tensions in the slums and the countryside were a prelude to the end of colonial rule in Morocco and was prepared to leave. He sold his factory to Ibrahim Nassiri and left, never to be seen again. Ibrahim built a large house for his family in the Place of Dying Palaces, a neighborhood where new wealth and palaces once abounded.

For the next fifteen years, Ibrahim thrived. Ibrahim Nassiri became the King of Plastics and the Head Inventor in this protocapitalist venture. He invented plastic products adapted to local demands and pockets. He invented the small plastic hammam pail, the large plastic tub, and the flat plastic fly swatter. But the bestseller was the round plastic comb. It was all the rage in Casablanca and a stroke of genius. The comb came in hues of pink, blue, yellow, or green. It fit perfectly in the palm of the hand and could be taken anywhere. It was useful in the hammam or in front of a mirror. It was made for the curly black hair of Moroccans and sat nicely into their empty pockets. With a couple of vigorous strokes and carefully administered hair oil, a rebellious curl could be subdued and flattened. The subject could drive and, freeing one hand, discretely and quickly brush his or her hair.

The Nassiris had stumbled upon their own Golden Age. They were the lords of the round plastic comb. All the constellations of the universe shined pleasurably on the comb, as it brushed women's long curly hair until it gleamed. They opened shops in bustling Derb Omar and the Habous, the traditional Arab Quarter built by the colonials in the late 1920s, and distributed their products across the country.

Their euphoria did not last long. When the late sixties and seventies rolled in, so did the imitators. The harsh competition and jubilant imitations soon pushed the family business close to bankruptcy. To make matters worse, and because bad things often happen one after another, the global price of plastic rose, and plastic products were dumped on the Moroccan market and its ecstatic consumers at a devastatingly low price. The factory stopped working at full capacity and their market shares slid to nothing. The magic was gone.

The austere Scholar stops, rolls his scroll, and bows to the Gossiper who, thrilled, takes over the story.

Ibrahim Nassiri was married to Aisha Skalli, a Sharifa, or direct descendant of the Prophet Mohammed, who came to Morocco by way of Sicily. Like many families of the Andalusi caste, Ibrahim's family had sought a Sharifa for their eldest son. A wife like Aisha was the natural bearer of the Baraka, the ancient blessing of the Sharifs, one which would protect the merchant family's fortune and good name. She was raised to be the mistress of a large house and to carry its keys with arrogance and pride. She threaded the house's keys into a ribbon she wore around her neck. She held the keys to the front door, the kitchen, the master bedroom, the storage room, the laundry room, and, most importantly, the long, dark hallway crossing through the center of the house and in whose shadowy depths the spirits lurked. When she entered the spirit-haunted hallway at night or in the morning, she carried with her a bottle of sea water whose contents she sprinkled in corners to ward off the evil djinns. Aisha exaggerated her walk and rolled her hips so all could hear the keys ring and sing. Everyone knew that the lady of the house was approaching with her bundle of keys that locked and unlocked every room in the house.

What no one knew was that Aisha was an instinctual genius of all things plastic. In reality, she was the voice behind her husband's wondrous inventions. Her weekly excursions into the changing world of the hammam tickled her imagination. She saw the washers and scrubbers struggle with the vast copper vats and the equally cumbersome copper pails. She saw the women's long curly hair break the traditional wooden and the long European combs. She observed the changes in the hammam, the desire for lightness and speed, practicality and comfort. She watched the modern world move into the hammam and press it to change, adapt, and continue living. She whispered to her husband what he needed to know, what to invent.

This would have made perfect sense to all those who knew him if they had only suspected it. For Ibrahim Nassiri was not known for his creativity or for his attention to local practices. This was the Nassiri secret, part of the magic Aisha offered to a husband she had vowed to honor.

When his wife had borne him many children, two of whom survived, he looked to marry a second time. When he introduced Aisha to his bride-to-be, and her co-wife, she smiled and welcomed her. But her heart broke like glass, and all the broken pieces breathed one word—"Mother. Oh Mother."

Aisha's mother, Nakhla, with the dark skin and the fierce embrace. Her mother the child who had been abducted by slave traders and torn from her landscape of stone and earth to become a slave to a powerful man from the north of the country, before he took her as one of his many wives for bearing him a son. Her mother who tucked her in at night and spoke to her of her home, Timbuktu, a land deep in the Sahara desert, with its flourishing trading centers, kasbahs, palaces, mosques, and granaries in which, during wartime, their most prized belongings were stored, including manuscripts that were dearer to her tribe than gold, grain, or salt.

Her mother who told her of the peculiarities of Saheli Islam, and how it was only much later that an intransigent Islam from the North came south to level all difference and crush all joy. She told her of the time before that, when the veiled men and free women of the desert oases conquered the North and imprinted Andalusia itself.

She told her of a past so free that knowledge of the Green Book fed into knowledge of bodies, sensuality, and desire. She told her of the passionate architect who built palaces and mosques of mud—brick, mortar, plaster—and wood.

Finally, she told her of the great, secret powers of the women of the matriarchal tribes of the Sahel, descendants of Lilith, the first woman, before Eve, free and untangled, who spoke words in the way that birds fly the high skies. She told her of an ancient manuscript that, if studied and read correctly, would reveal itself as Sacred Law. It was a manuscript that plunged into the most distant past and found the source of equality between all human beings. Its power resided in its ability to punish those who ignored its commandments. The manuscript was lost many centuries ago and was never found. Few even remembered that such a story existed.

One day, Nakhla gave her daughter Aisha a small corner of a page from the manuscript, the only evidence of its existence that was ever found. This was a treasure held by the women of her tribe for centuries and passed down from mother to daughter. But, she warned her, use it wisely, avoid using it altogether. It is little understood, and many legends cloud its essence— the consequences could be terrible.

Before Ibrahim brought home his child bride, Aisha had believed in her own strength. She did not know what breaking down or doubting beyond repair meant, and had always been intrigued by such weaknesses in others. What Aisha now felt was an an irretrievable flattening of days, life, and joy. She was trapped with an unfaithful man in a land where being unfaithful was both legal and tolerated. Male adultery was the norm.

A life built together must be built on this terrain, this swamp of diffuse, misrecognized humiliation. So what did Aisha do when her husband brought her a younger, fresher co-wife?

There was very little legroom. Divorce willed by the wife was quasi-abhorrent under strict orthodox Maliki law. Women had to seek other ways. They could retire from the fight but leave their children's interests unprotected. They could try to conquer their husbands all over again or they could ally with the second wife in an uneasy truce. In that defining moment when her life was transformed forever, these were all courses that Aisha considered. Then something erupted inside her, and her full potential surged forth. She touched the many keys around her neck and turned them counterclockwise. "My house is locked, my house is locked, my house is locked, my house is forever locked," she swore and spat four times on the floor—south, north, west, and east. Then she took the page of the manuscript her mother had given her and burned it.

After four days, the bride was found dead in her bed. Ibrahim, who had tasted youth again, craved it anew. He brought another bride home. She was lovelier and even younger than her predecessor. Aisha smiled and welcomed her. Four days later, the second second wife was found dead in her bed. Ibrahim waited a while, then brought a third bride home. Four days later, she too was found dead. Families of Ibrahim's caste now became wary of giving their daughters to Ibrahim Nassiri, no matter how wealthy or noble he was. He began taking wives from poorer backgrounds. The brides came from families desperate for money or who had never heard that the dashing fifty-year-old groom was a homegrown Bluebeard. All were found dead exactly four days after their arrival. Doctors said they died of melancholia.

Ibrahim finally understood that something unnatural was at work. He went to see a fqih, reputed for his science, to stop the enchantment.

Said the fqih:

"No one is powerful enough to fight against the magic used against your brides. It is a dark magic, one of the oldest known to our ancestors. Only a person learned in the ancient manuscripts of Timbuktu could compel a woman's soul to desire death so fully.

"The manuscripts of Timbuktu have long been feared by men of science. They trace back to an old Sumerian myth that some claim became inscribed in the scrolls of the Torah, to the tale of Adam and Lilith, his first wife, made of the same matter as he, his equal in every way.

"The story of Adam and Lilith is an evil story, blasphemously claiming that man and woman were created equal. Lilith is a she-demon whose mission is to destroy Adam's happiness with his true mate and second wife, Eve, created from one of his ribs and inferior to him in every way. It is rumored, but none have seen the manuscripts, that the lost manuscripts of Timbuktu were written by Lilith herself.

"The magic used is, I'm sure, the magic of the lost Timbuktu manuscripts. The manuscripts claim that the world was created for two beings, same and equal, built of clay and soul. Once these words, written in an ancient demonic tongue, are heard, they will never be forgotten. The women who fall under its curse are in a state that is neither sleep nor wakefulness. Wives, mistresses, and concubines feel such yearning for that lost freedom that death becomes the only answer. They are plunged into a perpetual trance that takes their soul hostage and pushes them into the arms of death. All you can do now to save your honor is to take your pleasure outside the house. You can never bring another woman into your house, and you can never take a second wife. God help you."

Upon hearing the fqih, Ibrahim went wild. Though he could not prove it, he knew the curse came from Aisha. He knew this because of a story Aisha once told him, in the early days of their marriage, about her mother Nakhla and her matriarchal tribe. He knew that his wife came from a place of forgotten power that she was now reclaiming.

"That is what I am," Ibrahim raged to the fqih. "A man. I have hair on my thighs and torso, a turban wound around my head. I perform my ablutions and pray five times a day in the direction of Holy Mecca. My djellaba is of the whitest, purest cloth, and I stand tall, taller than most men I know. I am a man. I eat mutton with my right hand and give alms to the poor every Friday. I bow to no man except to the Sharif who crosses my path and nods in my direction. I made the family business productive and enriched my bloodline with two sons. I have every right, every hard-earned, God-given right. Four wives, countless concubines, are my birthright. It is only a matter of wealth and will. Who dares to curse me? Who dares to stand between me and my privilege...?

"It is Aisha. Aristocratic, cold, above the law, she would have no qualms in killing an innocent girl, especially one who is not as highly born as herself. In her family, men do not work. They read and write exegeses, study for years, and advise lords and sultans. They don't know what work is. Even if they are poor and starving, they do not demean themselves to work for a living. They *read*. When I was younger, I went to the land of the Hind. They, too, have their Sharifs, they call them Brahmins. They piss on their people—merchants, warriors, none compare to the lofty Brahmins. Just so for the Sharif, just so for my wife!

"She will pay, I promise."

So Ibrahim became cruel to Aisha. His heart turned against her, and he became pitiless. He forbade her to leave the house or to have guests of her own. He did not allow her to buy refined cloth for her kaftans and serouals, and he stopped giving her emerald necklaces, pearl earrings, and heavy gold belts. He rarely joined her in her bed and made sure she knew that he was still living like a man. There was violence in all his actions toward her, but he refrained from physically hurting her because he still feared what she would do if humiliated too deeply.

The Gossiper pauses and bows to the Scholar. Under Zohra's eyes, the two merge into a feminine, larger-than-life shape. A large woman, who Zohra knows only too well, takes over.

After the deaths of his many brides, Ibrahim Nassiri's business began to suffer. The cause of the decline was unclear. It may have been triggered by rising competition or by the appearance of new products and markets. It may have been caused by Yasmine Nassiri's wealthy husband who, annoyed by his in-laws' aristocratic pretensions, refused to lend them money. Or it may have been caused by a jealous wife's curse gone awry. That is precisely what Ibrahim believed—Aisha was to blame.

Though only their own class would consider them poor, they were no longer wealthy. Their name was still respected, but people spoke of them as if they were ghosts, passing by their house as they would by a mausoleum. "A great family lived here once not long ago," they whispered to their children. "What happened to them is a mystery. Their house is cursed." But the Nassiris, like other passing families similar to theirs, managed to hang on to a part of their legacy. It would linger for a while, only disappearing when new tribes and new names would come along and write over a past they had no use for.

So Aisha raised her children in a hostile house. Her son Driss, after a brief education, went to work with his father in the factory. Ibrahim was disappointed in his son. He found him greedy, calculating, and lazy. He didn't love him. But he loved his daughter Leila. Her presence made their domestic hell bearable. Leila was the only element in Ibrahim's and Aisha's marriage that was good and true. Ibrahim did not intervene when Aisha sent Leila to a French school, nor did he protest when she encouraged her to continue her studies abroad, to find her path beyond their stilted lives. Ibrahim even prayed that a Cartesian education would protect his daughter from the realm of witchcraft.

Aisha often sat with Leila beneath the orange tree and spoke to her of imprisonment and freedom. There was another reason why Aisha wanted her daughter to leave Casablanca. She knew that the magic she had used against her rivals would come back to exact its revenge on what, or who, she held dearest. Leila was the one she loved above all.

When Leila returned to Casablanca with Adam, Aisha didn't eat or sleep for forty days. She knew it would only be a question of time before the dark forces came for her. When Leila and Adam disappeared at the height of the Bread Riots, Aisha believed that her daughter was lost to her forever. When Adam returned from the demons' lair without his wife, that belief turned into certainty. Despite all the facts, Aisha and Ibrahim still held hope for her return. But as days turned into months, their hope began to wither.

An ashen film fell on the walls of the house. No matter how thoroughly Aisha and Zeinab, the child-maid, scrubbed the walls, the particles of dust lingered there. Weeds and dark flowers curled in the walls' crevices to inform all newcomers of the slow decay within. The family pictures, too, had aged and faded. The once luminous mosaics on floors and walls were either broken or missing.

But in the midst of all this slow death, the garden flowered and bloomed ferociously. Roses bloomed for more than a day. Olive, fig, and almond trees, pomegranate and apple trees, all gave perfect fruit. At its center, hidden from view, was an old and beautiful orange tree. For the Nassiri household, the garden was both a provocation and an escape.

Aisha secretly believed that the fertile garden was fighting its own terrible battle with the desolate house. Sometimes, daydreaming beneath the orange tree at the center of her garden, she wondered why the garden was fighting so ferociously and with such joy? What was it waiting for?

The doorbell rang.

The large woman disappears, and Zohra is left standing with Leila at the front gate of the Nassiri house.

~

Zeinab, the young live-in maid, entered the living room where Aisha was listening to the recorder. "There are two women at the door asking for you. They won't say who they are."

Aisha went to the gates to meet the two women. She opened the great doors and looked at the two figures standing outside, their faces hidden beneath their veils. Then they dropped their veils, and there was Leila.

Leila, Leila, moon of my life, Aisha's mind reeled. You have returned. Leila's movements were hesitant and slow. It was as though her bones had turned to liquid beneath her skin.

Next to Leila was an old woman whom Aisha had never seen before. There Zohra stood, with her grey hanging kaftan and piercing eyes. Leila had returned with hollows under her eyes and a wild woman at her side. Aisha now understood the full consequences of her pride, the darkness she had unleashed against her own child.

She took Leila's hand and kissed her open palm. Leila's hand, which used to feel soft and clean, now felt rough and metallic. She couldn't bear to look her daughter in the eye. Hadn't her own resistance taught Aisha that tradition was stronger than human will? Hadn't she seen the hues and colors of her life fade into greyness? She was still being punished for wanting more than the life of an upper-class wife. When her daughter was taken by the woolen demons with cold eyes, she thought she would never see her again, that Leila would be thrown into the abyss and be forever lost to her. When she returned, Aisha understood that the Leila she once knew was lost somewhere beyond the hollow eyes and the shuffling walk. She also thought she saw a golden belt wound around the two women's waists. The tie between Leila and the old woman was a powerful one. But the sortilege she had wound around her home was an equally potent one, and Zohra would be forbidden to remain in the house without her permission.

Zohra looked straight at her.

"Ya Oum Leila, I ask for your hospitality."

"We thank you for bringing back our daughter, and we will give you anything you want, anything but permission to remain."

Zohra whispered in her ear:

"I can help you protect your daughter and her child."

"Her child?"

"Yes, she is with child."

"A child who needs more than her family's protection?"

"She is not any child. She is a most improbable, most special child. A child of the past and of the future, of forgotten myths and alternate destinies. Unlock your house for me, undo your charm for a vagabond who has seen how the stars and planets change over the centuries. Let me enter."

Aisha pulled a key from her necklace of keys and presented it to Zohra. "You are welcome in this house. Here is the key to your room. You may come and go as you please." But leaning toward her, she added, "There is a long hallway that leads to your room. It is a peculiar hallway. The djinns and ghosts have claimed it as theirs and their constant gossiping is never harmless. Protect yourself."

She clasped her daughter, and the three women crossed the high gates.

~

When Ibrahim Nassiri saw his daughter, he felt the foundations of his house shake. Her return was a cataclysm, a meteor falling over the Kaaba and splitting the Holy of Holies. When Ibrahim saw his daughter enter the house with slow step and hollow cheek, he finally understood the meaning of sacrifice. He saw how fully the demons had broken her. Ibrahim thought of God and His tortuous ways.

You have taken a great sacrifice. You once showed mercy to another Ibrahim and to his son. You did not allow for that sacrifice to happen. Why did you not spare my daughter? You have taken almost everything from me—my fortune, my pride, and the ringing echo of my name in the streets. She was sacrificed to the demons who rule this city, to the demons that *are* this city. Why make her so full of light to return her to me sadder than night? Truly, now she is Leila of the Night.

For Ibrahim, there was no possibility of rebirth or redemption. What had been broken could never be fixed, and his shame could never be washed away. But he did not yet know that a life was growing inside her.

The Garden

In an old-fashioned living room at the end of a hallway, a sofa had been turned to face the garden. Leila lay there, quietly taking in its bloom, its freshness, its magic. She had forgotten about gardens when she was *there*. She had forgotten about time and change and cycles. When she was a child in this house, she would dream of the fragrant orange tree at the heart of the garden. It was a strange, unexplained attachment. She had returned from France, she confusedly knew, for the sake of the orange tree and the way it turned silver under the moonlight.

She felt a presence at her side and shifted to find Adam standing there. His presence, she could not help but think, was wafer thin, almost inconsequential. But she couldn't avoid him any longer. She had to tell him. Time was passing, and she had to tell him the truth.

Adam stood beside Leila feeling as old as the world and looking almost as tired. He was a shell licked clean by the demons in the lair. They had gleefully hollowed him out and thrown him to the void. He had not had a single dream since he had been returned. His nights were filled with dreamlessness, and he was left to face the demons, now in full view, forever in front of his pupils. Adam was so lost in his own emptiness that he was unable to sense Leila's agitation or the anxiety with which she was now looking at him. He thought he saw his own void reflected in her burning eyes, and he missed the secret they held within. Then he remembered something from the demons' lair that he could share with Leila.

"I saw a little bird when I was in there."

"I saw it, too."

"It was delicate and graceful. It had no right to be there. It told me that I would soon be free. Then it was gone, and after an eternity *they* let me go."

"Did you feed it?"

"No."

"I fed it and it curled itself against my neck."

Adam was quiet. Leila took a deep breath before beginning.

"In the demons' lair," she said to her husband, "they made the day dark, and night was lit up with bare light bulbs hanging from the ceiling. So at night, I made myself believe that those light bulbs were the brightest of oranges, and during the day, I imagined that I had fallen asleep under the shade of my orange tree—except the shade became gloom all around, and I didn't know what still lurked in the dark.

One day, or perhaps it was a night, I dreamt I ate and ate those oranges. At first I would peel them and pop them into my mouth. I avoided the bitter rind but crushed the seeds between my teeth. Then I began eating the oranges whole—my mouth opened so wide I could engulf an entire orange. And I did. It disappeared in there like a shadow in a cave. My belly became fuller and fuller, bigger and bigger. The oranges sat there like stones in a sack, and my stomach looked like the stomach of the Big Bad Wolf after the huntsman had opened it up, filled it with stones, and sewed it back up again. All these oranges just sitting there in my belly, refusing to be digested, to disintegrate."

Adam looked intently at Leila's belly, as he listened to her. He imagined it filled with crushed seeds and rind. While he stood facing his wife, the lead in his blood penetrated his heart, and his hair turned white. He opened his mouth but found he could not speak. I think I am broken, his heart called to him. These past months have broken me, and now I think you're asking me to fight again, to choose something. But what? Leila, Leila…you who escaped the beasts and found an Ait Daoud for protection, do you think we are all like you? Do you think we can all intertwine our lives to our fates and win? I did some terrible things in order to return from the darkness. You have returned as well. But you've brought many things back with you, and there is a veil between you and me.

Now your body has acquired a new scent, perhaps even a new taste. You speak to me of oranges, seeds, and rind, and all I know is that Adam has lost his Leila. Stay under the orange tree—yes, why not? We'll stay here, and I'll watch over your rest and healing, your head nestled in the hollow of the tree bark. That heady fruit inside you will grow to the size of a football and become round like the moon and red like a watermelon. But my tongue feels heavy, and my vocal chords are tied in a knot. I feel my mouth opening, the skin on my face stretches into whirlpools of color, and I scream without a voice.

Adam put his hand to his throat and felt a burning there. He tried to speak but found that, though words and thoughts could form perfectly in his head, he was unable to utter them. And that is how Adam Tair lost his voice—in the living room overlooking the garden of his in-laws' great house, as he listened to his wife's dream and understood that it was real. He wished to leave. He resented her, and her survival. But his will had deserted him. In fact, at this moment, he wished only to lie down and go to sleep.

He took Leila's hand and pressed it against his throat. Feel my burning throat, Leila, and the knotted cords beneath, his eyes pleaded. My tongue is circling in my mouth, but I cannot speak. We'll stay here in your parents' house, and the witch will guard you. We'll stay as long as you like, watching the days go by and the nights settle in. Believe that I did not ask for this silence. It has ravaged me, his thoughts said.

But Leila did not believe what she saw but could not hear. One day she would understand that Adam was not the master of his fate. But on that day in the dark hallway of her house, she saw her husband's silence as a betrayal, and as a terrible weakness. *Beside the river, athirst, Asleep thou liest*, Rumi has warned us. Between silence and metaphor, spurred by violence, Adam and Leila had managed to drift apart.

~

Farther down the hall, in a room the size of a shoe, Zohra, her eyes closed, was listening to the far-off conversation. She could hear all its parts, its silences and unspoken exchanges. She understood it fully, in a way that neither Leila nor Adam could. She knew what Leila would reveal. She knew that both had been poisoned by lead on the night they were taken, but that neither understood where that heaviness and melancholia sprang from. She saw the curse simmering in their blood and knew that it was too potent, even for her, at least for now. She knew that it would stay there and bury itself in their entrails. She also knew of its particularity, as she had seen its work in others. It transformed its prey into quiet, unobtrusive beings who went gently through life and let their days crumble into their smallest components without ever puzzling about their meaning.

Despite all the suffering, she smiled: for this couple she recognized from the dawn of ages, for the child who would soon be here, and for the story that was told centuries ago but that was wilfully forgotten.

Content, Zohra looked around the room in which the family had placed her. It was a room that was somewhat between a servant's quarters and an impoverished guest's retreat. Clearly, the family did not know what to think of, or do with, Zohra. She was not the kind of woman who people welcomed into their homes. She was the kind of woman people go to in times of trouble, but one they chose to avoid. A beggar, a prostitute, perhaps even a rebel or a thief, who would want her? Zeinab, the Nassiri maid, had prepared the small room at the back of the house for this woman who was neither guest nor servant, for this woman they wanted to remain invisible—she for whom society's codes are at a loss and risk breaking.

Zohra somewhat enjoyed this ambiguity. She burped and stuck out her stomach. Then she called out to the emptiness:

"So, Sheherazade, you forgot about me for all these centuries, and now here I am. You've remembered me. At last. You need me. Or were you simply drunk? Still, I thank you for winking me into this story of stories. I've waited for a long time. I should have known that your vanity wouldn't keep you away from us for more than five hundred years. Do you know what you are unleashing this time? For one thousand and one nights, you have opened portals between us and them. The djinns, demons, and talismans are still here because of you, your ego.

For that mad king, Shahriar, you unleashed the power of words. But why did you never tell the story of stories, *her* story, the one that bound us to you in the first place? Why did you choose to go to him? I do wonder where your mother was when your father gave you away to that madman. This I say to you. I will play my part, the part you are writing as we speak. But I warn you, be careful of the powers you unleash on our world. Remember it is ajar."

Zohra turned around herself, a luminous dervish dancing for the sun and moon above, and the seeds and earth below. She burped again—it must be that Orangina soda they insisted she have in the kitchen. Her art thrived in that space that emerged in the plays between light and dark, sleep and awakening. It was a golden flower, with roots that plunged deep into the meteorites lodged in the earth's memory.

Zohra was a witch, fed on resistance and working-class defiance. She had seen faces emaciated and aloof from lack of love. Her shrewd mind recognized the attempt at domination. She had heard of houses like these—grand, old houses ruled by patriarchs. Their owners often came to see her, sitting meekly at her feet. She had always refused to go to them or to leave her shack. And now she was in one of these households, stripped of her past and freedom. Her room was a foreign habitat, which she could neither breathe nor feel.

Turning slowly around herself, she sprinkled rose water in the air. Then, she coiled her wild hair and tied a black and gold scarf around her head. From the bottom of her bag, she took out a wooden jewelery box with engravings on the side that closed with a clasp. She placed it near the bed. It was a simple box that no one would notice—and if by any chance it *was* precious, with secrets and treasures known only to its owner, what better hiding place than no hiding place at all?

~

Zohra walked out of the room and into the grey hallway. She whispered to the djinns and ghosts she knew were lounging there to let her through, to refrain from harming her. She dropped salt in the corners. She thought she heard hissing and protests, but she continued her work. She continued through the house. She felt the ill-luck that had repeatedly touched it. The walls had an ashen hue, and the tiled floors beneath her feet had lost their shine. The rooms were large, and sadness lingered in the air. She felt, rather than saw, the house. She sensed that crimes were once committed here and that hatred was part of the everyday. A soft light came from one of the wooden doorways ahead of her. She opened it and saw the beautiful garden that lay behind it. It was lush and beautiful, and pressed the house. Vines and bougainvilleas climbed up the walls, and rivers of roses flowed onto the stone terraces.

She stepped into the garden and smiled at the joy that emanated from it. She was also surprised to find that this joy did not break through the sadness that prevailed within the house but only hit against it, turning it into a nostalgia, a yearning for something lost. She found the orange tree that Leila loved so dearly. She came near the trunk and felt its potent force. She spoke her greeting, and its branches swayed, bringing a golden fruit near her mouth. She took that fruit and with infinite care peeled it and let it melt in her mouth. When the tree swayed, it also revealed a natural niche in its trunk. Zohra put her hand in it and found that it was covered in moss. It also felt warm and humid. She felt she could leave her hand there forever, cradled in the tree's softness.

"Leila is heavy with child," she whispered to it. "And what a child! It is *the* child, the one from the first story—*our* story. Her coming has required great sacrifices. Violence brought her into this world, the bloodied flower of chaos. But it is love that has reclaimed her as its own. It may well be that savagery is needed to pluck stars out of the firmament and to transform a doomed trajectory into an enlightened path."

The House

Leila was once Adam's love, closer to his heart than God himself. She was the alif, the one, the first. She was the beginning of all things, the first exhalation, the first and third letter in the Arabic name of God, Allah. Her love was absolute presence. She was the straight line extending from earth to sky, without end. The alif that is sensuousness and life, the first exhalation and the last breath, but an illusion after all, for the line extending to infinity will at some point curve and disappear. She was the alif that contains the second letter, ba: the beth, the home, finiteness. The alif that holds the thought of its own demise.

~

Leila and Adam settled into the Nassiris' dust and memories, and tried to shut out their fears and recurring nightmares. One night, Leila was awakened by moans and a melancholic humming that seemed to come from outside her door. She got up from bed, opened the door, and walked toward the moans and humming. She soon found herself in the corridor that led to Zohra's bedroom. When the moon was full, the corridor was crisscrossed by the falling shadows of trees. In between the shadows, women with bright robes and white veils were whispering frantically. When they saw Leila, they fled soundlessly up into the shadows.

Leila felt a sudden pity for these wispy, unhappy creatures. All the ghosts had fled, except for one. She seemed to hesitate before drifting toward Leila, her eyes lowered and her hand holding the veil to her face. After circling around her tentatively, she spoke to Leila.

"Welcome home, Leila of the Night."

"Why are you moaning, poor thing?"

"I'm moaning because that's what ghosts like me must do."

"Why are you here?"

"The mistress of the house had me killed."

"Why?"

"I was beautiful and very young. Can you still see my beauty through these shrouds? Everyone agreed that I was the most beautiful. Your mother looked like a shriveled old nut next to me. Her husband married me and promised me precedence over her. He was going to turn over the keys of the house to me. So she arranged to have me killed."

"My mother?"

"Yes, that crazy goat."

"You're very arrogant and full of yourself for a ghost. You must have been dreadful alive."

"Beautiful women must be arrogant to be taken seriously. Otherwise, they will feel like ghosts before they're even dead. Didn't anyone ever tell you that?"

"I was told that beauty is in the eye of the beholder."

"That's nonsense. Beauty is a consensus. And my beauty was admired by all."

"Don't you feel remorse?"

"Why should I feel remorse? The one who brought me here should feel remorse. I had no choice. My only choice was to groom myself and be as beautiful and arrogant as I could. The woman who used the ancient manuscripts should feel remorse. I'm not the only one the Patriarch brought into his house and bed. Your mother's sorcery plunged us all into a state of despair so deep that death was a relief. And now the cohabitation with the djinns, that's no easy matter either. They're difficult and moody. They think they're gods. The djinns are all mad, did you know that?"

"There are other ghosts like you?"

"At least a hundred."

"You're lying."

"Maybe. But this house is worse than Bluebeard's, I tell you. It's worse even than the mad sultan Shahriar's palace, and with no Sheherazade to stop the cycle."

"But then it stopped."

"It stopped, but everything stopped with it. We did have our revenge, after all. We are the dead brides from hell. Life itself stopped. We killed all joy and expectation. Except for you, dear one...and that silly garden. No one can touch that."

"Why me?"

"You're special. No matter how bitter we've all become in this prison, we can recognize an opportunity when we see one. And you, Leila of the Night, with your full belly carrying a most unique child, are that opportunity. You don't have to fear us. And we will take care of the djinns for you."

"Do the djinns want my child?"

"They want your child, yes, but not in the way you think. They believe that your child is the one from the oldest story in the world, a child of most extraordinary fate...The last time that they were this excited was when Sheherazade talked them out of their bottles and caverns under the sea."

"Are they evil djinns?"

"Djinns don't know good or evil. Plus, you can't really depend on any of them. Loyalty isn't a word they understand.

Their world runs parallel to ours, and their hair stands on end when strong emotions shake ours. They just want entertainment."

"Oh, then they will be most disappointed. There are no strong emotions left in this heart, or this house—only ashes of lives past. I too am a ghost. I crave sleep and forgetfulness."

"Leila, the living should never think they know death. We are what is not, we are what you are not. The wisps and fumes you see are not our essence, they're the trace of our absence. You still have a man in your bed. Get as close to him as you can, breathe in his warmth and his skin. That is what you will miss most someday, what you will moan and go mad for."

The ghost drifted away, and Leila was left alone in the cold corridor. She thought of these women who were ghosts when living and remained ghosts beyond the grave. She thought of these women chained to a man and his household, and how they created worlds increasingly more sophisticated and detailed to retain control of their existences. She thought of how they conjured territories and borders, mountains and poisonous lakes, castles and dungeons, fine silks and intricate brocades, and their houses became places of wondrous intrigue and willed isolation. She thought of the beautiful, sad ghosts who had drifted past her with their colorful dresses and veiled souls, and wondered if she too was that? Of the doors between the living and the dead, of the creatures that troubled the boundaries and made you doubt where you stood. Of the broken dreams and the superficial ecstasy, of the giggles and kohl, the envy and bruised desires...She thought of her mother who, with all her strength and ancient knowledge, never tried to free herself from a tyrannical husband but instead reaffirmed his hold on her. And she thought of the child growing inside her and prayed for it to be a son.

Leila returned to her bed and to her husband's silence. She curled up against him to breathe in his warmth, only to feel an even greater estrangement than before. Adam had ventured even deeper into his world of silence and was behaving like an animal in wait. He was a subdued being whose mind had gone elsewhere to rebel and hunt. Even in his sleep, he offered little comfort. Leila could sense the wilderness beneath and the primal call for solitude. She believed in his acceptance of the child, but she also sensed that his decision to become a father to a child conceived in violence had broken something inside him. The lead poison injected into him while in the demons' lair was forcing his mind and body into submission.

Adam felt Leila's presence at his side and took in her warmth and quiet breathing, but he could not bring himself to turn and hold her close. The silence and the poison had pressed his mind back into unknown territory where howling wolves conversed with hunched intellectuals in broken streets and dark alleyways. He had been turned inside out, and his gaze was now projected inward, into the endless depths of the primeval mind where the orphan he once was, and always would be, helped him pin stars to the velvet sky.

The orphan took his hand, and they both looked at the stars they pinned and the constellations they created. They named the constellations and arranged the constellations into words. Adam drifted deeper and deeper into the wild steppes of the mind and discovered the infinity of the inner abyss. He discovered the point where one line intersects with another to create a plane and where the individual consciousness connects with the universe. Silence was his ultimate refuge from a disquieting reality, as he curled his body into a ball.

~

Every morning, Ibrahim Nassiri sat at the round table in the large Moroccan room and had his breakfast, which consisted of olive oil, homemade bread, honey, and orange juice. He had either coffee or unsweetened mint tea, depending on his mood and daily schedule. He had once insisted that his family join him around the breakfast table. When Leila left for Paris, Ibrahim started eating his breakfast alone. Today, he decided that the family would sit around the breakfast table once again. He believed that tradition and daily rituals would keep madness at bay.

Ibrahim sat at the round table, with the olive oil, homemade bread, honey, and orange juice, and waited. A large tray of both sweet and unsweetened mint tea had been set near his right hand. He was ready. Aisha, Leila, and Adam walked in silently and sat around the table. Ibrahim poured rose water from the silver samovar over their hands. After Ibrahim offered them tea, he took a loaf of rye bread and sprinkled salt on it. He divided it into four pieces and gave one to each member of his family.

"Today we break this bread together as a symbol of a marriage renewed, a daughter returned, and a family reunited. In these difficult times for our country, we have been luckier than most. Our suffering is behind us, and now the time is for healing. This too shall pass."

He invited them to eat. The house was quiet and bathed in the sunlight filtering through the garden. Leila mixed the olive oil with honey and dipped her bread. The taste of the warm honey and bread in her mouth brought forth a flow of memories. Once, she had believed in her father's kindness and in the power of his protection. She remembered the daily ritual purifications and the recitations of the Kuran. The crescent moon hung above their house, while her father performed his ablutions and prayed, all trace of pride and vanity gone from his humbled body. My Proustian *madeleine*, with its own exquisite bitterness and hardened center, she thought. Memories are where truth comes to die.

Men like her father, she now knew, were pragmatics. They transformed faith into dogma and bent justice to their will. They were constantly searching for the most convenient compromise between their appetites and their fear of God. Ibrahim felt a prickling down his spine. He felt, and he was not a man who felt much, that his daughter was judging him. He looked at Leila and saw that her eyes were crystal clear. He shivered uncontrollably, for the clarity in her eyes was unbearable. And he became angry. He understood that his daughter, defiled and pregnant, was indeed judging him.

"What are you staring at, my daughter?"

"I am merely looking, Baba."

"Are you judging me, my daughter?"

"I am merely looking, Baba."

"Looking? Then truly see. See that I, an old man, am now the guardian of a mute, a shamed daughter, and an unborn child."

Ibrahim was filled with rage: the same sudden, violent rage he once felt when Aisha stood between him and his pleasure, all those years ago. A violent rage that threatened to destroy what was left of his family and his home. The house hissed and creaked, as the air became heavy and the trees shook. Aisha put her hand firmly on Ibrahim's arm.

"Beware, Ibrahim. Look around you at what is about to happen. Your anger is palpable, and its consequences will be dire."

"Are you threatening me?"

"I am warning you."

Ibrahim sat still. He quieted down. He inhaled and exhaled his fury and suffering. And he inhaled once more.

"That's enough. The tea is cold. The olive oil and honey are spent. I have not gathered you here to battle our fates and our mistakes with you. I have gathered you here today to tell you that our family will be coming for the birth of Leila's child. That is good. For everyone, the child is Adam and Leila's child. The full truth of the events of these past months will never be disclosed, not to anyone. It will be a secret that must be protected by all members of this household. I want Zohra and Zeinab informed."

The hissing and creaking subsided, and the trees cooled down. The house and the garden had, it seemed, agreed to an uneasy truce—a truce while masks were raised and stages set. Adam and Leila stood up, while Aisha went to find Zohra and Zeinab. Adam put his hands in his pockets carelessly like he used to when he once was a young mathematics professor in the Parisian Latin Quarter with a potential for rare brilliance. He walked out of the room feeling the extent of the responsibility ahead and his incapacity at pulling through for wife and child. As for Ibrahim, he stayed alone, his hands moving above the table to the beat of a melody only he could hear. Or perhaps he was realizing that he too was a pantomime in a story written by immaterial scribes who held them all with invisible threads. He had a bitter smile on his face, for he understood that he had lost his daughter.

~

Aisha's heart was secretly beating for the house that would be full again. Yet she did not know how to welcome life where previously there was only death and decay. She thought of the ashes, shadows, growing fissures on the walls, and lingering moans, and she made up her mind. She went looking for Zohra and found her standing in front of the orange tree.

"This tree is the heart and soul of the garden. My husband's family brought it with them when they left Fes."

"It is a most special, but stubborn, tree."

"I come to you today, Zohra, to keep you to your word of protecting my daughter and her child. We have family coming for the birth, and they will be staying here for a while. The house could be cruel and reject such visitors. It could terrify them, sadden them, or even haunt them. I need your help protecting this household and its inhabitants."

"I did make that promise. But if I am to help you, you must trust me and trust whoever or whatever I solicit to help me protect you."

"Yes."

"…It is done then. Don't worry anymore. You carry all the keys of the house around your neck?"

"Yes."

"Then allow me to touch the key to the door that leads to the street beyond, that I may be granted permission to bring someone into the fold of the house."

Aisha nodded and presented the key to Zohra who rubbed it between her two palms.

Aisha then went to find Zeinab. She remembered when she once ruled over ten servants and her house was the envy of friends and enemies alike. She remembered when the holidays were ten-day affairs and the courtyard became the backstage of grand, glorious productions. Ten sheep would be brought in, slaughtered, hung, and cleaned. Their entrails, meat, eyes, tongue, and head would be prepared and presented in steaming Chinese porcelain plates. Grilled, sauced, oven-cooked, or skewered, on couscous, with vegetables or dried, the meat would be consumed for ten days and nights. The lentils were sorted for small stones, and the couscous was sifted. The bread was kneaded and laughter soared. The women sat on the floor or crouched on their heels and made magic. But as the years passed and their lord-like influence waned, Aisha let the servants go and stripped her lifestyle of its mundane delights. She was left with Zeinab.

~

Zeinab had been brought to Aisha ten years earlier by an older woman who asked her to take care of the child like one of her own. In return, the child would help her with all the household chores. Zeinab was fourteen years old when she started working for the Nassiris.

Zeinab Ben Issa grew up in the Sraghnas in the southern Moroccan region of the Haouz. Her village was at the foot of the rolling hills that line the entrance to Marrakesh. Her family was large with four brothers and five sisters. She was one of the youngest of the ten children. Bright eyes, swift feet, and unruly hair, she was a beloved child. Holding her tightly by the hand, her grandfather would walk with her to pick almonds and olives from their almond and olive groves. He was often silent, but sometimes he told her of old heroes and their raids against enemy tribes or foreign occupiers. Other times, he would pick up his awwada, short wooden flute, and play ballads while they rested under a blooming white almond tree.

When she returned from the fields, her mother would warm some water she gathered from the well and scrub her down, holding her tightly against her. Her mother's hands were rough and scratched against her skin, and Zeinab would burst out laughing, putting her head in the hollow of her mother's arm…"Mama, Mama." She went to school but for a brief while only. The school was far, the path difficult, and the teacher often absent. So her mother and father let her roam freely in the plains and hills, caring for the sheep and goats, while her grandfather secretly taught her how to play the awwada and charm the herds into following her blindly and sure-footedly.

But then the days of heat became long and unbearable, while the almond and the olive trees stopped yielding their fruit and the bark darkened and died. The sheep and goats had to be taken farther and farther away from the village to find pastures, and the water became scarce and muddy. She remembered, ever so vaguely, a night when the tribal elders sat in a circle in the middle of the village and talked among themselves for hours and hours. Very soon after that, people started leaving the village to go far, far away. Perhaps they too were taken farther afield to find greener pastures. Men they did not know would come in their trucks and transport people to work in fields that did not belong to them anymore.

One day, her mother woke her and two of her sisters earlier than usual. She made them a warm tea and gave them bread and olive oil. Her father had his back turned to them and would not look at them as they ate their breakfast, half-asleep. That day Zeinab must have been about seven years old. She never knew her exact age, but she knew *that* day was one when all she could think of was play.

An older woman she had never seen before came to pick her and her two sisters up. The woman promised her mother that she would take good care of them, as though they were her own children. In the car waiting for them outside were other little girls Zeinab recognized from her village. The old woman drove them all into what seemed like an inferno to these children of plains and wide expanses. They drove deeper and deeper into Casablanca, through greasy streets and looming buildings, until they arrived at a rundown apartment building. They were stacked in one room, fed some old lentils and bread, and told to wait. Very soon, men and women began to come, money exchanged hands, and the little girls were taken off the woman's hands. Zeinab could hear her tell the clients, "Be good to the child. Treat her like one of your own children, like I did, and God bless you all." A couple came for Zeinab very soon, and she never saw her sisters after that.

They took her to their home, a small apartment not far from the sea, and showed her what they expected from her—cleaning, washing, taking care of their child, cooking, and sleeping on a small mattress by the oven where it was warm. It was up to her to keep the kitchen clean at night, for that was where she would be sleeping from now on. They shook their heads at her ignorance and country ways. They taught her about running water, gave her what was left of their meals, and woke her violently when they found her asleep in the middle of the afternoon, her head on the kitchen table. She was probably dreaming of her grandfather's flute and the white bloom of the almond trees in springtime.

She remembered wanting to play with dolls and trying on the child's pretty things, but the mother beat her after the child complained. She tasted chocolate once, and her only toys were the broken ones that the child's mother threw away, toys that she would pick up from the trash and carefully hide under her mattress.

She was already experienced when she came to work for Aisha and Ibrahim. The situation was not too bad, compared to what her life had been the previous seven years. She was now about fourteen years old. Aisha taught her to read and write. She had a small room, a bed, a table, and a small bathroom below the house, near the garage. She ate well and was spoken to gently and quietly. The ghosts scared her at first, but they became prized and cherished companions. They gossiped a great deal and made her giggle. And tonight, ten years later, she announced to them that the extended family would soon arrive for the birth of Leila's child, and the ghosts sizzled with expectation.

Zeinab made her bed in the small room below the house, behind the garage, and went to sleep, a smile on her face. She was probably still dreaming of the peaty smell of burning coal in her home village and the fresh, high air of the rolling hills in the winter.

~

Night had fallen, but Zohra was still with the orange tree. In the solitude of dusk, unseen and unheard, she finally whispered to it.

"I asked the mistress of the house. Now I am asking the mistress of the garden. Allow me to invite *him* in, that he may draw on your power to protect and perfume the house. You have refused, so far, to let me see what your mossy center truly hides, or even to converse with *her* on certain matters. Allow us to take your goodness to anoint the house, its hosts, and guests."

A branch of the orange tree swayed, and a luxuriant scent filled the air. The branch bent toward Zohra, and a perfectly formed orange fell at her feet. Zohra picked up the orange, and it burst open under her touch, revealing the luminous crescent quarters inside. Understanding that the tree had just given its permission, Zohra bowed and left, muttering under her voice about the vanity and susceptibility of certain spirits that she will not mention by name, lest *she* turns against her.

Back in her room, Zohra mixed the orange's sweet juice with salt, milk, and olive oil, and heated the potion on a softly burning candle. She then added cardamom, clove, and musk, and raised her hand.

"I call upon you, Hamza the Creator and the Destroyer, to remember our ancient ties and return from your wanderings to me. I ask for your double protection as Guard of this house and Gardener of this garden. I beseech you, Hamza, to return from your solitary wanderings and be of this house."

Her words spoken, Zohra fell into a deep, long sleep.

Crossroads

*T*he little girl walks in to find Sheherazade washing her long, black hair under the moonlight and listening to Leonard Cohen's "Hallelujah." Her pipe is smoking at her feet, breathing in and out with every hallelujah. Sheherazade dries her hair.

"Love is like a broken harp echoing through the night. It's beautiful but arcane, pure but doomed, transcendent but baffling."

"Love isn't for me, Old Mother. What's this song you're listening to?"

"It's a song that hasn't been written yet but that's been echoing through the night for as long as I can remember. It speaks of love and innocence lost, of beauty spent and kneeling faith. It speaks of things that you're still too young to know about and about broken breaths in the wilderness. It's about memory and remembrance, and most of all about God."

"How can this be? A song that hasn't yet been written but that you remember from many nights ago and that breathes love and God…"

"The world is a vast stage. It is what it isn't. It appears to be one thing, while it craves to be another. When one point connects to another, a line is drawn, infinity is created. But that's an illusion, for neither line nor point have depth. But then this line extends into infinity, and that too is an illusion, for space is finite. At some point, the line will bend, or you will bend it, or you can imagine that it will bend because

I just told you so. Well, let's imagine that the line bends because the universe is bent and that the line had no choice but to bend to its course. Take this possibility even further and imagine that what is being bent is not just space but time as well. Eventually, the two points in the line could intersect, the line could become a multiplicity of points that intersect at some time and point. Then the possibility is created that a song that has yet to be sung has already been imagined while simultaneously existing at some point in some plane."

"Old Mother, if this is possible with a song that exists now and in the future, that's been imagined and performed, but also not yet imagined and performed, is it possible with stories, too?"

"Oh, everything has already been imagined. Everything is already there. Imagination is the universe. You will find it if you bathe in the moonlight, pluck a star from one of the infinite pools of the finite universe, and look into it with a faith ready to be broken and renewed...But something is happening in our story. We must look into its dark pool and find what fills us with wonder and a faith renewed."

"What is happening, Old Mother? My body is tingling and my hair feels like a cool spring running down my back."

"At a crossroad, at the brokerage of two paths, at the heart of the story, in one of its foils, in one of its folds, in the midst of a dying breath, She is about to be born."

"She? Who's she, and why only now, so deep into the story? How will she find her purpose when the story has matured without her?"

"You think it's been told without Her? The story has always been Her. But She first had to be imagined, doubted, wanted, rejected, dreamed, and remembered before She came into this world and this thread of words."

"I have a great pain in my chest. The air is thinning, and I feel the weight of the world on my shoulders."

"Every breath you draw is Hallelujah, the poet is right. Will you accept this? Do you accept to see and be part of what is about to unfold and can only unfold with you?"

"Yes, I do, Old Mother."

"Out of love?"

"Out of love."

"Will you bend while others see you as straight, and will you be straight when others think you are but a bend in the course of the world?"

"Yes, I will."

Sheherazade smiles. She opens her arms to the little girl.

"Look at her. She is getting ready. The child is coming. She is finally on her way. Welcome to the world, My Daughter. Child of resistance and rebellion, of myths forgotten, broken crossroads, and new destinies."

The little girl bows and embraces the older woman. As they hold each other in a tight embrace, thunder rolls, the moon darkens, and the earth trembles.

"What is happening, Old Mother?"

"That is Hamza entering the world with his terrible strides."

"Who's Hamza?"

"Hamza is the life giver and destroyer. He is twenty-five thousand years old. One of his hands is green and the other is ashen. He is taking his position as guardian of the house and its hosts. All is in its place now. We can begin."

She smokes her pipe in a frenzy. Its fumes quickly penetrate her mind:

> *Kan ya makan…there was, but oh there was not…*

Hamza

Hamza thundered down the empty street of early morning. His brown djellaba opened on his military boots and faded blue jeans. He breathed in the crisp air and took in the cool sunlight with flair and joy. He had drifted from city to city and country to country for many years before finding his way to this empty street bathed in the cold light of dawn.

Hamza saw and felt things in his own peculiar way— through a cloud of instinctive and intense emotion. The world was sprouts of feeling or deflated aftermaths, miraculous growth or devastated solitudes. Thunders and typhoons were in his mind, as were gentle breezes and tropical rains. He felt things more than he understood them. His nose was long and his nostrils wide, and he liked to say that his nose was the seat of his intuition.

His heart was made of poetry and his hair of wildfire. He liked children and animals, and preferred to stay away from shrewd, calculating adults and complex interests. He whispered to trees and flowers, and they grew for him, tingling up pleasurably. But when he was angered, he flared, an Odin of destructive power. His gentle eyes fired up, and those in his way cowered in fear. He was the absolution of excess, a life-giving and a death-giving force. He was tall and built like a giant. His right hand was the color of ashes, and his left was a soft green. He carried a curved bronze sword engraved with calligraphy, stars, and moons. No one knew where he came from. But if language were a sign, then he was an Arab, for he was known to cry and bury his head in the warm earth upon hearing Arabic poetry.

~

Hamza stopped by the gate of the Nassiri house and rang the doorbell. The key turned in the lock, and Zohra stood before him, her coiled hair now running down her back and a smile on her lips.

"Greetings, Hamza. I've been waiting for you. Tell me why you've come before I let you in."

"My Lady, I've come because you summoned me here. You gave me a gift once, a long time ago. I never forget a gift. I've come to return this gift by guarding a garden and its house."

"Welcome to this house and garden, Hamza."

Hamza followed Zohra into the house, and his body shook. He felt anger, despair, and hate emanating from its walls. His right hand tingled. They walked through the house into the garden, and he gasped at its beauty and joy. His left hand tingled.

"Do you understand what's happening here, Hamza of the green hand and the ashen hand?"

"I feel there is a war here between creation and stagnation, between a garden and the house on its ground."

"Yes. I need the house and garden to be at peace while guests are being welcomed for the birth of a child, a most extraordinary child. I need the garden to protect the house and its human inhabitants."

"I cannot bring either house or garden to peace. I can broker a truce that will last the briefest time, barely a breath in the course of the world."

"Your skills as caretaker of grounds have been sung throughout the ages. You have created the oldest garden in the world and planted trees of beauty and wisdom. You have planted the gardens of Grenada and British Columbia, Baghdad and Edinburgh, Suzhou and Babylon. Where your boots have treaded the earth, deserts were transformed into gardens and wilderness into civilization."

"It hasn't always been for the best, old friend. The world should be left at peace sometimes. Chaos is not always a terrible thing. When we plant trees, we must also build walls."

"Do you build walls?"

"No, I plant trees and throw thunder. But I bring in my wake those who build walls. That's just the order of things."

"Look well at the garden, Hamza. Walk with me into its heart. Look at this orange tree and its blooming flowers. Do you not recognize this handiwork? Do you not feel its age and power?"

Hamza looked up at the gnarled orange tree at the heart of the garden. He could feel its beating heart and lush roots. He could feel the spirit within, a spirit he knew well. One who knew how to hide and appear at will, who could be passive, a beautiful tree in a medieval painting surrounded by a golden man and woman or a brown trunk around which a snake curled itself. A rebellious, wild spirit who was both knowledge and temptation, creator of laws and outside of laws, beyond good and evil, and a receptacle of love…Hamza sobbed and his mind reeled.

"I planted this tree. When the world was wild and free, I found a seed and I pushed it into the earth, for that seemed right. My left hand became green and the tree grew. It was the first tree of the world, the first planted tree, the result of my desire to dominate and create, to impose and be plentiful. But being the first planted tree, its roots remained wild and untamed. It craved a world before human domination, and it strained toward a time of darkness and black holes. My heart felt that the tree was untamable, that I needed to plant other trees that would not think of themselves as the first, the one, the aleph after the zero—trees that would be two, three, a dozen, a forest. I whirled thunder at it, but it did not break. And then my right hand became ashen. The tree was not destroyed, but there was a hole in its bark where the thunder hit, a soft, mossy center and that held all the tree's beauty and mystery. How did the tree find its home here?"

"This tree is a branch of the tree the family brought from Fes, which is itself a branch of the tree brought from Grenada, and before that from Baghdad, Udaipur, China, and, at the very beginning, a small island near Persia where it was planted—the first tree in the first garden of the world—by you. Will you help?"

"Are you telling the truth?"

"Why should that matter? Will you help?"

"Yes. I will."

"Then I will let you lock and unlock the gates between the house and garden as you desire."

"I will stay for forty days and nights after the birth of the child. Then I must leave."

Zohra nodded and left Hamza alone with the garden.

He walked around, whispering to its trees and flowers. Soon he disappeared in its midst and became an illusion drifting across the grass and weeds. He spent a day and night there, sleeping under the old, gnarled orange tree, which lowered its branches to form a protective wall around his tranquil body. He woke up in the humidity of early dawn and kissed the earth beneath his feet in a long, humble prayer. Then he walked through the garden and into the house.

The smell of roses, orange water, and freshly cut basil permeated the air. There was a near serenity that he hadn't felt the day before. He could still feel the anger and hatred, but could also sense books closing on old grievances and dark portals receding into the walls. It was a truce—though slight and uneasy—that had been forced upon the djinns, and ghosts, and upon the house itself.

Hamza passed his green hand along the walls as he walked and felt the mosaics and cement warming under his touch. He crossed dark corridors and half-lit rooms, which sizzled and protested as he walked mightily through. Then he found himself in the kitchen, and saw Zeinab.

He paused and stopped, as thunder and lightning blinded his senses. Images and experiences he thought were forgotten resurfaced in his memory, and he saw dark cedar forests and rugged mountaintops, fires lit under golden stars, and a sole voice rising through the dawn. He looked at Zeinab and was submerged with the reality of her. He smelled love and tenderness, dying almond trees and shriveled olives, huddled children and cold kitchen floors, harsh urban hearts.

His consciousness of himself—as far back as he had existed as the being known as Hamza—mingled with the trees and flowers he had planted. His was a moist, mossy consciousness, more like a pool of still water seeping into the earth than a solid entity that proclaimed its uniqueness. It was not a consciousness of opposition or distinction but one of curling branches and budding leaves, one that inhaled carbon dioxide and exhaled oxygen. He was the counterpart of all other living, breathing beings, who inhaled pleasurably that which he exhaled. But now, he wanted a single, unexchangeable purpose.

At that moment, his floral consciousness decided that it would exhale oxygen for this one person hunched on a cold kitchen floor looking up at him with inquisitive eyes, and for this one person only. It decided that all gardens, all the destroyed wilderness throughout the years and the seduction of pungent scents, were all soulless activities when compared to the jolt created by this one person whom he did not know. He would never acquire a consciousness like you and I, of course. But he had discovered a truth about himself, and about the world, that he had never suspected before. He felt like transforming the kitchen, its floor and dated utensils, into a secret mangrove that would hide the two of them from the world forever—a mangrove that would allow them to go on the longest of rendezvous.

Hamza looked at Zeinab from under his bushy eyebrows, struggling not to burst out crying tears of pent-up dew and rainwater. In a gruff voice, he saluted her. If he were wearing a hat, he most certainly would have taken it off and bowed with all the panache that his oversized body could muster. He wished that he had a hat. Zeinab hid her discomfort at this gawking giant by smiling at him. He introduced himself to her: Hamza, the new guard-gardener, hired for a forty-day period. He then assured her that, when he was not protecting, planting, or pruning, he was at her disposal. He could help, say, sift through the lentils with her. Four hands were always better than two, and he would be most glad to be of assistance to her, madam…?

"Zeinab, my name is Zeinab, and I am not a madam."

"No, of course not, I apologize for my words. You are too young and beautiful to be a madam. Accept my apology, Miss Zeinab."

"I am not a miss either. I am simply Zeinab."

"How beautiful and perfect, of course, you are simply Zeinab, desert flower. Your name means desert flower, did you know that? You are the flower that grows in the harshest environments and who gives hope to the desperate traveler who needs hope almost as much as he craves drink and rest."

Zeinab took in Hamza's blubbering and felt his words penetrate her heart like a cool spring irrigating an arid landscape. He looked like an oak and smelt like peat. She took in his formidable stature, his green hand, his grey hand, and his open heart. She saw him for who he was—a thundering giant, filled with joy and fury, with the ability to destroy and create. A magical, miraculous creature who had appeared on the threshold of her solitary kitchen and hovered there, incapable perhaps of leaving her. She breathed deeply to find that the air was pure and clean. It rushed through her veins, opening up her arteries like so many minuscule windows to the world. The air popped through her veins like the popcorn she once made for the children of her employers but which she was forbidden to eat. The windows opened and she breathed, truly breathed, for the first time since her childhood in a small village of the Sraghnas. She breathed in the oxygen Hamza had exhaled and realized, at that moment, that she had not taken a deep, unhindered breath since that morning when her mother made her and her sisters their last breakfast. She felt the knives and thorns leave her heart and mind, and understood that she had been slowly dying all these years.

She remembered taking used razor blades she found in her employers' sink and cutting herself repeatedly just to see herself bleed. She remembered cutting the meat and vegetables in the kitchen and wondering what it would be like if she plunged the knife deep in her stomach, or if she opened the kitchen window on the sixth-floor apartment and jumped. Those had once been her greatest fantasies and, ironically, her immense, secret rebellion against her fate. She felt strong and defiant with this great secret of hers. I know things you don't. I want things you didn't tell me were good or right. She yearned for that absolute peace where she could lay down her head and sleep through the insults, the orders, and the violence. She wanted to forget and to be forgotten. She hoped for dissolution and oblivion in a world beyond the grave. She had also been curious, as only teenagers can be, of death. The other world would be a place where she could float about freely, touching the stars and talking to God and his angels. She would explain to them why she had to do what she did. She would tell them she knew that they would understand and welcome her inside.

All she ever wanted was to be inside: the room instead of waiting outside, the bed instead of making it, the living room with the guests instead of waiting on them with a tray too heavy for her small build. Here, she would finally be inside, warm, and at peace. She would, of course, be free. She thought of it as her great escape and of herself as a bird who would one day escape through the prison bars. One day, Zeinab told herself, one day I will wake up and end it all, and they will all witness my great escape. Or perhaps they won't even notice, or care…What do people like them do with people like me when we are no longer needed? I think they may get rid of us as though we never existed. It's all pointless. I will rock myself to sleep on my mattress placed on the cold kitchen floor.

Hers was a half-buried consciousness, which did not dare recognize itself as such. It had been stifled by years of hard work and lost play, but now it was reemerging. She was not a small bird who would escape into the blue sky as she had always thought. She was a desert flower who bloomed in the hottest of sands and the roughest of environments. Yes, she finally recognized herself in the mute adoration of this giant who had blundered into her life. She felt something wild and forbidden. A desire for that chocolate she ate once in hiding before it was snatched from her. She wanted to laugh. All she could think of now was that delicious, brown, and stolen chocolate melting in her mouth. She had had chocolate since, on one of her days off or as a treat from Aisha. But none could compare to that first bittersweet chocolate that she had stolen and that had then been snatched from her.

She emerged from her daydream to find Hamza sitting next to her on the floor sifting through the lentils with his left hand. She took his hands in hers and kissed them.

"Do your hands hurt you? Does it cause you pain to have one green hand and one grey?"

Hamza swallowed mightily and with dry eyes replied.

"No one, in all the years I have roamed this and other worlds, no one has ever asked me that question. Yes, they hurt. They hurt like a curse unless they are doing what they must. When the green hand plants, it's at peace. When the ashen hand destroys, its pain subsides. But it can never be both. I have never felt painlessness in my two hands until…now…until you took my hands in yours."

They contemplated the meaning of Hamza's words and the possibilities of escape and happiness they provided. Zeinab was twenty-four years old, and Hamza was timelessness itself. But at that moment she felt like an old soul, and he felt like the young man he never could have been.

"There are ghosts and djinns everywhere. This house belongs to *them* as much as it belongs to us. Be careful."

"Houses and gardens are not what they seem. I see them for what they are. I see you. I love you."

Zeinab was quiet. Nothing in her past experiences had prepared her for kindness and love. She was ashamed, for she felt that all the words that came to her mind would sound coarse and uneducated. And she did not know who this man was or where his tenderness sprang from. She placed the sifted stones on a corner of the sheet and put the lentils in a straw basket. She worked quietly and carefully.

"A child is coming. You must protect that child. The house whispers about this child day and night. You must protect it, for it is a child of miracle."

"Miracles and myths are never what they claim to be.

Stories are told and heroes are born, but sometimes true words and acts of courage are forgotten in the abyss of time."

"You speak of things I don't know. Some people are touched by magic."

Hamza stood up, infinitely sad, took Zeinab's hands in his, and bowed.

"I must leave you for a while. I'll fulfill my mission with even greater purpose now that I know I must protect you, too. The guests are arriving soon, and the child is on its way."

"When will I see you?"

"Every day."

Hamza strode out of the kitchen, lowering his head to be able to pass through the door. His limbs trembled like leaves in the breeze as he continued his reconnaissance march through the house. He spoke to the ghosts and the djinns about the danger of his ashen hand and the uneasy forty-day truce that had just been established. He then walked toward the front of the house, close to the garage and Zeinab's room, and set up his post there.

~

It rained and thundered for one day and one night, but Hamza stood his ground. The neighbors claimed they heard a dog howl in front of the Nassiri gate, but no one ever saw that dog. There was only Hamza, with his drenched hair and beard and his roaring laughter at daybreak. After a day and night of sound and fury, the thunderstorm subsided and gave way to a slight wind and a yellow-white sun. The time had come.

Birth

I am here now, lying on the bed with my eyes wide open. I feel trapped in this body whose functions these past nine months have been beyond my control. My body has been subjected to all kinds of manipulations, proddings, infiltrations. It isn't the pain that's most unbearable, but the sense of exposure, of absolute vulnerability. There is nowhere to hide, no darkness to cover the nakedness, no respite. Physical, animal, exposable... terrain of social experiments gone awry—my body is all those things except the one thing I want it to be: mine, individual, and recognizable.

I believe it's the realization that my body doesn't fully belong to me that is slowly killing me today. I suspect that this realization *is* the lead poison they injected into me. There is but one step between knowing that your body is not fully yours and doubting whether you are truly you. What do I know about myself, in the end? We are the collateral consequences of mechanical workings beyond our understanding.

My vulnerability has deepened since I realized I was pregnant. The kid with the flat stomach and the adult with the flat womb, I am now with child. With detachment I watch the metamorphosis of my body as it fulfills one of its prescribed functions. I feel at once violated, powerless, and amazed at its capacity to run through a checklist of events inscribed in its

DNA without my knowledge. My body is a library so vast that an entire lifetime would not be enough to browse through its volumes.

The pre-labor cramps have started, and I'm breaking into a sweat. Lying down, I notice that the ashen film that covered the walls, carpets, and furniture has disappeared. Being withdrawn from myself, I notice that the ghosts and djinns are silent and the house is at peace. My hips are wide open. I feel a hand on my forehead and one on my womb. I chose this homebirth because of my new fear of septic rooms and metal instruments. And Zohra is my midwife come to deliver my child. She puts a piece of paper into my mouth and whispers: "A talisman for you, my love. The four corners of the paper are inscribed with four letters of our alphabet—alif, ba, ta, and nuun. These four letters will shield you from harm and limit your suffering."

I feel the paper melting under my tongue as I close my eyes under her cooling touch. Adam and my mother are beyond that door, and I am open weakness. The doors between the world of the living and the world of the dead are always ajar during delivery, and I secretly desire to take one of these doors and walk out into the unknowable. Zohra rubs my limbs with rose water and recites phrases of protection and power. She tries to ease my wounded body, but the pain is getting stronger. My body escapes even farther from me. It has become my intimate stranger with its cruel language of pain and passing presence. The wound is open for all to see, and I feel pricks and thousands of needle points in my lower back. Flashes of white, death lingering at my doorstep, cool water on my forehead, olive oil and honey in my mouth…Then, a soft cry and an explosion of orange blossom scent everywhere.

"A thousand congratulations."

"The child is here."

"It's a girl."

Birth

Zohra held the child in her arms. Ibrahim, Aisha, and Adam surrounded the bed, as Zohra cut the umbilical cord and put the placenta in a jar. She would later bury the placenta under the orange tree. She would watch as the night filled with the scent of flower blossoms. She would feel the roots of the tree seep deeper into the earth that holds it and close her eyes as the tree branches brushed her face in acceptance and gratitude for her gift. The tree roots would then reach farther into the earth, and water would rush up into the bark, branches, and white flowers to gorge them with scent and light.

Ibrahim put his mouth against his granddaughter's right ear and recited the Sourra Al-Fatiha from the Kuran. He then repeated the prayer in her left ear. Aisha and Zohra prepared the water for the child's first ablution. They mixed henna and mint leaves into the water and bathed her in it. Then they rubbed her down with olive oil and wrapped her tightly in a blanket. Zohra put her in Leila's arms and told her to feed her.

Leila was tired from the birth but also from the poisonous lead whose grip on her psyche was now acute. She could feel an ache, a sadness, take hold of her body, her skin, muscles, and sinew. The child at her breast was an anomaly, an additional intrusion into her physical space. She was a nfissa now: for forty days, she would be considered a young mother, vulnerable to infections and cruelty, encouraged to remain in her house. She only now understood the full meaning of that word. Nfissa did not mean the new mother, it meant the open grave. For forty days and forty nights, she was an open grave through which all the winds of death and despair could pass.

With the tip of her tongue, she tasted the bitterness from the ink of Zohra's talisman. A small paper, four square corners on which were inscribed four letters of the Arabic alphabet to delimit a space for protection against evil forces and desires. Four corners, a perfectly rational delimitation of space with

95

one letter for each corner. A Cartesian device placed in the darkness of a rounded mouth to shield her from unnameable monstrosities. It was utterance stripped down to its simplest form and placed in the pained mouth to conjure the power of text. Dissolved letters that circulate through the body-as-text—the body through which laws and their transgressions are endlessly enacted. She felt the four letters trickle down her spine and copy themselves on her skin like a pale reproduction of the Guttenberg press. The letters pressed upon her skin and momentarily absolved the tortured inscriptions the world had subjected her body to.

Leila looked down at the little girl in her arms. She saw in her daughter only frailty and weakness. A girl born in a country of wolves and monstrous sheep would know only pain and disillusionment. A child conceived in violence and scorn could only be pitiful and meek. The little girl had tapered fingers and crooked, uneven legs. Her skin was almost transparent and her frame ever so slight. Leila thought that she could break in an instant, and a deeper part of her answered that perhaps it would be better for her if she did break. Zohra stroked Leila's hair. "Your daughter is powerful, Leila. Her body's frailty is a veil shielding a power and courage that will prove beyond compare. Her uneven legs are to allow her to walk the world in her own way with her own imperfect rhythm. Her body touches the air and earth with its own gravitational pattern, and she will know, simultaneously, what it means to be strong and less strong, tall and less tall, transcendent and downtrodden. Her legs are uneven because she is like the world. Do not fear her difference and do not be pained for her."

Then Zohra lowered her voice. "She is our miracle. She is the one we have been waiting for but were told we must forget, the one who should have been in our ancient texts but was erased, the one who would have shown that the alternative path was the right path but who was never allowed to exist. The child of earth and night, of resistance and integrity, of sacrifice and endlessness, our most wanted and most needed child..."

Leila struggled with the pain caused by the contact of mouth on swollen breast and wondered when her weird, secret, unnatural desire for flight would disappear. Aisha watched as Leila fought to create a connection with her daughter, while Zohra prepared henna in a bowl. When the warm brown mixture settled, she tattooed Leila's palms, feet, and womb with the odorous henna.

"To protect you from furious despair and incurable disease, to weave a bond between you and your child, and to shield you from the evil eye, you will remain in this room with your daughter for seven days and nights. On the seventh day, the guests will arrive and the naming ceremony will begin."

She presented her with a date: "Eat this date that was picked from the venerable palm trees of the southern oases to nourish you with courage and sweetness. Do not worry, for I will remain by your side for seven days and nights."

Leila's body and mind were alternatively wracked by hot and cold flashes. Hot liquids, cold solids, and ritualistic tattoos had transformed her being-in-her-body into another consciousness of existence and physicality. For one as cerebral as Leila, her body's weakness and surgical passivity revealed the power of body. In these moments of great vulnerability, Leila no longer recognized herself and doubted her ability to persevere and return to the light. She thought that she could hear the Patriarch rage at her side. "What is this child? Its legs are uneven. What is this monster my daughter has brought into our house? My house is cursed. This is punishment for keeping a child who is probably the spawn of some hoofed demon!"

Leila could sense, more than she could hear, her mother's anger at her tall, blue-eyed husband. She held her child tighter, breathed in her skin, fingers, and soft hair, and thought of the mysterious link between life and fragility. She slept surrounded with the scent of orange blossoms, fruit, and honey, dreaming of forgetfulness.

~

Night fell on the city, and the household prepared itself. Zohra called out to Hamza, and soon he was at Leila's door. He came into the room at midnight with his curved, calligraphed sword and an orange-blossom branch. Zohra crouched on the floor and began.

"It is midnight, Hamza: listen to the worlds of day and night whispering alongside each other. In my tribe, when a child was born, the elders used a sword to get rid of Lilith and protect mother and child. The sword would cut the air in half and draw a circle above the resting mother and her child to keep Lilith away. The sword created a closed space for their protection. In that closed space, tales were told, myths and mysteries revealed. From these words would later flow, quite naturally, the newborn's chosen name.

"I am not asking you to use your sword to ward off demons, ghosts, and witches nor to create a closed space that at once delimits and defines a threatening outside. No, none of that here...I am asking you to bring life back into a broken spirit, to breathe green air out of your lungs to fill hers with life and warmth. I am asking that you remind this weakening mother that there must be light before the darkness descends on us for all eternity. It is not Lilith I am scared of. It is those fierce inner demons that are pushing her toward the brink and drinking the sweet milk intended for the daughter. It is midnight. Listen to the world of night take over the day. Inscribe your magic on its darkness."

Hamza held the orange-blossom branch up with his ashen hand and moved around the room as though sprinkling its fragrant water into the air. His hair stood on end like a treetop stretching toward the cool breeze as he breathed in and out with frenzied cadence. He then knelt at Leila's bedside and slipped the orange-blossom branch under her pillow. With his green hand, he used the curved sword engraved with stars, moons, and calligraphy to conjure the night sky above the bed. It was a dark, deep night with soft stars, a faraway moon, and a universe of calligraphic poetry. In his voice of thunder and leaves, he recited the story of a flood that divided the world in two halves with boxed compartments and hierarchical belongings, and of a vast arch.

Then he added:

"But the flood has not yet happened in this millennial time that is ours, and the arch has not yet been built. For the trees and the will to build it are still dreams in the mind of their maker. Tonight, the world is a luminous night sky with crescent and full moons, lingering planets, and cooling stars. On its jet black tapestry, inscriptions of timelessness and light have been carved."

Hamza called forth:

> *She who is not named*
> *She who should not be named*
> *Expelled outside the circle of light and words*
> *She is here*
> *She has been brought back in.*

Then he vowed, "I use my sword Zulkitab to carve words and worlds into the night and the branch of orange blossom to illuminate it with delight. It is the beginning of utterance. The name will soon appear."

Zulkitab trembled with anticipation in Hamza's hand.

Leila opened her dark, fiery eyes. She was both Leila and Lilith, a young, forlorn mother and an ancestral being of power and resistance. She was thousands of years old and the product of a generation and its contradictory codes. "I am here," she said. Hamza took her hands in his.

"This is the beginning of the naming, of the uttered word. What name will your daughter carry, Leila of the Night?"

"Maryam."

"Maryam. That is a good name: plucked out of the emptiness of night, it will wrap itself around your daughter and infuse passion into her being. This naming must remain a secret. Do not reveal her name to anyone. In seven days and nights, the name will be chosen for the naming ceremony. Only then will she be known."

Hamza left the room and with him departed the crisp, green forest air and ancient innocence.

Three Gifts and a Curse

On the seventh day after Maryam's birth, the family arrived with their hands full of gifts: kaftans, linens and embroideries, a gold necklace, saffron, incense and sweets. First came the patriarch's brother and sister. Mehdi came alone, as he always did. Then came Yasmine with her businessman husband, Mohamed Afrah, and their three children. Leila's brother, Driss, also came. He was with a woman no one had seen before and who made Aisha gasp and the ghosts whoop.

Andalusian music played, lanterns lined the entrance, and thick, waist-high sticks of sugar were placed in the hallway. Dates and milk were offered to the guests, and musk mixed with Indonesian incense, a rare treat, was passed around in a bronze coal burner. Ibrahim, dressed in an immaculate white djellaba and yellow leather blaghi, welcomed his family. He sat on the brocaded sofa lining the rectangular Moroccan room— the heart of his house. He was surrounded by silver teapots and coffeepots and almond and honey treats. On a perfectly polished silver tray, there stood five silver rose water sprinklers filled to the brim. On a raised wooden dais above them, as only traditional houses still cared to do, the Andalusian musicians strummed their 'ouds and sang the Ala Andalusia and the Gharnati.

Ibrahim greeted them with a complex mix of pride and pious sentiment he had not experienced since the launch of his first successful factory production. He remembered the joy he had felt when the first round of plastic combs were produced to appear shiny and perfect. Soon, a voice in his head tempered that exuberance. "Lhamdullah, thanks to God who has allowed for this moment," he had reminded himself. "I must be humble before the will of God." Today, Ibrahim felt a respite from the anxiety and shame of the past years and remembered that his was a great family, one of the greatest in the land. Beyond all their ill-fortune, their cultural heritage could still be wound up and deployed like an old music box playing a forgotten childhood melody on a cold day when all dreams seem to have passed. He kissed his wife on her forehead and greeted them all once more with the usual formulae and their unique blend of poetry, sayings, and religion.

The women trilled to dispel the evil spirits, and the men washed their hands with the rose water to purify their souls, while Mehdi smoked from a golden cigarette holder held casually between two fingers. The music suddenly stopped, and Ibrahim called the assembly to prayer. Mehdi put down the cigarette on the small wooden table set in one brocaded corner and took his place behind his mighty older brother. The women left the room, and Ibrahim began the prayer. Mehdi put his head down on the floor as fervently as every other man and opened his palms to his Lord in submission.

When the prayer ended, Yasmine walked to Mehdi and stood next to him. She was a tall, angular, haughty woman in her late fifties. Her skin was white and pulled against her cheekbones to reveal a hawkish nose and lined mouth. She was wearing her usual black suit, white shirt, and black tie. Her short hair was stylishly curled. "I am Greta Garbo," she would provoke. She had been trained as a lawyer but stopped practicing law a while back and now spent most of her time in women's rights' associations. Her husband called it "her charity work," but she didn't care. She had never cared what others thought of her. They would all probably faint if they were in her head or walked in her queer shoes. The other women had donned the Moroccan kaftan with large gold belt and long double robes of silk and satin. But Yasmine was, and always had been, "the Garbo," and was known to flaunt and enjoy that androgyny tremendously.

Yasmine did not speak a word to Mehdi, but her mouth was curved up in irony and contained bile. Mehdi could see the flash of a white tooth from the corner of his eye, and he could not help the stiffening of his body. She was standing too close to him. It must be said that, in the privacy of his late night musings, Mehdi had become convinced that his sister was a blood-sucking predator. During flashes of paranoid questionings, he clearly saw her sinking her teeth into his masculinity and taking it in for her own nourishment.

Mehdi lit another cigarette and, for reasons only he knew, blew smoke into Yasmine's face: "Here's to our deadly blue angel, whose cruelty taints the world" he breathed and walked away. He passed in front of her husband, Mohamed Afrah, and thought how he was an affront to the decrepit old household with his air of affluence and quiet power.

Mehdi had long hesitated before accepting his brother's invitation to the naming of Leila's child. He had always felt oddly off in this house. He had spent his childhood and youth in Ibrahim's shadow. His growth had been stifled, choked behind blue trousers and masculine sobriety.

Ibrahim was domination itself, shedding darkness on everything that was not him. Ibrahim instinctively knew how to take what he wanted and, as he grew older and stronger, learned the subtle art of bending others to his will. That is, until the dark years fell on his house. As children, Mehdi and Yasmine were never able to fully emerge from their brother's shadow. Yasmine gravitated around Ibrahim like planetary dust, while Mehdi chose to claim the margins as his blackened territory. They lived their lives in pale imitation and fearful avoidance of a charismatic Ibrahim. The future patriarch required his human sacrifices. They became emaciated and succumbed to bitterness. Their lives lost their sweetness, and their eyes their luster. They were the martyrs of their brother's potential. They were victims yearning to be Ibrahim, longing for their mother's touch and their father's pride. Ibrahim was oblivious to their suffering and behaved as though, one day soon, they would work for him. Inheritance became a matter of callousness and power, and no one was surprised when Ibrahim took over the family business, promising his weaker siblings to take care of them always. That, of course, would not be the case.

Yasmine eventually found a way to save herself. She became lean and tough, blasé and inconsiderate. She gave up social conventions and ladylike propriety. She enjoyed wearing suits, straight pants, and ties hung loosely around her neck. She smoked and jutted her pelvis forward when she walked. Mehdi envied, hated, and adored Yasmine. She was an odd, inverted version of himself. She was his Alice stepping through the looking glass. She was the cat grinning in front of his introverted misery, the wild tea party crashing on his carefully honed analyses. He cringed at what she did with her native gift of femininity, but inwardly he admired her decision not to be sweet and gentle. She became the mirror image of Mehdi's queerness and the stamp of his awful difference. And like Mehdi, she had spent the first eighteen years of her life planning an escape from their stifling home as fast and as irrevocably as possible.

Yasmine loathed the Nassiri house. She could not stand the scent of naphthalene and lavender emanating from the grand cabinets filled with threadbare sheets, blankets, and tablecloths.

She despised their new-found poverty and looked down upon her sister-in-law for losing her husband so completely. She herself had married a man for his money, and he had married her for two reasons: her name, and her disgust with it. "More Scarlett O'Hara than Greta Garbo," Mehdi had sneered at her during her lavish wedding ceremony. She shrugged an angular shoulder and pushed through the crowd toward the path she had so deliberately chosen for herself. It was no coincidence that she had chosen law—a complex, tortuous, and unpredictable discipline in a country like Morocco. It gave her a labyrinthine power that few people could master, let alone assail.

Unlike Yasmine, Mehdi was not a survivor. He was a hedonist. He was a navigator of seams, seeking pleasure where few believed it could be found. As a child, he learned to be an unobtrusive observer of others, and soon people began to forget he was even there. His quirks and queerness faded in the semidarkness of others' subconscious, and with time, he started to feel safe. He watched, analyzed, learned. His childhood and his youth in the familial house were long incursions in human nature and in the acquisition of a worldly, cynical acceptance of others' foibles. Mehdi became the crucible holding his family's stories. They boiled and bubbled in his overactive imagination, while easing his solitude with his family's torments and desires.

He was like the turtle retreating into its shell at any ominous sign of danger. This allowed him to study hard, excel, and in secret, parade in front of his mirror with items he had gleaned from his mother's and sister's discarded clothes. He was also the first member of the Nassiri family to acquire an advanced professional degree from abroad and, by age twenty-eight, he was commonly referred to as "Doctor," or its Arabic equivalent, "Hakim." He bore his medical profession like a camouflage for his peculiar nature. He chose to heal others so that his internal fissures remained out of harm's way. His passions and desires were hidden behind a white uniform and grey glasses, and this to his greatest pleasure. He walked out into the garden and inhaled its golden dust.

Here was his childhood home with its many, ugly secrets brushed under a Persian carpet and a closed door. He thought of all the shameful doings in darkened hallways and behind crooked trees: the gasp, the trembling release, and the unbearable shame that followed. Mehdi had long, strong hands, which he washed carefully and often. His fingernails were always clean and cut short, and a vintage gold watch adorned his right wrist. He had a respected medical practice, and his patients enjoyed his calm, professional manner and capable hands. He was known to be a good, pious man who took the poor and impoverished at a minimal fee, or even at no fee at all. His office and desk were of rosewood, and the rich smell of American cigarettes suffused the air.

Mehdi used his hands in an efficient and experienced manner. They prodded, touched, and felt patients dexterously, and threw light where previously there was only shadow and pain. But Mehdi's hands had secrets and shadows of their own. They felt, caressed, and moved upon skin forbidden to their touch. They gave and took pleasure in terrified disguise. His body had mechanistic urges beyond his control. Yet deep beneath the fear and shame, in that part of him where there was only quiet and calm, he felt pure joy. He was as crystalline as the flawless diamond no one dare violate, in perfect synchrony with the truth of his primary self.

Mehdi believed that the wall he had put up between his public front and his inner atelier of sensual deviations was unscalable. He believed his secret was safe. But one day many years from now, at the age where men and women begin to think of peace, Mehdi's secret will be discovered. The demons will take him to the mental asylum of Birsoukout in the

Casablanca countryside, and the world will forget about him. But, dearest darling, there is no need to rush into that story, for now here he was, breathing in the golden flower dust of his childhood.

~

As Mehdi faded into the garden's sunlight, the hosts and guests fell into the uneasy rhythm of family gatherings. Airs were mastered and conversations were honed to their cutting edge. Watches, shawls, and golden broaches were twirled expertly, and humid cigars were heated between palms. Driss, Leila's brother, was heating one such cigar between such sweaty palms. At his side was the beautiful woman whose disruptive presence had rippled throughout the household. She was looking at the house with a strange expression in her eye that Driss mistakes for admiration.

"The house is all that is left of our family's wealth."

"The house is alive. It's echoing your family's sadness and secrets."

"This family is cursed."

"What kind of curse?"

"A curse on love. Love comes here to die."

"What is love, really? Yearn instead for desire…"

"For our family, desire is nostalgia—a mysterious, aching need that can never be fulfilled. Love and desire come here for their burial."

"If you don't believe in curses, they will let you be."

"Growing up here has made me want peace. Something I know I will have with you."

Shawg smiled. Her black hair was twisted in a low chignon against her neck, and rings gleamed at her alabaster fingers. She was the kind of woman whose maturing femininity had managed to keep the usury of time at bay. Her breasts were full, and she had that heaviness of the hips that can be so moving in older women. She made men seem weak and vulnerable. Driss was completely under her spell—bemused by the depth in her eyes and her natural sensuality. She was his femme fatale, his childhood daydream, and his nightmare come to life. He knew he could forsake God and country for her, and yet he could never be sure of what she was thinking.

As can be expected in love stories like theirs, Shawg was bored. Seeing Driss in his family had definitely sealed their fate. Nevermore, nevermore, cawed the raven inside her. To be exact, "Shawg" was not even her real name. She had never liked her name. Do not say so, she was told by the women preening her for the men who would soon love her. Your name is beautiful, powerful. Your name is the name of the wife of the first man created by God. But she found it ugly, vulgar even, reminiscent of the brute sexual act, of fucking, "hwa" in Arabic. The wife of the primordial man, but oh how she hated that name and the destiny it would afford her.

So she chose the name "Shawg." Shawg, the nostalgia and painfulness of desire, the decadence of craving and the poisonous gift of life itself...Today, Shawg no longer wanted her fiancé, for she realized that she could only despise a man who settled for safety over excitement. And so it was that—during this brief moment of inner reckoning and as only beautiful and predatory women can do—she decided she must change her life and find another man. She turned from Driss, and her eyes fixed on Adam.

She looked at him long and hard. For reasons perhaps you will never understand, she saw something extraordinary in this broken man. He affected her in a way she did not think was possible. She saw his difference and suffering. She saw where he snapped and where his genius still survived. She thought an old thought: I could save him. In my hands, he could heal, he could even be great. She glowed and sizzled from this new perspective. She asked Driss:

"Who is that man over there, standing by himself?"

"That's Adam Tair, my sister's husband. He was a genius, a great intellectual. Something happened to him here. He didn't amount to much. Pity..."

Shawg had grown up in a lower-middle-class household in a poor, industrial quarter of Casablanca. Her father had been a teacher and her mother a lowly clerk in a small textile unit down the street. She had enough education to believe in its importance and was hungry enough to understand the even greater value of money. She belonged to those families who tend to gradually fall into poverty and precariousness but who continue to dream that better days are right around the corner. At thirteen, she was already smarter, stronger, and more beautiful than most women in her neighborhood, than most people in the world. What had to happen happened. She became one of those women who take money in exchange of pleasure.

She walked the streets at night, let men fall at her feet, or bend her over a cold bed. She then gave her money to pimps, investors, and parents. She swallowed her pride and lowered her head. With time, she became a prized object of desire. She traveled North Africa and the Middle East, and her success was great. She had to admit that at times she had enjoyed being who she was, and she became cruel to others—just because she could. But now, at thirty-five, she was finally rich and free. After years of sacrifice and humbled soul, of keeping her mouth and her mind shut, she could finally choose for herself. Others had always chosen for her. Now, she decides for herself.

And today, she chooses him, Adam. This she decided as her skin gleamed in the light of day.

Adam returned her gaze. How could he not? Adam looked at Shawg and remembered the shaved hair and long tress he wore as a little boy. He remembered how he'd rub his bare head and tug on his tress when he was reciting the Kuran to an angry teacher. He recalled the taste of fresh water from the nearby spring and the orange and olive trees whose branches clung to his uncle's house. He remembered the stolen oranges and olives, and how he ran as far as he could until, breathless, he'd fill his mouth with the forbidden fruit. He closed his eyes and tasted the melancholia of lost memories and unlived childhoods. Everything became quiet, as though the world had not yet been created and the universe was a great emptiness from which emerged one silent star after another. When desire appears, all else is burnt. When Shawg appeared to Adam, everything erupted. He was consumed with desire and the craving for complete possession. She was the answer to his hardened disappointments.

A terrible pain exploded in his chest. It felt as though someone had reached inside him and torn a rib out of his ribcage. He heard a voice near his ear (well, not *any* voice, *that* voice) telling him to accept the pain for it was the sign of a miracle to come. His breathing became constricted. He touched his chest below his heart and felt a softness where earlier there had been a rib. He tasted lead, and the wilderness in his mind became quiet for a while, listening to the new pain of the lost rib.

Adam did not know who this woman was, nor did he fully understand his reaction to her presence. She had appeared before him with all the promise of a Renaissance-era painting. She was made of light and color, and her skin glistened while everything around her became obscure. She carried herself as though there had never been any woman before her, as though the destiny of the world depended on her. She made Leila look complicated and sad, unable as she was now to taste happiness or go up in flames at the mere touch of life. Much to his own amazement, the years spent with Leila now seemed unhappy ones, and that unhappiness, he was beginning to suspect, was due to *her*.

His heart beating, he wondered what his life would have been if he had not met Leila and if she had not convinced him to return to their country. He felt angry and betrayed. His ego rose out of its speechless slumber, and he thought of all the wonderful things he could have done with a brain like his. Leila now seemed a primitive being to him, a demon of the night sent to destroy him and exile him to the darkest corners of hell. He saw her and her child as chains keeping him away from heaven. Something inside him, something faithful still to his past and to notions of loyalty and right, reminded him: You made a promise to a woman you have loved for over thirteen years. You made a promise to your wife and child to protect them always. But another side of him, eager for pleasure and freedom from responsibility, hissed: Don't you deserve joy? What has life with this woman brought you? Exile in a country that you were trained to leave behind, the wasting away of your talents, imprisonment, torture, demons, silence, and hell itself. Time has come for you to taste life again. This child, it is not even your child. A monstrous child who will carry your name!

The pain in his body had now risen to his head. A multitude of voices struggled to be heard and to speak—each with their opinion, their interests, and their advice. Some did not even address the matter at hand and instead just excitedly chatted away. It was as though all the djinns of the house had scrambled into his head for their enjoyment and his bewilderment. They played and spun webs of confused and confusing arguments. Some justified yielding to temptation and spoke principles that reminded Adam that the worth of a man lay in the honoring of the given word. Other, more sophisticated voices cited contradictory Kuranic verses as a backdrop to the right course to follow. One lone voice clamored that the Green Book had risen from the injunction to read and that therefore the given word trumped all other considerations. The voices in his head soon became a carnival of hollow advice where bad faith paraded.

Adam thought of the word he had given Leila and of how his word silenced every other word. He had forsaken utterance in the name of the given word. Perhaps he had made the mistake of recognizing a child he should never have recognized as his. He had lost his voice and hovered at the edge of ancient woods like a wolf. The body, after all, never lies. It reveals through its broken sinew, trembling limbs, and reddened skin every repressed desire and uttered lie. And his body, he now believed, had refused to recognize the child as his. But, yes, he had given his word, and the child would soon be baptized as his own. Adam paused in the midst of breaking a promise he had made over thirteen years ago and which he had reiterated six months back. It was suddenly clear to him, even though he would always deny it, that he already knew which path he would choose. The brilliance of his solution made him shake, and still his internal whispering continued: Oh, Leila, what would *you* have done if happiness had chosen you? I cannot choose, I cannot forsake either path. He sighed and a semblance of sound trickled through his lips. He felt a tugging at his wrist and, looking down, saw that the amulet given to him by a little girl one night, in the labyrinths of the Casablanca Medina, was gone.

~

Leila was sitting in her room as the women prepared her for the naming. They washed her in a bath of herbs and scented water. They dressed her like a bride and poured warm rose water and oil into her hair. They fed her the heart and fat of the sheep, sprinkled with red saffron from Taliouine, the village between the valley of roses and the mountain behind which lay the great medieval jail that, to that day, still held its prisoners. They gave her sellou, a crushed mixture of almonds, orange blossom, sugar, flour, and sesame seeds. They made henna in a bowl and beat kohl to a pulp. They tapped souak (the lipstick only married women ritually wore) on her lips, drew a line of kohl beneath her eyes, and repainted henna on her hands and feet. Leila remained immobile throughout the preparations, secretly rejecting these rituals and despairing for the spontaneity that seemed to be forever lost, for that privacy that was fleeing from her at every breath she drew...

Finally, the baby was washed and dressed in white European lace and satin that came all the way from Madrid. A drop of henna was placed in the center of her palms and in the small curvature of her feet. The newborn brings with her all the fear of an unknowable elsewhere whose chaos must be condensed into words and fleeting tattoos. Leila held her child who, the instant she was born, was taken from the realm of nature into the cartography of culture. She kissed her and cooed her own words in her ear.

Meanwhile in the courtyard, Ibrahim waited, his butcher's knife in hand, for the family to gather. He wore his white djellaba and held the sheep by the nape. He had performed this ritual for all his children without a second thought. With the help of another man, he had grabbed the sheep firmly and quickly slit its throat. He had watched it writhe on the floor and looked on as the blood trickled into the gutter. He had felt the power of God flow through him. He had praised God and named the child. Today, however, was different.

As he stood there holding his thick knife, he expected to feel that surge of adrenaline and that pride he had felt all morning. He expected to feel that extraordinary communion with the Lord that is obtained by observing His dictates. But no divine grace stamped his actions today. He craved for it with a powerful thirst and a devouring need. He hungered for the simplicity of the absolute sacrifice and the transcendence achieved through the shedding of the innocent's blood. He wanted the devouring thing itself rather than its pale alternative. He wanted the barbaric rather than the civilized, the sublime rather than the sublimated. He was filled with the desire to kill for his God.

At that moment, he wished his granddaughter would cease to exist. He was wracked with the double certainty that she was not fit for the world and that pain would accompany her throughout her life. He wanted to offer her as a sacrifice instead of the sheep and reverse the passing of time. He wanted to stand on the rubble of the mountain and present his burning sacrifice to his God.

Then he looked as Leila walked in holding her daughter. She came in with Zohra and Aisha, and was followed by Hamza and Zeinab. They appeared to him as an army, a band of companions who had elected themselves her protectors. He thought he saw, but he must have imagined it, shining swords at their sides and in their hands. Then he saw it.

He saw the child for who she was and who she was meant to be—and he trembled. He saw the light guiding her. This is the end, he shivered. He recognized the end of certainty, of hierarchy, of authority. He forgot about raw sacrifice and human death, and lowered his head.

"*In the name of God,*" Ibrahim cried, and, holding the sheep tightly in his arms, slit its neck. As the blood flowed and the body shook, he gave the child her name: Maryam. The name came to him naturally, "*Maryam,*" an elusive name with a multiplicity of meanings: rebel, bitterness, loved one, killer, saint, guardian. Maryam, a perfect name for she who was conceived in darkness and fear, she with the handicap and of the forgotten destiny.

At that very moment, a scent of orange blossoms exploded into the air and distilled its lustrous perfume upon the assembly. Each and every one was filled with a delightful, singing serenity. After some investigation, it was discovered that the orange blossom scent came from the child herself.

And that is how Maryam Tair came into this world.

~

Zohra knelt and gently touched the sheep's spilt blood with her finger, asking for the animal's forgiveness. She then drew a small crescent moon on Maryam's neck, behind her right ear, and whispered, "So you may hear all the suffering of the world and be compassionate always."

The family formed a circle around the child. Mehdi, Yasmine, and Driss came closer. The scent of orange blossom was everywhere. It brought peace and clarity to those who inhaled it. Mehdi was close to Maryam now, close enough to feel her difference. He began to sense the winds of change rise and imagined that they would carry people like him to safer shores. But his feet had been anchored to a cold earth for far too long, and he feared he would not be able to wait for that liberation nor experience the moment when people like him would walk this country without any shame or fear in the world. Driven by forces beyond his control, he prophesized:

"You will bring hope to those you meet. You will open the doors of the dream world and help people fight fear and hatred, anger and ignorance. You will make the margins bloom with beauty. You are *perception*."

Yasmine came next. She looked at Maryam and sensed her power. She thought of all her stunted dreams and the calculations that arose from her failures, like so many banners against despair. She too felt the frustration of lapsed time, but she had to admit that she had never truly despaired. She was the cold warrior with the blue-grey, vapid essence animating her. Driven by forces beyond her control, she prophesized:

"Your mind is powerful and free. You will drive your questionings off the beaten path. You will push your reasoning to its logical conclusions. You will crave knowledge. You are *thought*."

Adam waited behind Yasmine. The silence that had filled him these past months was dissipating. His voice had been returned to him. He was calm and burning all at once. He knew what was in his heart and what it would soon drive him to do. He had lost pity and loyalty along the way. His delusions had created a permanent strain on his psyche, and he had finally chosen to let go. He was in a constant state of panic whose only outcome was cowardice. Driven by forces beyond his control, he prophesized:

"You will see the world for what it is but also for what it could be. You are a magical, supernatural being who will heal the cracks in the world. You will embrace the image but also what lies beneath. You are *heart*."

"Ameen," echoed the assembled guests. They began walking back to the house when Shawg asked Leila, "May I hold her in my arms?" And before Zohra could stop her, Leila put Maryam in Shawg's arms.

She held her close, so close. She breathed her in and stroked her cheek, but all she felt was envy. Her face drained of color, and her eyes lost their light. She thought of the injustice of a world that granted such beautiful gifts to a weak, ugly child and that had allowed a person like her, a person of power and beauty, to wrestle with adversity and disdain. A shiver ran down her spine while hatred filled her heart.

"Perception, thought, heart, they will not come to you easily. You will have to fight for them. You will walk alone. You will fill others with wonder, but no one will come close to you.

You are fragile, driven by guilt. Your heart will never know the fullness of love. You are love forever seeking plenitude in the tormented quest for the loved one. You are *dissonance*."

Shawg then dropped Maryam into her mother's arms and stepped back.

Rebellion

"Grant me my divorce, Adam."

Leila sat with her hands on her knees and her back straight. She had been sitting for an hour listening to Adam's tale of woe and rebirth. He was distant and matter-of-fact. When he started, Leila was perplexed, and that perplexity increased as she heard the story of his life, of their life together, narrated with words she herself would never have chosen. She began to wonder whether his prolonged muteness had given rise to a distortion in language or to a loss of meaning. It took a moment for her to understand the purpose of his speech.

"Grant me my divorce, Adam."

"I have spoken to your father this morning, Leila. He and I agree that what is best for you and Maryam is that you remain my wife."

"You have fallen in love with another woman and you wish to remarry. I accept. But give me my honor back or I will go mad."

"Don't raise your voice at me, Leila. Your behavior is irrational. There's no need for a divorce. A woman like you in a country like this, you would be ruined without a man. Put your feelings aside and think of your future...and your child's future. You need me."

"I will go mad, Adam. In the name of what we once had and of what I believe we still have, let me go with what is left of my pride."

"No. They will say I have abandoned wife and daughter. They will say, after what you've been through, that I've abandoned you."

"Who is this *they* who have the force of law in your eyes? Is it God? Since when does the great Adam care what others think of him?"

"I will not grant you your divorce, but you are allowed to stay here in your parents' house. You don't have to live with... her. And my daughter, nothing will change. She is mine. I have recognized her as my own. That's more than most men would have agreed to, given the circumstances of her birth..."

"A man? You think this is what a real man does? You were more of a man when you lost your power of speech. Or was that a lie, too? Was everything a lie? Has she bewitched you? I think I'm going mad. This is just a bad dream. How could you change so fast? How could you forget what we shared, just like that, in the blink of an eye? Oh, I am beginning to believe in she-demons and black magic."

"You must calm down now. You're being hysterical, you're unrecognizable."

"This is not hysteria. This is rage. Marry your whore then, but let me go."

"You speak ill of another woman, you spit on her virtue. Know then that she is pure, that she wishes to wait till we are married. Keeping you as a wife is the best solution for us all. You and I have not been happy together. Leila, remember our pain, our solitude. Remember my delusions and your empty days. We deserve happiness. But I am an ethical man, and I will continue being your husband. It is done."

"Oh, grant me my divorce. In the name of our love, of our

days together in Paris and the dreams we once shared and that you now deny ever were, let me be free."

"Free? You're a mother and you speak to me of freedom? Speak to your father. I can't reason with you anymore. This is how it must be."

"I'm breaking. Look at me. We are taught to fear divorce and a solitary life. But this—bigamy, polygamy, call it what you want—is hell. The shame of being told to share, or kept in for pity's sake, told that you can be dispensed with at any time. Only a pervert could suggest such a thing. And to me, I, Leila. Do I seem so weak that you think I deserve this, or will accept it? Give me my freedom so that my daughter can grow up beside me and not be ashamed of her mother."

Her voice had risen. She was screaming, screeching like a caged bird desperate for the freedom of the world. She clawed the air and tore at her clothing. Her eyes brimmed with tears and her soul with wounded pride. He had broken her heart.

Adam drank in her fury. He looked at her wild hair and her torn clothing. He saw her teetering on the brink of madness, and he began to retreat, slowly, his hands raised to protect himself from her. Yes, Shawg had been right. She had warned him that Leila would behave like a hysterical woman. She told him that she had seen it in her—that fragility of temperament beneath, that anxious look recognizable as the key to an unstable mind. He walked away thinking of neurotic females and the quasi-natural, unavoidable moment when women just seem to *snap*.

He could not, however, deny the darkness that had taken hold of him ever since he made the decision to marry Shawg. He had discovered selfishness and had toned his behavior accordingly. And, as Shawg told him in one of the darkened hallways of the great old house, he deserved happiness more than anyone. He may have been a great man, and he probably still could be—if he listened to his own needs for a change.

And Shawg was good, wasn't she, for she had immediately agreed that he keep Leila as his wife but under the condition that she remain under her parents' roof. Could he deny, furthermore, that for the first time in years, he was a man again. He got hard when she smiled or glanced his way. He felt excitement and even, he blushed slightly, the desire for power and physical domination. The rush, the miracle…yes, for now he could speak, scream, sing his happiness. It was all so new. He was twenty again, in love, young, and ardent again. God had given him a second chance—he refused to waste it. Especially for a woman who was spent, whose life would sway from one melancholic sacrifice to the next. The muscles in the right side of his face began to twitch. He put his hand to his face and rubbed the twitching muscles to relax them. The twitching only increased, and he stood there quietly, waiting for the spasms to pass and terrified that he may lose his voice once more. The spasms finally subsided, leaving him feeling uneasy and on edge. He pressed back on his anxiety with a hardened heart and lascivious thoughts. After all, hadn't his voice been returned to him as a prelude of bliss to come and the promise of ecstasy? And only Shawg could ease his doubts.

~

Leila touched her hair, face, breasts, stomach, inner thighs, and legs. Her hands were cold, and they left a trail of shivers down her body. She thought that she heard the tinkle of glass in the distance, but it was only the sound her heart made as it broke. She bit her lip, and blood dropped on the faded Persian carpet. But it is not just my heart, it is my pride. I am not only hurt in my softness for him but in my sense of pride. He's trying to break me, isn't he, to justify his betrayal. He's showing the world how mad I am that he leaves me but keeps me chained to him for my own protection. And the woman he chose—a woman whose fake sophistication and vulgar wealth would once have repelled him! But I must be mad, or naïve at best, to think a woman like her could ever disgust a man. She is what a man dreams a woman to be. She is Eve, light to my darkness, warmth to my abstractness, hopefulness to my sadness. He has left but he has not left, he is my husband, but he has imprisoned me in my father's house with my daughter.

I am breaking in so many ways that my center no longer holds. I am numb from the pain. I once met a couple in Paris. They were convinced that true social freedom started with sexual freedom. But what I want is freedom from sex, from *him* and the humiliation he has caused me. True freedom is being alone. I pray that my daughter never knows that dependence on another human being. I pray that she be free from the terror of being let down and relegated to the condition of the unwanted first wife. I used to be free...or I thought I was. I painted suns on my cheek and wore flowers in my hair. We used to dance till dawn, but now, see, I am thirty-three and am already old. My life is used, useless, unused.

Do you remember, Sheherazade, do you remember the description of the harem of one of the greatest palaces in the world—Topkapi? There was no luxury, no oriental luxuriance for the women living there. Cold rooms with bare walls and low ceilings like the monasteries of Eastern Europe. They were made to live like monks but were hunted like prey. It was a community of fleeting friendships and cruel betrayals. They worked hard, ate, and slept little. They had the ascetic lives of nuns until the sultan graced them with his favors, and life became softer for a while. Most women were forgotten there for years until they grew old and filled the palace walls with their solitary breaths. There were hundreds and hundreds of rooms, and I am now in one of those rooms, prisoner of the great political machine that is a man's lust. To think that my daughter will one day submit to the violence of the world, and to think that I will be a constant reminder of the chains that bind us. How could she ever be free, how could she ever achieve something more if her mother agrees, today, to bend?

Leila sat facing the garden, deep in thought. Her rage and pain gave her a respite, while she forced herself to think clearly. She got up to look for a cigarette lighter and found that Aisha and Zohra were in the room. She didn't know how long they had been there or what they had witnessed.

"Your father is waiting for you in his office. He told me about Adam and your brother's whore, and what he has agreed to."

"He has."

"It's your father's revenge. He has agreed to this farce to punish me."

"Baba loves me. He believes this is the best way to protect a sullied daughter and a bastard granddaughter."

"You father is an idiot. Idiots understand other men's compulsions but don't try to curb them. Ibrahim has forgotten the true meaning of sharaf, of honor and blood. You are a woman of an ancient bloodline on your father's and on your mother's side. The blood in your veins is powerful, a maker of kings and queens."

"Mama, stop. There is nothing that history or family can do when a person chooses to love another person. But honor, yes, honor is something else."

"We can get rid of her, child. I will open the skies for you, and you will see her writhe and collapse at your feet. Let me do this for you."

"No. It will not accomplish anything. History will repeat itself in an endless, vicious cycle, and women will remain stuck in this inferno for all eternity."

"Don't preoccupy yourself with other women. Don't be naïve. In the end, you are alone with your destiny. Revenge is the best antidote for rage and humiliation. Sometimes, you have to debase yourself to get what you want. Remaining noble will only lead you to be forgotten at best and despised at worst. Time is not on your side. Freedom is a dream."

"We're always blaming the thief, the woman whose heart we don't know but who becomes our enemy because our man would rather be with her."

"It's difficult to blame the object for being stolen. Of course, it's the thief we blame!"

"But Adam is not an object, and he is not a possession. He let himself be stolen. He chose another woman for her beauty and strength, for the happiness he imagines he will have with her. He is the one to blame. She doesn't owe me anything. She took something that was not hers. But if she was able to take it, it means it was not mine either. Does it matter in the end? It's what he wanted. He has decided to save himself."

"Think about Maryam."

"I am...so very much. All I think of is her. Possession, possessiveness, marriage ties, these are all forms of enslavement. I will not have my kid be any man's slave. And what will she think when she hears her mother killed another woman to keep a man? No, I cannot...I know what I must do."

Aisha turned to Zohra to plead with her.

"Reason with her, she's not making sense. Tell her that nothing will ever change, that the world has been the same for centuries and as far back as we can remember. Women must fight their battles with the weapons at hand, in the way of the weak."

Zohra remained silent. She was looking beyond them at an imaginary horizon, and she saw what they could not. She arched like a tense bow, then spoke.

"Come rest in my arms, Leila. Yes, just so…hush, my beloved. You will do what's right for yourself and your child."

A silence surrounded the three women. Zohra's eyes had turned a filmy blue, and her arms were wrapped around Leila like a protective shield.

~

Leila rose to perform her final act of obedience. She went to her father's office and knocked on the closed door. Ibrahim was waiting for her, his white hair and white hands clearly outlined in the shadows of the room. The objects in the room were bathed in the soft shadows cast by the setting sun. Their corners cut the air like the ragged edges of cliffs cut the skyline. Perspective appeared flattened, and presence was denied warmth. Leila stepped hesitantly inside this space with the feeling that she had just penetrated a cubist painting. After her shattered heart, it was now her body's turn to crack and break into hundreds of jagged shapes diluted into the flatness. She looked into her father's face and breathed in the incense burning near his right hand. Her eyes melted behind the pain of remembrance and the fear of what lay ahead.

"Is it true, Baba?"

"It is true that, as your father, I have made a decision for you and for my grandchild."

"You have sacrificed me. You have agreed to keep me tied to a man who has chosen to leave me."

"A man? He is not a man. He is a dog. He would never have protected you, and he will let others abuse you and your child. This is the only way to keep you from harm's way, to keep the demons and the bloodsuckers at a distance from you. You are fragile, vulnerable, a ready prey for all the wolves to feed on. I wanted to keep you safe. Here with me…safe. That man no longer carries you in his vision of the future and of himself.

I don't give a crap about him, and neither should you! But for your sake, you must remain his wife. You must have that status. A woman who has gone through what you have gone through in times like these, and in a country like this one, is worth nothing!"

"You want me to remain a despised first wife and my child to grow in the shadow of a discarded mother? What you are offering is not protection, it's a slow death."

"I'm offering you a home."

"You're putting me in jail."

"Enough! I will not be questioned. You will obey me. And one day, you will thank me. Now get out."

Leila's head reeled from the impact of those words on her broken heart, her shattered body, her fugitive spirit. She looked one last time at her father and turned to leave. She paused in her footstep. She went back to him and kissed his hand, "Baba." She then walked to the room she shared with Maryam since her birth, less than forty days ago.

Forty days, a gap in time, a newfound thinness in the earth's crust as I stood with my newborn child in my arms, and together we discovered the extreme vulnerability of life. Forty days where it is known that a mother and her child can fall back into the darkness to which they still belonged for those forty days. I held her in front of the precipice of my own solitude and paused at the edge, while a terrible, terrifying lightness hissed at the brink of my consciousness and told me of the body that falls through the air and of the joy it brings. But then as I was dreaming the fall, her scent of fruit about to bloom, of hope and perpetual possibility, wrapped my wounded ego in a blanket of love.

Leila kissed Maryam's mouth and rocked her softly till her eyes closed. She then sat at the table and wrote. She wrote till her fingers turned blue, till her wrist ached, she wrote till her mind became numb. When she was done and the ink was completely dry, she brushed the words off the paper and into the milk. She watched as they twirled and settled between the ivory molecules. "Perfect," she sighed. "It is done." When Maryam woke up, she held her in her arms and fed her the milk. She whispered little nothings to her. The words dropped in her ear like pearls in a pure stream. Leila told Maryam many silly, absurd, and delightful things she had never told anyone before. She shared lightness and delight with her and let those fizzle joyfully through her, a powerful protection against loneliness and fear.

"I must leave you, my darling. It is my act of love for you. You must believe it to be true. My one, only, and ultimate proof of love for you. To reveal your strength, to provide you with your own destiny. I want more for you. I want you to experience the devouring leap forward and the understated delights of the introvert. I will watch over you from the tears between worlds, and perhaps you will see me and I will see you…There is one last thing you must know. I have written a story and inscribed it within you. You are the bearer of the oldest story in the world. You hold the pages of a willfully forgotten story whose power is now yours. When the time is ripe, the story will reveal itself."

Leila turned to see Zohra standing behind her, her face stripped of any emotion. She placed Maryam in her arms and said, "You are now Maryam's Godmother, Zohra of the Ait Daoud. Your tribe is the mighty tribe of the Guardians. Protect my daughter with all your power." Zohra kissed Leila on the mouth, deeply. "She is now and forever in my keep. No harm will come to her."

~

While this scene was being written in the sunlit room overlooking the garden, Hamza stalked to the kitchen, intent on finding Zeinab. It had been thirty-nine days since he had been called to the house. He had raged against the djinns and the ghosts, slid his sword Zulkitab across the stone floors till sparks rose, scattered gathering diseases, and defied the cold-eyed demons that had hungered to enter. He had debated with the trees about good and evil, planted daylilies, jasmine, birds of paradise, asters, alyssums, impatiens, lupens, ferns, marigolds, orange blossoms surely, and brought peace to a house built on strife and greed. And every night he kept watch outside of Zeinab's door, near the garage.

On the fortieth day of the child's birth, the doors between this world and the next will close, and she will be safe. On the fortieth day, he will leave for a new adventure. On the fortieth day, he will have to say goodbye to Zeinab forever. He walked into the kitchen with beating heart and the sound of waves in his ears. The ground shook under his feet and sand swirled around his boots, yet he coughed softly to announce his presence. Startled, Zeinab stopped her cleaning and looked up. She straightened her back and waited, her eyes large and bright. Hamza took her all in, and his backbone bristled like leaves in the wind. He bowed and presented her with a bouquet of flowers larger than she. Zeinab thought that she could hide in there, and her employer would never find her. Hamza touched the bouquet with his right hand, and it shrunk to fit snugly in Zeinab's hand. "Hmm...I think I may have overdone it a little. I created it for you." He paused and, encouraged by her smiling silence, he continued. "I have been watching over you." Zeinab smelled the bouquet in her hands, and the flowers chanted their names for her in their floral tongues. Zeinab buried her head in their petals and tasted happiness. Hamza said softly, "The desert flower has found her home." But tears soon filled Zeinab's eyes. Hamza stood there at a loss, wondering why such sadness when he only cared to make her happy.

Zeinab had forgotten the taste of happiness. To be exact, it had been hammered out of her since she was seven years old. To rediscover that giddiness and contentment was like rediscovering goose bumps on her skin or the taste of chocolate in her mouth. But it also meant that she must come to terms with hope. She would need to let her guard down and allow dreams to rush to the fore. She would be more vulnerable than the seven-year-old child she had buried at the back of her mind. As for Hamza, he was mortified by the helplessness in her eyes.

"Ya Zeinab, I am not who you think I am. I will take you with me, and we will build together a small house in the mountains of your childhood. We will reclaim the land that your tribe has lost and transform the desert into a paradise. Not that I mind deserts. Deserts have the bravest and most beautiful of shrubbery. You will be a queen. Not a fairy-tale queen with a crown and jewels, a queen who can make her land lush and grow olive and almond trees at will. You will have the purest joy of all: that of seeing the planted seed grow and bloom. Come with me. Leave this place and I will stop everything for you. I will grow old for you, and with you."

Zeinab had scars on her lower back from a beating many years ago. When she was thirteen, a woman had beaten her with a leather belt because she had seen her husband leave her room in the early morning. Zeinab was never quite the same after the whipping. She had recurrent nightmares of a dark man dripping with oil lowering his weight on her bed. A kindly neighbor heard her scream and offered to take the child out of the woman's hands. She was immediately let go. Since that day, whenever she woke up, her lower back would ache as though she had been whipped with that old leather belt in her sleep. The neighbor then took her to a woman whom, she told her, was once a great lady but had fallen on hard times and needed cheap labor. This is how Zeinab began working for the Nassiris.

Ever since her first encounter with Hamza, the nightmares had stopped, and the scars no longer burned. For all she could think of was him. She believed him when he said he had watched over her, but she feared him when he said he wanted to take her away. A man's touch on her skin would certainly burn it, and a man's weight on her would crush her.

"My life cannot be fixed, Hamza. It has been broken for too long. I don't know what happiness means. I wouldn't know how to bring joy into your life."

"You are my joy. Don't you see, you don't need to do anything for me. I am not your master, you are not my slave. You will be free. When I am with you, my hands stop aching and I am whole. I have looked for you throughout the ages and across worlds for thousands of years. I did not know what a painless life was until I met you. I did not know I hungered for you until I laid eyes on you. You are who you are. And you are the one for me. That is all."

"I don't know what freedom means. I know it's terrifying. I don't know whether returning to my homeland would break me or fix me. I don't know that I need to be free."

"Don't you love me?"

"Yes, I believe I do."

"I am the Destroyer and the Creator. I make way for humanity in this world, and I create wondrous life. I destroy wilderness and curb thunder to my will. I offer you my hands and my sword, my powers and my love, and still you fear! I ask you one last time, Zeinab of the Sraghnas—will you leave with me?"

"I would probably never make it out the door."

"Oh! If you could only see what I see. If you could raise your eyes to my height and see the vastness of the world reflected."

Zeinab remained silent, for how could she tell him that she had seen the world in his eyes and that it terrified her. How could she explain to him that resilience had replaced courage in her life view. She knew that he had changed her forever, but there was nothing she wanted to do about it. She held the flowers close to her heart and watched as golden tears flooded Hamza's eyes. She thought she saw a large boat floating in his pupils, a boat welcoming all the animals of the world in pairs and one lonely man. Then the mirage disappeared, and all she could see was a bawling giant.

Hamza kissed her hands and bade her farewell. As he was about to step through the kitchen door, he turned to her and said, "The flowers will never die. They are my love for you. My soul is in their veins, see, there, the stems are grey and green like me," he explained, his face crimson. Then Hamza left, his boots thudding the ground, tears rolling from his eyes in gallons, and a tsunami of pain in his heart. Possessed by a formidable sadness, he went to the old orange tree, planted Zulkitab in the ground, and lay face down in the earth. He sobbed like a lion and beat the soil to a pulp. He ate the flowers, dirt, and roots while sinking his hands deep into the belly of the earth for comfort. When he woke up the next morning, his arms from his wrists to his shoulders had turned a warm, dark brown, and his burning heart was cold.

~

Something else happened during that one day and night when Hamza grappled with his despair: he forgot his sword and his mission. He wiped out djinns, ghosts, and giddy gardens from his mind and postponed the protection of the house and its inhabitants.

In the early morning of the fortieth day, the orange tree lowered its branches toward Hamza's sleeping body and shook his limbs this way and that. Hamza woke up from his dreamless slumber to the sound of wailing women. He pulled Zulkitab from the earth and ran toward the house. He pushed through the people gathered around and found Leila lying on the terrace with slit wrists. After an interlude of whirlwinds and icy rains rattling his brain, Hamza turned toward Zohra and fell on one knee.

"I failed, my lady. I did not protect her, and now she is dead. Grant me a punishment that I may expunge my guilt."

"No, Hamza. She chose this for herself. This is as it must be. You have protected this household as you should. You have allowed the child to get stronger. I thank you."

"I was weak. You do not know my weakness."

"You too are allowed weakness. You may be immortal, but you are not infallible. And your infallibility was written into the story before you yourself encountered your own destiny in our midst. You're free to go. We are even."

"Thank you, my lady. You may call on me for Maryam's protection as needed, and I will come."

"Goodbye, Hamza. Zulkitab, protect our friend from harm. May the forces inside you balance one another once more and for the good of all."

Hamza kissed Zohra's hand and left the house with heavy step and filled with doubt. His sword became soft in his hand and curled around his wrist, lapping at his arm like a dog seeking to comfort a beloved master. As he left, Zohra felt the ghosts leave the house as well. They had had their sacrifice after all. A first wife, a daughter of a first wife who kills herself, what greater vengeance, what greater delight…They giggled and sang as they ascended or descended, depending on your preference for their fates. All were joyous except for the young ghost who had come to love Leila and their midnight talks.

~

Adam sat in an armchair in a darkened room. His head was bowed, and he looked, once more, like an old man. He did not feel regret or sorrow as you may imagine, my child. No, he felt awe. His mind had submitted to external pressures and disappointments a while back. He had curled in upon himself and let the darkness and the fantastic in. By the time he was taken, he could no longer rely on logical arguments or ethical syllogisms to guide him. He had collapsed because Leila was not there to help him through. Upon meeting Shawg, he had mistaken his own frailty for Leila's. He began to think of her as the chains holding him back from greatness. Today, while others were mourning Leila's death or whispering about its sacrilegious nature, he understood it fully. It was an antireligious, anticlerical, and antisocial act, but it was not surrender. It was an act of defiance whereby she exercised her power to say no. It was, most of all, an act of love. She was the strength to my weakness, and now I must bear the load of living in solitude. I must also show a new woman that I am all she thinks I am: strong, brilliant, misunderstood. His face started twitching, and he raised a mechanical hand to hide the muscular madness. The chair upon which he sat became hard and cold, and the unhinged grandfather's clock on the wall stroke an ungodly hour. It was time for him to leave this household.

Shawg was watching him coolly, cigarette embers sizzling between her fingers. She knew, with the desperate instinct of a woman in love, that Adam was changing his mind about her. She said hurriedly: "My love, Maryam belongs with us. We are her family now. We must take her with us. I will take care of her like my own child."

He held her hands in his and embraced her. But Zohra appeared before them and hissed: "No one is taking her. She stays here with me. And where she goes, I go. And you do not want me in your house, Adam of the weak ribs. I will eat life out of you, mark my words."

Shawg took in Zohra's fury, but her pride refused defeat. She followed her.

"This child should not be loved this way. It is impossible. I…"

"You cursed her? But your definition of love is a narrow one. You equate love to desire and want. But love is the stuff dreams and revolutions are made of. And as for myself, your curses cannot work on me. I am old and your curses are child games to me. Now get out or I too shall curse you, and my curses are worse than death!"

The family grieved over Leila's body before exiting the house in silence.

~

A few days later, inquiring through the notary about the state of his daughter's affairs, Ibrahim found out that her one material good, the Centre Ville apartment he had placed in her name, had crumbled. Further investigation revealed that the fissures in the apartment walls were caused by an invasion of moss and grey weeds. The apartment appeared to have been deserted by its inhabitants for decades instead of the one year that had lapsed since the demons walked in and took Leila and Adam Tair from their home.

Sheherazade

Sheherazade is dressed in black. Black leather boots, black leather jacket, black riding breeches, and black silk shirt. She is holding a riding crop, and her hair is long, electric, and silvery white. At her feet is an exhausted flying carpet. The little girl is sitting by the fire carving symbols on a double-edged sword wrought for a giant.

"Where were you, Old Mother?" she asked.

"My niece Pythia, the Oracle of Delphi, told me in one of her rants of a medium that would one day be invented by a New World wizard. I went to see it. It has a mirror that is as dark as a pool of still water. The mirror begins to shine, and bright blue lights appear. It's a screen. I wanted to see what lay beneath. So I became a virus and dove inside. The machine has many uses, but the most wondrous and terrifying of all is a use that exceeds it. Pure magic it is. It has the ability to compress and compile all the knowledge of humanity. A Babel of languages, imagery, and symbolisms, it immediately takes possession of you and hurls you into trancelike imaginings, fleeting and dense. Pythia claims that it can flatten time, space, and desires into one plane of windless linearity. She fears that mystery will dissolve into certainty and that her knowledge of the past and future, of human destinies and dramatic flaws, will be made obsolete. She believes that the New World wizard harnessed the power of butterflies and spiders to bolster his magical invention."

Sheherazade's body begins to shake uncontrollably, and her eyes roll upward. The little girl runs toward her, but Sheherazade stops as suddenly as she began.

"I still don't see why trances are so important to her. When Nietzsche was born, Pythia also predicted her own demise. Yet there she still is, and Nietzsche is dead somewhere. I'm not certain she gives a good name to the rest of us…I was warned it would be one of the side effects of that magical machine and its weblike quests."

"What did you see, Old Mother?"

"I saw a butterfly leaving Leila's neck as she fell to the floor. It flapped its wings and circled the world, spreading its golden dust as it went. With her last breath, strange events occurred, and the wizard's machine recorded them. Stars rained from the sky, meteors hit the earth, hail fell on deserts, and the sun shined in the darkest hours of the night. Women from across the land and from lands beyond the Dead Sea and the Indian Ocean rose up. Women from lands once immortalized by Ibn Batuta and Leo Africanus and since forgotten broke their chains. They wrote, stood, united, marched, refused, denied, negated, rejected, defied, defined, mocked.

"All households from Timbuktu to Cairo, and from Teheran to New Delhi, were in turmoil. Indeed, the news spread like wildfire— word of a mother's sacrifice and of the birth of a child conceived in hell and saved by love. A child of destiny who should have been born at the beginning of time but whose existence was elided by other stories and higher scribes. But now figures explode in the firmament, and grey matter laces the black-and-white certainties of the past. Narrative tattoos on feminine bodies writhe and the blood-ink fades. Finally, clauses in texts of law disappear or are reformed overnight, while bearded men wipe their glasses or rub their eyes, and perhaps one or two others chuckle."

"Is this true? Does this medium record truth?"

"It records what it encounters."

Sheherazade winks at the frustrated child. Sunflowers appear in her silvery-white hair. Opening her arms like a flower in bloom, her pipe curled around her arm, she turns toward the sun. The little girl looks at the symbols she has just carved on Zulkitab, the double-edged sword.

"Tell me more, Old Mother. Tell me about symbols, words, and the forging of destinies."

"You have always been here, my beloved child. Whether as dust, as a repressed memory, or as a mother's dream, the possibility of you is the reason these stories are told. Your presence now is the pool from whence these words have risen. But now you are no longer trace or shadow, you are here, at the heart of my world. So listen closely…"

It is 1984. Maryam Tair is three years old, and the twins Shams and Hilal are born.

Desire

It was early in the afternoon, and Maryam had fallen asleep under the gnarled orange tree in her grandparents' garden. An older woman was sitting next to her. She was over two hundred fifty years old. Everything in her stance suggested that she was guarding the sleeping child. Fallen orange blossoms lay on the yellow-green grass. Zohra picked up the dying flowers and stroked them gently. She looked up at the ancient tree and saw the sap bleeding from its bark. The tree was expressing its despair for the state of nature through all its pores.

Since Hamza's sobbing, broken-hearted departure, drought had hit the land. Trees and flowers were dying, and crop yields were meager. Zohra's village and others throughout the country had experienced a relentless exodus toward the industrial cities of the coast. Dry winds cracked the resolve of even the strongest of folk, while the hyenas sobbed into the hollow night.

In the northern regions by the Mediterranean Sea, the demons had attacked once more. Deaths and nocturnal disappearances became common events, while loud metallic birds dropped destruction on the land below. The pine trees lining the hashish slopes of the Rif Mountains became the demons' lair. The pine trees had been the ancestral homes of the white owls who, chased away by the demons, told stories of their exile and woe, far and wide.

~

Zohra looked at the sleeping child, and her heart ached at how weak she seemed. Maryam was asleep, but it was not a peaceful sleep. In fact, her sleep had always been an anxious, restless one. Her scent of orange blossoms mingled with the scent of the old tree and of the faded flowers sprinkled on the ground. Zohra had taken off Maryam's clumsy brown shoes, and her crooked legs lay revealed. A burning light flashed behind Maryam's closed eyelids, while an acute pain exploded in her legs. She woke up, barely able to breathe. She looked at her uneven, painful legs and called for Zohra. Zohra took in the child's trembling body and her enlarged eyes.

"What is it, child? What have you seen?"

"The brothers are born. They are the sun and moon. They are different but also...the same. They believe they are the alone in the world. No, they believe they are first."

"But it is not so. They are no longer first. The story has changed. You are first. The illusions are being dispelled."

Zohra rubbed Maryam's legs to ease the pain that rose whenever there was a change in the fabric of the tale or she saw something new. She then carried her in her arms back to the house. She had sworn to protect her and train her for the unbeaten path ahead. Yet Maryam's physical frailty and detachment from things at times weakened Zohra's resolve. The disturbances and the unknowns brought about by her birth were to Zohra like the reigning in of a thousand wild horses. Having been made aware of the existence of the demons, people had started to resist their enchantments. The leaden cloak that isolated the country and provided it with a sense of impunity had been slightly torn. People stretched to see the blue sky that cracked through, and they felt taller, their backs straighter.

So Zohra feared for Maryam. She began to wonder if she had read the signs correctly, if the stars had not fooled her, or if her ancestral memory had not been distorted by the ages. What if Maryam's coming were an end and not a beginning? What if the human fury, silent springs, hunger, and poverty that plagued the land were a sign of the end of things? But then the scent of orange blossoms burst in the air, and it became difficult for Zohra to doubt. She looked down at the little girl in her arms and thought of what lay in store for them. Zohra pushed her hair back into the black-and-gold scarf wound around her head and felt a rush of liquid energy flow into her veins.

~

In three years, the Nassiri house had aged beyond recognition. Leila's death had marked its walls and soul. The greying mosaic and crumbling cement told of a father's rigid reading of duty and a mother's fall into the shadows of revenge and hatred. Leila's sacrifice was a rupture with the old ways and an act of passion and excess. It was also the tool with which she cut out a piece of blue sky for her daughter. Her absence overflowed into the household's architecture to bare its lies and unspoken betrayals.

Beyond its own history, the house was also succumbing to the continued difficulties of the Moroccan plastics industry. The Nassiris, despite all their goodwill and hard work, were unable to gain back their lost market shares. Ibrahim watched his beloved invention, the round plastic comb, be duplicated to infinity on every stand, stall, and market in the kingdom. His sleep was colonized by nightmares of flattened plastic and oily residues. He saw himself as Sisyphus eternally pushing a pink, round plastic comb up the hill, only to see it roll back down again. Success flinched from him, and money melted at his touch. Yet despite his family's pleas, he refused to sell the factory. His brother-in-law had offered to buy it at an absurd price and transform it into a modern factory—rather than the horror museum of industrial failure it had turned into—for the processing of meat and poultry. But, more out of snobbery than actual business strategy, Ibrahim refused. Now, incapable of keeping the house afloat, the family had closed down entire wings, let leaky pipes leak, and allowed the blue-green mosaic to fade and break.

The refusal to forfeit was madness, of course. But one could also think of the refusal to admit defeat as a weird kind of resilience. An unpractical, illogical, and doomed resilience perhaps and yet...There was still hope in this house. Absurd ideals and crazy plans were concocted to stay on top because, well, Ibrahim and Aisha did not feel like giving up. So, it may be strange to say, but in this old, decrepit, sorrowful, awful house, there was a lingering joy that could only be traced back to...*her*.

Ibrahim and Aisha could never look at their granddaughter without thinking of Leila. They saw in her the same light and curiosity. But Maryam did not have her mother's beauty. There was a broken sensitivity about her that confused a family who still thought of themselves as lords and masters. Ibrahim cringed at her dark skin, blue-rimmed pupils, rough hair, and uneven legs. He saw in those legs the hoofed demon that could be Maryam's biological father. But Aisha saw in her the blood of her mother's tribe and the beauty of the Sahel. She saw in her physical handicap the ability to understand others' pain and imperfections. She also saw in her granddaughter the constant reminder of her own shortcomings and mistaken turns. Finally, both Ibrahim and Aisha secretly believed that as long as Maryam was under their care, no real harm or catastrophe could ever befall them. They felt protected, graced with a perpetually blue rag of a sky.

Today, something was amiss. Ibrahim and Aisha watched as Zohra brought Maryam into the house. Zohra laid her in her bed and prepared incense for burning. She hurriedly mixed a bowl of scented henna and drew ancient symbols on Maryam's legs and feet. Gradually, the pain subsided and Maryam was able to stand up. Zohra turned toward Ibrahim and Aisha.

"The twins are born. They are boys, as was expected. Maryam saw a sun and moon. She does not yet know that they are her brothers. Adam and Shawg will soon send someone here with the news."

"What will these births change?" asked Aisha.

"Oh, Adam will taste paternity. Sons will make him feel like a man, and it will be easy for him to deny his daughter. He finally has the justification he has been looking for."

"You do not discard a human being without consequence. The forgotten will come back to haunt you, one way or another." Ibrahim interrupted.

"Yes. But Adam has been seeking for a way to absolve himself. Strong, healthy boys may give him just that excuse."

"These boys, they are the sun and moon, you say. The sun and moon rarely shine side by side," said Aisha.

Ibrahim left Maryam with Aisha and Zohra. They waited for her to be fully at ease that she may sleep, but Maryam was restless. Aisha strummed the 'oud and hummed an Andalusian ballad. Still Maryam was restless, her body cold and her knuckles white. Finally, Zohra asked her, "Did you see anything else, my little one? Don't be afraid, tell me." Maryam stared at a corner of the room and said, "I saw two brothers who loved each other kill each other. I saw death. It was sitting in a chair near the window, with high heels and red nails....I saw pain."

Zohra wanted to explain that Maryam's description of death did not quite fit and that what she saw may well have been a bored storyteller come to sit in on her characters while relaxing at their balcony. But instead she held her close and told her a story. "Oh, what you saw is indeed complicated. Listen to my words that you may go to sleep."

A long, long time ago there was a king called Adam who had two sons. One was a shepherd and the other a farmer. The shepherd roamed the world freely and went where the pastures were greenest. He respected all things, ate frugally, and howled at the moon when the call of the wild was at its strongest. His time belonged to nature, and he gladly succumbed to it. But his brother, the farmer, planted crop after crop, year after year. He tamed animals, built tools, stocked crops, and planned ahead. He began to impose his own time on nature and expected nature to succumb to him.

One day, their father called his two sons: "One of you molds himself to the earth as it changes through the seasons. The other ploughs the earth and tries to force the earth to mold to him. I am an old man, and I wish to retire from the world. I must choose an heir to my kingdom. Tell me, my sons, how would you rule the lands I will leave under your care?"

The eldest son, the farmer, replied, "I will rule my kingdom with an iron fist. I will plough, sow, and reap every piece of land, cut trees, and control the river's flow. I will trade our wealth far and wide, build palaces and a strong army. I will make our kingdom the most powerful kingdom in the world."

The youngest son, the shepherd, replied, "I will lead my people to harmony. I will lead them toward shelter, food, and safety. I will be their guide, and their well-being will be my sole mission as king. That is my answer, Abi."

The father was quiet, deep in thought. He finally spoke: "Cain, my son, you would be a great king, feared by your enemies, respected by your allies and admired by all. You would build an empire. But that empire would destroy you as it would destroy the earth. And you, Abel my beloved, you promise to be the shepherd, to put happiness and the everyday above power and greed. My kingdom would never be a great one, but it would be a good one. My kingdom would never be envied by others but nor would it ever be craved. That is wise. A part of me yearns for power and glory, but my mind is made. As much as this decision breaks my heart, I choose your way, Abel."

Cain roared his pain and anger into the moist earth. Mountains fell and rivers overflowed. Something inside him broke. In his rage, he plunged his sickle in his brother's heart and killed Abel. His black hair became a flaming red. He then turned to his father, Adam, and declared, "I have death's mark on me. But, do not be mistaken. You are the one to blame for choosing one son over another. You have brought the shadows upon us all. Heed my words, old man, for I will build an empire, my enemies will quake before me, and the earth, water, and skies will bow to me."

And Cain left and built a great empire. But he carried the mark of death on his shoulder, and, it is said that on moonless nights when all are safe in bed, Cain can be heard weeping for his brother Abel.

Zohra fell quiet and wiped the tears flowing from Maryam's eyes.

"Hush, my baby. It's just a tale. There are many other tales and many ways of telling the story. Others say that the brothers had an older sister who was special above all. She had her answer too—an answer that was willfully forgotten by everyone, by her brothers, father, and by the world. An answer that was quickly erased from every manuscript, lip, and memory. But one day, she will return, her answer will be remembered, and she will change the very course of the universe."

~

The doorbell rang and soon Zeinab returned holding a closed envelope in her hand. Aisha opened the envelope and read of the birth of Shams and Hilal of the house of Shawg and Adam Tair.

"We have received the news. The twins are born."

"Have they requested her presence?"

"No."

"Then we will not go. And God help us."

"If only Hamza could guard us once more. If only he could protect this house from the evil that lurks."

Zeinab turned toward Aisha with slow breath and tightened mouth. She stood there with her hands limp at her side, her body leaner than ever, and her heart empty of desire. When she pushed Hamza away three years ago, her inner self was revealed to her, *bang*, just like that. An arid wind blew through her entrails to echo her loneliness. Her sorrow was a drought burning her inside out. She understood, as she watched Hamza storm out of the house, that she had just missed her only chance at a good life.

Her reasons for rejecting him were not clear to her. She had the suspicion that it may not be him that she had rejected. No, she had rejected her own right to a dignified existence. A maid, a slave—what the world had decreed she would be. The dry winds rattled within, raising dust and uprooting Zeinab's convictions about life. A stable roof, masters who in a certain light could be considered kind, food on the table, an eleven-hour workday with a twenty-four-hour rest day, during which she had recently found the courage to explore Casablanca, after more than a decade of living there. The search for, and recent attainment of, stability had been the thread woven throughout her years as a housemaid. All her efforts, her will, had been directed toward the achievement of this goal: stability. When Hamza came with his offer of a life of love-friendship-magic-freedom at his side,

150

she pushed him away. How could that even be? But if the mind chooses to lie, the body cannot. And from the moment she turned away from Hamza, her body began to shrivel.

Aisha noticed Zeinab's whitened lips and hollow frame, and asked her if anything was the matter. Zeinab said to her, "Lalla, I want to pick up reading and writing where I left it off, years ago when I asked you to stop teaching me. I want to become a literate woman." Aisha nodded and promised to pick up their lessons where they had left them, all those years ago. When Zeinab left the room, Aisha smiled, for she had very few chances to do good. And what greater good is there than to teach a dependant how to read and write? I'm a good woman. Hierarchy is good, she told herself. Yes, but if only Hamza were here. But he is gone and his cycles are not our cycles.

~

Aisha and Ibrahim were getting old. They did not only feel it in their aging, escaping bodies, but in the knowledge that accompanied their every step. Old, old—we are old. Death walks with us, eats with us, sleeps with us. We may think it is our shadow the way it clings to us, but it is there even at night, especially in the dark.

If only Hamza's cycles were our cycles. If only we regenerated after every winter and knew the rebirth of spring. But in Morocco, there is no spring or fall. There is winter and summer. Our cycles are not his cycles. We are engorged, we burn, then we die. Death is fully in the shadows, or we are fully in its shadow. Would you care to become ghosts, the world politely inquires of us? We know how inconsequential we have become with our crumbling walls, our copper pots, and our dried lavender sachets hidden in our djellabas.

We are fading, as are the oral historians who recite our country's genealogies and the exploits of our heroes. We are fading because so few have written about us and even fewer have read about us. Our name, which we thought was eternal, is also fading. Yet they will find us when they least expect it. In some crooked alleyway or as they try to flee from the modern, an archaic reaction, more itch than instinct, will burst forward, take them back, to their greatest surprise. That is who we will become—satires of this country's past, hated at best, or worse, forgotten. But we will remain there, in the deep furrows of this land, worms of decay singing of a past life.

So we are old, and we have lost our daughter. We see things we perhaps would not have seen earlier. We see these things without having to leave our house much. We hear of Adam, sometimes. He never comes by, and if he did, surely he would not survive our embrace. Adam believes it is possible to bury us. But you cannot bury people until they are dead, and even then... He has lost his way trying to forget his past. Far from us is Adam with his successful wife and his fancy apartment. We know about his apartment through busybodies who hurry to tell us news they think will hurt us. They sit and watch our faces to see if the color drains from it or if the eyes turn pale with envy. But we are old school. Our faces are unreadable as we express the customary good wishes and Godspeed.

Sometimes, Aisha would ask Ibrahim if he thought Adam was happy with his new wife. She had always believed that he was a man incapable of happiness. Yet a voice inside her repeated: what if he is? What if he is, would that mean your daughter always stood alone, in life as in death?

"But, there you have it, Ibrahim. Leila was capable of happiness. She was liquid joy before she met that man. Look at what he, at what *they*, did to her. She stood no chance against their powers of destruction. I want to go to his home and take his sons from him that he may know how it feels to lose a child," thumped Aisha's heart. "This is what haunts me."

Shawg and Adam

Shawg and Adam lived in a modern apartment building located between the luxurious residential area of Golden Hill and the bustling business avenue of Silver Dome. Their apartment screamed modernity and European magazine subscriptions. There was a TV and VCR at the center of the foyer, a large leather sofa, colorful love seats, floral wallpaper, wall-to-wall mirrors, blue ceramic vases, a plated-glass dining table and corresponding black chairs, short, round lamps with pink shades, and a grey carpet that covered the entire place, including the bathrooms. In the far end of the living room was an ornate desk covered in sheets of blank paper and dusty books, a hodgepodge of glorious asymmetry.

Their home was a screen for a cluttered TV commercial where the veneer of overripe elegance could shatter like glass. But, barely perceptible, beneath the pink lamps and the flowery fabric, was a roughness that rasped against their skins. A draft blew through the apartment and regularly sent a chill down their spines. Only a surrealist artist, inspired by nameless tortures in a country divided by civil war, could have imagined such a home.

Today, Adam, his hands in his pockets, watched a man speak on TV. This man was stunningly elegant and spoke like a Nordic Loki turned into an Eastern Lucifer. In an odd discourse, he laced subtle, paranoid analyses with threats in Moroccan street talk. He was addressing his words to people he seemed to know well, whom he called alternatively "my children" and "human waste." His voice was soft and still. When the speech ended, the screen turned black, and a kindly man's face popped up with the caption: "We are watching over you." The blackness of the screen began to fade, and a flapping of wings could be heard in its greying distance.

Adam stood there watching till the very end. He had just seen the Great Patriarch on television. He felt nothing. He thought of the little girl who had given him the amulet in the Old Medina of Casablanca, and he tried to remember the love that he felt then. He felt nothing. Some deep, primordial empathy was weakened the day he lost his rib to passion. The day when he embarked on a new journey, only to fail in his attempted rebirth...As time passed, his late night deliria returned, and in the wilderness of his mind he believed that Shawg had taken his rib, his soul, his genius. Oh, it was *people's* fault. It had always been people's fault.

When he was young, people made him believe that he would be great one day. He worked and waited for that day when his value would be revealed to the world. Instead, his classroom turned into a cell, the university into a prison, and the streets into a labyrinth of loss. Maybe he would have done something with his life had he not been plagued by his potential greatness. He may have wanted power, but he insisted on excellence. In his country, power and excellence rarely went hand in hand. He had been pushed aside into a small classroom, a small life, and finally into the demons' lair. So it was because of them, those people who had misunderstood and shunned him, that he had turned his back on those weaker than he. The muscles on the right side of his face began to twitch violently.

He raised his hand to hide the tremor and thought, "Now I have my sons, Shams and Hilal. Their mother says they are the sun and moon, and we are their earth."

Adam walked into the bedroom to find the twins sleeping on either side of their mother. Shawg's bed was vast, and she was covered in a grey-and-white fur blanket. She held her hand out to Adam: "Come, my love. Come see your sons."

Shams had flaming red hair, and Hilal was born with a splash of silver hair. Shams was golden like the Oum Er-Rbia river when it flows through the fertile valleys of the interior, and Hilal was white like the high snows of the Atlas Mountains before the herds come to feed at the first thaw. Adam did not come too close to his wife and sons. He was an outsider in a world of plenty, filled with want and emptiness. He could smell Shams and Hilal from where he was standing. They smelled of wet clay and earth. They had a damp, cold scent about them that called for a warming fire. But neither he nor Shawg had any fire to give their sons.

Shawg closed her eyes and smiled, her pale lips as luscious as that day when she first walked into the Nassiri house. She told Adam of a dream she just had. She dreamt she had seen Maryam. Maryam knew about their sons, and about the sun and moon.

"Ah...her soft orange-blossom scent, it was everywhere. How I have missed it. I think of it every day, Adam. Her scent has haunted me since her birth. The boys, they smell like mud, don't they? But in my dream, with her there, they were heating up like clay baking in the sun. Pregnant with the brothers, all I could think of was her. What madness, this little girl who has bewitched me. Or perhaps it is her Saheli sorceress of a grandmother, her Jew of a godmother, or her demon father. In the dream, I craved her so, I breathed her so...as though she were near, as though she were here."

Shawg continued.

"In my dream, I saw Maryam touch the boys with her hands and breathe in their scent of clay and earth. She was in great pain. I was flooded by the magic that emanated from her as she touched our sons and stared into the horizon. I felt she was here, and I wanted her here. I wanted to grab her and hold her prisoner in our house, that our sons may always feel warm and strong. So I asked her to remain near me, that I may bathe in her orange-blossom scent. I held out my arms to her, but Zohra appeared and stood between me and my desire. Her hair became uncoiled snakes, while her eyes burst into flames. I felt myself turning into stone, cold and hot all at once. My dream ended with Aisha leaning toward me, her eyes filled with hatred:

'Beware your desires, Shawg. It is in your nature to crave and want without respite. I should have killed you when I had a chance. Don't give me a new excuse to destroy you.'

"Then I was released from the dream. But, you see, Aisha didn't understand. I don't know how I found my way dreaming of her. I don't want Maryam. I only wanted to feel her tranquillity, to breathe in her scent. Perhaps I also wanted their big sister to watch over Shams and Hilal. She perceives things that you and I cannot. Now, go, let me rest. There is too much male in this room."

Adam left without telling his wife that he knew she was lying. He did not believe her dream. He thought that she wanted him to take Maryam from the Nassiris and bring her to them.

Adam found Shawg's desire for Maryam perverse. He thought that, like him, she would want to forget that Maryam Tair ever existed. He had never fully understood his wife. She was overpowering and highly ambitious. She would introduce him as her "genius, misunderstood husband," but she would sway when another man came close. There were shadows in her thoughts and a dark logic to her words that made her increasingly enigmatic to him. She did not, he knew, crave Maryam's innocence. No, what she wanted was to taste the mystery at the heart of Maryam's existence. Shawg's obsession with Maryam had grown with the birth of Shams and Hilal. It was a hunger that would keep her up at night, her entire body aching with that need. But Adam no longer understood that kind of irrational, destructive need. He now flattened any excess to a mad sidestep. He did not see...there was much he did not see and refused to see. He delved deeper into his own meanderings and pushed aside the anxieties that flapped around him.

Shawg remained with her sons. Her pride in having given birth to two boys was vast. Women would envy her status, and her past deeds would be forgotten. She was now wife, mother, and a woman of means. She was safely inside the door. She had arrived. She covered her mouth and hands with a scented handkerchief. The boys' wet, earthen scent was overpowering. It draped over her body, seeking warmth and not finding it. She sniffed her sons, and her eyes widened in panic. She had just noticed it. If it were not for their hair and skin, she would not be able to tell them apart. Her eyes closed, using her nose only, that most primitive of senses, she would not be able to tell Shams from Hilal and Hilal from Shams. Shawg was ashamed. She wanted to reject her sons, push them far from her. She could not stand their skin on her skin. She thought of herself as an unnatural woman, a mother who could not bear to have her children at her breast. But her anxiety went even deeper. She was trapped in an age-old story whose sequences were known before they unfolded. The boys she was nurturing would one day turn against each other to bring destruction upon the world. But there was something different this time around in this cyclical story of the world, and that difference was a threat to Shawg's role.

With the birth of her sons, Shawg saw her life in a different light. She touched her dry skin, heavy breasts, and sagging stomach. Who would recognize the statuesque concubine in the high-strung, overweight mother she now was. Instead of frustration, Shawg felt relief. People would now leave her alone, at least for a while, while she put away her broken masks and painted new ones on. She had based her life on seduction, only to come to the conclusion that men's penises were as weak as their minds. She could only now admit this to herself. She had wanted power and accepted submission to achieve it. She had wanted money and accepted sacrifice to accumulate it. She had wanted pleasure but had only known its craving.

Sex had often been a painful experience for her. At first, she thought that sex must either be brief or brutal. She let men take control of her and accepted that pleasure was a myth or a rare gift given to women she would never meet. When she gained power and began to choose the men she wanted for herself, she expected greater pleasure. There were some fleetingly tender encounters, but an orgasm, never. She wondered whether it was her choice of men or the molten lead that pressed upon them all, reducing the oxygen necessary to exude desire and breathe in pleasure. She tried every trick in the book. She brought another woman into the mix, let herself be handcuffed, tied, and whipped. She spanked, blindfolded, and dominated. She did cocaine and ecstasy, brought in props, went to specialized nightclubs and sadistic chateaux, strip-joints and seedy bars, peaty ports and cool airplanes. She experienced and let others experience with her, and still the elusive orgasm remained out of reach. She took potions prepared by witch doctors and visited shrines of saints famous for their ability to induce pleasure in cold women. By then, she was convinced that those who spoke of such things were either lying or exaggerating a small twitch of pleasure they may have felt.

One day, she fell upon a book with a blue cover and a title inscribed in gold letters. She was neither a reader nor a teller of stories. She thought of books as a waste of time and stories as a way to escape from the necessity of following a singular course with a well-defined goal. The book was called *One Thousand and One Nights*. Well-hung djinns, naked princesses, and bawdy artisans stood out from the ancient text. Her heart pounded. It described shameless desire and humorous betrayals with such lyricism that she could not believe that this was a text written by an Arab and a Muslim, and that these stories were told by a woman named Sheherazade. Arabs do not describe sex with such relish. The Arabic language does not write words like cunt, penetration, cunnilingus, throb, or penis with such obvious intent to arouse. In speech, vulgarity abounded. But speech can be translated into drunken song, relegated to the crudest domains of our human activity and then dismissed as lowly. Men and women of her culture thought of sex as dirty and thus thought of ways to make it as dirty as possible.

Shawg did not know that her civilization, now defined by religion and class and gender warfare, had once delighted in the awakening of the senses, in the exquisite beauty of the human form in the throes of desire. She did not know there were many Sheherazades. Her mind expanded, her body felt warm and new. Her senses were so awakened that she could feel a drop of sweat trickle down her lower back. Sheherazade, she read, was the storyteller telling tales to a king holding her captive. Her intended audience may have been male, and her stories may have been a mere survival tactic, but today she was speaking to her, Shawg, through him, King, and the original intent ceased to matter. That day, she did something she had never done for herself before. She put her hand down there, in her forbidden place and gave herself pleasure. The text had lit up all the facets she was made of. She found pleasure through words inscribed on the pages of a book that was over a thousand years old and whose continued re-editing was beautiful in itself. That day she discovered the subtlety of joy, a curtain raised on the infinite possibilities of desire.

But as all things go, the excitement of the discovery waned. Try as she might, she was not able to recapture that initial moment of pure happiness. She understood that pleasure had to be a conversation and that reading books, well, was more of a two-way monologue than a creative dialogue. She searched again. She tried mystic Sufi groups, women, poetry readings, painting, and sculpture, but all to no avail. She decided to settle for a man whose family name spoke of El Andalus, a civilization where pleasure, art, religion, and science gracefully poured into one another. He himself was a shadow of things, a Platonic cave walled in from its physical ideal. But Shawg was tired and thought that with Driss Nassiri she could, at least, begin to rest. She agreed to marry him. She came with him to his family home. As she was about to resign herself to whatever lukewarm existence was in the books for her, she laid eyes on Adam. A witch once told her that the devil himself strung at the cords of her life. When she thought she had found peace, he would touch the strings that held him to her and play her like the meekest of reed flutes. It was not coincidence or luck. Instead it was a precisely orchestrated plan that made two doubting, dissatisfied people find each other. It was the work of a meticulous and cruel architect. That is how, when she first saw Adam, Shawg threw everything to the winds. She allowed herself to dream of pleasure and intimacy once more, only to find that Adam was incapable of feeling or giving pleasure.

She continued her quest. She did so with a lost purity and with bitterness eating at her. It was her revenge, the useless shaking of the chains which held her in. She went with other men and tasted the odd thrills of betrayal. She did not care what Adam knew, or perhaps she wished he would show his anger or hurt, but he never did. He remained quietly in the sidelines, estranged from their own lives.

Now, she had two sons who smelled of wet clay and an anxiety she never felt before in her life. And could it truly be that her story and Maryam's story may never be woven together? Shawg knew that she would always dream of Maryam, and she hoped that Maryam dreamt of her, too.

Fire and Water

*S*heherazade is lying on her side wearing a silk veil and crimson lipstick. Her upturned hand holds an ember-filled pipe. Annoyed, she lets her hand fall to her side and resumes a normal position. I am the tainted odalisque turned inside out. I follow the transformation of my inner self into an object of contemplation. This is a ridiculous exercise. I feel the couch draining my life force out of my body. I am sinking into its depths, and the inertia is contagious and dangerous. A perfectly still, quiet woman in the musty opulence of the brothel... Delacroix must have had a death wish.

She stands up and pushes her veil back slightly to look like a movie star at the wheel of her convertible MG. The background whizzes past her to create an impression of movement, while the car and she remain immobile. She has replaced one still-life tableau with another. She snorts at herself in the mirror, and her image ripples its discontent back at her. The Sheherazade in the mirror strikes up her arms and twirls around herself, presenting her backside to the world. Sheherazade peers into the mirror, and sees a dance of mirrors within. Beyond the shallow surface of the image above is a proliferation of images.

She sees herself in all her forms, in the ways she dreams herself to be and in the ways she knows she is. She even sees the images battling each other for primacy, while the gravitational pull of the mirror pulls them deeper in. They appear to her as a community of flattened dolls.

At the very back of the sequence, she sees a little girl with blue boots and serious eyes. Sheherazade is about to tell the tough-looking kid in the mirror of a dead past. She thinks of the sixties. It was a time in the Muslim world when women believed in emancipation, when short skirts, on-screen kisses, cigarettes, and femmes fatales were commonplace. Afghanistan was chic, and Egypt was the movie capital of the Middle East. There was poverty, of course. The glory days were never truly glorious. For it was then that despotism crystallized and the seeds of future revolts were planted deep into the earth. Soon, they would all have to pay the price for their failed experiments in modernity. And that time had finally come.

Today, and for the first time since she left her great palace and immense power, she feels vulnerable. So instead of holding on to the mnemonic threads of the past, Sheherazade strips herself of her veil, tunic, pipe, and rouge. She appears with shaved head and transparent body. Her hands become translucent, and her eyes pale beyond measure. She quivers at the verge of shadow and inexistence to trick the mirror into returning her soul. She is interrupted by the blue-booted young girl.

"Old Mother, tell me, why does Shawg dream of Maryam?"

"It's a question of desire, my dear. She is haunted by her."

"But why?"

"It's in Shawg's nature to burn. She lives with fire in her heart and, with her last breath, a final regret. There is something about Maryam that she cannot quantify and thus cannot possess. She will bring about her downfall, and then her heart will break. Now hush my baby and watch as the story that is your story unfolds before you, while the words drop into your eyes like pearl drops in the early morning."

The little girl opens her thoughtful, serious heart to the tale at hand.

Grand Tribunal

Clockmakers' Town
Casablanca, February 2011

The sentencing. Time is elusive. It writes itself in and out of our memory. Maryam is standing in a court of law. Her glorious blue boots are old and torn. She listens to the verdict.

"Death:

for destroying government property,

for protecting criminals,

for supporting homosexuals,

for disrespecting the law,

for loving a gay uncle,

for saying no,

for being raised by a witch,

for being a witch,

for performing acts of magic,

for being magical,

for seeing under the veil,

for saying no,

for cherishing a ghost,

for owning a diabolic engine,

for helping the insane,

for reading minds,

for being strange,

for saying no."

But Maryam is already elsewhere, her attention shifting to the whirring of wheels.

School

Maryam rode the same bicycle for many years. By the time she was fifteen years old, the bicycle was rusty, and its chains clicked and clacked breathlessly. She had learned quite early on to be independent. Living in a house with grandparents and a two-hundred-eighty-year-old mother-nanny had been a blessing in disguise. There was no other option but to allow Maryam to wheel herself around. It took her a while to get the hang of the bicycle. Her body would sway to one side, and the bicycle would fall over. She enjoyed her freedom.

Every morning, she would ride her bicycle to her school, the Carmel Saint Augustine, in the adjacent neighborhood of the Place of Fading Oases. The Carmel Saint Augustine, once a Catholic school run and taught by European nuns, was now a state school administered by Lebanese nuns and taught by local teachers. Maryam loved the tall cathedral-like tower and impressive columns. Her boots beat against butterfly-colored mosaics as she hurried down the cold corridor. When she was very young, Zohra or Zeinab would walk her to school, but since her seventh birthday and to her delight, she was entrusted to her bicycle. Maryam was so attached to her bicycle that she gave it a name, "Aoud Errih," which means

"Wind-Rider," and the name breathed a soul and personality into the rusty, moody bike.

It purred, whirred, barked, and growled, depending on its mood. Maryam had found a sturdy leather belt with which she strapped her books and backpack onto it. One day, when she was no older than ten, as she was walking across the path lined by centennial trees leading to the school's main building, she thought she heard the trees whispering among themselves. She was used to the old orange tree in the garden back home and its frequent whisperings when no one but she was near, but she did not know that other trees could talk to human beings, too. Of course, she was not any human being. She was a child and a special, dreamy, lonely child. The trees were swaying, dangerously off course. The language of trees is a language from heart to heart. It is perceived rather than heard and reaches to the attentive child's primal core. Maryam perceived sadness, urgency in their breathy calls. She walked slowly through, respectful and slightly in awe. They were trying to convey a message to her, a grievous message, but she was not able to decipher it. The trees were warning her of a danger, but she could not put her finger on it yet. She continued walking, holding Aoud Errih close to her body, her two hands clenched on its handlebars.

Inside the school walls, the tension became palpable. Groups stopped talking, and eyes followed her as she walked by. Sister Josephine, known for her Levantine kindliness among both students and staff, held out a hand to Maryam and led her to a quiet place. She spoke gently to her.

"Have you ever heard of Birsoukout?"

"Yes, I have."

"It seems that one of your family members was taken there. We do not know when exactly, but we just found out. That is all we know, child. It seems there is something very very wrong with your family member. It is something terrible that we must never speak of. He is an extremely ill man. I will pray for his soul tonight, and I suggest you do the same because, if what is said about him is true, he is lost to the world."

Sister Josephine kissed Maryam on the forehead and walked away. Maryam was left alone in the school's front lobby. In those days, the name Birsoukout roused fear in people's minds. Terror and confusion trailed in its wake. The mental asylum of Birsouokout was a dreadful place in which were parked all kinds of deviants, schizophrenics, and otherwise mad, ill-adapted individuals. It was a space that remained in the margins of normality, somewhere beyond the everyday consciousness of surrounding physical landscapes. People's awareness of Birsoukout was stunted by the anxiety it caused and by that forbidden question we all ask ourselves at one point or another: "What if I too were mad?"

Birsoukout lingered in that repressed domain of our beings and our societies, existing to stifle rebelliousness. Maryam did not know any of this. In fact, she would not even understand this, for she wasn't wired that way.

She started to run. Who could it be? Who had been taken there? She ran and all around her tumbled an avalanche of whispers and hisses. Her mind was perfectly aloof now, taking in all sounds, echoes, and barely voiced thoughts. A filer for the asylum, a student's mother, had warned the school about the new inmate. She had recognized, in the new patient, the name he carried, *Nassiri*. She was not surprised, she had to add, *that* family had always been unstable, ever since Sultan Boabdil cried like a woman on top of a hill overlooking a deserted battlefield. There was a gene in that family, a deep perversity. But she was trained in impartiality, wasn't she. She could not say. A family like this one, graceful beyond compare, who liked art and music, I mean they *must* have *that unspeakable thing* in their blood. The girl's mother was a strange one. She died of a broken heart. She killed herself, really, she preferred death to submitting to her husband's and father's will. She said no. She finally said no. And the kid's father, he is with a prostitute, and isn't *she* herself a bastard child? Yes, she is.

Maryam's mind was made up. She ran out of her school, grabbed her bike, which was trembling with impatience, and biked out of there. She could hear the trees' deep vibrations as she biked through: He sways, sway he does, as do we, we sway too, dangerously to the left or dangerously to the right, he sways, and sway he should not. Trees sway, but that is good. Alone, alone we are, and alone we shall remain. He sways toward someone and that he should not. Go, go get him before it is too late. He will go mad there.

Aoud Errih vibrated under her as they whizzed out into the real world.

An acute pain shot through Maryam's legs. She was stronger than she used to be, but her legs still burst with pain when her mind opened up to realities beyond imagination. She did not walk, act, or think like anyone around her. She often seemed lost in her own thoughts, dreamy, or in communion with voices and words only she could hear. Yet this invisible thread woven into her existence carried its own burden. When it manifested itself, it pricked her like the thorns of a cruel rose. It drilled possessively into her being, causing her great suffering and a profound, unshakable sadness. But she did not stop. She continued until she reached the high, crumbling gates of the Nassiri house. She pushed and the gates creaked open. The garden was glorious at this time of year. In Morocco, there was no spring season, but the garden did not seem to care, and it bloomed with a pervasive joy. But inside the house, idle moths and the smell of naphthalene drifted by, filling the atmosphere with their soft decay. Today,

Maryam sensed that there was something direr than the gentle wasting of days.

Ibrahim was absent. Aisha was listening to Zeinab read to her from a newspaper, and Zohra was simply sitting, gazing toward the door, as though expecting someone. She was expecting her ward, so it was no surprise to her when Maryam burst in, sweating and in obvious pain. Zohra laid her on a sofa and began rubbing her legs.

"It is getting better, you are getting better, controlling the pain, controlling your body. Have you seen, have you heard, we have just been told."

"Yes Umi Zohra, I have heard about the mental asylum and its newest patient. But who and why?"

"It is Mehdi Nassiri, your great-uncle. They found him and found out things about him, unspeakable things that will bring shame upon your family."

"What unspeakable things? Is anything unspeakable?"

"To them everything that is threatening is unspeakable. He is in a dark place now, and there is no getting him out. He confessed. He has been stripped of everything."

"What has he confessed to?"

"It is not clear. But it is too late, he is already forgotten."

"When did this happen?"

"We just found out. It could have been days since they took him. But you must return to school. You must save yourself for what lies ahead. You must learn. You must rise. Go back. You must stay focused. Forget about him. Your struggle lies elsewhere. Look at the poor girl over there. There are thousands like her. You must rise above."

Maryam listened to Zohra's fiery words and turned to look at Zeinab, that representative of a multitude of poor, unwanted women.

~

Aisha was listening to Zeinab's raspy voice read the newspaper. Ever since her last resolution to become literate, Zeinab had struggled with the written word and the concepts it conjured. Her mind dreamed of things, of images and emotions. It structured things in a pragmatic, utilitarian way until she began to grasp written text. A new world appeared to her. A confusing world where form determined meaning and logic battled with metaphors. She was often lost and frustrated. She experienced reading like a daily reminder of her failures and shortcomings. Being unable to wrap her mind around the complexities of text and the connection between reading and imagining, Zeinab was close to despair. Simply put, she thought of herself as stupid. More importantly, she began to believe that everything that had happened to her had happened because she did not have the intelligence needed to shade herself from harm. As a result, her voice became raspy and her body broke down a little more. It stooped, dried and hurt. She was ashamed. It was as though a hand was pressing down on her neck and forcing her down. She felt trapped. True, she could now read street signs and billboards, she could travel the city by following directions rather than navigate thanks only to colors, known landmarks, or the kindness of strangers.

What Zeinab found most unbearable was the realization that she knew very little and that it was too late for her. At times, she yearned for ignorance and its shadowy peace. But that ignorance, long before she could read, had been shattered by Hamza's love. She was beginning to perceive that Hamza was not who she thought he was. She understood, one night, that he may have been a god, a mythical creature, a magical hero whose place was in a novel, not in the real world, and yet here he once was, standing awkwardly in her kitchen. She then began to wonder why a creature as powerful as Hamza had not simply taken her, as others before him had, except this time it would be an act of love. Finally, she became angry. Why did he not come back for her? Did he not see the pain and isolation she was in? He, so mighty and all-knowing, why did he not see her and come for her? Her anger turned to despair.

What she did not know is that giants like Hamza, eternal, forever green and forever grey, accompany the world in sadness and, as paradoxical as it may sound, were resigned to its many injustices and fallacies. He did not come for her because she did not call him back, and he found solace in his endless walks through the vast expanses of the world. Though he felt, in that most primitive side of him, how her dried heart still sighed for him, he could not go where he was not called.

Maryam felt Zeinab's loneliness and loss. The archangel Gibreel had once ordered man to read: "Read. In the name of God that created humanity from an atom." It was an epiphany, perhaps a raising of an ancient restriction. This order, which shattered a strict taboo against the availability of the text, was not a path to liberation for Zeinab. It was, Maryam could sense, a constant source of pain. She would never attain that level where her reading and writing skills could be a source of work and dignity. She was trapped in the grey domains between knowledge and ignorance, questioning and fatality.

Maryam went to Zeinab and placed a hand on her arm: "Ask. Ask for him, he'll come. He loves you." The paper in Zeinab's lap fell to the floor, and she raised eyes filled with doubt.

"Hamza is not of this world. I understood that too late. Now that he is gone, he will not return. His cycles are not our cycles. When he returns, I will be an old woman. I already am an old woman. Look at me. Do you think I would dare call him back that he may see what time has done to me?"

Aisha watched as the paper slid from Zeinab's hands to the floor. She could not hear their exchange, since Maryam had protected it with a fleeting wall of silence. But she knew that something beyond her comprehension had just taken place. Aisha had never felt close to her granddaughter. Maryam was special. She was not soft or lighthearted like other children. She seemed to carry the weight of the world on her shoulders and would often retreat into a deep, impenetrable silence. Her presence was a constant reminder of a cherished daughter's absence. Her imprint was everywhere. Walking through the old, decaying house, one would be surprised to find a room bursting with possibility or a window wide open on the outside world. There were also corridors as silent as Sufi retreats or walls lined with old books like an Italo Calvino story. Things were changing, and their house felt like a laboratory.

Then the door opened and Ibrahim walked in. He had spent all morning going from police station to police station, trying to find a solution for his brother, Mehdi. Mehdi had been charged by a court for degeneracy, abuse of a position of power, and sinful behavior. He was in his apartment when they came for him. Neighbors said that he was sitting in the dark when *they* broke in. The lights were off, but that may have been because Mehdi had not paid his electricity bill in a while. The situation was all the more complex, as Mehdi's office was in the same building as his apartment. His neighbors knew his patients, and his regulars knew his neighbors and his habits.

Mehdi remembered the patient pulling his hand down toward his unzipped pants, but he could not be sure. His guilty conscience could be suggesting to him that he had been prey, not predator. His memory was perhaps frantically searching for an alternate story line in which he was not to blame for what had happened in his office that stifling summer day. But he *was* to blame: he had taken advantage of a patient who had come into his office in trust, and he had let a routine medical examination slide into a shameful and sinister act. Rumors of praxis gone awry spread through town like wildfire feeding on dry winds. Patients stopped coming, and the demons began to circle around his life like vultures around decay. Mehdi knew the fate that awaited him if ever the rumors were confirmed, if his darkest secrets were dragged into the public square. He had heard whispers of the humiliation and the endless prison sentences. He had heard of the demons that came to feed on the exposed suffering. The patient in question, a young man with smooth skin and golden eyes, sounded the alarm and alerted the doctor's neighbors. He remembered, did he not, the patient pulling him down toward his trousers, or did he indeed take advantage of a trusting body waiting for a routine auscultation? Mehdi was still swooning from the warm embrace, the hot, erect penis under his trembling hand, in his mouth, his eyes closed, his body living. When Mehdi opened his eyes, instead of the satisfaction, or even slight, pleasurable guilt he expected to see in the young man's face, he saw anger and hatred. It was pure, mad hatred, and it hit him hard in the face and through to the heart.

Mehdi stood there quietly as his world crumbled around him. He thought of all the walls he had built between his deepest secrets and his profession. He had plastered walls between his elegant apartment and his austere office. Brick by brick, he built serene waiting areas, neat bedrooms, and sober offices. He condemned the passageway between his apartment and his office and always had a traveling bag waiting by each front door. Behind the neat closets and aseptic chairs, he had allowed himself hidden corridors and secret attics. He spent his evenings listening to Bach or Rachmaninoff and smoking Montecristo cigarillos. He enjoyed golden cigarette cases and silk handkerchiefs. He was a regular in the small intellectual and artistic circles of the city. American writers and foreign artists, regulars of Tangiers and Marrakesh, enjoyed his company, and he inspired them. He read Marcel Proust and Albert Cohen repeatedly. Jazz was good, too. Then there were nights when he would get carefully dressed, close the door behind him, and disappear for hours and sometimes days. He was kind to his neighbors and taught the most intelligent of their children about literature and art. He invited the building concierge in for a cup of English tea on cold, difficult days and gave her warm blankets for winter nights. People thought of him as European and sophisticated, but he was respected for his gentle manners and unfailing politeness.

Mehdi had spent his life building walls, carefully and meticulously. That day, they fell like sand castles with the first wave of the high tide. That young man, his patient, he felt he knew him. He felt close to him, and safe. Mehdi was a man of experience, a prudent man who had never taken any unnecessary risks. But there was something about the young man in his office, something familiar and exhilarating. They may have met at one of those parties where the participants are masked and bodies are taken at will. There was an innocence and a freshness about him that made Mehdi's heart break. And then the look of hatred and disgust in his eyes. Mehdi was taken aback, and shame, always there, right below the surface, overwhelmed him. He covered his face with his hands, but it was already too late. The nurse came in, the secret was found, and there was nowhere left to hide.

When the police finally came to his door, they found a dignified man in his early sixties sitting in the dark listening to Bach's Goldberg Variations with an unused razor blade in his left hand. After an initial investigation, they determined that the man was a Nassiri and a doctor. They questioned the patient, the nurse, and the neighbors. All corroborated the accusations.

The neighbors even told the police that the good doctor would try to invite their children into his apartment and that they had always known he was a strange, queer man. It was no surprise to any of them that he was, well, *found*, discovered as it were. Only the concierge remained silent, remembering the warm blankets and peculiar tea Mehdi Nassiri would offer her when the cold season began. So she was quiet, retreating from the witch hunt but also from any unnecessary declarations of support. Yes, the winter season was upon them.

The police handcuffed Mehdi and were about to take him to the police station when the cold-eyed demons swooped down upon the scene. They stood in front of the policemen and with their mad cackle, they hissed:

"To the Madhouse, to the Madhouse will the son of the Nassiris be taken. For his sin is madness. But not any madness: a madness that dreams the destruction of our absolute power. To the Madhouse of Birsoukout will the Queer be taken."

They held Mehdi between their claws, flapped their plastic wings, and were gone.

Ibrahim heard the rumors and went to look for his younger brother. He inquired, and money exchanged hands. He did not know precisely when his brother was taken. He did not keep in touch with him. Mehdi was an urban dweller, while Ibrahim was a failed feudal lord treating the city like a rural stronghold. During his search, he was caught in a whirlwind of conflicting emotions. A degenerate? His gentle, brilliant, caustic little brother a degenerate! If only he could make *them* fall to their knees and beg for a mercy that he never intended to give. If only they would see the blood that flowed in his veins and the wrath he was capable of, he so powerless and weak today, an old man still believing in old stories like a hermit dying of thirst believing a mirage. Fassis always dream of their childhoods, of the extraordinary gap between the city they grew up in, Fes, and the city they settled in, Casablanca. They often think of the little Arab boys they once were and the suit-wearing urbanites they became. They, who once caught old buses to indigenous schools, under the watchful eyes of a mother and sister left behind, under the suspicious eyes of the French administrators, and under the stern eyes of an authoritarian father who trained them in commerce in a small shop built into the walls of the Medina of Fes, taught them how to sell kohl and traditional Saudi lipstick to women, silver trays to aristocrats, and leather to soldiers.

Ibrahim would go with his father to the souk and take pride in the selling of wares. He was an apprentice eager to learn the secrets of the trade, chiseling every moment into the perpetuation of an ancient mercantilist code.

But not Mehdi. Mehdi was not weighed down by the desire to mirror the past. He had always been different. His childhood was like no other in the household. He would hide in his mother's closet for hours, lingering in that delightful moment between sleep and wakefulness. He devoured books and welcomed all kinds of friends into the house. Sons and daughters of European administrators, musicians, girls and boys from every type of household would come by, sneak in, and cheerfully convene there. He did not care about politics or ethos. He was curious and brilliant, and yes…simply different. Did that make him a degenerate? Ibrahim was at a loss. Would they have him believe that the signs had always been there and he had not seen them? Lies, all lies, machinations to humiliate them, perhaps a jealous colleague reaping revenge or a jilted lover pushing him down. Mehdi was in Birsoukout. Oh, he would not survive. He was a finished man, Ibrahim knew. It was too late.

Ibrahim walked into the house that he still called his own, until that fateful day, God forbid, when he would have to leave, if the djinns did not kill him first. "We will never get him out of there. But if it is true what they say, what he did, Mehdi has brought shame upon himself and upon his family. And yet I cannot but pity him for he was only looking for a way to fill in the void of his difference."

"It is impossible to get him out. The members of this family who can afford it have refused to help him. He is being made an example of. The state refuses to have degenerates out in the street, and he has marred our family name. The family feels that the shame he has brought upon us all is too great for forgiveness. Mehdi is a very sick individual. It is best he be forgotten. Now let us eat."

Aisha spoke to her husband with scorn in her voice.

"There was a time when no one would have dared touch a member of this family."

"And now justice is served. History has caught up with us, and it has chosen its martyr."

"The best of you."

"Yes, perhaps. Or just a man with his failures and faults. He is guilty of this crime."

"Mehdi has committed no crime. His loves are not your loves, and your decision is to banish him. It is Yasmine's husband who refuses to squeeze out a couple of pennies from his purse. That's all."

"No. This matter is deeper than that. It is about honor. It is done. Mehdi does not exist anymore. He has never existed. He too will soon forget he has ever existed."

Ibrahim plunged his hand into the tajine set in front of him. With the first three fingers of his right hand, just as his father taught him, he cut the mutton and dipped his bread in its fragrant saffron sauce. Aisha looked at his hand as it delicately stripped the meat and curved around the heavy sauce. That is when they heard it: the faint, distant ringing of a bicycle bell and the clink-clank of axle wheels.

Maryam carried the bicycle out of the house, through the blooming garden, and into the street. She rode it faster and faster, ignoring the click-clack of the protesting bicycle chain. She rode toward Birsoukout. She did not know, or perhaps she did, that the road she used was a road famous for its harboring of dissenters, dreamers, and lovers. Almost fifty years ago, in the high heat of June, people rose against the first modern factory of the country, a factory producing sugar from sweet, syrupy molasses and whose darkening heart had already chosen those powerful enough to bend to its will. Maryam did not know that people had discovered a new kind of enslavement and a new kind of resistance simultaneously, all those years ago, and that the discovery had taken them to the road she was now so furiously riding.

She did not know because no one could have told her. Since those events half a century ago, this road had become a road of progress and development. It now led to new factories, crossed glistening railroad tracks, and pressed beyond the hamlets hidden from view. The violence of the process had exhausted itself with the passing of time. It was, for lack of a better word, fate. Progress was the acceptance that suffering must be forgotten. Progress was rational. It weighed cost against benefit and chose *forward*. Progress was fate. The only thing remaining of those days of uprising was the road, beaten down by the machines, whitened by the wind, and made hot by the sun.

Perception

So Maryam took an ancient road in a country that had chosen to forget its past. She let herself be filled with the knowledge that she too could be conjured away, as Aoud Errih carried her farther and farther from her home.

~

When the sun had passed high noon and begun to fade into the horizon, Maryam finally saw the small French-built school and shop that lay at the edge of the mental asylum of Birsoukout. The school and shop were bathed in the reddening light of dying day, and to their right lay Birsoukout. The gates were made of wood and were unguarded. Maryam did not know what to expect of a place whose mere name brought terror to people's hearts and made heroes frail. "Dogs or mean guards, demons, but what do I know of them all? Aoud Errih, you have brought me to this place with such speed. You must be so tired. Rest here, you be the guard. I'm going in." The small bicycle shuddered and fell to the floor, as in protest. "It'll be okay. If I'm not back out by morning, go get Zohra." She looked affectionately at the rusty little thing on the floor and put it gently against the wall by the gates. Then she whispered, "Thank you for bringing me here. I love you."

The gates were half-open. The dreaded hospice had the easy approach of a simple rural house, harmlessly aging in the backroads of the Casablanca countryside.

Maryam walked in. The courtyard was empty and no one was in sight. She walked on, but still she encountered no one. The place seemed deserted. The air was too still. Maryam felt the brightness in her heart begin to drain away. She stopped and inhaled a long, deep breath. She wondered why the stillness and deserted aspect of the place filled her with such sadness. It was like no place she had ever been to. It seemed neither aggressive nor oppressive. The silence was not a full-bodied, heavy one. Instead, it was a silence made of emptiness. The place, she realized, was silent because it was in the business of producing nothingness. She stood there silently, her shadow long and delicate on the cracked pavement. Her eyes were very large and rimmed with blue. They always had been. They expressed every feeling or thought she had with the transparency of a pure mountain spring. Zohra often said that her eyes revealed too much. She should lower them often, she'd say, to protect herself against the outside world.

They grew even larger as she understood the peculiar silence that reigned in Birsoukout. It was an arid silence. The walls loomed high on either side of her. Twisted shrubbery grew on these walls surrounding the buildings and the courtyard within. Maryam looked under the greying plants to check her hunch. There she found the water faucet, brown and rusting from years of neglect. She turned the faucet, but no water came out. It was as she had suspected. There was no water in Birsoukout. In my house with the red brick walls, she thought, no matter how dark it may become inside, the fountain in the garden sings. The water trickles into the basin and sings. It is happiness itself. On hot days, I even plunge my head in the fountain. My eyes closed, I enjoy its freshness and coolness. Grandfather tells me that God proclaimed that water belongs to everyone. But this is not the case in Birsoukout. In Birsoukout, the water is taken away. It is a dry place and so very empty...

Maryam wiped the rust from the water faucet on her school uniform. There were buildings ahead of her and to her left. They all seemed deserted and lifeless. She began to wonder if she had not come to the wrong place. She hit the ground with her feet—*thump-thump-thump-thump*—and watched as the packed dirt rose around her. She opened herself up to this place that may not even be a place. Her legs ached, but the ache was becoming a familiar pain. It was a pain that accompanied her every transformation, understanding, and clarity of sight. It brought with it the necessity of resilience and patience. But it also deepened her solitude. In the midst of all the magic and story weaving, Maryam had always been alone. She was the suspended center in a swirl of maddening events. She had always felt different. She sensed that people did not react to her like they normally reacted to other children. Her vulnerability was not the kind that drove people closer but instead the kind that drove people away. Zohra was the only one who loved her unconditionally. There was something wild about Zohra's love for Maryam. It was ferocious and, at times, brutal. It did not fulfill the craving for tenderness that Maryam had but instead intensified her sense of difference. Everyone else trod around her with care and hesitation, as though they feared she'd contaminate them or reveal to them an unbearable truth.

Her loneliness hit her full force as she stood there wiping the rust from her fingers onto her blue skirt. She was alone in a place that breathed nothingness. Her inner world touched magic daily, but she was unable to share the intensity of her emotions with anyone. If only they knew, if only they cared to know. She walked into the first building and then into the second one. They too were deserted. Her confusion and doubt grew as she returned to the main courtyard. Her eyes wide open, her senses on the alert, she thought she felt a faint breeze touch her skin. It must be my imagination, Maryam thought. Then the breeze touched her skin again, but this time it was stronger, warmer, more insistent. The breeze stilled into a presence at her side, but it was not an evil presence. It was the spirit of a woman.

A woman with short dark hair and the deepest eyes in the world. Ghost or djinn, an apparition from Zohra's bedtime stories, Maryam ventured. Yet there was something tough and kind all at once about it; she almost smiled. "Your mother," the woman said.

"Here I am, my beloved. I sense the depth of your solitude and doubt. Now come close and listen, for my time with you is short. Don't be fooled by this place. It is in hiding. A powerful scribe has placed a spell on it that shields it from being seen as it is. The scribe is here. Find the scribe, *perceive* him as you perceive me, and you will find what you are looking for."

Leila's ghost began to fade away, but Maryam tried to hold it near. Her heart was full and about to burst with want. "Wait, please, there is so much I need to know. I am *alone*. When I was born, I was cursed with loneliness." She wanted to say: "You left me." But the pain caused by the thought was too great, and Maryam was unable to express it. Leila turned to her daughter. "I know, habibti. I know you feel that way, but you are loved. You are my greatest dream and my fundamental love. One day, you will see what can be done in the name of love."

Then Leila was gone. Maryam stood still and in disarray. She fought her tears and her feelings of abandonment, and discovered, there at the core of her being, in the smallest of nutshells, an invincible strength. She took that minuscule nutshell of strength in her hands and saw that it was made of pure gold, of tough moon and diamond stars. She understood that she was stronger than she could have imagined: formidably, delightfully, fearfully strong. She felt that strength course through her body all the way down to her shoes.

Maryam had always had to wear ugly shoes, made to hide her handicap. They were painful and only brought attention to her legs. People often made fun of her handicap, and she shielded herself to ignore their disgust. When she looked down, she saw that her ugly shoes had become gorgeous blue boots that fit perfectly against her feet and calves. And, of course, they allowed her to walk as she was always meant to do: unevenly, unfettered, and with a grace all her own.

She stood straight and quiet in the deserted courtyard. Her senses were stretched to their utmost in order to sense what lay beyond the veil of nothingness. As she stood there stretching her perception like a web across a sleeping cave, she began to hear it. It was faint and light, but she knew it was real. The noise became stronger, and it resembled a pen scratching paper. No, it was the click and swoosh of a typewriter. Her eyes adjusted to this new sound and to the reality it carried within it. She walked toward it and saw a small man with balding head and round glasses hunched over a typewriter, too busy typing to look up. She stood in front of him and cleared her throat. He looked up, and Maryam shivered. The man had the mundane appearance of a government clerk but the eyes of a dead thing. She understood that the nothingness that was this place came from these eyes. She braced herself and then addressed the man.

"There is a spell. It makes us believe that this place does not exist. Type it out."

"Why should I do that?"

"Because I have started to see beyond the emptiness. Those are the rules. Something cannot both be and not be."

"Yes, perhaps. But you will regret knowing what lies behind. Why are you here?"

"I came for my uncle who was wrongfully taken here."

"Wrongfully? You believe others are here rightfully?"

"I must believe something."

"Beyond the lifting of the spell, you will find that nothing is as it seems. This spell is one among many, and you are very young. So young for a place like this. Aren't you afraid that I will write you in as one of our inmates?"

Maryam came very close to the dead scribe. She looked down at the paper and saw that the paper was blank. She turned around him, her boots singing on the cold stone beneath and her orange blossom scent diffusing its fragrant nostalgia of things as they should have been but never were. The scribe screeched like an unplugged grenade and covered his nose with his hands.

"Those are not the rules. Unfair! Unfair! Take that horror away from me."

"I cannot. My scent—I myself cannot smell it. But I see that you can."

"I will write, but just move away from me. Your smell is disgusting, impure. It is...alive."

The dead scribe, let's call him S, sighed and raised his hands to the typewriter. Letters and words began to appear on the blank piece of paper, and the nothingness dissipated to reveal the agony beneath. Maryam watched as light became shade and shadows replaced the emptiness. Forms began to step out of the darkness. Though they walked and surely breathed, they showed no other signs of life. Their heads hung low, and their clothes floated on their emaciated bodies. They were neither chained nor whipped nor controlled in any way that she could see. Where were the guards, doctors, nurses?

Some faces turned toward her, and instead of the madness she was expecting to read, all she saw was fear and despair. She did not know what "mad" meant. Was it the anonymity she saw in the faces and bodies before her? She knew that her uncle was not mad. She remembered him from his rare visits to the family house. He'd sit with her and speak to her of Nietzsche and Sheherazade, but also of Boabdil, their family's spiritual founder, and of Maréchal Lyautey, who had reigned over Casablanca decades ago and had built the road leading to their house. She wondered whether his encyclopaedic breadth of knowledge could qualify as madness for those who did not get his many references and meanderings.

Night was falling. The country cold was settling in her bones, but her heart was warm. The faces came closer to her, and their open mouths stretched up and down in a soundless scream. Soon, she was surrounded.

"What is that?"

"A child."

"A child?"

"In here?"

"Not the first time."

"She won't last long then."

"Is she lost?"

"How did she find us?"

"She must have found S."

"Or S. found her."

"Unheard of."

"What does she want?"

"Ask her."

"No, you ask her."

"She found us. That's all that matters."

"Hope."

"We are the margins."

"Not to be seen."

"To be forgotten."

"We don't exist."

"She must be different from the others."

"Is it a she?"

"She reminds me of someone."

"Of me."

"She's lonely."

"She's in pain."

"Poor, poor thing."

"Like us."

"But she's different from us."

"Her scent. It's..."

"Life."

"Light."

"Water."

"Lightness."

"Joy?"

"Kindness."

"Yes, kindness."

"Perception."

"Appetite."

"Remembrance."

"I'm...remembering."

"Stories."

"A story."

"What does she want from us?"

"Why are you here?"

They were very close to her now, close enough to touch her face, her body, plunge their hands in her hair, on her heart.

"She's not scared."

"Her heart beats quietly."

"She's so warm."

"I feel something. It reminds me of..."

"A hazelnut in autumn."

"Books by the fireplace."

"Laughter."

"It must be made of pure gold."

"Of tough moon."

"Diamond stars."

"And Milky Ways."

"She's not scared."

"She's not repelled."

"She...perceives us."

"She cares about us?"

Maryam spoke above the whisperings, worried they would never stop.

"I am Maryam Tair. What are your names? I am looking for my uncle."

"There are no uncles here, no family, friends, or names. There is only an *us* sheltered from the world as a *they*."

"His name is Mehdi, and he should not be here."

"Who should be here?"

"No one should be here."

"Or perhaps everyone."

"I shouldn't be here. I had a life once."

"How I miss children."

"How brave you are."

"A superhero!"

"A supergirl!"

"A superhero with a physical handicap? Are you mad?"

"As a matter of fact, I've been told that I am."

"He is, he is."

Night was falling, and still Maryam did not have the answers she had come for. Then, in the corner of her right eye, she sensed a shift, a break in the atmosphere. She turned her head and saw a man walking toward her. His steps rang clearly on the broken floor. He was different from the others: he held his back slightly higher than his fellow inmates, while his eyes did not reflect as deep a fear and despair as theirs did. They stepped aside reluctantly to let him through. He spoke. His voice had its own distinct grain. It was rough and melodic all at once and, most importantly, still retained a fragment of personhood.

"Are you Maryam of the House of Nassiri?"

"I am Maryam Tair. But I am of that house, yes."

"A man was brought in some time ago. In Birsoukout, there is a period of time, or a place if you like, it's like Purgatory—purgatory for the insane. When we are first brought here, they take us to this space and time where we are broken down. It can be a short or a long process. I am still in that place. But you did something...You conjured me with the others, and here I am. Before I tell you what I know, tell me, how did you find us? No one has ever found us."

"I didn't find you. I just *saw* you. There's a scribe. He types all day, but it's blank."

"You mean S. He is responsible for Birsoukout. He writes the prescriptions, thinks up our punishments, and determines what we eat, feel, and see. We believe that he controls day and night, and time itself."

"Yes, that's him. I found him, then I told him I must see behind the veil and that he must let the non-writing become writing. He said yes as long as he never had to smell my scent again."

Maryam was smiling now, almost despite herself. She was enjoying this moment, and she could tell that the people surrounding her were enjoying it too.

"Does my scent bother you too?"

"It's life and hope and lightness."

"Thank you. Tell me what I need to know about Mehdi."

"I was in the purgatory, and a man was brought in. They kept him there with me for a while, and we spoke whenever we had a chance. I was a farmer once, and one day, shortly after

190

my father's death, my brother came to me and asked to buy my land. I refused. One night, the family banded against me and brought me here, to Birsoukout. Your uncle, well he had his story too. It was an odd story, full of shadows and doubts. He seemed *beyond* their reach. They could not break him, for they could not *find* him. One day they came for him, and I have not seen him since. They spoke of a 'hole from which there is no escape.' Before disappearing, he told me about his gifted little niece. He said that she was a magician and that she would save him. If you are who you say you are, then you will find him. He says he gave you a gift once. Find it. But hurry for you must be done before night falls. When night falls, the scribe will put away his typewriter, and you will become his prisoner."

The man stopped and turned to go, pushing the other inmates away from Maryam as he left. But they protested.

"How about us?"

"I want to stay with the child."

"I want to smell her scent forever."

"Why can't we go with her?"

"I want to keep her here."

"I will hide her."

"No. If the scribe finds her, he will squeeze her scent out of her and punish you for holding her. The punishment could go on for all time."

"You are taking away life."

"To each his destiny. I know now we are not meant to stay here. I have a better plan."

"What? What?"

"A blank paper. Let's take a blank paper and write."

"Write? I don't remember how to write..."

"I do, just barely, a little, like an eight-year-old child."

"But that will be enough."

"Yes."

"We will write that the end of Birsoukout has come."

"Let's steal the paper."

"And write."

"And wait."

"And hide."

"And leave."

"We will write of kindness and compassion."

"And intelligence."

"Competence."

"Gentleness."

"Discernment."

"And patience."

"Clean sheets and proper care."

"Freedom?"

"Justice?"

"Time."

"Yes, time."

"The end and the beginning of things."

"Let's go."

"How?"

"Did the scribe write this in?"

"No."

"Who?"

"Her?"

"I."

"I."

"I."

"I."

The bodies drifted away led by one who was saved by a twist in the story of Birsoukout and who chose to try that rabbit hole of change.

Maryam was left alone, colder than ever. It was almost dark. She didn't have much time before nightfall. She felt something crawling up her leg. It was a large black cockroach, "the Oil Thief" in Arabic. Its wings fluttered and shone in the dusk. Both fascinated and repulsed, she watched as it crawled up her leg, hip, and arm. Instinctively, she felt like brushing it off her arm and crushing it under her foot. She battled her disgust and forced herself to look at the shiny, hissing insect on her shoulder. The cockroach stopped and raised its antennas. Maryam forced herself to look at it and even let its antennas touch her cheek. She sensed the creature's intelligence and acute sensitivity to the world. The cockroach had always been the creature beyond the wall, the one you do not let in, or if you do, it's to trample it under your feet, over and over again. Its presence signaled a rupture of the home cocoon. She looked at it to find that this cockroach, now firmly seated on her shoulder, was keen to establish contact. So, and as can be expected in the face of new and interesting things, Maryam's disgust began to subside. Slowly, curiosity replaced her natural apprehension of this archaic bug. She understood that it was trying to communicate with her.

"Could it be? Are you trying to tell me something?"

"Shshshsh…my brothers and sisters are on their way. Look…shshshshsh."

Hundreds of cockroaches were climbing down the walls from their dark and moist hiding places. They crawled like a trained army unit on a camouflage mission. She understood that they expected her to follow them. Scurrying ahead, they led her into a nondescript building that Maryam had not noticed before. Once inside the building, they hurried up its left wall, and with hissing, fluttering wings and strong legs, they pushed and pushed until the bricks gave. The bricks collapsed to expose a small tunnel fit for a child. The cockroach on her shoulder rasped in her ear.

"Shshshshsh…my journey ends here. Here is a tunnel fit

for a small child. You must be brave and go in. At the end of the tunnel is a hole. In that hole is the man you are looking to save. But hurry or you'll be trapped in the tunnel forever, and not even a telltale heart will tell wherein you lay buried… shshshshsh."

"I thank you, noble cockroach, for your help. But why, may I ask, did you and your brothers help me today when your race and mine are enemies?"

"Shshshshsh…I did not know if I was going to help you or bury you when I started my journey up your leg. If you had tried to squash me, you would have failed and perished. I'm immortal. During my trek up your limbs, I could hear your every thought, sensation, and impulse. I heard the war that you waged against yourself and against your memory of creatures like me. And in the end, in the surprising end of your war, a new way of seeing won out over the old way. You surrendered to me. That's the reason I helped you. Now go, go. The sun is almost down, and the Scribe is already cracking his knuckles in glee…shshshshshsh."

The cockroach hurried down her outstretched arm, and Maryam lowered her head into the darkness.

~

Zohra was in the garden. She stood squarely in front of the ancient orange tree that was its center. She could swear its leaves were trembling with laughter. The tree shook, and its bark opened to reveal Sheherazade sitting in its soft, green core, legs crossed, palms pressed togther in the meditative pose of a yogi. Zohra turned her arms upward.

"This is no time for theatrics. Heed my call, Old Mother. The child is gone. Where is she? I must find her. I believe she may be in grave danger."

"She is in a place beyond my realm."

"There is no place beyond your realm, and if it were, it would be because you willed it into existence. You have woven it into your realm."

"It may be so. But that place comes with a scribe, and that scribe has powers I cannot control."

"Then tell me where she is."

"In your heart, you already know. She is in a place beyond words. In a place whose very name means the Well of Silence."

"Birsoukout!"

"Yes."

"Why?"

"Her heart yearned for Mehdi. Aoud Errih was available, the little bastard, so she went…"

"Her destiny lies elsewhere. You and I know the great tasks ahead of her, the great battles she has yet to wage and win."

"Do we now? Perhaps she has decided otherwise."

"Mockery of the sacred. It has all been decided since time immemorial. The world is dying, and she is our only hope. She is too frail now. She will only be ready once she is an adult, in full possession of her gifts."

"Who are you, Zohra Ait Daoud, to presume you know it all? Do not mistake your dreams for the truth written in the stars. Go find your godchild before it's too late. She is in Birsoukout, in an unnatural hole built on its premises to keep her prisoner there forever."

Zohra bowed low and returned to the house. She poured cold water from a wooden cup onto her head, face, hands, and feet. She burned incense, chewed on cloves, and put a drop of henna in the small of her wrists and ankles. She then went to the toolshed and took out a dusty broomstick. She mounted the broomstick and flew to Birsoukout. *Whoosh, whoosh* was the sound the broomstick made, the crisp air of fading day on her hair and skin. Zohra forgot about her confusion and frustration. She was relishing that pleasure of flight that is the forbidden, universal gift of the witch.

She flew south. Soon, she saw below her the walls of Birsoukout. The broomstick rushed toward the asylum and landed on its broken pathway. Holding the broomstick erect in her hand like a mighty sword, Zohra advanced toward the building. Her black-and-gold scarf rang as she walked, its ringing a war cry in the empty silence of Birsoukout. She called out the Scribe.

"I am Zohra of the Ait Daoud, descendant of the mighty line of Solomon and Sheeba, and I order you to release Maryam Tair."

The faint click and swoosh of a typewriter filled the air, and the small man with the round glasses appeared in front of her. He stopped writing and looked up, his unreadable eyes fogging up his glasses.

"A witch in my domain, and willingly so. I have broken many powerful witches before you, since time immemorial. You will be a prized addition to my roster."

Zohra stood very still, sensing the dangerous power emanating from the bureaucrat. She understood that he was not a mere scribe or the administrator of a damned asylum. He was the creator of borders and margins. He was the grand inquisitor who judged, boxed, packed, and threw away. His experimental treatments on his patients stripped them of all the attributes that made each one uniquely human. He spun scenarios where good and evil were banal and interchangeable. His words wrought the most frightening nightmares ever conceived. His daily notes meticulously traced the breakdown of the human spirit into its smallest components until dissolution was reached. His mission was a most terrible one, for its goal was to distill suffering and alienation in the marginalized few so that the majority might believe in its own self-righteous truths.

"You are..."

"Yes, I am."

"You have crucified, burned, and drowned my people throughout the ages."

"It seems I have not fully succeeded yet."

"You will never succeed. Do you not know who it is you are holding? Her very existence is proof that your end is near."

"Night will be here in the blink of an eye. It's too late, old woman. Time has come, and the war is over."

He raised his thin, white hands to the keyboard, but Zohra was too quick for him. She sprang forward and rammed her broomstick into the typewriter. The scribe screeched his anger, but it was too late. Words had disappeared from the keyboard: the words Maryam Tair. Zohra held the broomstick against his neck.

"Tell me where she is, Scribe."

"She's in a hole in the building on the left. The veil is lifted for you to see. You can now find her, but it's too late. Now get out of my domain."

"Not yet. Write, Scribe, write that today marks the decline of Birsoukout and that this was accomplished by a female child and a witch. Write, Scribe, the judgment that was pronounced!"

Lightning struck, thunder rumbled, and Zohra's hair stood on end, Medusa herself. As she ran toward the building, night fell and darkness was all around. She was too late. But as the wolves began to howl and nondescript creatures began to appear on the horizon, she saw Maryam. And Maryam was holding a tired old man in her arms. It was Mehdi Nassiri.

"Quick, we must leave this place before the creatures come."

"Umi Zohra, what about the others? There are so many. We cannot just leave them behind."

"They will be free, in due time. This hell is at its end."

Zohra held Mehdi on the broomstick in front of her, as Maryam ran to the gates. She called out to Aoud Errih, and soon she was rising through the air on her bicycle behind Zohra's broomstick. Aoud Errih let his bells ring, while fresh rain fell down to the earth. Looking down at Birsoukout, Maryam saw water springing from the faucets on the brick walls and orange trees lining the previously barren courtyard. Zohra ululated in the night, a wild woman freed from all social constraints except the one she imposed on herself, which was to care for a ten-year-old girl who brought exhilaration and purpose to her life.

~

They arrived at the Nassiri house in the dead of night and hid trembling bicycle and overheated broomstick in the toolshed. They then called to the people of the house to open the front door that they may enter. Aisha opened the door to see, standing in the rain, Maryam, Zohra, and an old man she did not recognize.

"What refugees has the stormy night brought back to me? Allah be blessed, for I thought I had lost you forever."

"We ask for your hospitality for this man."

Aisha looked at the old man and thought she recognized him. Her instincts warned her that if she did not agree to Zohra's plea, she could lose Maryam forever. She drew the doors open wide.

"Your companion is welcome in this house, for as long as he needs to remain."

Only when they were safely inside and the light shone on their faces did Aisha recognize the man with Maryam and Zohra. Ibrahim, startled from his sleep, was pleased beyond words.

"What has the rain brought in, indeed? Has my crumbling house become Noah's Ark?"

Mehdi had aged decades in a few months. He looked fragile and emaciated. Only his face retained traces of his past elegance, his subtle intelligence. The hospital had taken its toll on him. No, he thought, not the hospital. The accusation and the humiliation that followed. The guilt was there, it has always been there. For it is a disease, is it not? So why then am I convinced that I am not ill and that I can only be pure if I succumb to who I am? But the proof of my own secret affliction, spread out into the open for all to see, that is unbearable.

The hospital was a death-prolonging punishment, but Mehdi had already resigned himself to his fate. Suddenly, the scent of orange blossom, fresh and full, filled his soul and triggered his brutal awakening from surrender. Then he saw a little girl. Who was she? She looked familiar. She had helped him up and urged him to flee with her. He whispered to her, "All poetry is gone from my life. It will never return."

"You must rest, brother. Stay and rest awhile."

"Am I welcome here?"

"You are welcome."

"You are a member of this house, and this house is reclaiming you as one of its own."

Mehdi was carried to a room, bare and small, but with a window overlooking the fragrant garden curling around its wrought-iron bars. The night was short and good. When Mehdi woke up, the memory of his humiliation swept over him. The ache seeped into his bones and translated into pain as it touched his limbs. It was difficult for him to distinguish between the mental ache and the physical pain of broken hands and crushed limbs. It is all gone. I will never be who I am again. Poor, old fool with your silly boy crushes. He too was feeling the bitter taste of rind in mouth, like Leila once did. He called for Ibrahim and Maryam, and they came.

"Why are you helping me, Ibrahim?"

"I am helping my brother, Mehdi Nassiri. I am the head of this family, and my duty is to protect you when you ask for my protection. Who dare they think they are, to touch one of us! We do not bend or die that easily."

"How about you, Maryam? Why did you help me?"

"I helped you because I was told you needed my help, and I knew that I could help you, Uncle."

"Ah...Who told you so?"

"You wouldn't understand...It's a voice, but not one that you can hear—it's a sensation, a feeling. I don't quite know how to express it myself. But it often guides me."

"Then perhaps I didn't dream the wind in my ears, my hands on a broomstick, and my back against the chest of a whooping witch!"

Her eyes twinkled.

"And Aoud Errih ringing in the rain."

"And here I thought poetry was dead."

"Only if you believe it to be, Uncle."

"I thank you, Maryam Tair, for you were brave in a way no adult would ever have dared to be. I am forever in your debt."

"I am simply returning your gift. There is no debt between us."

"A gift?"

"I met a man in the asylum of Birsoukout who knew you. He said you had called for me, for a child you had once given a gift to. What is that gift? Have I returned it properly?"

"A gift to a newborn child whose destiny appeared to me the moment I laid eyes on it. Yes, indeed. I gave you, I saw for you, perception. I prayed for you to know the true meaning of perception, for at that moment I felt alone in the world, and I needed to be perceived. And you did. You came to a place beyond the world, you lifted the veils that hide the margins from view and you found us. You have ignited a spark, and it will grow until Birsoukout falls. You *are* perception. You are truly who they say you are."

Disillusionment

*T*he Old Woman of the mountain is silent. She is sweating as though from drug withdrawal. The little girl interrupts her silence. She feels alone.

"Forgive me, Old Mother. How sad their victory is. Maryam learns that her destiny has been written for her and that she is not free, while Mehdi is freed only to find that what he loved most about his life is forever lost."

"It's a story of triumph and sacrifice. That is as it must be."

"When Maryam rode Aoud Errih through the clouds, I hoped that she would break her trajectory and fly over the moon."

"That isn't freedom you're describing, little one. It's annihilation."

"Her loneliness is a slow annihilation. Her godmother protects her without understanding her. She is truly alone. Perhaps you too do not understand her."

"Do you doubt my knowledge of the tale? Your instincts guide you to a place you believe to be beyond my reach. That may be so. You will be free soon enough, to my great despair and probably your own. But for now, I am your mother, the mother of all storytellers. And you must keep me for a while longer."

"I want to bury my head in your lap and find sleep. Old Mother, I don't want to leave just yet. I must hear the story till the very end lest it unravel in my mind forever."

"Mothers are archives. When they're gone, we must organize our memories ourselves. Are you ready to pay the price of freedom?"

"I'm filled with discomfort. I'm troubled. But as I lie here breathing in your scent of wildfire, parchment, and dust-filled flowers, I'm beginning to awaken. Let me linger for a moment more, Old Mother. The world is out there."

"The world is in here. Inside my mouth is the entire universe."

"Then guide me."

"Guide you away from my mouth, from the words I breathe and the stories I weave."

"No, Old Mother. Guide me through them that I may recognize my story in the tapestry of stories."

"I am guiding you, my child. I, Sheherazade, am putting my power at your service, out of love for you."

"I'm lost. If you are guiding me, why am I lost?"

"That is the paradox. The existence of the guide is our greatest myth, a front, a lie, a role created to hide one's own fear, doubt. A life wish in a sea of death. It cannot be free or pure. Why should it be? We need to draw lines, divide, encode, and recode. But I am guiding you, beloved."

"Yet I am lost."

"No, you are learning. You are beginning to see. And now you must be patient, as well. We must return to our story. It's waiting. Hear the rumble below."

"Wait, Old Mother. First ease my pain: tell me about Mehdi Nassiri."

"Do you want me to tell you that he is a broken man who will succumb to his fractured life?"

"If that is his fate."

"His fate is a peculiar one. What happens to Mehdi Nassiri is another story that has yet to be written. But this I can tell you. He is a child of the Cycle. His ancestry holds a phoenix of purple-blue and red hue. He has fire and ashes in his veins. The nostalgic blood of Boabdil has consumed most of the royal bird's passion, but the ashes continue to burn. He will rise from the ashes of his existence, and his broken body will emerge anew. But that's another story. Now, come close to me. Listen to the hammer falling in the courtroom and the rumble of the audience."

"I hear the tearing sound made by a thin fabric as it is being ripped."

"It's the grinning of the devils. Their scissor-like smiles are cutting the air through and through. They are taking pleasure in her judgment."

"We must help her."

"No, we must be patient. The judgment must be pronounced. Its absolute injustice will explode in the cosmos and reveal the unbalance at the core of the world. We are at her side. Look, there we are sitting on those benches near the heavy doors. She's beginning to sense us. We are there with her. Let's resume, for she's waiting for us."

The little girl buckles her boots and ties her hair in a knot. She paints her eyes with kohl and sets her face in stone. She then sits on her haunches like an animal in wait. As for the Old Woman, she suddenly grabs her pipe, lights it, and pumps it furiously. She breathes a sigh of relief and, immediately invigorated, stands up and begins gathering the large black feathers falling from the sky. She makes wings of the feathers and slides them onto her body to become a most mysterious bird of midnight black.

Grand Tribunal

Clockmakers' Town
Casablanca, February 2011

The charges roll on. Maryam sighs and looks down at her great, shattered blue boots. She sees how they are changed, and sadness engulfs her. They were not *any* boots: they were her chosen paths in a world of thorns and evil intentions. When the cold-eyed demons came for her in her cell, they tried to tear the blue boots away from her, but couldn't.

"Witch, witch," they had hissed. "You deserve what's coming to you."

The boots are my second skin, they are made of stardust, velvet sky, and resilience, her eyes flashed back at them. They take me where I must go in the darkest nights and protect me from the vagaries of time. A witch you call me, if you say so. But if I am a witch, I am the greatest witch in the world. And you will soon tremble before my power. No words came out of her mouth, and for those guards who could not see into her eyes, she was mistaken for a terrified young woman defined by her frailty.

There were many others like her, they commented. For the past year, since late 2010, young men and women had gone to the streets and defied the existing order. They had woken suddenly, without any warning sign, and risen against their superiors, the price of bread, the price of injustice, the price of tyranny. But they had also risen up because they believed that no price would be paid for their insubordination. They swung joyfully through the barbed wire erected by the law and were convinced it was all play. There was a youthful quality to all this latter-day subversion that was incapable of recognizing consequences. Here was another flighty subversive who would appear stunned at the heaviness of the penal machine. The surprise would soon turn into terror and a dry-mouthed, yellow-hearted fear.

Most of them bailed, dropped, or asked for their families. But, for most, it was too late. The dungeons could not hear their childhood yearnings, and the cold stones swallowed their tears crying for light-heartedness and green fields. There were times, the guards admitted to themselves, but these were rare and few, when one such twenty-first-century hippy would surprise them with his or her resilience. They would watch and wait for that moment when the individual would break and the soul would be taken away by the surrounding horror, but it would not come. They would watch for days and longer days, they would become masters of cruelty and invent the most creative of tortures, but all in vain. They would persevere, and their perseverance would pay off. After a lengthy, doubt-filled wait, the prisoner would finally break. There was even a couple they had freed to serve as an example to other hot-headed, naïve idealists.

But Maryam was different. She was not breaking and she was not resisting. They began to think that she was either uncomprehending of the situation or...she was a real witch. They had never held a witch in their barren claws. Witches were not interested in revolution, their manuals told them. They were interested in twirling mystification throughout the land. But if she were a witch, why were her ideas so clear and her body so young?

Maryam was able to decode their brutal logic in the way they looked at her, threatened her, and tortured her. The demons believed their youthfulness had made the new subversives reckless. The demons thought that these kids, who had been raised on Hollywood, Coca-Cola, and sun-packed afternoons, would surrender after a day in the dungeons of fear. How surprised they all were—including the makeshift revolutionaries—when they discovered the peculiar brand of toughness some were made of. They neither quickly folded nor immediately cowered in submission. Though they were tough, in the end they did lower their heads. But these experiences in imprisonment and repression had brought to light something new and utterly unexpected. It was revealed, in the midst of all the terror and confusion, that previously free-spirited kids with all their cool and their style, were capable of coming up with tough attitudes and resistance, which indicated one thing and one thing only: presence—undeniable, unavoidable presence. What all parties discovered in the dark dungeons was that courage can spring from the most unexpected of sources in the most unexpected of ways. And that, my love, is a discovery that cannot be occulted. It brings to light surprising truths about the human spirit and the passing hold of consumerism and tyranny on individuals once they have discovered that they are individuals. But in the end, most folded, were let go, or disappeared forever. Only Maryam remained.

Her frail, unbalanced body, blue boots, and thoughtful blue-rimmed eyes came with a warning: do not treat this prisoner the way you would treat any prisoner. She is the child of Leila and Adam, the elder sister of Shams and Hilal, and the living sign that history is the fruit of a willful manipulation of texts. It is she, Maryam, the enemy, the witch, the forbidden one. These dungeons were her first home. Yes, even demons must consult their archives. The seed was planted in one of our cells, perhaps the very one she is now being held in. She may be your child or even mine, for Leila, her mother, remained our prey for many a long night. A moment of suspended violence, of pure pleasure upon which we fed our crimson delight...Her destruction must be complete. She is the anomaly, the forbidden fruit that blossoms into hope, the accident that brings history in its wake. Her judgment and sentencing will be made public so that the world can see that hope for change is dead.

Since she was taken into the demons' cells, Maryam had understood the true meaning of darkness. It was as though the light, sun, and air had been sucked into a vacuum, and she was forgotten in the emptiness that remained. She was imprisoned in a black hole, leaking pestilent fumes and tortured with mad water, but her mind was elsewhere. She was lost in absence, condemned to oblivion. And yet it was all strangely familiar. Maryam did not lose her mind nor did she submit. In this very moment, forgotten in the dungeons of time, she thought of her life. Barely thirty years old and as old as the world. In this place bereft of compass, she was finding her true north. She could not be broken, for her magic lay in the void left inside her solitude. You can try to destroy my powers, but you will fail. They reside in lack rather than in plenty. I know how to bend time and events, and I have learned to perceive the imperceptible, think the unthinkable, and love beyond love itself.

But a mother's tenderness I have never known. Two strong arms made soft to hold me in, I have never had. There is nothing to be taken away from me. I have known one rough, wild, inscrutable woman who taught me the ways of the witch and a matriarch who believed revenge and irony were a woman's best weapons. They were dominating, elusive influences in my life, but mentorship was a relationship they never understood. They were inconsistent in their training and filled me with doubt rather than knowledge. A father's acknowledgment, I have never found. I have known one old man roaming in the path of Boabdil, sighing over a lost greatness and obsessed with the sound of rusting tin in the pantry. There is nothing to be given back to me. My life has been a succession of failed attempts at finding love. I believe some may have tried to love me, but there is a curse on my head and I am doomed to roam all the worlds in solitude.

"Death:

for eating during Ramadan,

for drinking alcohol,

for eating ham,

for rejecting Islam,

for praying in a Mosque alongside men,

for saying no,

for being physically deformed,

for doubting absolute power,

for disagreeing with the majority,

for sitting on the moon and confirming there was no God,

for flying higher than an airplane,

for saying no,

for thinking,

for calling herself a citizen,

for considering herself equal to men,

for disrespecting our traditions,

for being different,

for saying no."

Maryam looks down at her magical, weathered boots and shuts out the angry crowd. She is searching within for that kernel of calm to protect her from the ambient evil. All she ever wanted was to be anonymous. Her magic had been a burden and a responsibility, rather than a blessing. She had not yet understood that her desire for anonymity rendered her gifts greater, more miraculous.

In the midst of the rage-filled room, she hears the crisp rustle of turning pages and looks up. There in the back of the courtroom, near the heavy bronze doors, sits a woman with round glasses resting on white hair tied in a bun and a young girl with heavily made-up eyes. They hold a large book in their arms, and their heads are lowered. The old woman is busy reading to the young girl, oblivious to the violence of the courtroom and the finality of the sentence. Maryam is swept with longing for this scene, which she dreams has been created for her.

Yasmine

It's July 1999, and Maryam has just turned eighteen years old. The new millennium is around the corner, but the land is in mourning. The Great Patriarch, lord of all warlords, has passed, leaving his children fatherless. Or so the state radio and official TV stations stated. When the Great Patriarch's soul left the earth, the cities closed in upon themselves, and the tribal countryside dreamt of raids and looting once more. Or so the state radio and official TV stations stated. The many lords ruling over their families, farms, or factories were weakened, or pretended to be, until further assurance that they would retain their power over their dominions.

Maryam did not know what having a father meant. She lived in a house where patriarchal authority was represented by a slumbering old man who recited Andalusian poetry and sighed his longing like warm air on a hot summer day, and where women used magic to transform their decrepit household into a battle of good against evil. In the Nassiri household, things were not—were never—what they seemed to be.

So it was that she turned eighteen when the land was mourning its feared leader and perhaps secretly hoping that change was around the corner. As for Maryam, she was holding her high school diploma in her hands and realizing that this piece of paper would be the only acknowledgment that she had crossed from childhood into adulthood. The breeze touched the great orange tree at the center of the garden. The leaves rustled, the branches swayed, and Maryam's body yearned for a return to the dark earth.

Then the familiar tingling took hold of her body, and her legs began to ache. She waited for the vision or the magic to appear in front of her, but instead she saw a hawk-like woman coming toward her. The woman was smoking a long cigarette with a gold holder, and a boyish haircut framed her thin, haughty face. She tapped the cigarette, and ash fell on the ground by Maryam's feet. The woman's shoulders sagged a little as she crossed her elbows on her chest.

"There's no need to stare. I am your great-aunt, though you probably have no recollection of me."

"You are Yasmine. Your brother speaks of you in his sleep."

"Yes, I heard of the way you saved Mehdi from the asylum. Your feat is legendary. People believe again. Maryam the Savior, the Compassionate, my ugly little niece who saved a weakling from the claws of fate."

"I was helped."

"So it's true then. Are you who they say you are? Are you the One?"

"I'm nobody. I have things inside me, and they seem extraordinary to others, but I don't know who the One is."

"I had a dream last night. There was an old woman in it. She told me it was time that I come for you, that you had reached that age. What is your age?"

"I'm eighteen years old."

"The age when women of our land are officially told that they are now, and will always be, minors. Adulthood is not for us: our rites of passage are from one prison to another and are leaps of faith. We pray for a husband, then we pray our husbands are kind to us and feel blessed when they are. If they are, we believe in magic and take pride in our uniqueness. We live our lives as twirls of witchcraft and fated chance, and only succeed in tightening the bolts on our cages."

"Was that your fate?"

"No, it was not my fate. And if you so desire, it will not be your fate either. I can teach you how to be powerful, how to fool the powerful and elude consequence. Do you want to know how?"

Yasmine pulled on her cigarette. From the corner of her almond eyes, she watched her niece. She was not at all as she had expected. She had expected a strong, beautiful woman with the arrogance of a princess and the fire of a commander. Instead, here was a young girl with the bearing of a child and a disharmonious body. Maryam was humble and quiet, and seemed detached from her destiny and abilities. Who, Yasmine wondered, would this girl ever lead into battle?

Maryam looked at the dry seventy-year old woman and smiled at her. Her smile was gentle, kind, and, to Yasmine's surprise, amused. Yasmine looked into her niece's eyes and saw what she had failed to see before. Maryam had seemed frail and unassuming to her—a person who could be cast aside without a second thought, for her presence or absence created barely a ripple in the room. But as Maryam stood there quietly smiling at her, Yasmine caught a glimpse of the unbreachable strength beneath. She began to understand that Maryam was not what she seemed, and she felt shame. Her mouth was filled to bursting with the scent of orange blossom, and she could taste its fragrant acidity. At that very moment, she also understood that Maryam could see straight through her into her darkest thoughts and most unspeakable desires.

Yasmine had always been a tough one, a hawk, a queen, a bully. She held most people in scorn, her husband and family included. She thought men were greedy and women meek. As a lawyer, she had chosen to fight for women's rights, only to come to the conclusion that laws befitted the people they served and that most human beings preferred to be numb than to be free. Simply put, she had given up. She was now a high-society woman who defined life as afternoon teas and frequent trips to Europe. She was a poser whose cynicism shielded her from her own bitterness. Her distaste of others deepened with age, but she drowned it in pleasantries and whiskey. She had taken a liking to luxury and status. There was a very specific kind of power granted to people like her in a country like hers. She was married to a wealthy man and had an old name. In her city, these guaranteed almost absolute privilege and, with time, had dimmed her desire for personal achievement and excellence. In the end, she shrugged her shoulders and, with breath warmed by alcohol, decided: Why bother?

Yet at the back of her mind, in that place where long-forgotten memories choose to lurk, were images of that child she had once held in her arms and who had forced a strange prophecy from her lips. Those words had come to her, rushed through her body, and found life on her tongue. They had changed her. She did not know where they had come from or why they had chosen her as a vessel. She was haunted by these words, by the paths they created. You are thought, she had whispered to the baby, her mouth touching her ear. Did these words then release her from her own obligation to thoughtfulness and analysis? Had she sacrificed to this child her own ability to think and question?

Yasmine heard that Maryam Tair was a magical being. She heard of the ten-year-old girl who had flown into the demons' asylum and freed the damned. She heard of the bicycle Aoud Errih circling the moon, and of Zohra the old witch who became tame to protect her. She believed that these legends

214

would die down and that her niece would soon be forgotten. She gave in to vanity and to the pleasure of being respected for one's wealth and origins. She began to believe in her own greatness. There were times, admittedly, when she would stay in the half-dark of her room and drink herself to oblivion. But she would soon remember what mattered, and what mattered were people of her station.

Yasmine did not know her niece. She barely noticed her the few times she came to her brother's house, when Maryam was still a young child. In fact, she still shuddered before going for a visit. The smell of lavender and naphthalene, which she once so despised, had faded, but a new scent inundated the house and filled her with an inexplicable sadness. It consumed her with nostalgia and an unbearable depth of feeling. She smiled when told, "That scent, Yasmine, what you are breathing into your lungs, is Maryam. Remember her birth. The scent has not left her since." Yasmine had chosen to forget about her niece and deny all stories she heard about her.

But lately, a recurrent dream was cutting through her sleep. Night after night, the dream came to her and emptied her days of their flavor. The dream was a message for Maryam. She would not be granted peace until she delivered it.

So Yasmine came to her niece to deliver the message. She also came because the rough, alive side of her wanted to cross swords with Maryam. Yasmine wanted to convince herself that Maryam was nothing more than an old wives' tale. Standing near her niece and taking in her steadfastness, Yasmine understood that Maryam was not easily swayed. It was almost strange. It was as if her words had had no effect on the girl. She had opened a door for her, but Maryam did not even deign look through it. Why?

Maryam looked at the older woman and answered her silent question.

"Resistance is one way of dealing with fear. I am not interested in power. Why? How can I explain to you something I don't understand? I'm made this way."

"Aren't you ambitious? I hear that your powers are great, and you are only at the beginning of your journey. Do you mean to throw your potential to waste?"

"People are always hungry. They hunger for more, they want more. Then they get lost in their hunger and want. I am looking for something else. Something beyond the vicious cycle of greed and anxiety."

"You are still so young and self-righteous. Know that greed is not why I started this fight for women's rights. But that's where it has led me."

"That is where you have chosen to end it. Tell me, venerable great-aunt, why have you come to me on my eighteenth birthday?"

Yasmine had come with a dream-message and with cruelty at the tip of her tongue. She was about to deliver her message without a second thought for its consequences. Dream-messages rippled through time and space to create unforeseen, uncontrollable events. Yasmine did not care what Pandora's box she could unleash onto the world by talking to her niece. She had reached a point in her life where evil had become an exit from boredom. She had hoped to dominate this frail, handicapped young woman, but instead she found something she had not expected. The simple features were not closed, and the large, clear eyes were not shy. There was a detachment in Maryam's face, a rare distancing in someone so young. Yasmine thought of the right word to describe the expression, but she could only think of things it was not: it was not greed, or want, or envy. It did not exude vanity, power, or hunger. It was, yes it was, the expression of someone *aspiring* toward something—toward an unknown beyond the farthest horizon into the infinite radiance of the world. Yasmine understood then that she would never control Maryam's destiny, and so she delivered the dream-message, adding her narrative drop into the story unfolding before her eyes.

"I am the bearer of a message. In a dream I saw a raven sitting on my windowsill. It spoke to me about a prophecy that was made once, a long time ago. The prophecy spoke of a woman, the daughter of Adam and his first wife Leila. This woman has an extraordinary destiny, but her path is fraught with danger. That woman is you, Maryam. And I am here to tell you that you must leave, for you are in grave danger. You must go find your second gift before it's too late. You are now at your most vulnerable. You are eighteen years old. There is no rite of passage for women in this land. If you do not leave now, you will perish. You will fall into the legal swamplands of subjecthood. You must go to the land of the wild cedars and the great, grey mountains of the north and retrieve your second gift. That is the raven's dream-message."

Yasmine crushed the cigarette under her feet and took Maryam's face in her hands. She gave her a deep, long kiss on the mouth and whispered in her ear: "Alas, for you have rejected me. You would have enjoyed my company, and you and I would have had a grand time. My protégée..." A voice rose behind them: "Let go of the child, you used-up hag." Mehdi was standing behind them. Yasmine laughed at the frail old man who had uttered those words.

"What are you scared of? She's a legend, all eyes are on her. How could I possibly want to hurt her?"

"You're a predator. A spent-up, washed-up old lizard, but a predator nonetheless. You would feast on her, prey on her if you could. Why are you here?"

"Perhaps this is my atonement. My last noble deed."

"Come now, sister. We are too old for these manipulations.

Why did you come?"

"I had a message for Maryam. A raven in my dreams was its carrier."

"A raven is the messenger of death. What ill-omens are you sending her way?"

"If she does not heed the call of the raven, she will be lost to the world. She must listen to the dream-message."

"If she does as you say, she will surely die."

Maryam spoke.

"The raven is blood and warfare. But it is also light and creation. I have agreed to heed the raven's call. I will go to the wild forests of the north."

"It's a trap set for you by a jealous old woman. She is a cynic, and that's what cynics do. You may never return."

"That may be, but I must go."

"Why?"

"Because I had the same dream, and I know it to be true."

"You went to the edge of the world once and you survived. The powers above may not be as merciful this time."

"It is true, I found you at the edge of the world. And I discovered that I too belonged there, somehow. Now, I will penetrate the savage depths of the world and seek that second gift. I will also perhaps come nearer to understanding who I am."

But Mehdi feared for Maryam's life. Ever since his escape from the madhouse, he had been plagued with fear. He saw ill-omens everywhere and at times would stare at his own body as though it too were haunted. Yasmine interrupted: "Indeed, it may be your destiny to find your answers among the wild forests of the interior. I thank you, niece, for believing in my dream, and I wish you good speed."

Yasmine turned to leave, and her beige dress floated on her angular body like a drape around a theater loge. She left to Mehdi's words.

"That woman destroys all that is good. She turns joy into sadness and pleasure into pain. And yet you heed her words."

"They are not her words. A dream-message must be heeded, and the raven is the most powerful of birds. Its call must be answered."

"You have a future ahead of you. You could go to university. You could learn from books rather than from the wild creatures of the forest. You could leave this country never to return. You could plant roots in a country that has defeated its demons and that sees men and women as citizens rather than subjects destined to kneel and be silent. That is freedom, Maryam. You, you are pursuing ghosts and chimeras."

"I do not know if that is freedom. I do not know that any land has defeated its demons. I feel inside me the urge to go into the wild rather than anywhere else. I feel the need to create, to invent, to disrupt if that's necessary. I do not know that I am seeking freedom only, and I do not know that the roots I would plant elsewhere would agree to grow. Look at my legs, they're uneven and cause me pain. Yet they hold me up and take me where I need to go. They remind me of my weakness and my difference. And today, they are planted firmly in this soil, and they are turned toward the forests of the interior."

Mehdi's own frailties had defined him more acutely than had his strengths. His bones had weakened and were brittle, close to crumbling. With every passing day, he felt his body escape him a little more, and there was nothing he could do to stop it. He knew helplessness and lost struggles. He could see his life wasting away and turning to ashes, and yet he was unable to pull himself back up. Lately, the taste and feel of ashes were everywhere. His mouth was filled with it. His tears were grey and dry. A soft, grey dandruff fell like rain from his hair. The hair on his body had fallen off to leave his skin smooth and delicate. He felt the weight of the inexplicable at every moment.

He felt his solitude increase and his yearning for others grow. He was a sad old man, was he not, craving affection and fire but cursed with loneliness? Sometimes, he imagined he was a phoenix free to be as bright and colorful as he wished. He was a fool, sometimes. He knew the call of the void and its twin beckoning for renewed life and yes, why not, joy. So he nodded to show his respect for the young woman who was patiently explaining to him why she must follow a raven from a dream.

Maryam cut a strand of her hair and placed it in Mehdi's hand: "If you miss me or fear for me, hold this strand of hair. It will comfort you and tell you that I am fine. As long as it carries the scent of orange blossom, you can be certain I am alive and well."

She left the garden and the soft humming of the trees, insects, and creatures who resided there. She walked quickly toward the house, for she was eager to begin her journey.

In the arched passage leading from the garden to the house, Zohra was slightly bent over a broomstick, and she was sweeping dust out of the house into the garden. The dust lingered in the air when Zohra stood up, her two hands still cupped around the broomstick.

"Well? What did she want?"

"She delivered a dream-message from the raven. It said I must go to the forest of cedars to claim the second gift."

"Those are grim lands where evil magic runs high. They are the home of the tattooed butterfly tribe."

"They are also lands where goodness, cool springs, and storytelling found refuge after the One Story conquered the world."

Zohra ran her hands over Maryam's hair, face, and neck. Her hands were warm and smelt of cedarwood.

"Your hair, face, and neck are now familiar to the cedars. The memory of the cedarwood is within you and will guide us on our journey to the interior lands. Come, we must leave before the clock strikes midnight and the spirits fill the streets to mourn the passing of the Great Patriarch."

"Godmother, you always have a choice. If you wish to remain here, I will not force you away."

"I will always protect you, my little one. I may be old but I am strong. Do not underestimate a witch, especially in her old age."

Maryam kissed Zohra's hands and inhaled the scent of cedars that still lingered there. As she walked toward her room to gather her belongings, she could hear the clamor beyond the house's walls. The rhythmic voices, the flapping of wings in the air, and the dull mourning cries indicated that night was falling and the spirits rising. Maryam knew the danger that came with the descending darkness. The Great Patriarch had left a people whose mourning disrupted the stability of the land. It was fast transforming into litanies of fear and ritualistic transgressions. There was an anxiety in the voices that filled Maryam with sadness. Chaos was trying to seep into the holes left by the dead leader. Indeed, the air itself sang, the moment had come. The crowds beyond the walls were growing like snowballs rolling down a mountain. And Maryam sensed their hunger. She paused in her footsteps. She was perhaps hesitating, pulled by the call of the wild at her front door. It was also possible that she thought the answers she was looking for could be here, at the heart of the city, and not in the hinterlands of the north.

As her mind swayed toward the asphalt streets beyond, she began to feel a great force pressing against the large gates of the house. She could hear voices calling out her name. The voices became stronger and clearer, and waves of anger and hatred hit her in the heart. The voices beyond the walls were calling her a witch and claiming her head. She stood very still. Her legs ached, and her huge, blue-rimmed eyes ate at her face. She sensed a presence at her side. Leila's gentle, soft presence, which filled her with longing. She had not sensed it since that night in the madhouse of Birsoukout.

"Mother."

"My love, you can't stay. You're in grave danger. Leave now and don't look back."

"I will leave but I feel like a coward. When and if I return, it may all be too late, and my life could be a failed one, all because I ran."

"Patience. The center is not where we think it is. Our footsteps take us toward destinies we could never have dreamt of. But if you stay, you will certainly meet death. You would not be brave, you would be foolish. You could unleash a wave of terror against all those like yourself: different, incomprehensible, seen as vulnerable and unfit."

"What if Mehdi is right and I am turning my back on the action at hand?"

"Oh no, not so. Listen carefully. It's time you know. There is an ancient story about a man, a woman, and their child. Their names were Adam, Lilith, and Maryam. The wild forest of cedars was their first home. In fact, the ancient trees kept the memory of their story in their bark and sent its echoes throughout the world. That is our first home, Maryam. As close to the origin of stories as ever possible. The cedars are beyond time. No one knows what magic rules that place, and no one dares venture. But you have been called there. By returning to the cedars, you return to the source, and only then will you understand. You will have knowledge and use that knowledge well, I know. Go now, beloved. The cedars are waiting for you, and their leaves are rustling impatiently. Do not make them wait. Their anger can shift the course of things."

Leila came near her daughter and through her words tried to convey her love and worry. But as she spoke and as she tried to come close to her daughter, she faced her own emptiness. She remembered physical warmth like cooling water remembers the tea-leaves that once lingered, and she was haunted by its loss. She was as near her daughter as possible, and yet she would never feel that satisfaction of touch, smell, warmth.

"I must return to the place that holds me, my daughter. But you must leave and fast, before the night falls and the demons hunt you down."

Before she left, she conjured two bracelets out of the air and wound them around Maryam's wrists.

"Once, long ago, a little girl came to Adam and I in an alleyway of the Medina, in a dream. She gave us these bracelets and claimed that they would protect us. And they have, they were true to us. It is we who treated the bracelets and their giver callously."

"Who was the little girl?"

"The little girl was the dream of a child. I do not know who that child is. It is only right that the bracelets are given to you. They will protect you as they have protected us. They have returned to you. Cherish them."

She faded away and Maryam slumped, for she was beginning to question the necessity for resistance when your psyche belongs to a ghost of a mother who chose to leave you at birth.

The windows had turned orange with the dying light of day, and Maryam knew she must hurry out. She went to her room and silently closed the door behind her. There the voices were temporarily muted, and she could think. She would soon be leaving her home behind her, and with it, a certain treasured intimacy, anxieties, and fantasies. She looked around at her room, wondering what to take with her. I must learn to live with scarcity and give up the superfluous, she told herself. Her room was small and, by certain standards, bare. By the standards of most of her classmates, her room was vastly luxurious, the reason being, simply, that it was her own.

Just as her own household experienced hard times as the decades went by, so did her classmates' families. The wealthier students were taken out and educated in better schools. Their exodus opened the way for poorer families to send their children to the nuns. Most children were the sons and daughters of families who had only recently left the working classes or who were about to return to them. Artisans, nurses, secretaries, school teachers, merchants from the urban souk of Derb Omar, or young functionaries, most parents had to deal with the daily fear of collapsing revenue. For the Nassiris, material loss had become an inevitability. Ibrahim's factory had recently closed, and he was now selling the few parcels of land he had left, before finding himself with nothing but a sprawling domain he could no longer afford, but which he could not get himself to sell. He was hoping that death would come to him before complete ruin. Maryam's material conditions slipped with that of her school. But, like her school, the past opulence could still be sniffed here and there.

Beyond the material gap, she knew that her classmates did not consider her as one of *them*. One day, a boy told her: "You'll never be like us. You're like…a character in a story. But you're not like any character I know. I don't know if you're good or bad, but I'm scared to find out. I think you're probably bad, for you're strange and strange things are always bad."

Now, Maryam would strip herself of belongings and judgment, at least for a while. She would rid herself, by the same measure, of the guilt that often accompanies privilege.

The bracelets Leila had given her wound themselves comfortably around her wrists. Though she had never seen them before, they seemed oddly familiar to her. They purred softly, and a thought flashed through Maryam's brain: They are alive, and they remember me. They began to attach themselves firmly to her wrists, and the inscriptions hooked themselves to the skin—hot-white tattoos of talismanic protection.

She looked around her room to see what she could take with her and noticed a burnous and furry mountain overboots she had never seen before. The burnous, warm traditional clothing of shepherds and merchants alike, was thick and made of wool. The furry mountain overboots were like those the artisans of Fes and Rabat once made for horsemen set on long travels. She knew they were meant for her, though she didn't know who put them there. She had her burnous, overboots, and bracelets. She whistled, and the rusty bells of Aoud Errih the bicycle rang in the distance. She was ready.

Meanwhile, Zohra was in her own quarters, chanting slowly. After eighteen years in this house, ever a gypsy in her soul, Zohra was ready to leave. She was now looking intently at the wooden box by the bed. When she came to this house, all those years ago, she had set the box there. The wooden jewelry box, with engravings on the side and a copper keyhole, had remained there for eighteen years, unnoticed. Zohra now wished to take the box with her on her journey. The box clicked softly, and Zohra understood that permission had been granted. She raised it carefully, held it against her chest, and it disappeared from sight. She then noticed two woolen blankets on the bed and took them. She turned and left the room without a backward glance.

She went to the pantry and gathered food for the road: homemade round bread, Laughing Cow cheese, tuna, and sardines, all staples of urban Moroccans' daily diet. She was pouring water in a large gourd when she heard a voice calling out to her, "You're leaving me behind. Take me with you." Zohra turned to see Zeinab standing in the dusky hallway. She looked parched and old, yet there was a rare glimmer of hope in her eyes.

"I cannot take you with me. Only two blankets were given. If I take you with me, *he* will not watch over us."

"He?"

"Hamza. He will be angered if you accompany us on our journey."

"Is he so cruel to not forgive me?"

"It is not about forgiveness but about danger. You will surely be destroyed on our journey. Your time will come."

"When?"

"Not until Hamza finds his way back, if he finds his way back. Only Sheherazade sees. Your story is not yet written."

"My story is written. I am a prisoner and always will be."

Zohra watched pensively as Zeinab retreated into the distance. Then she picked up her broomstick, tied the provisions and blankets to its back, and stalked to the garden. She stood in front of the gnarled orange tree at its center. After a while, Zohra knelt. The leaves rustled, and Sheherazade's face appeared etched in the bark.

"I came to say goodbye, Old Mother. Grant us your protection."

"It's yours."

"Answer one question, then I will leave: Were you the raven in the dream-message?"

"Yes. Hamza was kind enough to lend me the props. Black wings, tail, and all. That woman has one rugged mind. But yes, it was I."

"Then I'm content. It's not a trap."

"Ah…but you always presume to know so much about good and evil, success and failure. And yet you don't."

"I know more than even you, O wondrous Sheherazade, think. I know that you have secrets of your own, I know that you have expectations that you mean to keep hidden from us all. I know that you see the world through this child who is much more to you than a daughter. I know that you dream of change."

"Outrageous! My stories are endless, and change itself is folded in their ripples."

"But you are a sorceress, Old Mother. Do not ask me to forget that. And I know Maryam is not just a pawn for you. I know that you have your secrets."

"Where is she? I must see her before you leave."

"I am here."

Zohra turned to see Maryam standing behind her. Said Sheherazade: "Come close, beloved. My eyes are not what they once were."

Maryam came close to the old tree and gently touched its bark with her hands, mouth, and cheeks.

"When you get to the forest of cedars, do not behave like a stranger or a visitor. You will be destroyed in an instant. Remember, you too come from the trees. Your scent is that of the seed blossoming in the earth, and your ancestry is not altogether human. Ride into the forest of the interiors as though you were returning home."

The tree shook, and the face etched on the bark disappeared.

~

It was almost night. Zohra and Maryam mounted their rides and flew into the air. They turned Aoud Errih and the broomstick north and plunged toward the interior lands. High in the skies they saw large flocks of birds speeding in the opposite direction, toward a Casablanca ripped apart by mourning and fear. When they were eye to eye, they saw that they were not birds. Witches, demons, and djinns of all orders and classes were rushing toward the city. From the most powerful to the most evil, they were flapping their wings and whirring their metal rides to feast on the humans below. They whooped and screeched. They filled the air with their rumpus and acted wild, but Maryam could sense the black holes beneath their extravagant attires and acts. They are absolute emptiness, she thought, come to feed on fear. No, that is not exactly so. It is not just fear they want. They come to destroy all hope that may rise from this cataclysmic event. They bring nothingness with them and fool us into believing their monstrous costumes. They are the void at work.

Meanwhile, in the quiet of the Nassiri household, Ibrahim and Aisha sat in front of their TV set, half asleep and once again unconcerned by the failed beginning outside their walls.

The Journey

Maryam and Zohra rode across the sky through the chilly night air. They crossed a winged man falling from a plane who looked strangely like the archangel Gabriel. He seemed headed for India. They continued forward in the direction of the Forest of Cedars. Huddled underneath her burnous and the warm blanket provided by Hamza, Maryam was safe from the cold. They flew all night until they reached a magnificent city of white and green.

Fes the beautiful lay at their feet, bathed in the morning light. Both Maryam and Zohra had heard many extraordinary tales of Fes. Encouraged by the cool light and the call of the minarets, they stopped in their journey. They landed on a terraced rooftop of Fes El Bali, the Old Fes. They placed their riding machines on the low white wall surrounding the terrace, spread out the blanket on the floor, and laid out their victuals in front of them. They sat to eat their breakfast of bread and cheese.

In her two hundred eighty years, Zohra had never been to Fes. Her centers of influence were the bastion cities of the lower Atlas Mountains, which looked toward the east, Algeria, and the desert. She was nervous just sitting on that roof. At her feet lay the city of artisans, merchants, and teachers. Urbanity was mastered here, and Andalusian civilization created its own rhythms.

They looked across the horizon toward the four fortresses whose role once was to protect the city from the tribal invaders of the hinterlands. They saw the olive trees and the orange groves. The emerald-colored palaces and the minarets sparkled in the light. They sat on the low wall of the terraced rooftop and sharpened their gaze. Their eyes adjusted to the city's architecture, and they began to see into the narrow streets and the square below their feet. The walls were crumbling, and rust had formed on the water pipes. Trash lay on the sidewalks, and the famed donkeys with their mercantile loads were thin and slow. There was no grace or gentility in the scene below. Children were begging for money from wide-eyed tourists, while young women stood in doorways, plastic slippers on their tired feet. Behind the women, in the faint light of the rooms, an old man or woman lay sick, dying, or worse, forgotten. Students haunted university halls emptied of professors, and factories were closed down while people looked for work. The city was sprawling, broken, and disenchanted.

Suddenly, Zohra held Maryam's arm, her eyes glazed. "Do you see it too, Maryam?" she urged. Maryam nodded, "I felt it. Now I am beginning to see it." A sound like rolling thunder could be heard in the distance. The noise was getting closer, as wave upon wave of protesting men and women, young and poor, hit the narrow streets.

"The people have nothing left to lose," said Zohra.

"This city is as cursed as our city."

"Perhaps more so, for they are all stuck in these thousand and one narrow streets and within these caving walls."

"Where is the Fes of our history? It's so hard to see the civilization when it is covered in grief."

"Its masters have all abandoned it to its fate. All they do now is dream about it from afar, but no one comes to its aid."

"I am starting to understand the story of the violence in my house, the cruelty that is part of our history. It has all been there since they abandoned Fes for Casablanca and the coastal cities, leaving the rest of the country behind. Umi, I have grown up in a household where nostalgia clocked our days."

"Your mother was not so. Aisha, your grandmother, is not so, or if she is, her nostalgia is of the kind that seeks revenge."

"Ibrahim is haunted by the past."

"Yes, but aren't all patriarchs haunted by the past?"

"This stop in Fes the imperial, the beautiful, the erudite, has rid me of my nostalgia for it."

"There is discontent here, but that is not all. There is hope—nostalgia for a better future."

"Your tribe, the Ait Daoud, have been here for over three thousand years, and yet they have managed to change their nostalgia into pride."

"Oh, but how often we fled or used magic to protect ourselves and our secrets. How precarious are origins!"

Maryam and Zohra fell quiet. Maryam sighed, filled with a new kind of fear. The veils between expectation and reality had begun to fall, and her mind was shedding its illusions. But with every new understanding, a new question arose. The more she thought about the city below and the place of regret in one's life, the more she questioned what she knew. How much easier would it be if she just accepted to return inside her shell and burden herself only with herself. But something within was pressing her on to a different path. The world is so vast, that inner voice confided, it is yet too soon to crouch. Think through, and with, your fear. It will always be there. But that too is knowledge, and it is part of you. Rise, the voice insisted.

Zohra was rolling a cigarette between her gnarled fingers. She put it to her mouth and inhaled its green and brown fumes deep inside her lungs. She passed the cigarette to her ward and told her to breathe in and out slowly "You must relax, little one. Inhale, this too is part of our nostalgia," she whispered. "We must hit the road soon, for this city has touched you in no uncertain way."

Then from right below them they heard a soft music, an ululating 'oud and a low voice singing about betrayal and the forgetful heart. The acceptance in the voice and in the slow music echoed through their bodies and brought tears to Maryam's and Zohra's eyes. Maryam's thoughts reeled: between the vibrant rage and hopelessness of the city and the gentle letting go in this woman's voice, there is but a thin wall, and it may be we are sitting on it.

She noticed that she had been grinding her teeth. Then she realized that what she was grinding were not her teeth but seeds. She spit in her palm, and the scent of pure orange blossoms exploded into the air. The scent was everywhere, and it engulfed them in its fragrant ubiquity. The music stopped, the cries from the street stopped, and time itself asked for a pause. It was a breath of transient peace, time itself taking a break to honor the inexplicable.

Maryam and Zohra heard footsteps coming up the outdoor staircase leading to the rooftop. This staircase was used by women who came to the terraced rooftop to hang washed loads of clothing. It was also the staircase once used by women to chat with their neighbors and tie their own colorful threads into the fabric of the neighborhood's tapestry. For these women of old Fes, the rooftops were their only constant contact with the exterior.

Zohra rose: "We have imposed on their hospitality enough. It's time we leave."

They picked up their rides and flew into the air before the woman with the humbled voice and intrigued footsteps coming up the staircase could see them. It is highly possible that she saw a large woman on a broomstick and a frailer one on a rusty bicycle fly off the roof and into the sky between the northeastern and the northwestern forts of Fes Al-Bali. It is also likely that she rubbed her eyes in disbelief and then smiled her reenchantment. She was now a little stronger to face the vast troubles that life had thrown at her. She felt oddly privileged that two witches had chosen her rooftop, and she decided that it was time she use the shrewd brain God had given her to try to find a way out of her misery.

~

Maryam pedaled furiously, while her mind readjusted to the losses and gains of the past day. They rode for many hours, a day and a night. The sun shone on them, but the air was chilly. Ice was starting to form on Aoud Errih's handles and chain, while the broomstick shuddered miserably beside it. They had almost reached the snow-filled domains of the cedars. It was time for them to start their descent, for they were forbidden to enter these sacred lands from the sky. They looked for stable terrain to land, and soon they saw, stretched below them, a vast plain covered in snow and ice. The plain was a tundra of snow and rock in the Atlas mountains known to the nomads as Affenourir and considered sacred. At its center was a great frozen lake that, in the springtime, was home to migrating water birds. Underneath the ice and snow, the rare green moss pressed into the cold ground.

Zohra and Maryam walked to the edge of the plain where the cedars began to grow and built a fire with the wood that had been felled from the trees by hands or storms. They huddled against each other for warmth under the howling winds dancing on the white and brown expanse. They opened their cans of tuna and heated the bottom on the fire, before dipping their fingers and eating their fill of the oily red fish.

Zohra shuddered, for the cold was biting. It must be that I am getting old. After all these centuries, time is finally taking its due, she thought to herself. But deep within her labyrinthine wisdom, she knew that the grim winter was not responsible for her sudden chill. It was something else, a premonition of a slow, gathering trap. She touched the wooden box nestled against her heart, afraid she may have lost it along the way. She looked at Maryam gulping down her food with such pure appetite and remembered the many worlds that separated her from her ward. She handed her another canned tuna with twinkling eyes.

"Eat, child. You need to be strong."

"Aisha would never have allowed me to eat such a meal, crouched on the floor, a pungent burnous for a coat and a million stars for a roof."

"And that is why you are enjoying this moment so."

"It is...a kind of freedom. I feel the strings that bind beginning to disintegrate."

As Maryam shared her wonder with a woman fed on poverty and tin slums underneath a sky of shadowy hue, a young boy appeared before them. He was holding a rope by one end, and on the other end of the rope was a lamb. His eyes were large and inquisitive.

"Who are you? Are you lost?"

"No, I don't think so. We have stopped here in this beautiful land to rest and eat."

"Beautiful? I never thought of it that way. It has good fish, and the birds are quite tasty, if you are smart about catching them."

They looked at each other, unsure about what to do next.

"Would you like to come with me? Our tent is not far. It's over there, above these cedars, on the side of the mountain."

"Where the fire is burning?"

"Yes."

"What's your name?"

"My name is Mohand."

There was pride in his voice. He had a rare grace in someone so young. Maryam and Zohra decided to follow the little boy to his home. They followed him through a dirt road they had not noticed earlier and headed toward the camp. When they arrived, they saw that it was not a camp proper. The tent was made of plastic bags and sheepskin, and its poles of rotten wood. Torn blankets were wound around the sides to keep the cold air out, and the pegs were held in place by heavy rocks and rope. Near this tent was a wooden shed for the animals: four sheep, two goats, and one old mule. This was the extent of the family compound. The family belonged to one of the transhumant tribes of the Zayan, the most powerful tribal confederacy of the Atlas Mountains, if not of the entire land.

In front of the fire was a man, a woman, and a girl about Maryam's age. The father turned his face toward his son. He had sunken eyes and high cheekbones. His emaciated features could not quench the gentleness in his eyes as he looked at his son.

"What have you brought home this time, Mohand?"

"Two lost travelers I found near the lake. Could they stay with us for the night?"

"What road has God chosen for you?"

"We must go to the land of cedars."

"It is a dangerous, forbidden land. You could get lost there for all eternity."

"Yes. We do not intend to remain lost."

"You can stay with us for the night. But tomorrow morning, we will break camp, and you will go where you are waited for."

The mother and sister remained quiet, their eyes lowered. The man, Ismail, then told his wife, "Go fetch a sheep for our guests."

The woman, whose name was Taylit, or princess in the language of the Amazighs, rose to her feet and fetched one of the sheep they kept in the shed. She was thin and her back was stooped, but her face was still young and soft. Zohra protested.

"No, my noble friend. There is no need for you to kill a sheep on our behalf. We have eaten our fill below in the valley. Keep the meat for your children. The winter is harsh, and the road ahead of you is long."

"It is our way. Let it not be said that Ismail of the Zayans did not honor his guests because an old woman took pity on him."

Maryam looked at the thin woman and the sheep already in the father's arms and took out the cheese, bread, and canned tuna from the bag on her bicycle. She spread it on the ground in front of the man.

"I believe that I too am from this land. There's no need for you to treat us like strangers in an inhospitable land. This is my home, too. Before Casablanca, before Fes, before Granada, this was my home. I ask that you share with us our food. It is simple, but it would be a true welcome. As for Zohra, her people have roamed the Atlas Mountains to their southern reaches. Her home touches upon the same mountain range you herd your flock. Do not sacrifice your sheep, Ismail of the Zayans. Do not sacrifice any sheep on our behalf. But instead, share our food."

And so it was that Ismail did not sacrifice a sheep for Maryam and Zohra, but instead, and to his family's great relief, they shared in their guests' fare. The food placed in front of the family and the two women was inexhaustible, and the stale cheese, bread, and canned tuna became tasty beef and delicious vegetables cooked in olive oil, large-grained couscous with spicy red sauce, lemony green olives, farm-made yoghurt, and honey-almond treats. The murky water in the gourds was now pure and crystalline. They ate their fill, and only when they finally stopped did the food disappear. All laid back in contentment except Maryam, who thought of the sheep that could have been sacrificed for her. The taste of meat was still in her mouth, strong and pungent. She felt the bitterness of the life spent course through her veins, and it piled on the many lives spent before it and the lives yet to be taken. People are hungry, they always hunger for more. The meat now sitting comfortably in her stomach told her of her people's predatory nature and of the pleasure killing and consuming the kill procures. The stars shone in the jet-black sky, and their silvery whiteness echoed the coolness of the earth.

The little boy, Mohand, was stroking his lamb, now fast asleep in his lap. His older sister was sitting beneath a tree, honing a piece of wood into a sharp weapon. Mohand stroked his belly and sighed.

"Are you a magician? My great-grandfather told me of a magician who could do what you just did with the food."

"I didn't do anything, Mohand. Sometimes, we are merely vessels. Tell me about this man."

"He was a magician, and his miracles were known throughout the world. He could transform water into lamahia and stones into bread. He could heal the sick and even walk on water."

"What happened to him?"

"No one really knows. One day, he just left and went east. That's when our troubles began. Maybe he was angry at us. But they say he could make dreams come true."

"What would you have asked him?"

"I would have asked to ride a plane and drive a car! I would have asked to see the ocean once in my life and perhaps one of those big cities travelers tell us about."

Mohand paused. Then, with a subdued voice, he continued.

"Sometimes, we get so hungry that we boil leather, and that's what we eat. No, I think what I would really ask for is to feed our old horse till it is full and sleepy. Protect my lamb from ever being taken away from me. Take care of my mother and father."

His sister rose to her feet. Khadija was formidable—tall and lean, and with iron in her eyes. She walked to where Mohand and Maryam were conversing.

"Magic is evil. It brings power to those who have it and fear to those who don't. Look around you. This land is dying from the magic of the powerful. We are the ones ordered to bend to those with power, and yet our name is as great as theirs! What poems do not mention the tribe of the Zayans?"

"You have the name of kings and high lords."

"Yes. But, in truth, our own tribe has forgotten about us. We walk through their territory, and they close their doors on our needs."

Maryam took all of Khadija into her wide-eyed gaze.

"And you, Khadija? What is it you would ask a man with the power to do good?"

"What I would ask for? To be a man."

Her brother started teasing her, "You are a man, Khadija. Braver than most men I know. Soldiers and lions run from you." But then he saw the expression in her eyes and he stopped. Khadija returned Maryam's gaze with diamond-clear eyes. She touched the secret spot between her legs. "No, not so," she said. "I want to be a man here. Here where it matters the most to *them*. But it's not just about them, it's also about *me*. I *want* to be a man." Maryam pointed to her own unhealthy legs across the chasm of their difference. "You and me, we're the same, trapped in bodies that escape us, pain us, and embarrass us."

Maryam fell silent, contemplating the mysteries of a universe that allowed these rare incursions into another's soul and the even rarer moments where you discover that the reverberating echo is in fact the other's nakedness revealing itself to you. Simply put, for the first time in her life, Maryam felt close to someone her own age, a girl too, imagine that—well, a girl not like any other girl she had ever known. But she wasn't like other girls her age either. Being near Khadija was natural and easy. She had read about, but never experienced, the sudden pleasure of immediate connection. A rich, dark emotion embedded itself in her heart, and she felt weak and strong all at once.

Experiencing such things was as foreign to Maryam as the image of a father's glasses resting on a newspaper on the coffee table. She had once been at a friend's house and seen the father put down his newspaper, take the glasses off, and place them neatly on the folded paper. She remembered quietly standing there until her friend pushed her into the kitchen for a quick snack. She had forgotten all about that moment until now when she laid eyes on Khadija and was consumed by longing. In the other girl's dark eyes and strong arms, she sensed the possibility of a life beyond the dictates of history, family, and duty. With her, she could have a real chance at happiness. How she wished to remain here for just a while and forget about the world, its quests and failures.

Khadija was also looking at Maryam, and she was holding her breath. Her entire posture was a hesitation between the now and the what if, between the real and the dream. There was hope in her held breath and beautiful mouth. The entire world danced in her eyes. She began to believe that change and wonderful things do not only happen to others but could happen to someone like her. Then she felt an inexplicable cold enter her heart, and she thought how crazy she was to feel such things. She looked at Maryam and saw in her the stranger she in fact was, and the connection between them snapped and broke. She turned her back on Maryam and closed her eyes.

Maryam fell into a profound melancholia. She was confused by the sudden change in Khadija and blamed herself for it. For a minute, she had forgotten, or chosen to forget as people often do, the curse of solitude that had plagued her since her naming.

"Tomorrow come dawn," Zohra's voice cut through the pain. "We will be on our way to the forest of cedars. Breaking bread with you was our honor." She turned to look at Maryam, who nodded. Zohra gave the husband and wife some cheese, bread, and canned tuna, and continued. "Allow us to leave these gifts with you. Whenever you or your children go hungry, place this food in front of you at the campfire, and it will fill your belly. It will remain abundant for as long as Maryam walks this earth." Then her voice fell to a whisper. "When the food runs dry, then you will know." Maryam heard Zohra's strange predictions through the haze of late-night musings and dusk-filled imaginings. Her eyes were already closing, but she sensed the truth in Zohra's words. She could not remain with the nomads. Her own trail led her elsewhere.

Taylit, the mistress of the camp, spoke for the first time in the evening. Her voice was clapped and chipped, as though seldom used.

"You've been kind to us. I've heard of people like you, people who inhabit the grey zones between this world and the next, the past and the present. We know of magic here. But it is a fearsome, primitive magic that obeys no laws and yearns for chaos. Why did you come here?"

"We are on a quest. We are following a dream-message that urged us to the land of the cedars."

"No human is safe there. Only the tattooed butterfly people of the forest or the lost traveler with a mind teetering at the edge of sanity will ever be found roaming the wild woods at night. Even the most powerful spirits hesitate to enter the forest."

"Yes. That is known."

"You must find the tattooed butterfly people. They are barely human, and they survive on an uneasy truce with the cedars. They may choose to help you. What is this thing you are looking for?"

"It is not a thing."

"Then you truly are on a dangerous quest. If the butterfly folk agree to help you, they may ask for something in return, and you must be prepared to give it to them."

"Thank you, sister, for your guidance."

An ache crawled up Maryam's legs. She knew that a vision was on its way, and she allowed the familiar pain inside her. She saw that the cedars were waiting for her coming. She saw that they were restless and awake. But she also saw something the tribeswoman of the Zayans did not tell them. She saw a sky filled with voices and writing. Stars were words and the night sky the screen on which they were scrolled. It was the universe's own manuscript of legends and myths about the dawn of a new world. It was spread out in absolute vulnerability for all to read, but who cared to read anymore? Who lives by the book anymore? Fragmented, shattered, following inklings every which way, the manuscript has burnt itself out for most readers. But not so for Maryam. She had spent her life looking for that fabulous story that would tell her of her beginning, guide her through its unforeseeable plots before leaving her breathless, exhaling that one final sigh.

She saw the story unfolding, rolling toward the land of the cedars, and she burnt to reach it. She pushed deep within her the softness she had seen in Khadija's eyes, because she knew that love was not for her. There, beyond the ridge, scribbled on the cedars' ancient bark, was a narration waiting for her arrival, thrilled by the possibilities that would emerge with her coming.

For the land of the cedars was a land of primal terror but also of ancient resistance. Its chaos was one filled with ever-renewed life. A forest of calm and beauty during the day, the cedars become terrible things when night fell, beating to a rhythm unbearable to humans but heavy with the call of a new world. And they were waiting for her. Yes, she would find the answers she came looking for. The pain subsided and Maryam slipped into sleep.

~

Zohra and Maryam woke up with the dawn. They washed their faces with good snow melted on embers and left the nomads' camp behind. Zohra gripped her broom like a cane, the full weight of her two hundred eighty years heavy on her shoulders as she walked. Maryam strolled along, whistling at Aoud Errih to fall in step at her side. They trekked for kilometers through muddy and often steep paths into the wilderness. Silence reigned all around, and the air turned to a steely grey. Signs of life decreased as they came closer to the land of the cedars. Only the rare falcon circled the sky, hovering with beak lowered toward the ground and watching its prey. The silence became heavier, a black hole quenching all sound from the atmosphere. Before them stretched the immensity of the plain, and the darkness beyond could only be the forest of cedars. The silence weighed on their shoulders, and they felt as though they were the only human beings left in the world.

Soon, the forest of cedars stretched before them. Dark and brown or silvery and gold, their branches like sinewy arms holding green velvet, the millennial trees rose as high as eyes could see. Maryam and Zohra paused in front of this brute force of the earth that spent its days immersed in its own existence, oblivious to theirs. They rode toward it, their hearts trapped in an eerie sadness. They reached the forest's edge and inhaled its musk.

They expected the air to turn into lead and the silence into void, but, to their surprise, the deafening silence was withering away fast. The soundlessness of the plain had lifted to give way to the light breezes stirring in the trees. The air rang with a buzzing that had no origin and no end. The winds clung to the canopy. The air, the sounds, the wetness, and the warmth all came from within the trees. The buzzing and the humming began to sound like whispers in beautiful, old languages that neither Zohra nor Maryam could understand but that made them silent and want to listen forever. They filled the air like silvery fumes, wispy lianas, or thickset clouds. They were the words of the tree spirits, weaving their stories, their myths, their wrath, their ancient justice. The travelers had entered a world intent on its own creation, one that hummed, buzzed, and whispered like no other place they had seen. It was a world that sang of dissonance and apartness.

Maryam and Zohra placed their rides against a great cedar and watched as its branches slid around Aoud Errih and the broomstick to hold them firmly against its bark. They entered and felt the stony earth turn soft and easy under their feet. They had come upon a world for which they were not prepared. They had expected to find fear and emptiness but instead discovered a place of disconnect. It lay in the midst of a wasteland but denied the drought and famine all around. It exuded an earthen, drunken scent that shattered all certainty. It was triumphant, out of time, on edge, and uncontrollable: pure, wild magic. They walked deeper and deeper into the forest. The trees loomed thicker and higher with each step they took. The fullness of the whispers shattered any possibility of silence.

"What answers can be gleaned here, Umi? How could I decipher the endless messages that fill the air?"

"It's a strange place that's not meant for humans. It has chosen to lie outside our domains, and we have come to disturb its peace."

"Is there reason to fear?"

"There is reason to fear annihilation."

"Annihilation is not destruction, Umi. That much I can sense."

"It is destruction of everything we believe ourselves to be. Of the lines between you, me, the demons, and the spirits. We are in a place that is playing with us. We are close to nothing here."

They walked deeper into the woods surrounded by the incessant noises of the trees. After what could have been an eternity, or a mere intake of breath, they found themselves in a sun-filled clearing. Their skins became luminous, bathed in light. Their steps were lighter as though a weight had been lifted. There was something ephemeral and unreal about the golden clearing they had stumbled upon. The tree words lingered high in the air above it. Maryam and Zohra were now at the center of the clearing. They looked about and saw ravens all around them, their beaks open and their wings deployed as though ready for the next message to be delivered to the waiting dream.

Thought

Maryam watched the ravens at the edge of the clearing and listened to the tree words high above her head. She was more focused than she had ever been in her life. Her senses were heightened and her eyes sharp. Her legs began to ache, and a prickling raised the soft hairs on her arms. "Something strange is coming our way, Umi," she said to the ancient woman beside her. Soon, the lightness became even lighter, and the hovering words turned into a fluttering of wings. The light turned white. Suddenly they found that they were surrounded by wispy creatures with large wings covered in geometric tattoos and with bodies rounded like the Venus of Willendorf. They released pollen, sand, and butterfly dust everywhere. Maryam breathed in a multitude of particles and could no longer see or sense Zohra at her side.

She raised her voice, "Who are you?"

The creatures shuddered. Despite their mass and large wings, they were touchy, fragile types.

"We are the Idaid. We are the children of this forest wild."

"You are the butterfly tribe of our legends."

"We are called that, yes. We also have many other names, some names mortals have dared utter and died, *hiiihiii-eee*... Why have you come here?"

"I came following the raven's dream-message. I was told you could help me."

"You are disturbing our peace in your quest of mind. You have tipped the fragile order of our things, you'll find. Perchance you have brought chaos and consequence in your stride. Why should we help you, child?"

They spoke in singsong voices, their unity of sound never complete, yet never broken, either. Maryam was hit by the foreignness of their speech. There was a hollowness to their voices that terrified her. She vaguely sensed Zohra's presence around her somehow, on a different plane as it were. So Maryam stood there in the clearing, on the other side of the world, surrounded by creatures whose dangerous nature she instinctively sensed. Creatures who did not care to distinguish between the old and the new, the real and the unreal; creatures who could suck her into their world to annihilate her and her fragile sense of existence.

She was close to dread, sweat trickling down her back. She understood that they would not help her, that they hungered for her. She saw herself in the very back of their opaque eyes, a prisoner of their ravaging wilderness. She was about to walk toward them and submit to the call of the wild when she saw the butterfly folk take an uneasy step back. They were looking at her uneven legs. They peered into her huge black eyes with the blue pupils and their wings began to flutter uncontrollably as they sniffed her from afar.

"You are not a mortal like other mortals we have seen. You too have many names, do you not? Daughter of Adam and Lilith. They could have been one of us, but they chose to leave us behind. What a risk for you to come to the land of day and night. Not fully human yourself, it appears. You are the One, perhaps. You have come here to find on that rickety ride, beneath your manners so mild, answers to questions, answers that can no longer hide, *hiiihiii-eee…*"

The excitement in their voice was mounting, reaching its breaking point, flirting with the high notes, wispy, lispy until it finally snapped. It was a screech rather than a word, sounding like a freed bird gone mad. Then, in the midst of that high-strung folly of vocals, they heard a sound that resonated like the ocean tide breaking on the rocks before the first sign of life transformed the planet's destiny forever. The sound seemed to come from the earth itself, below ground. Maryam closed her eyes and could feel the sound flowing from the earth to the roots, sap, trunk, branches, and leaves of the cedars. The spirits of the cedars had awakened, and they rumbled liked thunder and lightning.

Maryam heard it all, acutely and perfectly. She knew of the uneasy truce between the butterfly folk and the cedars. She felt the primal force of the trees overpowering the unearthly beings fluttering around her. The cedars were interceding in her favor, reminding the butterfly folk of their truce and its fragile base. The butterfly folk obeyed the cedars, reluctantly, with trembling bodies and twitching antennas.

"Fine," they screeched. "We will help the magical mortal, *hiiihiii-eee…* We tremble at the edge of the world and *hurray* for its end. We are immortal and will only perish, with joy, when the end of the world arrives. We are creatures feared by all—but not by you. Our power you deny. Our existence you allow. To you with your deep, deep roots, we are poor, wretched exiles, exiles disgusting and vile! Are we not so in your eyes? Poor, poor tribe without homeland, begging for you to be kind, to kindly let us here reside. Cedars of might and fright, even you shall one day die in the great bonfire of the end of time, *hiiihiii-eee…*"

Maryam's head hurt from the foreign voice and sounds ranging all around. The rumbling thunder and lightning rose to become a full-fledged tempest. The cedars were awake and angry. The butterfly people quieted down suddenly. Playtime was over.

"Okay, the bile has for now expired. Clap-clap, blocked by your perfect sappy-sap. But we are victims, the consequence of this bitching truce that makes us so wild. So enough, fine. But she must give us something first, this maiden fine—*we want the box*."

The tempest stopped.

"I don't know what you mean by a box. I don't have any box."

"What? Lies! Or…your companion perhaps may hide?"

Maryam fell silent.

For some reason she herself did not know, she was afraid of what was about to happen. A veil lifted and she saw Zohra now, clearly. She was standing at her side, slightly dazed from an ordeal only she knew of.

"The box, dear lady. We want the box! If you want the answers you came looking for, give us the box in your robes you hide…"

Zohra looked at the creatures surrounding her, and she too was afraid. She whispered under her breath: "What should I do, Old Mother? The heritage of Solomon and Sheeba, the heart of the secret…How can I give it up?" A voice only she could hear answered: "It's alright, my daughter. They will respect a pact. Give them the box, for the story must write itself, and Maryam must find her way. It is our only hope."

Her eyes full, reeling from the pain of separation, Zohra lifted her voice.

"I know who you are. I know of your treacherous natures. Your designs are not our designs. But the choice is mine, and I choose to give you the box. But you must promise my companion and me safe passage through the territory you inhabit."

"In our territory, you have nothing to fear from our kind. Now give us the box."

Zohra produced the box from under her robes. It was a simple box made of cedarwood, with engravings on the side. It fit well in her hands. It was as if the box had been made to fit in her hands and her hands had been made to hold it. Maryam watched as the old woman presented her box to the wild tribe hovering above ground expectantly.

"Don't, Umi. Keep your box. We'll find other ways."

"No, it is as it must be. It's being written as we speak. The box is not as weak as they think. It can defend itself. It has survived centuries, has it not?

"To the Idaid: Here is what you have asked for."

High-pitched yelps filled the air, and the small brown box shifted hands. Zohra's hands dropped to her side, and she looked old and frail. Maryam could sense the other woman's power leaving her body, bleeding from her pores, leaking onto the ground. She felt her suffering and loss, and she never admired or loved her as much as she did at that moment. Then as they looked, the box seemed to shift shapes. From a perfect square, it became a hazy oval. Zohra whispered, "Nothing is lost. Everything is transformed."

The Idaid turned the box this way and that, passing their antennas over the ancient script. Satisfied, they asked Maryam once more what she was seeking. "The second gift," was her answer.

"We are the butterfly tribe, the Idaid. Barely human, we are what lies beneath and what lies beyond, what came before and what came after. Do you acknowledge our might?"

"Yes."

"And are you willing to abide by the ties that bind? The gift is precious, quasi-divine."

"Yes. So be it. What is it?"

"Open your mind and the gift you will find."

A rush of images filled her mind. She saw Adam and Lilith as they once were in the clearing with the two lakes and the two trees. She saw how the thick cedar forest grew to protect this world from the unknowns that lie beyond, but how the temptation to see, learn, and grasp were stronger than any dream of happiness and unity. She then saw hatred, violence, their residues, the silver stardust that became the high-strung, curvy butterfly folk, and the endless cedar forest that became the forest of today.

Finally, she saw refusal. She saw Lilith rebel against an order invoked by a God of power and domination. She saw Lilith open her wings and disappear into the night, never to be seen or heard from again. She saw that Lilith and Leila Tair were one and that Adam and Adam Tair were also one. She saw her past—a possible past, a dream of a past—and she understood.

"You come from a place where fabrications abound—lies, lies, everywhere there are lies."

"Yes. It is a kingdom of lies."

"Why?"

"Why…Aren't all lands forged on lies?"

"Dig deeper, child. Why are there lies?"

"To hide the truth."

"What truth is being hidden from sight?"

And suddenly she knew. She had known all along. It was the forgotten memory of truth returning.

"The violence beneath…What the lies and fabrications are hiding is the violence beneath."

"Yes, that's right. Lies and violence, violence and lies. That's all there is. But you are a being of power. What do you wish for most in life?"

"To be anonymous."

"You retrieved a first gift. What might that be?"

"Perception."

Maryam thought of her childhood…of the violence. The violence that lay beneath every event in her life since her birth, and even before her birth, since her conception. She thought of the demons that terrified her city and the lords that controlled their domains, be they big or small. Her house and her family were a part of this. Their decrepitude stood in the way of fresh beginnings, but that was how things had to be. Their descent into poverty was a slow and painful one. Her family grabbed onto anything they could along the way to stop the inevitable fall. The carcass remained, of course, and the garden. The garden whose beauty and strength were a provocation to the decaying house it belonged to. There was witchcraft, that too she knew, superstitions, curses, spells. Ghosts, spirits, demons, and creatures from other shores and other worlds had been let in and now walked alongside human beings. They were tourists come to stay, careless with the riches they found and at times even claiming them as their own. Doors that should have remained shut had been opened: opened, she now could see, by all the fabrications, from the most mundane to the most damaging. These doors allowed in evil, but they also allowed in magic—as power, as a first step to resistance. She thought of the prickling of her skin when she had a vision, her many powers, her difference, and the first gift she retrieved from the asylum of Birsoukout: the gift of perception.

The butterfly folk fluttered impatiently around her. They were not a serene or patient people. Any little inconvenience could set them off, and they would transform into beings of pure terror. Maryam bowed to them expectantly. Their unitary voice flirted with a shriek.

"You have been made to give up much already in your brief life. What did you give up for the gift of perception?"

"I gave up belonging. I gave up feeling like other people, and I gave up being understood by others. I gave up being normal."

"Good, child. Your answer is fine. For this next gift, a much more powerful gift, prepare for an even greater sacrifice."

Maryam nodded pensively and stood still for a moment. She was thinking of the emptiness behind the Idaid's artificial unity. She thought as well of the classroom, the family, the urban hierarchy, of Birsoukout. Of excess—of humiliation, fear, waste. She thought of all the forces in the land and how they trickled in one direction and one direction only...

"What have you discovered here?"

"The violence has a reason: to destroy resistance, originality, thought. But there are other ways to keep the light low."

"Yes, oh my, you have decided to use that mind."

But Maryam did not hear their words. She was looking at the geometric shapes on the Idaid wings. They rearranged themselves to form letters and lines. Previously inanimate, they were moving about, full of life and purpose. She observed the shifting shapes until they finally stopped. Words had appeared. The strange thing was that the words appeared as Maryam was imagining them.

She thought and read the words:

"I came looking for a gift. I see now that I came to look for reason and I lost something. The world is born from chaos. We are as free as the threads that bind will allow us to be. I was called to the wild cedars and found multiplicity instead of unity. There is no God, no unity. God is not. A Sufi saint once said that if you look for God and your logic drives you to the conclusion that God does not exist, God will forgive you. I am now beyond the struggle curled in that prism. I see, I feel, I know."

"Yes," was their answer.

Then she finally let the words out.

"I lost God."

"Yes! It is the end, annihilation. There is nothing beyond the divine. It is time. Your gift is yours to take. It has always been there. It is the gift of thought. You are thought. But with thought, new sacrifices will be made. You will be lonely, on the outside. On the border of things, the margins, the grey, *hiiihiii-eee*. You'll be like the Idaid…but our opposite!"

"I will give up peace."

"It is only the beginning. But you still have a choice, if you so desire. You may choose to stop now, all questioning, all thought gone from your mind. You may choose to turn your back on the path written for you by a storyteller unleashed and wild. That is the tricky part with the gift of thought, you will find. The master storyteller is setting you free, but this you don't see and prefer to deny. You can decide to stop at this annihilation, and then it will all be over and here you can hide. You will be free, child, *hiiihiii-eee*. You would make us so proud. You could be one of ours, an Idaid. Be one of the Idaid."

Maryam was thinking feverishly. An absolute freedom, an annihilation of responsibility, and a severance of the ties that bind—isn't that anonymity, isn't that what she had always desired? The geometric shapes on the Idaid wings had shifted to form words. They were a code. She had decoded them. She could stop at the satisfaction of knowledge and the excitement of understanding, or she could digress. So she digressed, a pianist discovering the octaves on her new, beautiful piano. So, no God, no unity, the acceptance that the world is more and more complex. And that is good, Maryam's heart beat faster. Multiplicity, plurality are good. It is the inscription of a new resistance.

She turned to the Idaid: "No, that's not all there is. There is refusal, resistance, the inhaled *no* and the exhaled *yes* of change.

It's time for us to leave. You have your box and I have the gift of thought. We can go now."

Zohra and Maryam bowed to the Idaid who were old-fashioned folk. But the Idaid spread their wings to form one solid wall of tattooed geometry.

"Perhaps we don't want you to leave child. Perhaps we will hold you a time."

"You made a promise. A gift for a gift. The cedars are watching. Look, they're getting angry."

"*Hiiihiii-eee*...The weak are not always as weak as the strong think. We have a truce, yes. The cedars tolerate us, fine. But it is not in their interest to destroy our kind. They need us to keep trespassers at bay, lest they crave their might. We are the image of fear keeping the outside world away, one soul at a time."

The Idaid came closer, their wings steely and mechanic now. The shapes rearranged themselves into prison bars.

"She is like her mother, isn't she? Ooh she does not yet know the path she chose and the end that for her ahead lies. We wish to embrace you, to kiss you, to keep you for a while, *hiiihiii-eee*...Stay. Join our tribe."

The cedars shook in fury and lowered their branches to the ground. They hit the butterfly tribe and pushed them to the ground, making them cower and groan in protest. The branches carried Maryam and Zohra up through the canopy of trees. The two travelers inhaled the musky scent of cedars and the cleanest of airs. They lingered there for a second or two. Then the trees lowered them gently to the ground near the edge of the forest and returned to their places once more.

"Run, Umi, run," Maryam urged. "We are almost out of the forest. One more step..." But as she was speaking, the sound of high-pitched voices and beating wings filled the air. The two companions looked up only to find that the Idaid had come for them. Their antennas had turned into thin, sharp rapiers, and their wings were raised high behind their curvy bodies. In the half-second it takes to breathe, they plunged and buried their blades in Zohra. When her body fell to the ground, halfway in the forest and halfway out, they dragged her fully in. Maryam could hear the excited beating of their hearts through their soft bodies. That must be their hearts she heard, for hers had surely stopped.

"You made a promise to us."

"*Hiihiii-eee...*We promised you safe passage through *our* territory. She had one foot out. She was no longer passing through the land of our tribe. She was between this world and the outside. She was ours."

"The cedars..."

"The weak have weapons the strong can't even fathom. There is nothing the cedars can do. For the terms of our deal we have abided by."

"But why?"

"Why not? Our pleasure is to cause chaos. Our events have unforeseen consequences, that is the purpose of the butterfly tribe."

"Why her, not me?"

"She was weak. She gave up her most precious belonging, the little box, diamond product of history and time."

Maryam felt rage and anger rush through her. She wanted to use her powers to destroy them all. Powers she had always kept in check, powers she didn't know she had. The Idaid witnessed her grow as tall as the cedars. She was the manifestation of Al-Kahina herself, the great Berber warrior Goddess. She was about to unleash it all, furiously, uncontrollably, unapologetically, on the treacherous creatures when a hand touched her jeans below the burnous. "Stop, Maryam. It's not worth it. It's in their nature. Let them go."

The Idaid fled from the scene into the mysterious depths of their borrowed homeland.

Maryam knelt near the dying Zohra. She took Zohra's head in her hands, looked at the flowing blood, and wept.

"Umi. My only mother, you made me stop. I would have killed them all for you."

"I did it for you. You must fight the evil in you. The demons are not only outside, they are inside us. And you are too precious to surrender to them."

"What will I do now?"

"You must continue. You must return home and build a life for yourself."

"It's over then?"

"No, it's only beginning. You don't have all your powers yet."

"Umi..."

"Don't cry for me baby. My will to live deserted me when I gave up my box. I could feel myself dying when I turned over the treasure of my ancestors, of our common story."

"Then...why?"

"For you. That's love sometimes. Goodbye my Maryam."

Zohra could barely speak now. "Goodbye, Umi."

Zohra exhaled her last breath, and Maryam put her head down on the moist dark earth. "Umi, you left me alone in the woods. I am alone with my fear and my dread."

She found a branch and began to dig a hole under one of the cedars. She found that the earth was soft and eagerly gave way to her inexperienced hands. She could hear a low rumble that sounded like chanting trees. Once more, the branches came down for them. They carried the old woman from the Central Quarries, the woman whose roots plunged as far back as Solomon's Song, who lived in a slum of a sprawling city but left it because she believed a young woman's courage was the key to a new world. They carried her to her grave below their trunks and claimed her as one of their own. Maryam watched the ceremony between the earth, the trees, and death, and was filled with awe.

~

It was time for her to go. She found her bicycle where she had left it, but the broomstick was gone. She rode off with more knowledge and thoughtfulness than she could have bargained for.

As she was riding off, thunder and lightning hit the ground. The forest was illuminated by the sudden light that came from the sky. For most people, this looked like a natural phenomenon. But in fact it was the rage of the storyteller falling on the Idaid. Sheherazade fell from the sky. She rode the lightning and thunder all the way down. Later she confessed that she could have come down in a less extravagant way, but she was terribly angry and wanted the advantage of dramatic effect. She stood in front of the fluttering Idaid. Her hair was roaring fire, her eyes shot lightning bolts, and her body was made of cloud and rain. She was fuming.

"You've made a terrible mistake, Idaid. By killing Zohra, you've attacked me!"

"The storyteller remains on the outside. Be gone, by your own rules abide."

"You have unleashed me, you fools. By taking the box and killing Zohra, you have triggered unforeseen consequences. You've compromised the balance of things."

"You're on cedar territory. Even your power must here subside."

"Ha! The cedars are angry at the betrayal that occurred on their watch. Maryam couldn't touch you. She had to remain good. But…I can exact my revenge. I can reverse the pact."

"You speak in riddles, storyteller. Behind your words you hide."

"Then listen, listen well: It won't end this way. The box of Solomon and Sheeba returns to me."

"*No*...you have no right! The box belongs to the Idaid. It always has."

"Try and stop me."

With a casual flick of her hand, she took back the cedarwood box, its mysteries intact. A carriage made of a single seashell driven by sea horses appeared in front of her. She stepped in, her skin now pearly white, her hair long and red-gold, and with a battle cry rode her carriage into the sky.

~

It was later said that the broomstick was found in a garbage dump in the ancient stronghold town of Azrou, some kilometers south of the forest. No one knew how it got there. It was said that a woman with spiky pink hair and pointy boots came for it and took it away with her, never to be seen or heard from again. It was also observed that the ground shook one night and that a new cedar appeared, as wise and mighty as its sisters and brothers.

Mourning

"You left in the middle of the story. Where were you, Old Mother?"

"Righting a wrong, my darling."

"That doesn't sound like you. The storyteller usually remains neutral."

The young girl then smiles at Sheherazade. Nothing, she knows, sounds like Sheherazade.

"These are terrible times, my child. Sometimes, I'm not given the choice. I have to take sides. The unbalance is too great."

"Is there anything else?"

"Maybe."

"Love, perhaps?"

"Yes, love for these poor mortals and their doomed endings. Look below and tell me what you see."

"I see women rising in the land, gaining confidence in their battles."

"Yes. Maryam has retrieved her second gift, and its ripples have spread. She is bringing insurrection with her. The Idaid have helped tip the balance. But they will not gain what they had hoped for. What else do you see my beloved?"

"I see cities burning, bombings, drought, floods, mass migrations. Demons and violence, greed everywhere."

"There are no answers to their questions, and still they go on *trying. How can I not love them?"*

The two women fall silent. The young girl watches as Sheherazade takes a fistful of hashish and presses it into her pipe. Trembling, she lights it. The pipe flares and the flare spreads to the hashish. Sheherazade puffs and puffs and, as she is enjoying her moment, she feels the pipe tugging at her arm, pushing to be passed on to her disciple. Sheherazade resists, and the pipe bites her lip. "Alright, fine," she grumbles. Under the young girl's confused gaze, she says, "At this point, any initiation will do. Smoke up." Sheherazade and her companion sit there puffing on the pipe, listening to the crisp noise produced by the consumed hashish. The young girl's mind wanders to Maryam.

"What will Maryam do now that Zohra is gone?"

"Time in the Forest of Cedars is not human time. When she returned to the world, she found that five years had passed since she had left. She returned in January 2004— the date the kingdom's lawyers and religious men worked on the new family law, the law you saw women fighting for. But the new law is an illusion. It is change…"

"…on the surface only."

"Yes, change in this land is always on the surface. It's sleight of hand. Don't forget that ours is the abode of some of the greatest wizards, witches, and magicians in the world. Much is conceded, but never the essential."

"You mean, real equality…"

"In status, heritage, marriage, the law, the unconscious, and between all citizens, be they man or woman…or whatever one chooses to be."

Sheherazade falls quiet. Zohra's death has her reeling, her whole body aching with loss.

An insistent voice shakes her from her reverie.

"I'm curious, Old Mother. Maryam sacrificed belonging in the world in exchange for her first gift. What will she lose with this second gift?"

"Joy. She'll never know the true meaning of joy. But watch…and see what she does."

Departure

When Maryam returned, she went to her old house to find that her grandparents had aged considerably and barely recognized her. It was now January 2004. Ibraham's blue eyes had become a clouded grey, and he could often be heard having conversations with an invisible interlocutor he called "Boabdil." As for Aisha, she dressed in her old finery and tired satin kaftans, and crept around the house sobbing for her daughter. She had finally become a ghost in her own home. The Nassiris had turned their house into a crypt and shut out the world. In return, the world tagged them as degenerates and avoided them like the plague. When children passed by the house, they would throw stones at the still impregnable gates and run off.

As for Mehdi, Maryam's uncle, he too was there. He was still the thin, tired man he had become after Birsoukout, but he had gotten slightly better. The reason for his lifted state of mind was Maryam. He was waiting for her to come back.

Mehdi was inside the house when she got there. He smelled the scent of orange blossoms, heard a familiar, awkward step, and knew that she had finally returned. Maryam was stronger than he had ever known her to be, but a light was gone from her eyes. And Zohra was not with her, that much he noticed.

He was writing lines, poetry, a novel, memoirs perhaps, when she walked in. He put down his blue Bic pen.

"Welcome back."

"Thank you, uncle. A strange welcome though, I must say."

"Everyone thought you were gone forever. But I knew you would be back. I knew you would outwit that hag Yasmine and her birds of ill-omen."

"What happened here, uncle?"

"…Time, poverty, old age. This is the house of people who quit years ago. You've been gone a long time."

"I was gone for only a couple of months."

"You were gone for five years."

"I don't understand."

"You roamed the world, went to the land of cedars."

"Yes, only two months ago. And I came back."

"You came back. But time spent with the cedars is not the same as time spent with human beings. It may be that the five years *seemed* only months to you."

He urged her to find a place and make a life of her own. The house had been sold to a flushed real estate tycoon who bought it for his eldest son, still a student in the United States. The Nassiris and the tycoon had agreed to wait until the death of the old couple before the boy moved into the house. However, the new buyers couldn't contain their enthusiasm and had been coming by regularly to gauge the house and make plans for its remodeling into a neoclassic villa. Surprisingly, they liked the garden and were thinking of keeping it unscathed, except for the great orange tree whose roots sprawled above ground and which they found hideous and overbearing, and wanted to cut down. But before they had a chance to do so, a giant man with rough hands and Odin-like step came by one early morning and scooped up the tree in his arms like a sapling, loaded it onto a running truck that was waiting for him outside, and drove off, never to be seen again. Mehdi interrupted his chronology of events to dig around in his pockets.

"The giant gave me this for you. He knew you would come back. He also knew when. He said it would be when the new law regulating men, women, and families was passed. He said the law was a grand deception, but he was happy because it would bring you back to our city. Just as certain as the bell tolls in the Vatican and the muezzin calls out from his loudspeaker in the mosque, she will return when the law passes," he said.

Mehdi gave Maryam a leather pouch whose softness marked the work of the artisans of Fes. She unrolled it and found a sapling. "It comes from the orange tree. It's yours to keep and grow. He said to plant it in your new home. The tree will grow firm roots and look after you."

She rubbed the young leaves between gentle fingers and buried her nose in her hands. She remained in this humble pose for a long time, her eyes closed, struggling against tears that threatened disclosure. All I ever wanted was to be anonymous. The anonymous is forever yearning for a platonic ideal that she can never reach. The anonymous stays outside the fold looking in. It is the only perspective I ever found bearable.

Her empathy was pure, she could see into the heart of suffering. But this very empathy paralyzed her, while any action seemed futile to her. She was detached to such a degree from the rest of the world that she began to doubt the reality that surrounded her and her own existence. Her only hooks to reality were her empathy and her own growing powers. Zohra had guided her through her loneliness onto the path of magic and the surreal. But now she was on her own. She had chosen to take her second gift and the sacrifices that came with it. She felt dizzy suddenly. The world swirled around her, and its colors and shapes blended and faded until she almost lost her balance.

"You must leave now, you're not safe here."

"Why? Who would come looking for me after five years…"

"They sniff the air and smell your return. They hear it everywhere. They will come for you."

"I'm nobody."

"You're a nobody with extraordinary powers. You're the greatest threat. Anonymity feeds the coming insurgency." Mehdi laughed bitterly. "As for me, I think they got me. I think I'm finally going mad."

He gave his niece a key. It was the key, he told her, of a small bachelor pad he still owned in the Centre Ville not far from the Wilaya and the Tour de l'Horloge in the United Nations Plaza. "It's a studio, nothing fancy," he explained, blushing. "It was my shelter in my wilder days. I still go back sometimes, to vent my regret. It's yours now. No one knows about it, not even the demons. Now go and don't look back. Forget about us, about this house, about the past that is slowly killing us."

Zeinab watched as Maryam left the house. She then walked to Mehdi and, her eyes fixed on him, asked him a question that left Mehdi dazed and confused. Zeinab and he had barely spoken to each other in the near-decade he had lived in this house.

"Was Hamza here?"

"Yes, I suppose that's his name. Do you know him?"

"Did he ask about me?"

"No, he didn't. Should he have?"

Zeinab ran out of the room. Mehdi sat thinking how strange, unpredictable, and unknowable people were. She ran up the external staircase leading to the roof, spread a sheet on the floor, and poured unsifted lentils on it. She held the flowers *he* had once given her. She then raised her head to the sky and whispered to him.

"If you are there and you still remember me, come. I am ready for you."

Grand Tribunal

Clockmakers' Town
Casablanca, February 2011

The charges plough on. They plunge deep where it hurts the most. Every word pronounced is a hammer chipping away at her humanity, her self-worth, her intimacy. Maryam understands the tactics, and her body still aches from where they broke and invaded it. She has never been stronger. She feels the magic coursing through her veins. The three gifts have merged into a triangle of diamond-hard power, trembling for release.

She looks around the courtroom. Hostile faces surround her. But she is finally starting to see. This is what she observes. Two dark-haired women sitting in the back of the courtroom are whispering excitedly to one another. They are dressed in red summer dresses, and both are carrying white canvas bags over their shoulders. She looks more attentively and realizes that the two women are not sitting on the bench, they are hovering above it. They look up at her and wink.

Then she notices that, in the indistinct sea of angry faces, sprinkled in the audience, are masked figures. The masks are an ethereal white with rosy cheeks and a thin, long mustache atop a smile. They look like turn-of-the-century gentlemen of most enigmatic and baroque composure. Maryam had become good at reading minds and deciphering intentions, but these minds were not like others. They were wired slightly differently. They thought in networks and digressive clicks. They thought like pirates who had never gone to sea. She was assaulted by the symbols that lived in their minds, the codes, the very new abstraction. They were a new kind of army, a legion perhaps, but they chose to act as one.

What troubled her most was the constant refrain of resistance and insurgency that their minds were polluted with. What interesting, dangerous creatures, she concluded. As if hearing her thoughts, they stood up slowly, one by one, bowed slightly, and sat back down. "Finally," said one of the gentlemen, who was really a girl. "Twas time she noticed us," another voice harped. "Yup-yup," a third nodded vigorously.

A bearded policeman screamed from the back of the room.

"Silence in the courtroom. We tolerate no disruption here! One more sound and you are out of here, the lot of you!"

"Death:

for perverting our sacrosanct history,

for desecrating the Holy Book and the story of our prophet Adam, his one wife, Eve and their children Cain and Abel,

for doubting the divine right of the Great Patriarch to rule the land,

for wanting equal inheritance and marriage laws,

for feeling outrage where submission is scripture,

for saying no,

for being a homosexual,

for refusing to marry,

for refusing to have children,

for wanting to be an individual,

for reinterpreting good and right,

for saying no,

for being provocative,

for being subversive,

for saying yes to secularism,
for saying yes to freedom,
for saying yes to choice."

Maryam closes her eyes, her heart beats faster, and her lips open slightly as she remembers how once, a lifetime ago, pleasure made her faint, and she said yes.

Betrayal

They kissed on the mouth. The tips of their tongues touched, and Maryam closed her eyes. She held the long, tangled hair in her hands and brought the body in closer to her. After a time spent surrounded by the falling light of day, they released each other and lay still on the floor. Their skins continued to touch as they lay there, content and quiet. Maryam lit a joint, which they shared over the jazzy 'oud sounds of Anouar Brahem. She turned to look at the body lying at her side, only to feel her stiffen. This was not the first time she felt her stiffen after sex was over.

Voices and chanted slogans rose from the street, loud enough to be heard from the ground-floor studio in the Centre Ville in front of the Wilaya. Maryam got up and went to the window. She listened to the unions' calls for strikes. She sensed the demons circling around them, sniffing their prey. It was the spring of 2009. They had gotten more sophisticated, more modern. They no longer simply disappeared people or tortured them, though they did that too, of course. They corrupted them, turning one against the other, creating disunity where previously there was conviction. She could feel them disrupting the air around the protesters, using invisible waves to pass divisive messages and tantalizing promises. Neither will win in the end, Maryam thought. The demons will erode the protestors' will power, while they in turn will create deceptions that will return to haunt us. And the time of the haunting will be upon us soon, a voice whispered in her ear.

Maryam felt a strange sorrow take over her. And the woman with her now was adding darkness to her sorrow. She raised her head to find she was looking at her. She was slightly younger than Maryam, extremely delicate physically, and cruel. There was a roughness about her that, because of her young age and beauty, came out as bravado. Maryam had seen her primal hardness since that first day when she had seen her in the street, but she had chosen to ignore it. Great powers are not always a protection against ravaging crushes.

She had let herself be seduced because her solitude was too harsh to bear. She fell for her with the burning need of the thirsty man who, having crossed the desert, finds an oasis filled with crystal water, only to realize it was a mirage. She often wondered whether she could have fallen for a man, or whether desire, for her, was cluttered around the female form. Unable to find answers to her questionings, she chose to see her lover as simply that, her lover.

Today, Maryam could sense that she was nervous and on edge, as distant from her as ever.

"What's wrong, habibti?"

"The blues. The dumps after coitus. Hate this moment. Tell me a story."

"What kind of story?"

"A love story. The story of Adam and Lilith. It soothes me."

"I'm not sure it's a love story. It's a painful story for me to tell. I told you the story once and you promised..."

"Don't be an old bore, tell me the story."

Maryam eased into a wooden chair in the sparsely decorated studio. She had rarely felt so alone in her life. This is the story she chose to tell her.

Adam and Lilith were star-crossed lovers. They loved each other deeply and freely. Their love was so intense that it made the demons restless. The demons decided to destroy their happiness. They took them to the place that is not to be named and kept them imprisoned for centuries. When they returned from the place that is not to be named, Lilith and Adam tried to reunite and rebuild their lives. But the fates were against them. A beautiful woman by the name of Eve, flanked by archaic angels and sceptical stars, conspired to break them apart.

Under the spell, Adam fell in love with Eve and forgot Lilith. Eve was a beautiful woman, seemingly soft and gentle, sensual and willing. She was desire personified. It was easy for her to take Adam from Lilith. She announced that he had always been hers, that Lilith was a she-demon dressed like a woman, that their child, a little girl, was not his daughter but the daughter of nameless demons. She backed her claims with written sources and the highest authorities to prove that she, Eve, was Adam's legitimate wife. Adam cheated Leila, no I mean Lilith, of her place in the world and in his heart. He let the archaic angels and religious scribes rewrite his story and erase from our historical memory the first family.

His marriage with Eve gave him two sons, Cain and Abel, and daughters, all forgotten, all insignificant. But Adam and Eve became curious, greedy. They became intrigued with the mysteries surrounding them. Eve tempted Adam with the unspeakable. They committed terrible crimes in the eyes of the black-and-white order they had helped establish. At last, they found themselves in perpetual exile, endlessly seeking a homeland that they would never again find.

Maryam's cold lover crushed her joint in an ashtray, took a crisp almond from the plate set in front of her, and commented sarcastically:

"The story of Adam and Lilith is a story of sex, not love. Of crotches and vaginas, not doomed passions and bitter dregs. The only spell he fell for was his erect penis."

"You see what you want to see."

"Say it, say I'm a bitch. Ah...but you like it when I'm a bitch."

"You're being cruel. With you, I feel old."

"And powerless. I hold your fate in my hands. I'm your Eve."

She shook her blonde hair and threw herself on the coach. She became serious. Her nervousness had returned. She bit her lower lip, then asked her abruptly:

"How would we fit into this kind of story, Maryam? How would our affair look in the book of revelations? Two women, that's unnatural, impossible."

"There's nothing evil in our story unless you choose to see it so."

"We are a humiliation to ourselves and our families. What we're doing is wrong."

"That's not the problem, honey. The truth is that you don't love me enough. You never have."

"You're thinking of your curse again, aren't you? You think you're cursed! But there's something about you, something strange and different that can be terrifying, isolating, and that makes it easy to reject and forget you."

"You're harsh."

"You leave me no choice. I have to get it through your head. Your powers, they horrify me. There's something evil and unnatural about a simple mortal having so much power. You are, yes you are...dissonance."

"Whoever said I was a simple mortal? Whoever said I had all that power? Yes, dissonance, that's the curse. I am dissonance. I ring at an angle, never completely right but never completely wrong. I'm always at odds with harmony. People never love me, and they never quite know why."

Maryam paused, for suddenly she understood.

"Who is it? What's his name?"

"Does it matter? He's rich. He's building me a house. He wants a family. He is giving me a monthly allowance and promises two expensive vacations per year. One in the summer and one in the winter."

"There is no summer or winter in our country. All the seasons are the same."

"The world is full of seasons, and I want to see them all."

"You're making a mistake. Seeing the world is not worth being dependent on someone else."

"And this, this isn't a mistake? It's shameful and unwomanly. Can you fill my womb, can you give me a child, a name, a status?"

"No."

"What can you give me?"

"Nothing."

Maryam spoke softly because she knew it was already over. But the exchanged words shielded her momentarily against the pain of the break up. It's not that this...affair had ever been a relationship. It was more a game of cat and mouse in the dark. It had lasted years but remained superficial and, often, contrived. Maryam didn't know what attracted her to this younger woman in the first place. She suspected it may have been a matter of luck. Her own body had procured her so much pain that she had never thought of the body as a source of joy. She had been starved of physical pleasure since she was a child. She had been treated, and now treated herself, as a vehicle to higher, more abstract goals. Physical pleasure was unknown to her. When this confident young woman appeared to her in the street that day, over seven years ago and smiled at her with her cherry-red lips, Maryam realized how starved she had been.

Her dark thoughts were interrupted by a flow of words, panicked and sharp-edged. What got her attention, however, was the rare sincerity she sensed in the other woman's tone of voice.

"I'm scared, Maryam. I'm scared of being caught. I'm sorry. I believe in God, I believe Islam is the right path. I'm not like you."

"I know."

"People say there's something wrong with you, that you're not natural. They say you will bring destruction in your wake. They say that those who are associated with you will all be punished. You and I can pretend that I control you, but you know you will soon be elsewhere. That's who you are. That's what God, or Satan or whoever is behind you, intended for you."

"It's not about me, don't you see? Our lives are a string of wrongs we are made to commit toward others and that are committed against us. It's become unbearable, and it must stop. We can choose a different path, a moral one... We must."

"No, that's terrifying. Change terrifies most people. You'll see. You'll soon find out how terrifying you are to people. People just want to forget you exist, and the demons, well, they're lying in wait for you. You're in danger."

"We're all in danger. We live in a time when we have given up our lives to chance, evil magic, and illusions. Violence is everywhere and in everything. But there's hope, still. Where there's resistance, there's hope, and where there's hope, we can begin to heal."

"That's absurd. Where there's resistance, there's destruction. You will lose."

"No. There will be change. The world is now wired to

such a degree that change will happen so fast that it will be unstoppable."

"Goodbye, Maryam. A thousand times goodbye."

Maryam sensed a slight hesitation, a passing regret in her goodbye to her.

"Am I nothing to you?"

Then Maryam, ashamed of her sudden heated reaction, asked the question she knew to be the right one.

"No, that's not it. It's not because of a man. You're hiding something from me. What is it?"

"Let me go. It's too late."

The young woman got up, picked up her designer bag, and, with an expression that resembled pity, or compassion or even empathy, she told her: "I've never been good at anything. But this—landing a man—this I'm good at. It's a skill that fades with age. Look, I tried to warn you. Forgive me..."

Maryam unlocked the door to the apartment and held it open. She watched her lover step over the threshold and disappear from her sight, her blonde hair flowing down her back. Maryam knew that she had already forgotten about her. Her last words, however, puzzled her. She felt that the forgiveness required of her had nothing to do with the brutal break up but with something else. She sensed an even graver betrayal ahead than the one she had just been subjected to. She felt the familiar prickling in the legs and a dull ache course through her body. In the darkened sky, she could now clearly see the demons amassing, their wings and their metallic horses ready to descend upon the earth. The demons were hovering above, she could feel them. But she now suspected that they may be here for her, too. Soon, she knew, soon they would be here. And they would come for her.

Aoud Errih, old and rusty as ever, rolled toward Maryam and fell gently on her knees. It rang its tin bell and grumbled its discontent at the sight of its melancholic mistress. Maryam held the handle bars close to her and stayed still, listening to the demonstrations below. She casually rang the bicycle's tin bell once more and remarked to it: "Dissonance. That is what I am. That is what I seem. But dissonance can only work when there are others around. You combine me with others and, there you have it, discomfort, disruption, cacophony. But when I am alone, I'm not so. I'm another being altogether. I struggle to remain true to myself, to find harmony. So which person am I?"

Peace finally descended on the square. Maryam was alone now. She knew that she would never see her lover again. She knew, as well, that the doll-like world her ex imagined did not exist. Behind the gifts, the house, and the travels lay a perverse, pseudo-modernity where most women are little more than trophy wives or bartered commodities.

Maryam left her apartment and turned the key in the lock. Apartment building number nine, located on the once chic Rue des Anglais, was a quiet building with yellow walls and grey floors. The studio given to her by Mehdi was a neat, tidy little place, scantily, but efficiently, furnished. In a building full of teachers, bureaucrats, low-to-middle managers, it was no surprise that Mehdi had chosen to host his activities on the ground floor. He could come and go as he pleased, in exchange, of course, for one hundred dirham bills distributed to the concierge to ensure greater discretion. "I've seen much worse, Mr. Nassiri, trust me, I've seen much worse," the little man would excitedly tell him after every generous donation.

Innernet

Maryam was a teacher of American and English literature at the most famous all-girls' high school of Casablanca, the Lycée Tolban. She rode Aoud Errih to school and back every day. In days of particularly high Casablanca traffic, Aoud Errih would develop a small engine and speed between the blocked cars like any other moped in the city. Neither of them ever dared fly over the traffic. Maryam had in her class many brilliant, creative young women who, with every passing day, became more anxious as to the kind of future that awaited them once their high school days were over. Maryam advised them to keep thinking, to hold on to their independence as long as they could. But she saw many of her students succumb to the men waiting outside the high school with their fancy cars and thick wallets.

Maryam liked her new place. She liked its simplicity. She was also grateful to her uncle for providing her with a place to live. A studio in a decent building in the Centre Ville was far above the means of a schoolteacher in a Casablanca high school. She counted her blessings. The other residents, however, were not too pleased at the idea of a single woman living alone in their building. When she first moved in, they used to regularly spit when she passed by or dump their trash in front of her doorstep. But strange things began to happen. The spitters found themselves subjected to an unknown condition: excess saliva. Their mouths would fill to the brim with acrid saliva, and they would be forced to spit every few seconds. No matter how much they spat or how many doctors they saw, the saliva continued to overfill their mouths. After a few weeks, and after they started becoming cordial with the new resident, the condition suddenly stopped. As for the trash dumped on Maryam's doorstep, it began exuding the most delightful and enchanting of scents. When the culprits, overcome with curiosity, peered into the black plastic bags, they saw orange blossoms where previously there had been filth. And when, their hearts beating, they returned to their apartments, they found a great amount of trash covering all their apartment floors. "Witch," they all whispered, "she's a witch." And, "It's true what they say about her." And finally, "Single women should be forbidden to live on their own. Single women living in apartments on their own are all witches." But, of course, they could never quite prove it had been her doing. After that, they avoided her and, when they had to, greeted her politely and hurried along.

They couldn't help notice, however, that the building, once a desolate, bland place, now constantly smelled of orange blossom. It was wonderful. Furthermore, flowers began to grow on their windowsills, when previously, despite the residents' best efforts, nothing could be grown there. The sickly trees in the narrow courtyard became big and strong, providing a welcome shade in the hot summer months and green loveliness in the colder, greyer winter months. At the center of the courtyard there now was a glorious orange blossom tree that no one had ever noticed before. With Maryam's arrival, the building became a place, not exactly happy, but certainly serene.

~

That early Sunday morning, when Maryam's heart finally broke, she decided to go for a walk. There was no time she liked more than Sunday in the early morning when the city was still asleep and the streets were deserted and she felt transparent, invisible, her shadow paper-thin on the streets. It was the only time of day she could hear the city's voice telling its story through the concrete and granite. That particular Sunday morning, as she walked through the United Nations Plaza, she told herself that the violence and disregard that she had been subjected to by a person whom she had held in her arms for many years, was only a speck in the ambient violence and disregard that the inhabitants of this city were subjected to every day. To be a Casablancais was to become intimate with violence and shame.

So she walked, her hesitant, uneven step resonating unhindered on the deserted sidewalk. She walked toward the Wilaya, and the Tribunal de Première Instance at its right. She breathed in the exquisite white Casablanca of the past that perhaps only existed in the minds of its inhabitants who, despite its everyday cruelty, still believed it could be redeemed. She passed by the Tour de l'Horloge, a minaret-like tower dominated by a clock and built in 1910 by French colonial officer Dessigny to bring in "French colonial time and order" to the natives. Its initial purpose was now conveniently forgotten by all.

She then passed by the block where Adam and Leila once lived. She didn't know that, right in front of her studio, on the other side of the park, was the home her parents once shared. She walked by the now demolished apartment that Adam and Leila lived in when they loved each other, when a glass of red wine was enough to paint their walls with the color of life, and when poetry made and unmade their bed. But she knew none of this. She didn't know, for there was no one to tell her. The city itself had chosen to destroy that memory. Where the graceful art-deco building once stood, and after its invasion by the weeds that appeared in the wake of the Bread Riots of 1981, there now stood a skyscraper made of blue glass and white steel.

Maryam let her feet guide her through the city streets. Her steps took her deeper and deeper through Bab Marrakesh and into the Casablanca Medina. She passed by children, some only as high as her knee, sleeping in street corners or huddled behind trashcans. Casablanca was filled with these "street kids." In recent years, and this made many people angry, their number had risen at an alarming rate. For you must know that single mothers in this land were still put in jail, following the Old Law. Children may be abandoned for many reasons: lack of support, despair, fear of jail, or perhaps the gnawing realization that life, in the end, is worthless. The belief that certain lives were doomed, and that the world was too powerful for an individual to fight against it, had become pervasive. Maryam watched the sleeping children, and she too wondered about meaningfulness.

She roamed farther inside the Old City and inhaled its salt and peat, until she found herself facing a dead end. As she was preparing to turn back, she noticed a small brown door with a bronze hand of Fatima beckoning her inside. She placed her hand on the cool, sculpted talisman and pushed. She had entered a cavelike room. Standing by the fire in the dimly lit room were two women. They were dressed in red cotton dresses and appeared to be waiting for someone. The older woman, who had the matter-of-fact expression of a successful businesswoman, spoke.

"Welcome, Maryam Tair. We have been waiting a long time for you."

"Was I expected?"

"We've been waiting for you since the dawn of time."

"The past few days have been most strange...Time has stopped. Everything is a haze."

"That's the broken heart talking."

"How do you...? How dare you...?"

"Quiet, love. We know everything."

"Forgive her bluntness, sister. It's difficult sometimes to remember that this tactless woman is in fact Sheherazade."

Maryam's eyes widened.

"You are Sheherazade?"

"Look what you've done. You've shocked the poor girl. Well. It's one of my many names. But yes, ahem, it is I."

"You have many names?"

"As mad people often do, and, ooh child, I am madder than anyone you've ever met or will meet! That's how I cope...and hide. Sometimes I push the envelope, dangerous people come after me, and I need to hide for a couple of centuries."

"Sometimes, you think the story she's telling is going in one direction, and then you see it's going in a completely different direction, and when you are about to protest, you look at her and see that she is as surprised as you are at the turn it took."

Maryam stared at the two women, who in turn smiled at her.

"But look, something else happened when your heart was breaking. Something you did, that's tied to a breaking heart and whose importance you can't begin to fathom."

"What happened?"

"You too coped. You told her a story."

"Yes, not for the first time."

"It's not any story."

"It's a story that's half-myth, half-reality that I tell myself to ease my solitude."

"It's much more than that."

"It's a forbidden story."

"Every time the story is told, the demons become restless, and a human being's eyes open."

"It's a magical story filled with dissent and mystery."

"It's not any story. The power of disobedience is hidden within it."

Maryam remained silent. She was thinking.

"Have we met before? It seems to me that I know you..."

"Yes. You know us from the time when you were but a dream in the sleep of the world."

She then noticed an intensity in their eyes, a tension in their postures that had escaped her earlier.

"Why am I here?"

"Ah....finally. You are here because we have a message for you. We must warn you that the sacrifices you have made so far are nothing compared to what is expected of you."

"I know."

"I'm sure you don't!"

"Be nice to her, follow the plan."

"You will soon receive your third power, and it will be in the most unexpected of ways. Once you receive your third power, there will be no turning back. Do you understand?"

"I understand."

"You can still stop everything."

"No, I'm ready for what lies ahead."

"May we ask why you are agreeing to this?"

"I don't think I've been given a choice. It's the right thing to do. In a world of lies, the truth must be told, equality must be restored. That's all there is."

"And how do you know it's the truth?"

"I know because it's just."

"Ah, ethics. An ethical super-witch. A woman appropriating ethics and willing to risk everything for her ideals. Grasping the full complexity, the chaos of the world, and sticking to an absolute."

"Stick to the story."

"The globalized female. I love that. I bow to you respectfully."

"It's more than ethics. It's about honor and being honorable. I too bow to you with respect."

"You could have the entire world. That, too, is inscribed in your destiny. What would you do with all that power?"

"Power that proclaims someone as the ruler of the world is a dangerous illusion. The world belongs to no one."

"It appears we may not be mistaken this time. She's the one and she's ready."

"I am. I can't remain transparent forever. And I have nothing left to lose."

The walls shook and trembled. Dust fell on the floor, and sand cracked through the ceiling. Sheherazade and the young woman at her side were watching her excitedly.

"It's happening. She understands."

"She's taking her destiny in her own hands. She's finally here."

"But the walls are crumbling."

"Listen beyond the crumbling walls to the changing order. That's the real noise. People are listening, waking, rising. They're hungry, but for more than food. It's delightfully apocalyptic."

"There's another sound, Old Mother. Listen well."

"Are you suggesting my hearing is bad?"

"The demons are close. I can feel their presence, and it's her they want. We must get her out of here."

"Yes, I just need to get one thing done first."

Sheherazade proudly presented Maryam with a laptop. She whispered excitedly.

"Write, Maryam. Take matters in your hands. Your old auntie Sheherazade wants to see a good spectacle. Write the manuscript that flows in your veins. Write the story of the first true family and the unquestionable equality of men and women. Write how this first family was hidden from history and wiped from our collective memory. Write what the people of this land refuse as heresy. Write as resistance, write it all on this laptop, using the Innernet."

"You mean the Internet."

"No, the *Innernet*. It was invented by djinns who hacked into the system of a US company specialized in new technologies. As soon as you write your words down, they go viral. And not just on the web. It's a direct connection between worlds. It's highly disruptive. You'll understand when you use it."

With these words, Sheherazade and her companion disappeared, and Maryam found herself standing in front of her apartment building. It was early in the morning, that time of Sunday when she usually left her apartment to go for a walk. She began to doubt the events of the past twenty-four hours, but looking down, she saw she was holding a laptop in her arms. After a slight hesitation, she returned to the apartment.

~

She sat at her rickety desk and saw, mixed in with her pens and pencils, a thin smoking pipe. She picked it up and the pipe lit up, its fumes rising to the ceiling. Maryam put the pipe to her lips and inhaled deeply. Then, she opened the gleaming laptop. It wasn't like any laptop she had ever seen. There was a screen but no keyboard or charger. Hesitantly, she put her fingers on the screen and it lit up. The letters floated above the screen, so she raised her hands slightly and touched the elevated letters. As she wrote, so to speak, on thin air, the words became three-dimensional and plunged deep inside the screen.

The connection established between the computer and Maryam was not a casual one, the unquestioned use of an object by a consumer. It was a synergetic relation from which she sensed that the machine and herself would come out transformed. And the reason, she was beginning to see now, was that the laptop was not a machine at all. It was a portal between words and the unconscious, between the physical and the invisible. As she was writing the story of a failed, deromanticized equality, the portal was inscribing it directly onto people's unconscious. It shot words into the collective unconscious like a syringe shoots up vodka in a vein.

The stories little boys and girls grew up listening to in this land, a specific dream of existence, a belief in right and wrong, began to fade. What once was instinctive and natural now was becoming troublesome and even impossible. Ancient fears and repressed anxieties resurfaced to be battled in the open. Maryam's story was fast leaving her fingers as an offering to a multitude of individuals, all paralyzed by the same archaic nightmares of domination and power. A closed flap in their minds opened up, and they began to imagine another possibility, a multiplicity of other possibilities. It was dissonance at an all new level—as exquisite cacophony and honed resistance. Cities, towns, and remote villages began to wake up and question the unquestionable.

Upon completion of her tale, the computer screen died out once more, and the detached letter-board disappeared from sight. The pipe was nowhere to be seen, but perhaps it was hiding among her many pens.

At that very moment, out on the street, two young men were stepping out of a long black Mercedes and walking toward Maryam's building.

Shams and Hilal

The two young men stood in front of the apartment building, looking at the piece of paper in their hands. After they assured themselves that this was the right place, they rang the doorbell. One of the young men was tall and beautiful. He was informally dressed, and his hair had a striking splash of silver hair down the middle. His skin was white and smooth. The other young man was short and stocky, with flaming red hair and golden skin. Where one radiated kindness and serenity, the other was the living image of strength and self-confidence. No one would have guessed that they were exactly the same age, twenty-five years old, and that they were brothers, twins to be precise. They were as different as the sun and moon. They were here for *her*.

The two men stood on their heels as they waited to be buzzed in. They conversed casually on the doorstep, oblivious to the fact that soon one would destroy the other. As it was early Sunday morning, the residents were still asleep, while Maryam was concentrated on her storytelling and did not hear the doorbell. To pass time, they inventoried her characteristics.

"This is what I remember. I'll list the inner traits, you do the outer ones, Shams."

"Okay, I'll do the outer."

"Inner: Prodigious, perceptive, psychotic, creative, imaginative, a witch. Enigmatic, intelligent, introverted, ill-adapted. Solitary."

"Outer: Monstrous, insignificant, banal, unimpressive, short, slightly deformed. Curly black hair. Huge eyes with blue pupils. Blue boots and orange blossoms. Rarely smiles. Skin burns. Odd Superheroine, if you ask me."

"Well, I guess we're ready. No one's answering."

"Okay, knock."

"No, you knock."

Shams knocked and waited. They heard movement on the ground-floor apartment on the other side of the door. Hilal turned to his twin:

"A girl we've never seen…and now we have to bring her back, convince her to come with us."

"We must. Mum will be so proud."

"And Father does seem restless."

"He always seems restless."

"Old age…What can you do? It happens to the best of us."

"He must have been something special if Mum chose him. Just can't see it."

"Be nice, bro. He's never done anything wrong."

"He hasn't done anything, period."

"Knock again."

"You knock."

"We'll both knock. On three, go!"

The door finally opened, and Maryam stood there, looking at this odd pair.

"May I help you?"

"We are looking for one Maryam Tair who resides on the ground floor, Apartment Building Nine of the Rue des Anglais?"

Maryam felt a prickling of the skin and an odd premonition.

"I am she."

"Greetings to our sister!"

"May we introduce ourselves to you? The twins, Shams and Hilal, at your service."

They bowed exaggeratedly and kissed her loudly on her two cheeks. Maryam hesitated before inviting them in. They paused at the building's threshold as though afraid to enter.

"We trust we are not intruding upon you at this ungodly hour?"

"Not at all, I was about to make coffee if you would like share a cup with me."

As she walked in, she glanced at the desk. She was relieved to find the farsighted laptop had hidden itself from view. The brothers glanced around at her home and, though surprised at its commonness, were too polite to mention it. Maryam smiled to herself for she could sense their confusion.

"Not too impressed with the witch's lair, are you?"

"We don't mean to be rude, but it's so...common."

"Yes, commonness works for me."

"But there's this scent everywhere..."

"You're referring to orange blossoms. That would be me."

"Are you truly a witch?"

"Witches do not exist, Hilal," scolded Shams. "Stop your nonsense!"

"It depends on what you mean by witches. There's no evil here."

"They say you're possessed."

"Possessed? I'm everything *but* possessed."

Shams's face was closed. He had left this superstitious nonsense far behind him when he moved to Palo Alto, in northern California. In fact, he firmly believed that all magical occurrences would one day find a logical, scientific explanation.

She offered them black coffee and sat in front of them. She decided to wait for them to give her a reason for their visit.

293

She had not seen her brothers since their birth twenty-five years ago. Twenty-five years already. She had not seen anyone from the Tair household for twenty-five years. Certain nights, she saw their mother Shawg dreaming of her, and she could feel the intensity of her desire. She remained quiet, struggling to keep the images and experiences of her childhood at bay lest they drown her.

"We are here because our father is very ill. He has asked for you."

"He wants you at his bedside."

Maryam's entire body froze. She felt the ice enter through her mouth, down her dry throat, and into her heart. Who was this man who was making demands on her after twenty-eight years? Why did he think he had a right to even say goodbye to a daughter he had never been able to love? She didn't know much about Adam. She had heard, or perhaps even read, that he was once a celebrated mathematician, perhaps even a good professor. But that was all before the great fall. Before he and Leila were taken to the dungeons, and he returned a changed man. The Nassiris blamed him for Leila's death. The hatred between them ran deep. Zohra had shielded her from the hatred and bitterness that was their daily bread at the Nassiri household. She showed her that there was a different path. But today, in front of joyful, beautiful Hilal and the strong, well-adjusted Shams, she could not but feel a bitter taste in her mouth, an acquired taste it is said, after a life of loveless encounters. She felt cheated somehow. So she remained quiet for a while longer, her eyes lowered.

It was not sadness that prompted her silence. It was an unexpected shame. Negative, evil thoughts, angry, resentful feelings had unexpectedly swept over her and held her prisoner. In the wake of the negativity and pain erupting inside her, came endless waves of regret and darkness. She breathed and slowed herself down. She reached out to the cedars, to the tree growing in the yard and changing the very air they breathed, and to the goodness that had always accompanied her. She struggled against the hate and primal fear, and remembered who she was. Oh, but it hurt to do so.

She looked at Shams and Hilal. She saw through them into their very souls. What she saw in Shams filled her with fear and foreboding. Once again, she wanted to turn her back on this family who had only caused her suffering. But then she looked at Hilal, and what she saw there filled her with wonder and sadness for him. If life had been kinder, they could have been close. When she finally felt ready, she raised her wide, ever-translucent blue-rimmed eyes and said softly:

"After twenty-eight years...he remembers he has a daughter?"

"People remember things on their deathbeds. They try to leave this world with as little loose ties as possible. We're here to ensure a dying man's last wish."

"Will you come see him, sister?"

"Yes, I will."

The twins rose from the sofa, and after two more hearty kisses on her cheeks, they left. Maryam watched them leave. Not a care in the world, she thought. How different our lives have been. Her skin started to prickle, and her entire body shuddered under a premonition of terrible things to come for Shams and Hilal.

Cain and Abel

Their task completed, Shams and Hilal returned to their car and drove home. Shams had already forgotten about Maryam. He knew that it would be easy to convince her. After all, it was part of his job qualifications to convince people. As for Hilal, he was intrigued. He had seen the hesitation and the furious desire to refuse, to bring pain to one who had denied her all her life. But just when he thought that she would turn her back on them, something in her expression changed, and, to his surprise, she agreed to come. He found the change confusing and atypical. Indeed, he had caught but a glimpse of her inner struggle and only knew her through the myths and tales that circulated about her. But he was satisfied with the positive outcome and deemed the timing was right to have a talk with Shams.

Hilal was an architect. He didn't choose to be an architect to build stunning towers or original homes. Since he was a boy, he had always wanted to be a builder. As a child, he would draw, color, or stack up row upon row of small houses and large gardens, joyous schools, and serious hospitals. Everyone agreed about his talent, and his mother, who loved him more than anyone else in the world, supported all his ideas and dreams, no matter how impossible. In a family defined by money relations,

Hilal was a mysterious exception. He wasn't interested in wealth, status, or reputation. He never pursued money and thus ensured that he would never have any. His mind was filled with cutting edge-technologies, building proportions, and rational geometries. He would look at any landscape and imagine what it could become.

Everything had always come easy to him. His peers and teachers adored him. He thought of architecture as the possibility of utopias, and of architects as the artisans of these utopias. He had big dreams, and he believed in their realization. His prime ambition was to build holistic neighborhoods in the poorer regions of the world, starting with his own. He imagined these new neighborhoods as perfectly autonomous villages, all linked together through wireless networks and codependent strategies. He also worked on viable plans for developing these new suburban or subrural neighborhoods without displacing the people who were already living there. That was why he wanted to talk to Shams. And that was the real reason he had returned to Casablanca. Convincing Maryam to go see a father who had abandoned her as a child was a complicated task for him. He felt uncomfortable asking a stranger, whom no one in his family ever mentioned, to come help a guilty man die in peace. But he thought that it would be a small price to pay for the chance to speak to his more successful twin brother about his project.

~

Shams was impervious to his brother's current state of mind. Though they were twins, he had never felt any affinity with Hilal. In fact, Hilal had always exasperated him. Hilal never had to fight for what he had. Talented, charming, and handsome, things had always been easy for him. Their mother had spoiled him, satisfying his every whim. That's why, Shams thought, he hadn't ever done much with his life, while he, at only twenty-five years old, was already extremely successful. He was a venture capitalist working for a firm specializing in new technologies located in Palo Alto, California.

He traveled constantly, and his was a self-proclaimed postmodernist lifestyle. He was sophisticated and worldly— if you consider having been to all the five-star hotels and restaurants in the world a mark of sophistication and worldliness. He considered globalization as an affair of the rich and dreamed of a world dominated by a monolithic understanding of luxury and service. At eighteen years old, he had read *The Communist Manifesto* by Karl Marx. He then wrote a paper arguing not only that Marx's "workers of the world, unite" vision was an unattainable dystopia, but that we were clearly heading toward a "bourgeoisies of the world, unite" kind of world. And that was a fine thing. At twenty-five years old, he was already a cynical middle-aged man.

Shams had a secret, one that he hid under his stocky legs, strong arms, and gold Rolex watch. He owed his great success to this secret. He was a master of the great, forbidden secret: that you may murder and profit. Once, not that long ago, a colleague came up with a genius idea for their company, an idea that Shams could never have come up with; Hilal yes, but he never. The colleague disappeared and was never found again, and Shams got a lightning promotion. After this first promotion, and his first million dollars, he decided to get a tattoo. It was a bundle of twigs on his left shoulder. He had heard that the bundle of twigs was the mark of Cain. But he didn't mind. He quite liked Cain—Cain was a winner.

The tattoo and the money made him feel like a man. But there was a darker side to Shams. He had tremors like his father, uncontrollable, sudden tremors that would seize him when he least expected them. He also had erectile dysfunction.

He considered the tremors and the erectile dysfunction to be Adam's legacy. He created a story for himself to render his life more bearable, and in that story Adam, his father, was a weak man who had passed on to his sons all his faults and defects. Shams was an enigma to all those who knew him. Yes, even to his mother, who chose to keep her distance from him. No one could have guessed that everything he did, everything he said, was fueled by a deep-seated envy. He, Shams, the successful twin, envied his brother Hilal to the point of obsession.

Hilal glanced at his brother, his perfectly manicured fingers and immaculate cuffs. He relaxed and gathered his courage. He knew, like only a twin can know, that his brother loved him and would help him.

"I'm glad we're here together, Shams. It's been a long time."

"Indeed."

"You and I, we've always worked well together. Do you remember when, as kids…"

An expression on Shams's face made Hilal pause. "I've been around long enough to know when someone needs something from me. Go on, tell me what it is."

Hilal told him that he had a vision for a new type of housing project. It was based on a utopia of egalitarianism for the precarious classes in the country. It was inspired by the great modernist utopias of the fifties and sixties but on a smaller, more humane scale. He knew of available land in the rundown peripheries of Casablanca. He had foreign investors who trusted him. He had a plan. With the new materials and technologies now available, he could build homes of the future in less than a year. He would build integrated villages and use half the land for housing and parks, and the other half to build schools, hospitals, ecological waste systems, community spaces, and cultural hangout areas. They would be self-run and environmentally friendly.

Well, why does he need me? Shams wondered. It seems he has it all figured out. But there was one problem. He couldn't afford to buy it. His investors were willing to back him for the creative architectural dimension of the project but were only willing to pay for half the land. He was expected to buy the other half. That's where he needed Shams.

Shams asked for time to decide. The car continued its smooth passage from the Centre Ville to the luxurious apartments of the Boulevard d'Anfa and the Boulevard Franklin Roosevelt. Shams and Hilal got out of the chauffeured car and walked across the green marble floors, eager to deliver the good news to Adam and Shawg. Their driver sat in the car staring at them as they disappeared inside the elevator.

~

What happens to Shams and Hilal is another story. Suffice it to say that, soon afterwards, Shams asked to see the land in question and found other reasons to stall before finally agreeing. He struck a deal with his brother, bought the land in his own name, and convinced the foreign investors that a utopia in a kingdom like theirs would never be sustainable. He then pushed his brother out and erected dinky, already rusty, leaky apartments for the lower classes. Hilal watched as his dream and reputation shattered around him. He stopped eating and became wafer-thin. He had lost a dream to a beloved, trusted brother. Hilal was shocked, not only by the betrayal and disillusionment, but also by his own blindness. What kind of man doesn't know his own twin? He can only be a naïve, worthless man who deserves his own misfortunes. Perhaps, one day, Hilal will emerge strengthened from this tragedy, or perhaps he will belong to the forgotten legions of men and women who went under hopelessly. But that *is* another story.

As for Shams, his success was short-lived. In 2011, he would travel to the Yemen to negotiate a business deal and disappear in one of the uprisings. Some say that a wild man can be seen roaming at night in the deserts of the Hadramaut, mourning for a brother beloved and betrayed. The shame and guilt had turned his flaming red hair grey, and his once strong, upright body now drags upon the hot desert sands aimlessly. The exile of Shams would last centuries, and who can guess how and when it will end, for that, too, is another story.

Aisha

The night that Shams and Hilal came to Maryam, her grandmother, Aisha, could not find sleep. Ibrahim had severed most of the ties that bound him to reality, and she was often alone, haunted by a life that was nearing its conclusion. That night, when both Mehdi and Ibrahim were asleep, she went to the garden seeking comfort. The crescent moon was red as blood, while the clouds stretched across the sky. In the midnight mist, she heard the cackle of a she-demon and the suggestion of peace in endless revenge. She swore it was the demon-queen Qandisha herself. Aisha let in the demon-queen's words. In the dark night, surrounded by the heavy foliage, she cried for a beloved daughter and a granddaughter she had been unable to care about.

In the garden, she could forget the ghosts that still haunted her house and her nights. The ghosts were all women: wispy, pathetic little things who had stood no chance against her power. She had sworn not to kill women anymore, not to yearn for another's death, and not to envy another's life. But tonight, she felt differently. She felt great evil creeping Maryam's way, and she heeded the Qandisha's call. The bloodred moon and the sighing leaves indicated coming sorrow. The orange-blossom tree was no longer there to drug her with its scents and promises of goodness. She saw Adam's and Shawg's shadows where the tree once stood. She heard the she-demon's laughter once more. She knew that these were all tricks to get her mind reeling, but the rage they conjured was real.

In her old age, she could still remember fragments of the Timbuktu manuscripts, the most precise of arcane manuscripts. She still knew how to split a person's soul from his body, cause one to whither and the other to wander. She thought again of the death she could bring to Shawg, but she remembered her promise to Leila. The she-demon hissed and Aisha's anger multiplied. All was quiet around her, and suddenly she found a way to unlock her rage. Killing a woman was out of her range now. But a man—no one had said anything about a man! The idea of killing a man made her heart blood beat. The idea of killing a man would be something new, exhilarating, dangerous, and oddly...just.

She returned to the house and locked herself in her room. She stayed there for many days. During that time, she didn't sleep, eat, or talk to anyone. When she finally emerged, she was holding a small, soft rounded object with undecipherable Semitic writing on its surface. She slipped the object into an immaculate white cotton pouch and hid it in her robes. Then she tied her hair in a bun, slipped on a simple black dress, and slid her feet in old-fashioned square heels. She opened the front door and inhaled the fresh air, wisps of freedom blowing her way, she who had barely left her house in half a century. As she was about to step onto the street, she heard footsteps behind her. It was Zeinab running across the pebbled driveway with a concerned expression on her face. "For an end to apathy," Aisha called out to her before disappearing through the doorway, her eyes large and excited.

~

Shawg was still a beautiful woman. She had prospered. Her prosperity had eased her into maturity with a vengeance. Her taste in furniture was as sentimental as ever: lavender couches adorned with lace cushions, pink marble floors and bathrooms, gold-plated faucets, and intricate bronze frames. These pieces screeched gentility. Yet if one were to enter Shawg's and Adam's home, one would feel oddly uncomfortable. Behind every luxurious item lurked a crudeness that grabbed the visitor by the throat.

On that particular day, Shawg waited in stillness for the twins to return from their mission. Her teeth were long and white, and scratched at her half-open lips. There were some people, she knew, who would always heed a call for help. It was her idea to convince Maryam to come to them by saying that her father was ill and in need of her. Shawg had dreamt of her stepdaughter every night since the day of her birth. Her days were spent with barely a thought for her, but her nights—and how could she help her nights—were filled with her. When Adam, trembling, told her that Maryam must come to them, she was quiet for a moment.

Then she said to him, "You must be dying."

"I'm not dying."

"Oh, of course you're not, but she won't come otherwise."

There was something macabre about his wife's plan. But Adam had secrets of his own, and today he had no choice but to bring Maryam back into his life. He began to shiver uncontrollably, and tremors wracked his face.

While Shawg sat with the stillness of a woman waiting once too often for a happiness that never comes, Adam remained in his room poring over a yellowed mathematics treatise. He had not opened a mathematics treatise in over a decade. Math, once the regulator of his days, had become a painful reminder of his failures. Today, he understood that its logic, its graceful constructions and abstract beauty still had a hold on him. He buried his face in the pages, and fragments of his past self knocked against his ribs.

Adam had that detachment of people who have been imprisoned, broken, tortured, then made to return to the world. He seemed to say: "Why am I here? Is this real?" He floated above reality, unobstructed by the chores or constraints of the everyday. He often bore a quizzical expression on his face. It was the kind of expression common in children and childlike adults unable to process their surroundings.

Where once mathematics had kept his inner demons at bay, now there was nothing to hold the darkness in check. He lived his life lost in the childhood trauma that he had repressed his entire life. The darkness and demons lurked around him, ate with him, slept with him, conversed with him. He was a small child again, left alone in the woods near his uncle's farm. The spasms in his psyche had invaded his body, and his face was now contorted beyond recognition. Was he to blame when the demons asked for Maryam and he obeyed? Could a child stand up to the fears that had made him who he was and robbed him of what he could have been? Adam's answer was no, he couldn't be blamed for what had been done and what was about to be done. And their promises in return…oh, what they had promised him in exchange for Maryam. Soon they would all see him for who he truly was.

He let his tears fall on the treatise. The wait would be over soon.

Shawg entered his study.

"The twins are back. She is coming."

"Good."

His voice was slow, matter-of-fact. There was no regret or confusion in his answer. As for Shawg, her mind was reeling at the coming of Maryam Tair. Her home had always been vulnerable to storms, an open wound, a scarred cocoon. She didn't know what having a real family, a safe home, meant. Shadows from the past, a jilted wife who commits suicide, and a daughter denied, all haunted her nights. She never felt guilty. No, why should she? If anyone should feel guilt, it should be Leila, for meeting the darkness so soon, or Adam, for giving in so easily. The tension subsided. Adam looked at this dangerous woman who was his wife.

"Maybe I am dying."

"What?"

"You told the twins that the only way to convince Maryam to come to us was by telling her I was dying. Maybe I *am* dying."

"Nonsense. You look better than you did in a long time. And you're working again."

"This? This is to stop my heart from breaking. It's simply my way of passing time while I wait for her."

Shawg did not ask why Adam had called for his daughter. She decided to hold her breath and wait. She was undoubtedly a strong woman. She had cultivated her strength on a daily basis and from a very young age. She was not born strong. She often wondered if anyone is ever born strong. Perhaps everyone is born weak, afraid, and only rarely able to transcend that fear. Perhaps when you only have one tool at your disposal, like an artist or a genius mathematician, you are more likely to succumb to that fear. But not she. Shawg had drunk her strength from the powerful image she created of herself. Her only reminder of the lurking chaos was Maryam.

She all at once wished for her disappearance and yearned for her proximity. Maryam was both the negation of Shawg's family and its condition of being. She was the living proof of its frailty, its breaking point. Today she would come to them, and there would be a miracle. An extraordinary element would be injected into their lives, of this Shawg was certain. A most beautiful butterfly would finally emerge from the cocoon, and all would be okay.

Locked in her fantasies, she missed the only question she should have asked: Why now, Adam? Why are you calling for Maryam now? Twenty-eight years have passed, and now you are calling for her. These questions hovered around them. Shawg might eventually have grasped these essential questions, but the doorbell rang.

The moment had passed. They both walked toward the front door, but Adam stopped Shawg. "I believe this is something I must do on my own." He continued alone, opened the front door, and instead of the young woman he was expecting to see, there, on the front porch, stood a woman with a saintly aura about her. Her hair was tied in a modest bun, and her black dress and square shoes were elegant in an old-fashioned way. Her eyes were gentle and kind, her face soft and lovely, her smile infinitely compassionate.

Adam felt the perpetual blues slip away from his body and soul. He closed his eyes to hide the sudden emotion he felt, and his lashes curved shadowy on his cheeks. The woman was quiet, but he knew she held all the wisdom of the world in her hands.

"Umi, Mother, Mother," the yearning vibrated within and without. Beyond a lover, a companion, a child, what Adam craved was a mother—he the orphan, the illegitimate, the lonely country boy. There, miraculously, there she now was. She opened her arms to him and he was irremediably lost.

"How are you on this day of days, my child?"

"The world has been crumbling around me till today… madam."

A joyful laugh like a bubbling river in the summertime: "Madam? I believe you know that I am more than that to you."

Under normal circumstances, Adam may have started to have doubts about this woman standing in his doorway. There was something oddly familiar about her, and her words rang emptily. But today, he chose to believe in true magic. Only a mother could make him feel this safe. The woman took a soft round object from her pocket, which she handed to him.

"I must leave, my son."

"No, Mother…"

"Only for now, for a while. I will return. I came to you on this day of days to protect you against the harm that is coming your way. Here, my son. Take this talisman, for it will protect you against all evil. By the ancient knowledge of Timbuktu and its children, this I swear to you!"

Adam hesitated, but his soul was at her feet that had stepped over the threshold into his home. A high screech pierced the air, and he turned to see Shawg running toward him: "Don't touch it. It's a trap! It's not what you think it is…"

But it was too late. The rounded object had touched Adam's palm. It popped, melted, dissolved, no it disappeared, absorbed by the skin, absolved by it, fused, diffused, mingled, flourished, married, embraced. The ancient Semitic writing sizzled, crisp on the skin, before whispering its incantations and turning black.

"What is this?"

"She's a witch, you fool. She has bewitched you, entrapped and ensnared you."

Adam and Shawg looked at the sedate woman standing at their front door, her very thin feet quite at odds with the old-fashioned shoes. The maternal woman of Adam's yearnings had disappeared. There, her eyes desolate as an abandoned cemetery, was Aisha Nassiri.

"She's a witch, Adam. She came to kill you."

"I do not kill. I facilitate death's labor. I bring justice where there is injustice, balance where there is imbalance."

"You are death."

"I am what others have allowed me to be."

"You are Aisha Qandisha. I've always known you weren't mortal. In your house, at night when everyone was asleep, I could hear the beat of hooves on the cold mosaic floor."

But Aisha was already far gone.

Shawg's anxious words followed her into the distance, and to Aisha they were as sweet as honey and as delightful as the first ray of sun after the endless winter. The witch can also do math, the words swirled in Aisha's head. All these years, I've counted, analyzed, imagined. I've deciphered, worked, studied, remembered what my mother once taught me of the manuscripts and the power of writing beyond the pillaging of brute contemporary forces. The magic of Timbuktu transformed, for and by me, into tools of vengeance. I've kept myself in check and considered the chances. I was told to stop for the sake of Leila and her daughter.

But my daughter has been dead for twenty-eight years now, and her daughter has been my own intimate stranger. She, the cause of Leila's suffering and disappearance…But there's a nature in all of us we cannot escape, a destiny perhaps or a particular skill. Mine could have been alchemy, it could even have been theology. But death chose me and gave me no respite. Death claimed me for itself, and the murderer's blood flows in my veins. I have chosen to be a killer. It's the only activity that gives me pleasure. It's my respite. It can be planned in the dark, honed in bathrooms, executed in private. Death knows no boundaries, no public or private spheres. For the prisoner, killing is the ultimate liberation from the chains that bind. Adam will pay. He, the core of everything, the apple of the world, the witness of all disillusionment, and of all that has gone wrong.

Adam was silent, his head was bent. How could he have not recognized his formidable mother-in-law in the candid lady at his door? He reasoned that it was because she had come to him as a mother. There was no magic on her end, only foolishness on his. The sizzling and whispering in his body subsided. Adam imagined that it was all a dream. But he could not always follow his imagination in its fantastic whims and escapes. He could not brush aside what had happened. A part of him was fascinated by the lasting naïveté of his relations to the world. He had chosen to believe that a miracle had sidled into his day to save him from the inevitable. But he knew, didn't he, that miracles didn't exist, and if they did, they wouldn't happen to him.

Shawg was looking at him with a strange expression in her eyes. He was as unable to decipher it as he was incapable of understanding what she was thinking or feeling. In fact, he was beginning to believe that he had spent his life merely guessing at the possibility of others' inner lives.

"I've changed, Shawg. I used to have talent, I had potential."

"You've been tricked by a woman who blames you for the black cloth she wears around her heart. She was too powerful for you."

Adam tried to feel that dark magic in his veins, but still he was met with a deafening silence. It's all a great illusion, he thought to himself: life, death, reality, magic. And I'm trapped inside it. Nothing has happened, nothing has changed. Yet here is my wife convinced that a sad old woman has the power to bewitch and kill.

"Nothing is happening, Shawg. She's mad. You've nothing to be afraid of."

"You deny feeling that *thing* melt inside you?"

"I recognize a melting feeling inside me."

They stared at each other across the abyss of their mis-recognition. Soon she will see me for who I truly am. And she will respect me and adore me once again.

The twins entered the foyer and sat on the sofa in front of the empty fireplace. They were engrossed in their own designs, oblivious to the strained atmosphere in the household. Adam paced restlessly.

"Where is she, boys, where is she?"

"Who? Ah yes, she will be here soon."

"She will soon be here. Mousy little thing. She strikes me as the kind to keep her promises."

"And to be on time."

"Well, she is late."

"Late for what, Dad?"

Adam paced anxiously. Time was running out. *They* would soon be here. Would he have to go to her? She may have tricked the twins into believing she was coming. The twins were unused to the ways of this land. They were too modernized, too Western, too hopeful. They believed in progress, in logic, in simple causal equations. They lived in clarity, in success, in optimism and optimization. They knew nothing of love, of pain, of betrayal. But she knew it all. She had that knowledge buried inside her since she opened her eyes to the world. She was graced with extraordinary powers and a unique spirit to face the repeated assaults against her. But she was trapped in ways they would never be. Adam winced, spasms deformed his face, and that is when the doorbell rang. There she is, he breathed. He felt no guilt, only anticipation, taut as a bow about to be strung.

The twins smiled, and Shams rushed to open the door.

Heart

Maryam stood in front of them, in the middle of the living-room. They asked her to sit, and she did.

There they all are: Adam, Shawg, Shams, and Hilal. They are looking at me as though I were a queer animal caged for their benefit. My skin is prickling, but I don't need to wait for what will be revealed to me through *those* channels, because I already know. I've known all along, and still I came. I came. I'm here in this home that could have been mine or that should never have been at all. I'm here in this family that left me out in the cold to fend for myself with grandparents trapped in reminiscence and regret. There was Zohra, my warrior godmother, but she left me before I was ready to be left again. There was Zeinab too, but she kept searching the stars for Hamza when she wasn't on her knees scrubbing floors. Here I am with the ghost of a past that eluded me. I had a garden. Do they have a garden? I had a tree. Do they even know what trees truly are? Do they know they are spirits holding us to our sanity, forcing us to breathe fresh air?...

I came because Shams and Hilal asked me to. My brothers. People think they are first. Stories make them out to be the kernel of everything that followed. They have erased me, my primacy, my oneness faced with their strong duality, their

313

complex dualism. I am here. My powers are vast, and I am their inferior. They see me as a charity case. Shawg doesn't. Adam is always and already elsewhere. He can't be pinned down or made responsible. He is the unpinned, egoistical butterfly. He's not ill. He's not dying. But I knew all along. I know death too well and departure too intimately. I didn't see it in the twins' virgin eyes. Not yet, but one day *they* will, and they will understand it too. I know why I'm here. I chose to be here. There is something else…I'm here because of the love I crave.

"You came, Maryam."

"I came, Adam."

"You must be confused, full of questions. Your brothers told you I was ill."

"And you're not."

"Not in the physical sense."

"You needed me, then."

"I did need you here. I'm grateful you came."

Maryam sensed the awkward pause in his sentence. But she didn't feel like digging deeper into its meaning just yet. The truth was, she knew why Adam was uncomfortable, and yet she still hoped he wouldn't carry his plan to completion.

The muezzin's call to prayer echoed across the city. From mosque to mosque, the call rose and grew. The words threaded into phrases and lengthened into exhalation. Birds stopped their flight in midair to listen to the familiar recordings of the prayer-rite. Their calm, rhythmic beauty was in utter discord with the broken scene within the Tair house.

Shawg watched Adam and Maryam with trepidation. Her round body, her warmth, her red pomegranate lips, her pearly skin had dried up in that brief exchange. To be precise, it was not the exchange that drained her so. It was Maryam. Her attraction to her was violent, quasi-ecstatic. She could neither define nor explain it. It was of a deep, mysterious nature, like the craving of the mystic for the divine. She had spent her life haunted by the elation she felt when she first saw her. "Go on man, tell her why you sent for her. Tell her why she's here…"

Adam looked at Shawg, his eyes dark as night. Tell her what, Shawg, he asked silently. Tell her that I love her, that I'm sorry. But that wouldn't be true. Because it is your nature, you forget that once you cursed Maryam. You cursed her with a loveless existence, a solitary, marginal, humbled life. Leila knew that I would never love this child. She knew my inability to love her. *She* would have left me eventually. But I left her first, and I've been looked down upon ever since. This child is not mine. I was forced to give her my name, but everyone knows she was never mine. Leila would never have let me have that knowledge, that respite. Her love for me would have abated without any possibility of return. She was loyal and frank. There were behaviors she was unable to accept. And I am beholden to all those behaviors, and have been for decades now.

Maryam's clear voice cut through the heaviness.

"I know why I'm here."

He looked at her. Yes, he realized, she knows.

"And yet you came?"

"In hope."

"What?"

In forgiveness, her eyes told him. He stared at her with incredulity.

"Why are you here?"

"Your sons invoked illness and a dying man's last wish to see an estranged daughter." Then, with great simplicity: "You called me here. How could I refuse?"

Adam remained silent. His fingers tapped his knee as the words paraded in his head: utopian, idealistic, naïve, foolish, impossible.

"Do you know what awaits you?"

"Yes. I've seen what lies beyond the door. But I can't accept it. I refuse it."

She fell silent. Her eyes had grown as large and blue as two full moons capturing the essence of all that lives. She put her right hand on her left shoulder, while her left hand rested on her leg: "I came, Father, as an act of love. Love is my revolt: Refuse the unjust, the unacceptable—that is love. Love is the *yes* secretly curled inside the perpetual *no* of revolt."

Shawg's heart beat like war drums before battle. Sweat appeared on her forehead, and the white of her eyes gleamed. She too had begun to sniff the evil beyond the door, already inside the house.

"That's enough, Adam. Let her go before it's too late. That's enough. I command you to stop lest you regret it."

"You don't understand. They promised me my life back. My talent, my potential and squandered greatness. They promised to return to me what the Storyteller has deprived me of."

"That's enough. Only the devil can return a life spent, and what idiot trusts the devil!"

It was then that they heard a discrete cough. They turned and saw three men dressed in grey suits and felt hats, sitting in a tight row on the sofa recently occupied by Shams and Hilal, near the now flame-filled fireplace. No one had seen or heard the three men enter, nor did anyone know how long they had been sitting there listening to their conversations like an eager audience at a private play. They all looked exactly the same with their grey skin and pale eyes. They were holding handkerchiefs to their noses. Adam and Shawg, Shams and Hilal, and Maryam stared at the three men in disbelief. A peculiar strain of sadness had crept into the house in their wake.

"There is a terrible smell in here. It smells like orange blossoms."

"Who are you? How did you come in?" asked Shawg.

They smirked professionally and adjusted their grey ties.

"Your husband, dear madam, Mr. Adam Tair, invited us in. We would never be so inconsiderate as to let ourselves in without a proper invitation."

"What do you want?"

Only a man, she thought, would invite danger into his own home. Her detachment from Adam was now complete.

"Shut up, woman. Enough with the questions," the second man responded, his voice harder, thicker than the first. "The tables have turned, companions. Now let them watch us."

"Indeed. Let's begin. We've heard enough," the third man picked up.

And the first: "You have your three children around you. A child you left behind and two beautiful sons. You should be proud, Adam, Son of Man."

They raised their voices:

"You're all here. Good. We've waited a long time for this. It's all thanks to your little father and his relentless ambitions. We're going to ask you a question, a riddle in fact. Take your time. Answer carefully. A great deal depends on your answer. Here goes: A farmer on his deathbed calls his three children to his bedside. He had a daughter and two sons. This humble farmer was a great king in disguise. He said to his children: 'I am a great king in disguise. I'm ill and about to leave this world. To decide who shall rule in my stead, I ask you the following question: If you were king or queen, what would you do with the vast domains I entrust to you?'"

The three men looked at Maryam, Shams, and Hilal, and they looked back.

"Well," said the three men. "answer the question."

"The question," protested Shams, "is part of the story. Why should we answer when the answers are already known?"

"Are they?" chuckled the three men. "Answer! It's an order.

You must and you will."

Hilal answered: "If I were King, I would rule my domains with equanimity. I would ensure food, health, and shelter for all. I would make sure everyone in my kingdom has a good life. I would be my people's shepherd."

Shams answered next: "If I were King, I would bend the land and its people to my will. I would build great palaces and a strong army. I would develop our economy and extend my rule over all the other kingdoms. My kingdom would be the greatest, most prosperous kingdom in the world."

The three men turned to Maryam: "Answer, child. It's your turn to answer. Time is running out."

Maryam shook her head.

"I refuse to answer."

"Oh, but you must answer. You have no choice."

"I do, and I choose not to answer. There should be no distinction made between the three children. They should all be equal. And for them to be equal, they should strive for equality among them and among all things. Possessions are illusory. We bend things to our will thinking we bring good around us, but that too is an illusion. We own nothing."

"We will give you one final chance: Answer!"

"I've given you my answer. There is nothing to be given or taken."

The atmosphere in the room turned to ice. The flames in the fireplace became thin blue crystals. Water froze in the glasses, and the walls became porous.

"How dare you disobey us?"

"Your model is not my model. My answer does not satisfy you as your question does not please me."

Adam began to tremble. Maryam had angered these dangerous three men, and they would surely punish him for her behavior. It was then that the three grey men revealed themselves for who they were. The grey suits, grey hair, and grey eyes disappeared, and there stood three sheepskinned, rough-eyed demons. They knocked furniture here and there, and raised their otherworldly voices:

"Yes, it's her. We take her."

"We knew all along. A game well played though. We know for sure now. It is she."

"She's ours. She's coming with us to the dungeon to be tried and tried and tried again."

"We won! Let it be known far and wide, Maryam Tair has been trapped, unmasked, defeated. Things will continue as before, since time immemorial. Nothing will ever change. Everything—everyone—will remain the same."

"Adam, you will have your part of the bargain, ha! But we hear an old witch came to visit you before we did. Ever wonder how she knew you would do this to your daughter? Enjoy your returned talent while you still can."

Cackles and darkness, darkness and cackles. They grabbed Maryam by the arms, pushed her head down, and stuck a long nail through her two palms before tying her hands behind her back. They pointed their steely claws toward the ceiling, and the apartment exploded around them.

But as they were about to disappear into the sky, a golden form, a bubble, light as air, delicate as a breeze, descended toward them. The bubble landed on the exploded rooftop, blocking any escape. Inside it was the grandest creature anyone ever saw. She was so grand one couldn't determine whether she was male or female. She was divine. She was dressed in shimmering gold and silver. On her forehead lay a crown of pearls, lapis lazuli, emeralds, sapphires, and rubies. Her fingernails were long and sharp, and for those who could see past her blinding light, they were not fingernails, but the most exquisite of writing pens. Behind her were two women: one as old as the world, and the other as young as the new day. The three descended, their legs crossed, their hands on their knees, their thumbs and fingers touching at the tips in three perfectly executed lotus poses. The older woman and the younger woman spoke, and their voices were filled with joy: "Behold, Sheherazade is among you."

Sheherazade stood in front of the three demons who, in her presence, looked once more like three banal bureaucrats.

"Tricksters, devils...thieves! Do you still think no one is watching you? I, Sheherazade watch you. And you have missed one fundamental detail."

"What? We miss nothing. We are trained in thoroughness. We leave nothing to chance, no stone unturned."

"You've missed the paradox."

"Paradox?"

"A paradox, you ignoramuses, is the existence of a contradiction. It is a portal, if you will, through which the most extraordinary of things may come to pass. So listen. Maryam is your prisoner. But mind, you've captured her in the only moment you could have: the moment when she revealed herself fully to you. But by revealing herself, by baring her soul to you all, she has done more than fall into your base trap. She has earned all of her powers: perception, thought...and now heart. These three powers were her birthright, and she has rightfully earned them. She is invincible."

"What good will her three powers do her now?"

"You will soon find out. It's time you familiarize yourself with uncertainty and doubt."

She turned to Maryam and took her head in her hands.

"Here, my beloved daughter. Here you have earned your third power. Through the perception of good, the understanding of moral principles, you have reached the highest of powers. For your kindness, your empathy, your courage, here is the third and the greatest of all powers: heart."

She kissed her on the mouth and eyelids, and whispered in her ear: "I will ease your pain. Soon, your physical suffering will be but a sad memory of the violence of this world."

Holding Maryam in their steely claws, the demons then flew into the sky, screeching and bellowing their hate and frustration.

Before leaving, Sheherazade turned to the stunned family of four, their pretense at normalcy shattered once and for all. Shawg and the twins were looking at Adam with a shocked expression on their faces. Sheherazade circled around Adam, her eyes filled with pity and compassion.

"A man lost in such a world. Such a beautiful talent and soul, crushed by adversity. What a waste. Know this: through your betrayal you have revealed your daughter to the world. No one can deny now that Adam had a first wife whose name was Leila, whose deeper name was Lilith, that they were equal in every way and together had a daughter called Maryam."

She then turned to Shawg.

"Misunderstood friend, estranged sister, tender enemy. Take care of your boys. Love and cherish them and forget about the transcendental you guessed but never grasped. Forget Maryam Tair. She will never belong to you."

Finally, she took Shams and Hilal in her arms: "Youth, strength, beauty…enjoy it while it lasts. Your story will soon be told."

Al-Batina

The Old King turned to his first and favorite child: "Tell me, my daughter, what would you do if I were to bequeath this kingdom to you?" The daughter, whose name was Al-Batina, which in Arabic means "she who is hidden," hesitated. She loved and respected her father dearly. But she knew that she couldn't give him the answer he was hoping for. "Abi, Father, oh my love, I do not want these lands, for they are not yours to give. They belong to the animals, the ebbing tides, and waxing moons. They belong to the changing seasons and to the men and women who borrow its gifts. There is no need to decree a dominion, for these lands are stateless, beyond our words and frontiers. They are to us as we are to them. I cannot take anything from you except the love you've given me."

The Old King's heart broke. For a thousand and one days, he sat on his heavy iron throne without eating, sleeping, or uttering a word.

After a thousand and one days, he called his three children, Cain, Abel, and Al-Batina, and informed them of his decision: "…My sons, I have not eaten or slept. Know that my decision has been a difficult one, but now it is made. I love you both dearly, but neither one of you will be my heir… My daughter, you ask that I leave this earth without a trace. You ask that I submit in every way. You ask that I believe there is no violence or desire for power in any living being. You ask that I bend my will to the will of the world. You ask that

I return the tides, seasons, winds to their original balance. My heart breaks. The future you are condemning yourself to is an uncertain and insecure one. But I can still know truth when I see it, and I choose you as my heiress."

And in the kingdom of Al-Batina everything was laid to rest: her crown was laid to rest, weapons and power were laid to rest, and the people swore an oath to uphold freedom and equality among all creatures, be they of this world or the other, and of all living things. And the word "kingdom" disappeared from the people's tongue.

Sheherazade is standing in front of the fridge with a big plate in her hands. She fills it with cakes, pastries, cheeses, fruits, nuts, and every kind of food she can lay her hands on. The young woman, her disciple, waits until she has eaten everything on her plate.

"I trust you enjoyed your food?"

"I'm binging. I'm extremely nervous and unhappy. I may just need a holiday, a breath of fresh air, a cool gin-and-tonic, and the Indian Ocean of my childhood."

"Your last stunt must have exhausted you."

"I think I'm…depressed."

She pouts.

"That's a good one!"

"No, I mean it. It's almost the end. I'm having withdrawal symptoms."

"Well, I can't say I'm not glad it's almost the end. What's ending by the way?"

"My role."

The younger woman smiles tenderly. Then a shadow passes over her face.

"I have a question that keeps me up at night. It's about Maryam. She could have engaged in heroic actions to change the course of the world. Instead, she chose to come to an old man's house, a worthless father, no doubt, in her eyes, and she let him trap her."

"She did what she believed to be right. That comes first."

"What happened to Adam?"

"Adam died soon afterwards. But not before he felt his talent rush back to him. He was sitting at his desk writing a mathematical proof when he died. Other people say he died of a broken heart."

"What do you think?"

"I can't be sure. Shawg believes it was Aisha Nassiri's black magic. She is beginning to understand Aisha. Her feminine powers are on the wane, her sons have left the country. She is alone with her regrets and the memory of her relations with men. She has begun to understand why some women resort to murder or the black arts. Women with Shawg's beauty and intelligence rarely need to resort to such stratagems, but it's good she understands. Perhaps she will learn to surrender her bottomless cravings."

"And the twins?"

"Shams and Hilal are another story. The mark of Cain, the mark of greed and murder, will not be on Shams alone. Hilal also will bear its burden. They have seen the most primal of betrayals, and they were its unsuspecting agents. Their egoism engineered it. All I can say is that what will one day happen between Shams and Hilal was sealed on that fateful day. They watched, motionless, as the demons took their sister Maryam away. A piece of them broke that day. But of course I can't be sure."

"What do you mean? You are the creator of these tales."

Sheherazade smiles her enigmatic smile.

"Is that what you think? Do you not think there are other sources? That these stories are there waiting only to be told…"

"You are the center that holds. When you begin your stories, you are transformed, and I hear the omniscience of your voice."

"You see nothing wrong in me?"

"I have come to see that you are far from perfect. However, you have been blessed with the gift of stories, and though it may be unfair, knowing you are, well, mad, I can't deny the transcendence of your voice."

The two women fall silent. The younger woman is thinking of the blithe madness of Sheherazade's voice, and suddenly she understands.

"The storyteller chooses to be mad and to tell her crazy story in that chosen state."

"Why would she do that?"

"She is waging a war against omniscience. Madness is her tool."

"It's her prized possession."

"Yes, Old Mother."

"In this century, madness is a necessity. Consciousness is split, it has exploded like the overextended threads of the spider web. The center no longer holds, and stories come at you, intricately intertwined, fragmented, and faded. I went mad to adapt to these times."

"Must mortals go mad as well?"

"They are survivors, these mortals. With the help of the djinns and the ghosts in the technology, they have created a portal into the world of stories. This portal, the Web, is a powerful storytelling tool. The clicks, the dizzying falls and ramifications of endless stories and fragments. Nothing gets lost, nothing gets transformed. There are no originals and no copies. It's all derivatives, reactivated at will, at whim, or even unknowingly. It's the end of the age of books and physicality. One click and it's forever there, in limbo. Everything is exposed, everything gets hacked, chopped, disarticulated, deterred. It re-enchants the banal. I fear that soon, I, Sheherazade, will not be needed anymore. The Web will replace the storyteller. The story of Maryam may be the death of me."

"Old Mother, you are needed. You are the tie that binds."

"The world doesn't want to be tied down. It wants to explode."

"Look below. People's hearts are breaking. Many will never be whole again, others will die of sadness. Stay with me for a while, Sheherazade. We have a task to fulfill."

Sheherazade's melancholia slips away, and her face radiates a pure joy. She takes the serious young woman by the hands and kisses her palms with great respect. "The apprentice has learnt her trade. I salute you, young mistress. Let's go down and remain with them. We've lost all objectivity. Their hearts echo our own."

Sheherazade wraps the young woman in her vast arms and begins.

"Maryam Tair has been put in jail until her judgment. In this system, you're always guilty, until you pay—the judges, the lawyers, the notaries, the officials. Only then is innocence pronounced. There's always a way out for those who can pay. But for Maryam, there's no way out. No money and no defense. It's night, and all the monsters come out. The prison is inside her now. It's filling her with shame and terror: knowing she is an individual, and being told she isn't."

Power and Shame

The Fortress
Casablanca, February 2011

The demons were restless. The dungeon guards were frightened, and some had refused to take their posts. They told the demon-lords to take *her* out of their prison. Expedite her judgment, get it over with, but don't leave her here. For as long as the demons could remember, the guards had never once disobeyed orders or abandoned their posts. It had been for the demons a source of great pride. But since the arrival of their latest prisoner, the ancestral order appeared to be in peril. The scent of orange blossoms was everywhere. Sunlight, vegetation, and cool water had appeared from nowhere, causing the dungeon walls to fissure and fall. The other prisoners, some of whom had been imprisoned for centuries, were beginning to raise their heads and backs in defiance.

The demons were angry. They had ways of breaking their prisoners. They knew how to inflict pain physically, mentally, and in that most essential, intimate part that establishes the human being—flesh, thought, and feeling—as a person. They rarely had to reach that kernel of the being to see their victims break. But *this* prisoner was special. They would break her absolutely. Yes, they would expedite the judgment now instead of leaving her to rot in jail. But before they did so, they would fill her with such fear and despair that she would beg for death.

In the dungeon, Maryam felt and heard the stones moan the prison's darkness and whisper its hopelessness. The assaults on her were now daily. The demons' cruelty was extreme, and their knowledge of pain and humiliation boundless. With every passing day, her sense of abandonment grew. Her legs prickled and ached continuously and her strength was beginning to leave her. And still the demons, who preferred to torture their prized prisoners themselves, did not succeed in reaching that intimate, essential part of her that made her a person. As they fed and gorged on her terror and shame, they found it increasingly difficult to enjoy themselves. Indeed, instead of the usual decay and sadness they were used to tasting, the taste of oranges, cedar, milk, and honey became overpowering. These sweet, fresh tastes were making them nauseous. How could a tortured being taste so sweet, so revoltingly alive?

One day or night, or dawn or twilight, the demon-lords gathered, their killer instincts on the prowl for an answer. They couldn't reach her. Why? The entire cosmogony was imperiled. They had to hunt her and tear her beating heart from her chest, for she held the message of a new world order. No, she *was* that message. Because of her, things were changing. She knew of the hidden stories. She came from the manuscript, the untold erased story. She was the child they had kept hidden for millennia.

They looked around at the luxuriant vegetation, the golden sunlight, clear water, and blue butterflies that had infiltrated their dark, dank dungeon and knew that things would never be the same again. Try as they might, they could not reverse the changes. They could only kill Maryam and end it. However, they had started to believe that if they could feed on that intimate, essential part of her that made her a person, they would become invincible. They were incapable of thought or logic, but they had a knack for sniffing out secrets. Gradually, they began to see that the link between the luxuriant nature that had erupted in the dungeon and Maryam was a deep, primary one. They began to sense a pattern, and finally it hit them.

Maryam was sitting in a corner of her cell near the entrails of the earth, well below the dungeon's foundations. Since her imprisonment, the dungeon's appearance had radically changed. Vegetation was exploding through the walls, water gurgled at its center, and butterflies shook their nourishing golden dust every which way. But she was tired beyond imagination. She could feel her will leaving her body steadily and inexorably. She was grateful for the energy lent to her by the earth, but she also knew that the earth could not remain in an unnatural place without it too being weakened. She would soon have to ask it to let her go. She sat in a corner of her cell, with every sense of self damaged beyond repair. Her body hurt, and seeing, breathing, smelling, touching hurt as well. She listened to the stones and their archaic, linear narratives of the past, present, and future: one long moan, one endless whisper, that was all the stones remembered or knew.

Maryam closed her eyes and wondered how long she had been held captive. As her mind slipped toward depths she did not know existed, she felt a soft, eerie, gentle presence by her side. She looked up to see her mother, Leila, wispier and thinner than the last time she came to her, hovering near her. Unlike previous times, Leila the Ghost did not come too close to her daughter. She was standing at a respectable distance from her. "All hail, my daughter, for you are succeeding where everyone before you has failed. Do not despair, for you are almost at the end of your ordeal."

Maryam struggled to speak. Her teeth hurt in her head, her loins, her irregular legs and thin arms, all had become foreign entities to her: "Mother, my ghost, I have been abandoned by all. How long must I suffer?" One of the blue butterflies fluttered to Leila and settled on the line of her neck where it touches her shoulder. "Listen, beloved. You are in great danger. The demons have discovered that your spirit cannot be broken, for it's not in your safekeeping alone. You must find the strength to hide it from them, and then your ordeal will end." To which Maryam Tair answered that she didn't know in whose safekeeping it was.

Leila's ghost could not remain long in this cell below the world. She passed her opaline hands over Maryam's head and told her, "The answer is in you, it's all around you. You know where it is." Then she was gone, leaving coldness in her wake.

Maryam remained deep in thought, her head resting in the curve of her arms. Her nose inhaled the scent that emanated from her skin. She breathed in and out. She breathed in the orange blossom scent and exhaled the shadows and fears. She thought of this scent that no other human being possessed. She thought of her crooked legs and of her peculiar relation to the world, to its creatures and its spaces. She realized, quietly and in the most unobtrusive of ways, that she had always known. She set loose a stone from the walls of her cell, softened it, and molded it into a bird. She told the bird to fly to the orange tree in the courtyard of her apartment building and, with its permission, cut a branch and plant it in an orange grove at the edge of the desert, a tree of life, one among many orange trees, forever protected from evil. Then the link between her and the world would be safe from harm. She held the bird lovingly, then let it go, and it flew away to fulfill its mission.

That night the demons were particularly cruel and thorough: "You have failed, nothing will ever change. You may have won in here, but you have lost in the eyes of the world. Now it's time," they hissed and bleated. "You will go to your judgment tomorrow, and the world will soon forget that Maryam Tair ever existed."

That last night in her cell before the judgment, the demons

let her be, and Maryam found a fragment of peace, at last.

The most important things are the frailest, Maryam thought over and over. They are the things that cannot speak for themselves, things for which there is no reward or judgment. I never belonged there, or here. Nowhere do I fit, nowhere does the world have a place for me. It's good they are letting me go tomorrow. I have a path I must follow. I chose this path. No one forced it on me. I heard that I should never have been born, and looking back, I believe it must be true. The world of men aligned to make my birth the rarest of probabilities. And yet… here I am. I've been hidden, denied, forbidden throughout the centuries, and yet here I am today.

Adam had a first wife. Her name was Lilith-Leila, and she was no demon. She was his equal, in a world of balance and transparence. Their love made a child, a girl who was then wiped away, just as her mother—too proud, too free— was demonized. History must have tripped. The scribes must have hesitated, the written text was claimed by one over the others to become the Green Book, and the kernel of doubt and unbalance entered the world in that one inadvertent moment of the raised, questioning pen. A box, somewhere, was opened, misunderstanding thrived, and power entered the world.

But my thoughts need to be silent now, lest the demons hear them and come for me. What more can they do to me… Will they make me beg, crawl? How will I ever know my own courage or cowardice? I, fated with the most ambiguous of sacrifices…

Then in front of her appeared a man of vast proportions. His head scraped the ceiling, and his shoulders were so broad that the stones bent inward for him. His beard was thick and red like the earth. He had one grey hand that held a double-edged sword and one green hand that he held out to her. He was the most magnificent being Maryam had ever seen.

"Greetings, Maryam Al-Batina, finally revealed. I ask that you forgive my raucous intrusion into your...temporary abode. My name is Hamza. Let me present to you my sword, Zulkitab, my left hand, grey, for its consuming-force and my right hand, green, for its life force. They are, always have been, and always will be, at your service."

Maryam stared at this old-fashioned giant, a Norse God in a coal mine, a Lorenzo de Medici in a world of Torquemadas: "Ah, that's good, a twinkle in your dark eyes. The stars will be down shortly. Soon, it will be midnight."

With those cryptic words, he fell awkwardly silent. He shuffled his feet and stared at his boots. Maryam questioned him softly.

"Why will the stars come down?"

"Hmm...I always say too much when I'm nervous."

"You're nervous..."

"To be in your presence, to succeed in my mission..."

His eyes filled with tears as large as a glass of water: "Look at you, so grown up and accomplished. So...wonderful. You know, I was there for your birth. My happiest and saddest time..."

Maryam stared down at herself, at her red knuckles and thin knees, her crooked legs, torn boots, and falling hair. Wonderful, grown up, accomplished? The kind giant must be out of his mind.

"You came for my birth?"

"I came to protect you from harm. That was my mission. That's my mission now. I must admit...I did not perfectly execute my first mission."

"I'm sure you did. You seem quite thorough."

"I left a gift for you. Aoud Errih. I made him myself. Did you like him?"

"Yes. I miss him."

"Don't worry about your bike. He's fine. Back where he belongs."

They were quiet for a while. Hamza's heart was heavy.

"I failed my mission. I was...inattentive, and I couldn't save your mother, Leila. She killed herself, you know."

"Yes, I know. Why was that your fault?"

"I was occupied elsewhere. I was busy...falling in love."

"That's okay, then."

They smiled at each other across the chasm of their difference, immediately connected and at ease. "Your stepmother's curse, it doesn't work on me. I can care about you in the blink of an eye."

They smiled at each other again and heard a distant clock strike midnight.

"Well, let's begin."

Hamza raised his hands. The dungeon disappeared. Thunder rolled, and lightning struck. The sky went black as ink and the stars bright and silver. It began to descend. The night sky came to rest in his immense hands. He held the firmament in his hands and sewed it into a cape. When his work was done, he presented Maryam with a cape made of the entire universe.

"We're lending you this. It goes to the one with all three powers: perception, thought, heart."

"We?"

"Those who feel, who remember, who write...It's yours for a while. Use it tomorrow. You'll know when the moment comes."

Maryam took the cape, and it became minuscule, fitting on the nail of her smallest finger. She let it hide there. She turned to Hamza with incommensurable gratitude, but she noticed a shyness, a hesitation about him.

"Is there something else?"

"Yes. I don't dare...You don't have to, of course...but there was a woman, at your old house..."

"Yes. Zeinab Ben Issa."

He turned a purplish red.

"She is my great love. I lost her once already. But I am told that the cycle is returned and…she's called for me. I could have another chance with her. That is, if you agree to let me cut out a piece of the firmament cape. That piece is my renewed chance with her."

"How could I refuse?"

"It will be painful."

"Take what you need, friend."

He took her small finger in his hand and cut a piece of the miniature cape. Maryam felt an excruciating pain, one of the greatest pains she had felt these terrible days. Then the pain passed, and she saw the pure joy on Hamza's face.

"I thank you, Maryam Tair, for giving me back my life at a cost for you. Now sleep, darling. I will watch over you and shield you from harm. Tomorrow is the day of destiny."

Revelation

Maryam Tair is at the stand. She notices that her chains and handcuffs are gone. The charges are listed, the jury must now decide the sentence. One by one, the judges pronounce the verdict. They rise and Maryam sees that their number stretches to the back of the courtroom endlessly. They are identical, an infinity of mirror images about to sentence her with the same infinitely echoed verdict.

"Death:
Death to the witch,
Death to the unbeliever,
Death to the subversive,
Death to the unnatural,
Death,
Deat…
Dea…
De…
D."

She is to be executed immediately.

~

It is May 2011. Maryam is thirty years old, but she knows that she is ancient. Images, representations of her, remembrances have been present since the world was but a speck, a fleeting possibility in the imagination of the universe. She is the denied, the repressed, the forgotten being, the redacted story, the erased word, the woman with power, the equal and extraordinary creature, the hidden and now the revealed. Al–Batina.

She raises her head and looks at the assembly. To her surprise, she sees neither fear nor hostility. Only silence. The masks of the smiling, mustached revolutionary are now plethora, and they seem keen on battle. The color red dominates, and Maryam is blinded by its vibrancy. She sees familiar faces. Some have lowered their eyes in shame of the unbeaten path she has chosen for herself. The Nassiris are present. Mehdi is there with Ibrahim and Aisha. He has opened the silver locket with Maryam's strand of hair and noticed that the scent has never been so powerful. Yasmine is there with her still millionaire husband Mohamed Afrah, as is Driss Nassiri, alone since Shawg had left him those thirty years ago for Adam Tair. The Tairs are also there: Adam and Shawg, Shams and Hilal. A blonde woman with black glasses sits at the back.

Members of the butterfly tribe are there camouflaged as delicate butterflies, thick trees are hiding as benches, half-moons posing as flickering lights. Wispy beings freed from the asylum, demons, ghosts, djinns, prisoners, street vendors, students, and prison guards are all present. Leila is standing nearby, and Zohra, too, her warrior godmother. And there are Hamza and Zeinab Ben Issa, his great love, together at last. Inhabitants of the Central Quarries and the impoverished tribes of the interior are there. Finally, Maryam sees the two women she has met in half-dreams and on days of great silence and even greater solitude.

The demons are coming for her. Their guns are at their sides, and their metallic horses can be heard stomping on the roof.

Suddenly they stop. They seem frozen in place, incapable of movement or decision. But Maryam does not see that something unexpected is happening. She is lost in herself, in her own physical pain. The prickling on her skin intensifies and stretches from her uneven legs to her cropped hair. It gives her no respite. The prickling becomes harsh. It is unbearable. The assembly rises. Something extraordinary is happening, but Maryam can't see it. It is her they are all watching. They are staring and not letting go.

The courtroom is filled with whispers and chatter. She hears the words "witch," "magician," "demon," and also "goddess," "beloved," "anointed one." She touches her arms, neck, and face and feels…words. She looks at herself and finds that she is no longer herself. She cannot say *I* or *me* with any certainty anymore. She has transformed into something other. This must be how the caterpillar-becoming-butterfly feels. It is a misrecognition, an unknowing, and a soon-to-be inconsequential memory of past states. She has become words. The prickling was the changing state, the manuscript writing itself on her skin. The physical pain was the precondition to the metamorphosis, to the completed becoming of the text. She is no longer flesh and bone, she is word and meaning. She tries to speak, perhaps in awe, perhaps to be comforted by the sound of her own voice, but soon she understands that utterance has become irrelevant, for it is present.

For there she is. She is the child, the manuscript, the resistance. She is the page and the words. Her entire body is script, and she becomes the expression of a force that transcends and encompasses her. She hears the calls for her death ring through the courtroom. She also hears the assembly rising and turning to face the demons.

She *is* the assembly facing the demons. She is the crowds gathering beyond and nature revolting, the orphaned child straightening his path, and the broken woman getting up. She is the unemployed facing the machine and the very poor gaining consciousness. She is the artist with heart, the leader with perception, the lover with thought. She is the wave upon wave of people rising, simply raising their eyes and straightening their backs.

She becomes larger than life, and she breaks the wooden stand upon which she has been charged and sentenced. Hamza's cape is now draped over her shoulders. The demons are still. They weren't demons at all. They were symbols, now unread. Something has broken. Absolutism has fissured and cracked.

Maryam watches them. "Mother," she whispers:

"Watch, watch them break. There was no lead in your blood. Only fear. Watch how it is fear, *our* fear, that has nourished them. Mother, be at peace. You may rest, for you have made me safe. Your sacrifice was not an ambiguous one. Who can deny love when they find it?"

Sheherazade is watching Maryam and reading her. As Maryam is about to ascend, Sheherazade's disciple puts her hand on the master storyteller's sleeve.

"Old Mother, I'm being pulled to her…I've never understood, but now I do. You have brought me home. I am finally home."

Tears fill Sheherazade's eyes.

"Yes, now you do, and now you must. You are being pulled, for you are her. You are Maryam Tair, and now your tale is told. It was told to you, for you, and with you. It was told and lived, breathed and written. You are revealed, Al-Batina, hidden and revealed. You are pulled, and that is good. That is as it must be. But the stars and moons and planets alone know how I will miss you, my beloved daughter."

Maryam rises above the courtroom. The cape deploys the universe it is made of. There are the stars, moons, planets, everything in-between and everything within. Then everything—the words, the stars, moon, planets, the creatures, and the meaning—everything disappears. It is blissful, creative annihilation: the inhaled *no* and the exhaled *yes* of creation.

The night sky fills the courtroom, the plaza, Casablanca, Morocco, Africa, the Middle East, Europe, and the world. Its blackness covers everything, and night is everywhere.

Atlas Mountains

Sheherazade is alone, her pipe back in her mouth. She holds a box in her hands, its clasp between her thumb and forefinger.

She begins.